**WRITTEN, DIRECTED, AND PRODUCED BY
CHRISTOPHER ROBERTSON**

COPYRIGHT CHRISTOPHER ROBERTSON 2022.
COVER DESIGN AND TITLES BY DEREK EUBANKS.
SECOND EDITION EDITED BY BRET LAURIE.

VIRGIN NIGHT IS A WORK OF FICTION. ANY RESEMBLANCE TO PERSONS LIVING, DEAD, OR OTHERWISE IS PURELY COINCIDENTAL. NO PART OF THIS BOOK MAY BE REPRODUCED, RESOLD, REPACKAGED, OR REMADE WITH SHODDY CGI BLOOD EFFECTS WITHOUT PERMISSION OF THE AUTHOR AND TERRORSCOPE STUDIOS.

WANT THE FULL VIRGIN NIGHT EXPERIENCE?
SCAN THE QR CODE BELOW AND LISTEN TO THE OFFICIAL, UNOFFICIAL
SOUNDTRACK FROM THE BOOK.

OR SEARCH FOR VIRGIN NIGHT ON SPOTIFY.

ALSO FROM TERRORSCOPE STUDIOS:

R-RATED
MY ZOMBIE SWEETHEART
THE COTTON CANDY MASSACRE
GOONS AND GREASE PAINT - SHORT
THE COMEBACK KID - SHORT

PG-13
THE OCTOBER SOCIETY: SEASON ONE
THE OCTOBER SOCIETY: SEASON TW

THIS BOOK CONTAINS:

HOMOPHOBIA.

VIOLENCE AND GORE.

RELIGIOUS INTOLERANCE.

SCENES OF AN ADULT NATURE.

AND SOME VERY JUVENILE ONES.

> "RELAX, TAKE IT SLOW, AND LET THE GOOD TIMES ROLL."
> —STEVE STIFLER, *AMERICAN PIE*

> "I NEVER THOUGHT I'D BE SO HAPPY TO BE A VIRGIN!"
> —RANDY MEEKS, *SCREAM*

FOR CRAIG.

WHO'S FACED COUNTLESS MONSTERS BY MY SIDE.

BOTH REAL AND IMAGINED.

CHAPTER ONE

ONCE UPON A TIME AT A RENTAL STORE

SOMETIME IN THE LATE 90S.

Imagine it's Friday night, in a time before streaming, when the internet was just for nerds. You're bored, nowhere to go, and there's nothing on TV. So you head down to the rental store. It's a chilly night, and the glowing sign of the store cuts through the fog like a beacon that says *forget your dull, everyday life and bask in the small-screen glow*. It says *we have popcorn and chips*.

Inside, trailers loop in tandem on mounted TVs hung over marked-up candy and soda racks. Most of the good movies are gone and what's left are seven-day rentals you've never heard of before. You're not going home empty-handed, though, so you pick one, just any random movie that doesn't sound too awful, and you take it back home—maybe picking up a pizza on the way.

Back home, you settle down, put the tape in, and though you fast-forward through the piracy warnings, you let the trailers roll: space truckers, dark heroes, and serial killers taunting detectives by strobe lights. The movie starts, and the credits roll. Historic photos, faded town maps with vaguely familiar names superimposed over them. Jumpy, jagged cuts to a grungy beat. The screen fades to black, and then, in the bottom right corner, in a straightforward white script, a date appears:

FEBRUARY 13TH, 1989 - VIRGIN NIGHT.

A Clear Lake County Sheriff's cruiser pulls up outside a half-renovated, two-story, freshly painted house. A few yards behind, there's a thick wall of trees and no sign of any neighbors. On the decking that leads into a kitchen stands a woman in a worn yet very flattering sundress. She smokes in a way designed to hide her habit from the children, screaming at play inside the house. As the car pulls to a halt, she stubs the cigarette out, though the smirk on the driver's face tells her she's not fooling anyone.

"Those things will kill you," the Deputy says as he slides out of his car. The name on his badge reads Tran.

"Says you," the woman on her deck teases. Her name is Debbie Tran, wife of Deputy Jimmy Tran and proud mother of two hell-raising twins, Vincent and Emilie. The children, at this moment, are acting out a Ninja Turtles battle across the entire first floor.

"Says the package, can't you read?" Jimmy jokes as he comes up the steps. He stops at the top, hands on his belt, and stands tall to make his point.

"The hell's that mean? You sayin' I'm some kind of dumb country girl?" Debbie hits back with a playful sideways glance; she lets her natural rural twang run free across her smirk. "'Cause if you is, then you went ahead and married one, so what's that say about you?"

Jimmy steps over to her and wraps his arms around her. "It says I love you," and he kisses her. A slight moan escapes her lips. As Jimmy pulls back, Debbie holds him in the hug. "It also says since I knocked you up, someone needed to make an honest woman out of you, and your cousin already got married to his pig."

"One of these days," Debbie says without missing a beat, "I'm gonna call in and say you only married me for a green card."

"Honey, you'll be the one in jail. I got kids that are American as an eagle riding a Harley on the Fourth of July; they gotta let me stay."

"Oh, Jimmy, I wish you could take me for a ride in your car and punish me for being such a bad girl," Debbie says as she bites her lower lip and looks into the kind, soft eyes of the man she loves. "I could smoke a whole pack in the back, blow it in your face." She parts her lips, and Jimmy has to pull away.

"There's nothing I'd love more than to take you 'round the back of some barn and make love to you like your other cousin did on your fourteenth birthday. But you know we got these kids…" As Jimmy pauses for effect, something like "Die, Shredder, die!" comes from inside the house, and the sound of something substantial hitting the floor follows. "Besides, you know what night it is."

"I know," Debbie says, "just being a tease is all."

"C'mon, let's go see to the kids before one of them puts the other through a window."

"Wait," Debbie says as she takes hold of her husband's hand. He can tell from the slight wrinkles on her forehead that she's not kidding around anymore. "I know you had to call in some favors to get tonight off. Thank you. I hate the thought of you out there on Virgin Night."

Jimmy wraps his other hand around hers and feels a slight tremble. "It's okay, Honey. I'm here." He pulls her in for another hug and breathes in the scent of her hair—menthols and jasmine soap. "Besides, there hasn't been an incident since before the kids were born."

"I know, and I'm being stupid. But, all the same, thank you. Boy, am I glad my Daddy didn't kill yours in 'Nam."

"And I'm glad your Daddy didn't marry you instead. I love you, you know. Even if you are just a dumb country hick."

"I love you, too, you goofy Vietcong."

The two of them head inside, and the sight of their father makes the twins forget about their battle. Together the pair launch themselves onto him, latching on like a pair of monkeys.

Debbie stands back and lets the kids have their fun. She doesn't fool herself that it's because she's been with them all day and they're just bored of her. She knows they have more fun with him and she doesn't mind. Jimmy's a kind, gentle, and strong man who somehow finds the time between fixing up a never-ending project of a house and working all hours to make his kids feel like they're the only thing in the whole world to him. The sight of him wrestling on the floor with them—that image will stay fixed in her mind for the rest of her life.

After the kids go to bed, Jimmy and Debbie fall asleep in each other's arms, and they stay that way—until the phone rings.

The shrill, electric chirp echoes through the house and cuts like a scream through a bad dream.

It rings for long enough that neither Jimmy nor Debbie can fool themselves that it's just a wrong number. Both of them lie awake, eyes meeting in the dark. Over his wife's shoulder, Jimmy can see the alarm clock, and it tells him it's just past two in the morning. He goes to move.

"Don't," Debbie says, and Jimmy halts for just a second before he finishes getting up. "Don't!" she says again, more forceful, and she holds on tight to his forearm. "Don't," she says, though now it's more like a plea.

Jimmy gives her a look that says he has to, and she knows it. Of course she does. He wouldn't be the man she loves if he didn't answer that phone, strap on his gunbelt, and go out into the night. Debbie knows, but that doesn't mean she has to like it.

"Hello," Jimmy says as he picks up the phone, feeling like it was a dumb thing to say, but what else could he do. He listens. Debbie's heart sinks as Jimmy's face drops. He nods and says, "I'm on my way."

"It's happened again, hasn't it?" Debbie asks, but she already knows the answer.

"Yeah. Bunch of kids out by the old camp." Jimmy pulls up his uniform pants and takes a fresh shirt from the closet. "They…yeah." Jimmy doesn't know what else to say. He's afraid of so many things but mainly that if he doesn't go now, he won't at all, and he'll hate himself for the rest of his life. "I—"

"Don't," Debbie says as she sits up in her bed. "Don't say it. Just do it."

Jimmy nods and leaves. On the way out, he stops by the twins' room. He needs to remind himself why he does this. They're getting so big, he thinks and tells himself he needs to get on with finishing the other upstairs room so they can each have their own. He'll do that this week, he promises and walks away from the gentle snores of his two small children.

The radio in his car comes to life with more chatter than Deputy Jimmy Tran hears on even the busiest of nights. He picks up his speaker and calls in. "Deputy Tran here; where am I heading?"

Through the static and noise comes a low male voice. "Jesus, Tran, thank god! I'm on route to the Williamson Farm, but I'm on my own, and I ain't exactly jumping at taking this fucker on by myself."

"It's definitely him?" Jimmy asks, even though he knows the answer. Nobody but nobody in Cherry Lake jokes about him, not on Virgin Night.

"Shit, man, when you see what he did to those kids? Nobody BUT him could do that."

"I'm on my way," Jimmy says and peels out of the drive. Debbie watches as her husband speeds off and prays to God she'll see him alive come the morning.

The Williamson Farm isn't far from Jimmy's place, but, all the same, he's not the first on-site. He recognizes the other car as Dickie Martin's cruiser before his lights shine on the man himself, shotgun resting uneasily over his shoulder.

"Brother, am I glad to see you!" Dickie says as Jimmy hops out of his car, shotgun also in hand.

"Where's everyone else?" Jimmy asks, disheartened to see no other police vehicles parked up.

"Gideon and Burke are about twenty minutes away. Jolly and Jackson more. Kelly's gone to round Horton and some of his 'good ole boys' just in case we need more firepower." Jimmy can hear Dickie frown at the mention of Horton Dumont. He and his gang of backward buddies weren't too fond of an Asian and a black man with badges telling them what to do. Dickie keeping his mouth shut says a lot.

"We know for sure he's coming through here?" Jimmy asks and doesn't want to hope they're in the wrong place. That would mean more innocent deaths.

"Started up by the old camp, then he tore through the Twenty-Four-Seven. There's nothing between there and the Williamsons'. After that, there's…" Dickie trails off as it sinks in where he will stop next. "Tran, look at me, man." When Jimmy doesn't respond, Dickie yells, "Look at me!"

Jimmy looks into the cold steel of Dickie's eyes as his partner tells him, "That ain't gonna happen," and Jimmy nods with him. All the same, he grabs the radio and calls in, "Tran here, can somebody get my wife on the phone. Tell her to get herself and the kids the hell outta there."

A jumble of static, then the voice on the radio says, "Ten-four, Deputy Tran."

"Tell her to take the old Woodvale pass, up past the point, and not to go into town, you hear?" Jimmy hangs up the radio then takes a second to get his focus back. "What's the plan?"

"Sue's tryin' to get old Joe on the phone, but he ain't picking up," Dickie says. "I'm thinking we gotta go up there and get him out before shit hits the fan."

"Wait, didn't Joe's daughter walk out on Horton last week?" Jimmy checks with Dickie, not liking where this is going.

"Yeah, racist piece of shit spent the weekend in the drunk tank after that. Why?"

"Did she take their boy with her or…"

Both Deputies slowly turn, looking up at the farm, and realize they can't wait for backup. There's a kid up there. It's too late, though; they're only halfway up the drive when the screaming starts.

The two Deputies pick up the pace and sprint the rest of the way. As they pass right by the old well and a beaten but well-loved truck, they find themselves mired in a rolling fog that seems to come out of nowhere. It swirls around the house, enveloping it as the light from the windows pierce through.

From somewhere inside the house, a rusty old voice yells, "Git the hell away from her, you sonofa—" and it's cut off just like that. A second later, the head of old Joe Williamson smashes through a window and soars through the air till it lands a few feet from the Deputies. The face still wears a toothy, defiant sneer above a long, pointed beard slick with fresh blood.

The Deputies don't have much time to react before a plump redheaded woman wearing just a nightie runs out the door, tearing through the fog, a little boy held tight to her chest. Her screams follow till she reaches the Deputies, and she falls, skidding to a stop.

"Keep going!" Dickie yells, but the woman refuses to budge. With her son held tight to her chest, she clings with her other hand to Jimmy's leg. "Go!" both of them yell, but it's no use. "Shit, take them to the car!"

"What about you?" Jimmy asks.

"I'll hold the fucker back, get her to the car, get it going, and I'll fall back," Dickie says and pumps his shotgun. Jimmy nods. He doesn't like it but doesn't see any other options. Just as he helps the woman to her feet, Jimmy turns back to the house. He catches sight of a massive silhouette ducking its head under the door frame; it's only a shape in the fog, yet it simmers with pure distilled evil.

"Hey, Shithead!" Dickie yells and fires once for punctuation. As Jimmy runs the woman and child to the car, he hears four more shots and just as many cuss words.

The three of them reach Jimmy's car, and just as he pushes them into the backseat, Jimmy hears another shot, another swear, and then an agonized roar. Shit. Jimmy slams the door hard, and the woman begs for him to get in and drive, but Deputy Jimmy Tran isn't going to leave his partner behind.

By the time Jimmy runs back up the road, Dickie has crawled past the old well. A long knife sticks through a knee at an impossible angle. Buried so deep it's probably gone straight through, judging by the lack of space between Dickie's torn pants and the handle. What kind of strength would that take? There's not even a wiggle to it as Dickie drags himself closer, and it doesn't take a doctor to see he's probably never using that leg for much after this night. Assuming they make it through.

Everyone who lives in Cherry Lake knows the stories, but to see it for real, "Jesus Christ," is all Jimmy can think to say. The monstrosity stands near the old well, barely moving, and even though all but hidden by the fog, Jimmy can feel the hate flowing off him. If menace and pain and vile walked...

"Run!" Dickie shouts as he scoots further away from him. "There's no stopping him, just run!"

Jimmy glances back at his car and the woman who beats her fists against the window within. He could run, and he'd make it, then reverse the hell out there. Go round up his family, but then what? Dickie dies for sure. How many other people would join him before it ends? How much of that blood would be on his hands? No, Jimmy knows what he has to do, and even though he doesn't like it, he knows it's what's right.

Jimmy pumps his shotgun and marches on towards hell. He fires, pumps, and fires again cowboy style, and it barely does a thing to the monster—but it's something. The blasts push him back, bit by bit, inch by inch, towards the rim of the old well. After Jimmy fires his last shot, he rushes the distance and delivers a fast, hard kick. The blow forces the bastard back against the well but not over, not like Jimmy hoped.

"Jimmy, don't!" Dickie yells. He knows his partner, knows that he's about to do something stupid and impossibly heroic.

Out of options and determined to keep everyone behind him safe, Jimmy takes a step back then rushes the monster with the full force of his body. The two of them topple over the edge of the well and fall into the dark together.

"No!" Dickie screams, but his partner's gone before he even draws breath. If it weren't for the woman and boy in the back of the car, he'd drag his ass over to the well just on the faintest of chances there's something he could do. By the time Dickie makes it to the car, leaving behind a snail's trail of blood in the dirt, he's about ready to give up and pass out. It's the hand gripping the edge of the well that stops him from doing just that. "Jimmy?"

Dickie's radio squawks to life, almost like an answer. Clicking the button Dickie asks again, "Jimmy?"

A wet cough answers, followed by static that cuts through his partner's words like a scalpel. "Di...gotta...don't..." And, of course, it's the last words that come through clear, the ones that break Dickie's heart and seal Jimmy's fate: "Forget me, stop him."

Fog spills out of the well like it's overflowing, and Dickie knows what's about to happen.

The woman in the back, screaming at him to go all this time, reaches a level of shrill that, under normal circumstances, would make Dickie's ears bleed. The thing is, that fucker climbing out of the well cost Jimmy his life, and Dickie can't let it be for nothing. He can't.

As Dickie takes the wheel, as he turns the engine over, the woman in back declares, "Oh thank god," and then her face turns sour as she sees Dickie put the car in drive. "What are you doing!? We need to get outta here 'afore—"

"Ma'am, what's your boy's name?"

"C-Caleb? Why?"

"Hold Caleb tight." Dickie revs the engine and charges the cruiser forward. The kid wails, though not half as loud as his mother, and the well in the headlights gets larger and larger. Just as the cruel shape in the fog begins to rise out, the cruiser crashes through, the old stones caving in as the front of the car comes to a stop wedged in the hole.

Dickie can't hear the screams from the backseat over his own thundering heart; he's about a minute or two from full cardiac arrest, and so he doesn't hear the other sirens or truck horns raging as the cavalry arrives either.

As the rest of the Sheriff's Department and the hometown militia pull up to the farm, we pull back further until all we see is the night sky and treeline lit by flashing red and blue.

Then the title card…

CHAPTER TWO

GREETINGS FROM CHERRY LAKE

JANUARY 11TH, 1998 - ONE MONTH TILL VIRGIN NIGHT.

Night fades as the sun comes up over Cherry Lake. We pan back down and cut through pretty streets lined with old buildings. Joggers run along the shore of a vast, beautiful lake, past a towering glass cathedral.

Inside, a packed congregation awaits, murmuring politely before the sermon begins. Posted around the hall are about a dozen young men and women, almost indistinguishable from one another in their matching white polo shirts. The man who ascends to the pulpit doesn't need the hanging monitors to call for silence, nor his staff to hush the crowd; his presence alone is enough. Clipped hair and beard, the slight hints of gray only adding more legitimacy to his authority, eyes of steel, and a warm smile as he strides out from the back with insistent confidence. This is where he belongs, and there's but one soul in the Church who does not stare at the man with enamored admiration—a portly young man who stands by the pulpit, looking like a junior, funhouse-mirror version of the Pastor. The boy stares at the floor like he doesn't want to be there, unlike the pretty, beaming blonde girl on the opposite side.

The Pastor takes his spot and turns his eye to his flock. Not a seat untaken, he notes, and even some standees in the back. They sit in their Sunday best; opal rings glint on the fingers of the younger congregants. There is nothing like the approach of Virgin Night to bring the people of Cherry Lake closer to God. Closer to him. He takes the papers that sit on his pulpit and raises them enough for the congregation to see. There's nothing on them; they're just a prop—any vital reminders he needs will be on the discreet teleprompters, but he knows what he's doing. It's all a show, this business of God, after all. Same as the crisp white shirt open at the collar, no tie, nearly luminescent against his soft, dark skin. Just like how he tosses the papers aside with a smile as he declares, "My friends," his voice booming through dozens of speakers—

—crackling through the radio in a truck that idles out by the main highway, "It warms my heart to see so many of you here today. Truly, it does." Several workers in high-visibility vests, bearing the Cherry Lake Municipal Department badge, discuss the optimum placements for the explosives. A few miles along the highway, another team marks several trees on the opposite side of the turnoff to Cherry Lake. When the time comes, both teams will work in tandem to cut off access to the town. Till then, troopers, both in uniform and out, keep a close eye on the main road into town, counting the number of people coming and going out of Cherry Lake. Like the two Deputies in a Clear Lake County cruiser parked behind a billboard for The Church on the Lake. Beneath the raised faces of the young man and woman last seen flanking the pulpit, the two Deputies keep note of any vehicle that doesn't belong to a resident of Cherry Lake. Through the radio, on the dashboard, the Pastor's sermon continues: "I want to start today by telling you a story—a tale about a quaint little town, I think we all know the name of..."

Across town, motels, hotels, and even Mrs. Mason's little bed and breakfast all prepare to close down for emergency repairs, fumigations, or whatever else they've come up with to justify shutting their doors to out-of-towners. Road work signs go up, but no work commences, though it's hard to tell if that's intentional or just business as usual.

In a VHS rental store, at the Cherry Lane Stripmall, a very bored teenage boy with one eye covered by a sweeping black fringe, the other heavy with eyeliner, watches the sermon on one of the TVs in silence. A bunch of posters for a trashy slasher series called *Blood Harvest* crowd the wall behind him. A black-and-white portrait of a man with one hell of a grin hangs above them, with a nameplate that reads Homegrown Hero: Jack Caligari.

Though the kid behind the counter wears no uniform, a small badge labeling him "Tran" clings askew to the pocket of his black gas station–style shirt, surrounded by pins for White Zombie, Marilyn Manson, and Nine Inch Nails. He scoffs, a smirk cracking the emotionless mask of his face as the Pastor puts his arm around the younger man by his side. It amuses the young man behind the counter and frustrates him that everyone other than the Pastor can see how uncomfortable the boy is.

On a scrap of paper, the surly video store clerk scribbles some lines on something that looks like a hand-drawn floor map of some large-scale building. The bell above the door tinkles, and the clerk looks up and sees a tall man, receding hair barely clinging to his skull, and an adorable little girl with a bow the size of her head sleeping against his chest. They give each other a knowing nod as the tall man hands over a nondescript brown paper package.

In the back of the store, two kids pretend to be interested in anything but the adults-only section that they hover around, but the clerk couldn't care less. It's a decoy anyway, something for the Churchies to get uptight about while the bootlegs under the counter—unreleased feature films, studio rough cuts, and pirated video games—are the store's true bread and butter. It's about the only way to compete with the Blockbuster across in—

Old Town, where fresh posters announce the Purity Prom one month from today, hosted at The Church on the Lake. They're everywhere—at the diner, the theater, even at the hardware store that reeks of oiled metal and spilled paint. Down one aisle, the organization of tools and equipment haphazard at best, a teenage boy in a beanie tests the weight of a hammer in his hand. A cruel and satisfied smile twitches at the corner of his asymmetrical lips. Malice gleams behind his baby blue eyes—he'd be unbearably handsome if something truly ugly didn't seep through from deep within.

Somewhere in the back, the Pastor's voice comes through a radio, faint and distant. "This town, you see, was blessed with a great many things. Beautiful scenery. Serenity. Prosperity. Light." Each sentence is punctuated with dramatic pause.

The boy in the beanie looks to the sides, and sure no one is watching, slips the hammer into the front pocket of his hoodie. He turns his attention, then, to sharper things.

At the edge of town at the Twenty-Four-Seven, the sermon continues on a ceiling-mounted TV. The disinterested man behind the counter digs inside his nose with great vigor as he watches a fuzzy image of the Pastor declare, "My friends, oh my friends, where light shines, there follows shadows. Follows darkness."

A hungover man, eyes red and hair unwashed, throws some cash on the counter and nods to his brand of smokes. The clerk doesn't need to look away from the TV. He takes a pack down from behind with his free hand and slides them across the counter without a word. The hungover man's on his way as the clerk nods along to the sermon.

He's three steps outside the convenience store when he bumps into a skinny, long-haired ginger kid in torn denim. "Watchit fag," the hungover man warns.

"Dude," the ginger kid says, "you're the one who copped a feel."

Half a second later, the redhead kid, now with a bloody nose to match, slams against the wall. He raises a finger as though to say "Hey now" just as a fist slams into his stomach. He doubles over, and the hungover guy with the angry hands grabs a fistful of ginger hair, forcing the other boy to look at him. A mistake, as it turns out, the redhead kid spits right in his attacker's face, and just before he gets it good, a rattling from behind interrupts.

By the side of the old garage stands a burly giant of a man, all thick beard, trucker cap, and the kind of energy that says he doesn't want to fuck you up but wouldn't have a hard time doing so if it came to it. The trucker tests the weight of the wrench in his hands, and though it's half the size of his arm, he hefts it like it's a toy. The hungover asshole pretends to fix up the beaten boy, ruffles his hair, and walks on like nothing happened at all. Nodding thanks to the trucker, the redhead limps away and smirks as he takes a pack of smokes from his sleeveless jean jacket.

We're back at The Church on the Lake now, as the Pastor wraps up the broadcast version of his sermon. "The point, my friends, is not to fear the dark. Where good walks, evil follows, and was it not a great man, I forget his name," the Pastor pauses for his congregation to chuckle, "who said I am the light of this world? He who follows me will not walk in the dark?"

Under his breath, and no notices at all, the Pastor's son corrects him with a whispered "Darkness," and then mouths the word silently over and over.

"But you must let the light in! As we have done with this magnificent cathedral. My friends both near and far, won't you join me? Won't you let the light in?" The Pastor holds his arms out as the seated congregation stands. They applaud, raise their arms, and chant "Amen" while a ticker beneath the Pastor repeats a phone number for donations on television screens across the state.

The Pastor looks to one of his technicians, who confirms the feed has been cut, and he nods. He returns to the pulpit, more somber and solemn. "My friends, it's been nine years since the last incident, since six people lost their lives, including Deputy James Tran, who gave his last to save us all. His heroic sacrifice made the last incident the least deadly in recorded history. A small mercy and a terrible loss. Though the Tran family is not with us here today, I ask you all to take a moment of silence to pray for them." All heads bow, though only one amongst the packed congregation prays in earnest for them. The Pastor's son prays for Vincent Tran especially, and for God to forgive them...

"Now!" the Pastor interrupts long before a minute passes, and only his son keeps the Tran family in his thoughts. "We, the sons and daughters of Cherry Lake, know what it's like to live with evil on our doorstep. We know the fear, and you know what? I. Am. Sick of it!" Whoops and cheers fill the auditorium. "Why give evil its night? Why cower in the dark? I say no! What do you say?"

"No!" the congregation responds.

"No!"

"No!"

"Enough!"

"Amen!"

"One month tonight," the Pastor clenches a fist and brings it down on the pulpit, "I ask that each and everyone of you joins us here, in this cathedral of light." He raises his arms to the massive open windows behind him, gesturing to the uninterrupted vista of the lake. "Defy the lurking evil of this town with our devotion at

The Church on the Lake's Purity Prom! Everyone is invited! Hallelujah!"

"Hallelujah!" the congregation responds as they rise to their feet.

The Pastor's son continues to pray, quietly whispering something that sounds like a plea for forgiveness.

CHAPTER THREE

JANUARY 30TH, 1998 - TWO WEEKS TILL VIRGIN NIGHT.

Cut to: Paradise Falls Trailer Park, where Caleb Dumont wiggles his way under his neighbor's trailer, well worn unlaced Chuck Taylors kicking up dust clouds in his wake. He holds a screwdriver firmly grasped between his teeth. The wide, skeletal grin the tool forces him to make goes well with the mess of red, shoulder-length hair that fans out all over. He looks something like a dirty, homicidal, anemic Ronald McDonald. Caleb's shirt and pants were already filthy, so he doesn't care too much about all the dirt and spiders. When Caleb sets his mind on something, no matter how dumb or insane, little else matters all that much. Anyway, a little grime only makes his slightly torn Offspring tank top look more legit.

Twenty minutes ago: Caleb comes home, and his Pop has nothing to say about the general state of his son's clothes or the fresh shiner on his right eye. He does have a thing or two to say about the phone bill, which Caleb assumed his father would be too drunk and too stupid to understand. He was right on both fronts, but he didn't count on his old man calling up the phone company to demand to know why his phone bill was higher than the rent on their dinky trailer. "And it ain't cause we callin' any of those titty numbers. I get all the cooch I need down at Tillman's, and my boy's a fag, so it ain't him," the irate man yells down the phone while Caleb gets off the bus by the edge of the trailer park. If Caleb could hear, he'd find it funny that for all the shit his old man gives, he's remarkably tolerant when it comes to using his son's sexuality as an excuse not to pay a bill.

As Caleb slinks inside the trailer, the customer service rep on the other side of the phone explains to Horton that the charges are for dial-up. A bit more explaining gets his head around the fact that it was his boy, using that dang computer of his that he'd fished out of the trash pile by the back end of the park, going on something they called the World Wide Web.

"Hey, Pa," Caleb gets out just before his father backhands him hard enough to sit his ass down hard on the torn and duct-taped sofa.

"Don't you 'Hey Pa' me when your faggot ass just wasted nearly two hundred dollars on a goddamn phone bill," Horton yells. He's tempted to whoop the boy some more but knows it'll do no good, and besides, his head's killing him.

"Pa," Caleb tries to explain himself, or at least come up with some on-the-fly excuse to simmer things down, but his father silences him with the threat of another backhand.

"Boy, I do not want to hear any goddamn thing you have to say right now." He gets in close. Caleb can smell the cheap beer on his breath and the stink of unwashed, weeks-old clothes. He can taste body odor and earwax. "Now, I know beatin' you ain't going to do no good. If an ass-whoopin' worked, then I'd have slapped the faggot out of you months ago, but seein' as how you still got pictures of that Dawson queer on your wall, that ain't the case. So I ain't gonna whoop on you no more than that, which you assuredly deserved."

Caleb feels momentary relief, but when his father doesn't step back, he knows there's more to come, and it's going to be worse than just a few smacks.

"Since you love your web world so much, I went and told them to cut the line." Caleb's heart drops. Shit, he'd take an ass-kicking any day; he needs to get online. "I said Horton Dumont don't need any faggot web stuff and told him we weren't payin', so it's gone. All gone." The man says it with such glee, such satisfaction. Horton sure knows how to hit where it hurts the most.

The plan, the whole damn thing—it's ruined. If Caleb can't get back online, can't finish his side of things, then it's all going to be for naught. He could take the defeat, sure, but he couldn't take telling Vincent that it was off. He'd rather take a thousand ass kickings from his Pa than let Vincent down.

Horton reads the concern in his son's face as contrition and backs off. He chuckles as he enjoys the cruel irony of his punishment, then Horton takes a cold one from the fridge in celebration, heading outside to enjoy it in the sun.

Caleb sits on the sofa for a moment, and the whole predicament sinks in. He needs to get back online. He needs to let Casey know the final plans. Just in case his father was all bullshit, a distinct possibility, Caleb grabs the phone by the sink and checks for a dial tone.

Nothing. Would the phone company cut them off that fast? Caleb doubts it, but it doesn't matter. Following the phone cable, Caleb finds where his father has ripped it out of the wall and sliced it in two. Even if they weren't cut off, that'd do the trick anyway.

"Fuck me," Caleb says with one side of the sliced cable in either hand. "Fuck me hella hard with a two-by-four."

Laughter carries through the air, through the window over the sink. George Higgins, their closest neighbor, has always irked Horton on account of how close the man moved his trailer to theirs last winter. While still, technically, within the boundaries, it's meant that their kitchen windows are spitting distance—something Caleb can attest to personally having seen his father make that shot on a few occasions. Both trailers are close enough that, with the windows open, Caleb can almost hear the garbled voice coming through the earpiece of the phone Higgins holds up to his ear.

Caleb drops the wire dangling from the useless phone and takes up the other side's slack. He follows it to the wall, then notes how it crosses much of the trailer on its way out the other side. Why, if he were to untack it from the wall, it'd surely reach over to Higgins' trailer.

So that's how come, a few minutes later, and after liberating the severed phone cable, Caleb finds himself sneaking under Higgins' trailer in search of some way to splice into his phone line. Dust falls into his eyes as the vibration of heavy footsteps above dislodges years of build-up. Caleb wonders what asbestos tastes like and reckons this is it.

The struggle seems for naught till Caleb catches sight of a familiar logo on a plastic box bolted underneath what he figures must be the bedroom. He's seen that logo plenty, and most recently when Michael's father had cable installed at their lake house. God damn, so Higgins had cable TV. Caleb had to figure out a way for his Pa to find that out for himself. The fit of jealousy would undoubtedly spur the man to find some way to get it just for the rivalry.

From the beaten and scratched look of the box, not to mention the jutting unprofessional jumble of cables, Caleb figures Higgins isn't exactly paying for it. Hell, that works even better, Caleb thinks as he manages to open the box without much effort. The fire hazard of spaghetti wires inside is just what he needs, and Caleb finds the phone line easy enough. It's the only wire that doesn't look like it's five seconds away from combustion.

Caleb waits till Higgins stops his pacing above him and holds steady till he hears the unmistakable creak and groan of a huge man resting his ass on a sofa that's on its last legs. The faint mumbling of conversation has stopped, so Caleb figures it's safe now to splice his phone line into Higgins, and with a bit of duct tape magic, that's what he does. "It ain't pretty," Caleb says as he looks at his handiwork, "but if it works, it works."

In his haste to get back inside and online, Caleb neglects to hide the phone line that trails through the dirt from Higgins' trailer to Caleb's bedroom window.

Caleb clambers up through the same window, the same way he got out lest his father figures out that he was up to something. Not that Horton would object all that much to Caleb stealing from Higgins, though. Inside his room, walls lined with posters of pretty-boy TV stars (Caleb makes no secret of his fondness for handsome boys with messy hair to anyone), Caleb boots up the old Apple computer he'd managed to fix up and waits for it to click and boot to life. Once it's awake, he hits the browser icon and watches as the connection wizard begins the dial-up. The beeps, buzzes, and modem's static make the connection impossible to hide, and Caleb holds his breath both for fear of getting caught and in hopes that it works.

The connection wizard turns green and—boom! He's on! The first thing Caleb does is open up AOL Instant Messenger and sees several unread ones from someone called Slayerette17, first asking for details of the meetup, then several more demanding to know what's wrong and if the messages are getting through.

Under the screenname JuanDongLover, Caleb responds and quickly explains the situation and the lack of internet. He gives her the instructions on where to meet them, how to get there, and then sits back—nothing to do now but wait.

Since he has some time to kill, and there's not much else to be doing, Caleb opens up his browser and clicks on a bookmark labeled "Totally Not Porn." After a painfully long time, a site with an obviously fake, fully nude photo of James Van Der Beek loads up.

"I ain't gonna wait either, Dawson," Caleb says as he slides his hand down his pants.

Meanwhile, just as Caleb's getting to know himself, Higgins picks up his phone to order some take-out. There's a decent-looking nudie film coming on Skinemax later, something about folks making a movie in some old southern mansion with horny ghosts. Higgins wants to make sure he's well situated by the time Kathleen Kinmont gets her clothes off. The thing is, though, the darn phone keeps making all these bizarre buzzes and clicks no matter how many times he hangs up.

Thinking there's something wrong with the line, Higgins works up the energy he needs to check on the junction box. He knew he'd regret letting that kid set it up under the trailer. That kid insisted, though, didn't he, so now Higgins was going to have to get his tired old ass under the trailer and—hey, wait a minute! The cable company doesn't bother with the folk who live in Paradise Falls, they know there's no money to be had here, so there was no real chance of one of their guys finding the stolen, modded box even if they stuck it to the outer wall like Higgins wanted.

"Huh," Higgins scratches his chins as he spots a cable coming from underneath his trailer. He follows it as it snakes through the dirt and up the side of that heel Horton's double-wide. Higgins peeks in through the window and what he sees momentarily blinds him.

The Dumont boy, beating his meat—all of it and the fire bush beneath on full display as he tugs hard enough to break the damn thing off.

Higgins screams.

Caleb screams.

Horton bursts into his son's room to see what the commotion is and comes to set his eyes on the sight of Higgins looking through his son's bedroom window while the boy tugs on himself. Now, Horton might be an abusive, drunk, homophobic, racist asshole, but some perv spying on a kid? His kid!? That's low, even for Horton.

"You stay right there, you damn pervert, while I come round and kick your ass!" Horton demands.

"Your boy's stealin' my cable!" Higgins insists, but it does no good.

Horton storms out of Caleb's room, through the trailer, and heads outside. The scuffle outside his window buys Caleb enough time to put his junk away and check AIM one last time before he makes a break for it. There's one unread message for him from Slayerette17: Cool, see you guys then! Caleb smiles and celebrates with a fist pump. He hightails it out of there while Horton and Higgins tussle in the dirt behind him. He's desperate to give Vincent and Michael the news, at least that's what he tells himself, but Caleb would be lying if he said he wasn't just as excited about showing the shitheels in Cherry Lake what he's capable of once and for all.

CHAPTER FOUR

THE SILENCE OF A LAMB

Cut: across the lake to the pretty McMansions that dot Cherry Lake's luxurious Southern Shore—to one particular mock colonial mansion, tastefully adorned with golden crosses.

"God, we thank you for this food. For rest and home and all things good. For wind and rain and sun above. But most of all, for those we love," sings a young girl's sweet voice, and we cut inside to the dining hall, where the whole Wallace family bow their heads. "Amen," she finishes.

"Amen," the rest of the family responds.

"That was beautiful, Ariella," Pastor Creed Wallace says from the head of the table, his mighty hands steepled as he smiles over them. "We should give thanks, too, to your dear mother." He nods to his wife at the other end of the table.

"Thanks, mom!" Ariella chirps, but the other Wallace child still bowing in prayer doesn't join in.

"Michael," Creed stares.

"Leave him," Vanessa Wallace says, knowing her son's peculiar ways don't take kindly to being upset.

In the awkward silence of the dining room, you can just about hear Michael as he repeats the grace prayer over and over. If you were paying attention, you'd notice he does it precisely thirteen times and then says "Amen" out loud, as though just catching up with the rest of his family. Realizing everyone is staring at him, he says, "Sorry, was I doing it again?"

Vanessa puts her hand on her son's. "It's okay, honey, you do you."

Ariella pulls her eyelid down and sticks her tongue out at her brother, but as her mother notices, she feigns having something in her eye. Vanessa scowls playfully as Ariella smiles sweetly.

Creed looks around the table quizzically. "No steak sauce?"

"Oh, didn't you get the message? I left it on your machine," Vanessa answers.

"Ah, yes," Creed pauses. "Michael and I had some Church business to attend to."

"Huh?" Michael asks, confused. His father's stare demands obedience. "Oh, yes, that's right."

"Anyway," Creed declares, "let's eat!"

After dinner, Michael notices he has a single stain on his blue button-down shirt, and even though he has a mission to accomplish this evening, he can't let it go. The problem is, Michael had already set out his seven shirts for the week on Sunday, which will upset his schedule. He'd planned to go blue to white this week, but he doesn't have a spare of either to fit in. Meaning he'll have to break the routine; taking a salmon one from his wardrobe and just knowing it's the wrong shirt for the day makes the fabric feel like sandpaper against his skin.

Michael's room is as neat and clinical as a $500 a night minimalist five-star hotel, and nothing, not even the Bible on his desk or school books, sits at anything less than a perfect 90-degree angle. He doesn't need to measure; Michael just knows.

Just across the hall, his sister's room sits open; clothes spilled on the floor. Michael tries to ignore the mess, but it makes him itchy nonetheless. He stands in front of an immaculate mirror and fastens every button on his shirt, then tucks it neatly into his slacks, the fabric pressed tight against his portly stomach. Feeling clean once more, Michael takes a deep breath and closes his eyes. When he opens them, his eyes land on something that's not right, something out of place that nobody else would possibly notice. Just at the corner of his bed, a tiny black triangle of something juts out, barely a centimeter, but Michael sees it clear as day.

He heads over to the bed and pulls what turns out to be a magazine out—the January issue of *PlayGirl* with a grinning Tom Selleck and a headline proclaiming him America's Sex Symbol.

"Caleb," Michael curses as quietly as possible.

His father will kill him if he finds this here. The others have been banned from the house ever since Michael's father caught them watching a Wesley Snipes bootleg in the basement theatre. Caleb made it worse, tried to talk them out of trouble by pointing out how cool it was to "have a sexy-ass black dude up front," and then added something about swallowing Blade's sword Michael didn't understand.

Creed Wallace rained hellfire that day. Also didn't help that the film wasn't even out yet, a studio rough-cut

Vincent got from his boss at the video store. Every word of his father's sermon was etched in Michael's memory.

"Not only did you bring illegal goods into my house, but you also partook in the glorification of a Satanic monster, a blood-drinking vampire, and worshipped an actor that personifies the celebration of the degradation of the Black American identity. We should be seen not as violent thugs but as powerful leaders of our own destiny."

If his father finds the magazine, he's either busted for sneaking his friends in or taking the blame himself. Neither option bodes well for what the three of them have planned.

There's nowhere Michael can think of that he could dispose of it without risk. His sister, obsessed with recycling, is not above sorting through the trash while tutting and chiding everyone for "killing the planet." She'd find it, then, wait a minute—there's his answer.

Michael glances over to the eruption of clothes and haphazardly discarded shoes in his sister's room and figures he could hide the magazine in there. Chances are, she'd never find it. If Michael didn't know that gambling was a sin, he'd be willing to bet good money that Caleb cleans his room more often than his sister does—that is to say, never.

He takes a few steps and then stops. The weight of what he's about to do comes crashing down on him. It would be wrong, even if he never got caught. No, Michael would just have to take this cursed thing with him and dispose of it outside, far from home. He can feel Caleb, wherever he is, giggling. Besides, what Michael needs to do tonight, what he's been trying in vain to avoid, will be sinful enough. He only hopes the end can justify the means, that in doing what he and the others plan on doing, he will be forgiven.

The sounds of laughter from downstairs fill the house and tell Michael that he's alone on the second floor. It's time to make his move.

Rolling the copy of *PlayGirl* up, Michael tucks it down his pants and adjusts it away from his front. He prays to God for courage and heads down the hall to his father's office. There is no door to it, not here nor in its counterpart inside the Church over on the northwest bank of Cherry Lake. Creed Wallace says it's to promote an open-door policy, that he, like God, is always there for his flock. Yet, whenever his father works away in the office, Michael can't help but feel it wouldn't be a good idea to test that boundary despite there being no door. It's one of his father's brazen displays of power that doesn't sit right with Michael, though he's nowhere near ready to ask himself why that is.

The office is all dark wood, with a heavy desk before a custom-made stained glass window—Michael searches for the courage to proceed. "Be strong and courageous and do the work. Do not be afraid or discouraged, for the Lord God, and my God is with you," he quotes the Bible under his breath. He repeats it another twelve times, just as fast, then with a deep breath, steps across the threshold.

A moment passes as Michael waits for God to strike him down, and when nothing happens, he proceeds to rummage around the room. Michael pulls open drawers and feels his heart race so hard he's sure it's going to pop the button on his shirt pocket. Drawers filled with papers, nondescript ring binders, nothing special or noteworthy. Then, as Michael tries to close the bottom right drawer, it sticks. He gives it a good shove, but it's no good. Something jams it up, and when Michael pulls it open again, a false back falls free and reveals a small, hidden compartment.

Inside, there's a simple mask carved from wood so dark it's black. It's creepy and weird, but not what Michael's looking for, so he puts it back carefully.

"Where is it?" Michael takes another look around the room and comes up empty. The silence from downstairs worries him though he knows he's safe for now. No way he'd miss anyone coming up those stairs. Turning back to the desk, Michael notices a small drawer right under the middle. He finds, tucked away inside a slim leather wallet, just what he was looking for—the Church's corporate credit card.

Michael grabs a slip of paper from the desk and quickly copies all the card's names and numbers, both sides, just like Caleb told him. He lays the numbers out exactly where they appear on the card, identically spaced. As Michael notes down the last digit, doubts begin to surface—what they're thinking of doing, and how he could put a stop to it right here. The others wouldn't even need to know. He remembers the sick feeling in the back of his throat when Vincent and Caleb asked him to do this. Stealing is wrong; Michael knows this. "Nor thieves nor the greedy nor drunkards nor slanderers nor swindlers will inherit the Kingdom of God," he quoted to his friends, and Caleb told him not to worry about "that Captain Kirk shit," that credit isn't real money, so it's not actually stealing. Michael didn't buy that, but the look Vincent gave him was enough—his friends needed it, and so Michael agreed. The whole idea seemed so much easier in Vincent's room, though. "Greater love has no one than this, that someone lay down his life for his friends," Michael mutters, and while the sentiment calms him, he hopes it won't come to that.

Michael hears footfalls on the steps down the hall. Not the energetic thunder of his sister racing up to her room and not the careful slight steps of his demure mother. They're the heavy, purposeful, and proud footfalls that announce the coming presence of Pastor Wallace. It's too late to back out now, so Michael puts the credit card back where he found it and shoves the paper copy in his pocket, but there's no way he'll get back to his room before Creed reaches the top. Michael gulps and prays for God to forgive him for the lies he'll have to tell.

Creed Wallace enters his office to find his son waiting for him. The boy stares through the tinted glass of the stained window with his head bowed in prayer.

"Michael?" Creed walks over and places his hand on his son's shoulder. Michael grits his teeth. That's got little to do with the situation. He just doesn't like to be touched. On top of that, he's confused about why his father lied about them spending the day together. "Can I help you with something?"

"Father..." Michael stalls.

Creed sighs. "Is this about dinner? My son, I didn't mean to make a liar of you, but there are some things your mother is best not knowing."

"No, it's not—"

"The camp? Again?" Michael doesn't want to have that conversation either, but Creed barges on regardless. "My son, you know that I bear no ill intent towards homosexuals. There are far more lost souls in this world than those who seek love in the wrong arms," Creed says, and Michael feels his booming voice fill the room. Creed doesn't need to shout, not even raise his voice an octave above his usual cadence to fill any space he stands in with his words. "I ascribe to the notion it is, indeed natural, and some scholars suggest its outlawing in the time of Moses was due to survival needs, and not morality."

He should just nod and walk away, but none of that sits right with Michael. "So why does the Church run the camp then?"

"It's simple, my son. Where would these young men be if not for camps like ours?"

"Home?"

"Home, indeed, with parents so aghast at their son's desires they're willing to spend thousands of dollars to somehow cure them of it."

"Are you saying the camps don't, uh, change them?"

"My son, if they did, they'd go out of business."

"Then what's the point?"

"We help young homosexual men find ways to blend in with society. To suppress and hide their desires. As we all must."

"That's, but people get hurt at these camps—"

"People get hurt no matter what. Suffering is inevitable. Hope is a panacea."

"So you sell false hope? Fake miracles?"

"Just as our Lord and Savior once did." Creed pats his son's shoulder and takes a seat behind his desk. "You think your father is wrong?"

"No, of course not," Michael says intuitively, but those seeds were planted long ago, and the doubts have grown like weeds inside his heart.

"Michael, my son, what do you want?"

"Perhaps if you allowed me to attend one of the Inner Circle meetings—"

"I see." Creed steeples his hands. "And suppose I were to engage in nepotism, promote you far beyond your station, and allow this. Allow you to slight those who have shown dedication and devotion, like your own paramour Miss Parker." A smile twitches in the corner of Creed's mouth. "What would you say?"

"I, um, haven't thought—"

"No! What would you say, Michael, do not stammer."

Michael gulps. "I'd say we should close the camps. Run outreach programs instead. Welcome members of the gay community into the fold, the Church could grow so much bigger if—"

"No," Creed states coldly.

"Father?"

"And if each member of the Inner Circle voted no, what would you do?"

"I, uh," Michael looks to the floor, "I don't know."

Creed sighs. "Michael, look at me. Look at me!" Michael snaps to attention and meets his father's piercing eyes. "You plant your feet and refuse to back down. Insist till you get your way. Back your convictions with courage. If you can't stand your ground with me, my son, what makes you think you can with the entire Circle?"

"Father..."

"Leave now," Creed instructs and turns to the papers on his desk. He picks one up and drives it down, hard, on a spike. The impact makes Michael wince. He hangs his head and does as his father says, slinking out of the office. Just as Michael steps over the threshold, Creed looks up. "You just proved my point."

Michael slips a hand into his pocket, checking the paper is still there and decides to take his father's advice.

Cut to: the Wallace property's back wall. The old stone bricks and climbing ivy might look ancient, but they've only been in place for the last few years. The whole south bank consists of miniature mansions and houses, made to look like they've stood there for centuries though more than half of them have stalled in construction. If you were to take a quick look at South Shore, you'd see money; if you were to peer in closer, you'd see it's mostly run out.

Michael clambers over the wall and lands with a gentle thud on the dirt path beside his house.

"Where you going?" a voice behind him asks, and Michael shrieks.

He turns around to see his sister, Ariella, her frizzy hair held back with a hairband and a cigarette dangling between her fingers. She holds it away from her body and blows the smoke with the breeze to limit what her clothes soak up.

"Nearly gave me a heart attack! You're smoking?"

"And you're sneaking out; neither of us is in the clear here, so where you going?"

"None of your business," Michael stands firm.

"Tell me, or I'll tell dad I saw you sneak out."

"I'll tell dad you're smoking!"

"I'll deny it; you've got no proof." Ariella flicks her cigarette over the barrier between the path and the still waters of Cherry Lake.

"Yeah? Where's your proof?"

Ariella pulls the hairband free, her long bouncy hair falls in front of her face, and she slumps her shoulders. "Daddy! Daddy!" she cries in a little girl's voice, "Daddy, I saw Michael sneaking off into the woods last night, Daddy!" Ariella pauses for effect, then shifts back to her normal voice. "There's my proof. FYI, he loves that Daddy's girl shit."

"Look, I'm just going to hang out with Vincent and Caleb, okay? We're just gonna watch a movie at Vincent's. Play some PlayStation. No big deal. So, FYI, get off my back."

"Do you even know what FYI means?"

Michael's silence speaks volumes.

"Caleb, though? Tell him I said hey, and we're good, big brother."

"You know that Caleb is gay, right?"

Ariella shrugs. "How gay?"

Michael reaches into his pants, utterly unaware of how inappropriate it looks, and whips out the copy of *PlayGirl* Caleb stashed in his room. "This gay!" he says as he holds the magazine up.

"Let me see that," Ariella says and swipes it from Michael before he can respond. She cracks it open, and her eyes go wide at what she sees. "Nice," she nods and bites her lip. "I'm keeping this too."

"Fine, but if father catches you with it—"

"Pfft, don't worry about that," Ariella says and opens the centerfold page. She lets it unfurl, and her eyes wander across the spread approvingly.

Michael shakes his head and then heads off, down the path leading around the lake's eastern side. Ariella doesn't notice that her brother is heading in entirely the wrong direction from where he said he was going. "Don't forget to tell Caleb what I said," she calls after him without taking her eyes from the page.

CHAPTER FIVE

THE GOOD SON

Pull back from the Wallace kids, across the surface of Cherry Lake glistening in the late afternoon sun, over the small island in the middle, to the Tran house up past the northeast shore.

Jump-cut inside a bedroom. It has the feel of a metalhead squatter in residence rather than the quaint country home it appears from the outside. Though it's hard to tell from all the half-drunk soda bottles, opened chip bags, haphazardly stacked CDs, and video game boxes, the floors are bare. The walls don't look like they've seen fresh paint in decades; between the gaps left by metal band posters and half-naked girls, we can see cracked plaster and bare wooden supports. Both legit and bootleg VHS tapes of horror movies and well-worn paperbacks sit in stacks along the wall with no support or organization. Wedged between some dog-eared Richard Laymons are local history books stolen from Cherry Lake High's library. On the floor, in one corner, rests a double mattress with no frame.

It's closing in on early evening, and Vincent Tran's still asleep, having stayed up till near dawn playing *Resident*

Evil. A bedsheet covers his whole body, dusted with a fine layer of potato chip crumbs and a scattering of video game magazines—the charmed life of a high-school dropout.

The bedsheet whips away, and we see Vincent on his back. Snoring and fully clothed save for his worn-out VANS half-cabs, discarded carelessly next to the mattress. He wears ripped black jeans, a *Dawn of the Dead* t-shirt, and his long black hair covers his face where it's not tangled in a pair of over-ear headphones.

A polished and well-cared-for boot taps Vincent's knee, but he doesn't so much as stir. It kicks him much harder than needed, and Vincent jerks to life. He panics, scrambles, and struggles to tear the headphones free without ripping some of his hair out. Heavy metal chords play so loud it's a wonder Vincent was able to sleep with the growling and bass.

Vincent clears his hair away and stares up at the intruder with eyeliner-smeared outrage. "What the hell, Em!?"

Emilie Tran stands over her twin brother with her friendship bracelet-ringed arms on the flannel shirt tied around her waist. "It stinks of weed in here."

Vincent rubs his eyes. "That's probably because I was smoking it. Nice work, Sherlock."

"Do you need a lift to work tonight? I picked up another shift. Are you wearing my eyeliner?"

"So what if I am and, nah, but I was gonna use the car—"

"Dude, you know the rules."

"Yeah, yeah." Vincent fumbles around the bed, looking for any leftover weed now that his sister has brought it up. "He—"

"Or she—"

"Who worketh taketh the careth."

"You agreed."

"I know, jeez, I know." Vincent sighs at finding nothing leftover to smoke.

"You even insisted on the lame old English stuff."

"That's what makes it legally binding."

Emilie sighs. "How are we related?"

"I—no! No, no, no, God no!" Vincent scrambles across the room, all but shoving his sister aside till he gets to a portable TV sitting on an upturned milk carton. There's a PlayStation covered in stickers next to it. "What the hell!" The TV and the PlayStation are both off. Vincent punches his thigh. "Who turned this off?"

"Oh, you must have fallen asleep and left it on. You can't do that, Vincent, it's a fire hazard," Emilie says. As she finishes her thought and looks around the room, she can't help but think a good blaze might be an improvement.

"You!" Vincent turns around and glares at his sister with unbridled outrage. "I had a perfect; I mean PERFECT run going. I was right at the end, no saves, no damage, and just under an hour on the clock. I was finally going to do it and knew I'd fuck it up, so I paused it for the morning, and then YOU, how could you!?"

"It's after four, and what did I ruin?"

"My PERFECT run on *Resident Evil!*"

"Is that the zombie game with terrible acting?"

"How dare you. HOW DARE YOU!"

"Well, sor-ee! Next time I'll leave you to burn the house down, 'kay?"

"You can make it up by giving me a ride out to meet the guys later."

Emilie rolls her eyes. "Fine, but be ready in an hour. I'm not gonna be late because your stoned ass fell asleep."

She turns on her heels and marches out of Vincent's room. "And stop stealing my eyeliner!" she yells as an afterthought.

"I'm not stoned! That's the problem!" Vincent calls after, but Emilie ignores him. An hour, he thinks, well, that's enough time to take another shot, and he turns on the PlayStation.

Close to an hour later, just as Vincent has Jill Valentine running through the start of Umbrella's secret underground lab, he hears Emilie scream for him from downstairs. He abandons the game and races down to see what's happened, though he has a pretty good idea. Vincent finds his sister standing next to their mother, reeking of booze and unwashed hair. The woman heaves into the kitchen sink, over a pile of dirty dishes, as Emilie holds her lank, greasy hair back.

Emilie looks up and says, "She's done it again."

"Fuck," Vincent curses.

"Can you—"

"I'll get her; you get to work." Vincent steps in and takes Emilie's place as their mother hurls again. Debbie's breath is staggered and labored. Emilie nods a thank-you and leaves her brother to care for their mother.

Vincent checks the splatter in the sink and curses when he sees no sign of the pills Debbie must have taken in the vile, chunky yellow goop. Debbie continues to breathe heavily, and Vincent scrunches his face up to pinch his nose off as best he can in preparation for the next wave. It doesn't come, though, and Vincent hopes he won't have to make her throw up again when a mighty heave thrusts Debbie forward, and she spews out another blast of foul liquid. There's a soft clink, and Vincent almost smiles to see a scattering of pills in the mix.

Through the ratty, torn kitchen window curtain, Vincent sees Emilie sit in the family's beat-up old SAAB. He gives her a thumbs-up, letting his sister know their mother had at least thrown up the pills, and through the dust-smeared window, Vincent can see the look of relief on Emilie's face.

Debbie gives a few more dry heaves, but it's clear she's gotten all of the crap out of her system that she's going to. Vincent resigns himself to the fact that he's going to have to spend the night looking after her, and since the guys will already be on their way to the hideout, he has no way of contacting them to say he won't make it. Debbie pushes herself up from the sink and places a sweaty, vomit-slick hand on her son's face. She smiles at Vincent, and, for a moment, it feels nice. Then Debbie coos, "Oh, Jimmy," and passes out.

Cut in on gushing water as it blasts from an old but still functional showerhead.

Debbie sits on the closed toilet lid, slumped over with her hands in her face. She sobs and mutters to herself, "Why do I do this? Why do I do this to you both?" Vincent doesn't answer. He knows that even the admission that she's harming her children is only another aspect of her self-pity. He's done listening to it and long past letting it get to him. Debbie, either unaware or just not caring that the toilet lid is down, begins to pee.

Vincent groans. Yet more of his mother's mess to clean up, and stops himself from saying anything, knowing that she wouldn't listen. He propped open the doors and windows downstairs but doubts they're getting the stink of vomit out of the kitchen any time soon. Not like they have family dinners down there anyway. He helps his mother undress and step over the edge of the tub into the shower. Debbie sits down and holds herself as the water runs down her back. At first, the idea of undressing his mother, of seeing her naked disgusted Vincent. Now it's become so routine it doesn't even register as weird, the mother-son dynamic most people take for granted erased by years of having to care for her. Not even anger at the idea she chooses to do this to herself rises in him; Vincent's so inured to the situation he nothings it.

Once Debbie's clean, dry, and dressed, Vincent helps her to bed. He makes sure she lies on her side, just in case she feels the need to throw up again, and, as he leaves, Vincent turns to see Debbie touching her wedding photo. "Oh, Jimmy," she sighs, and Vincent leaves her to wallow in her misery.

The sun's just about gone, and the cicadas are out in force as we cut outside the Tran house. Vincent steps out the backdoor, takes a seat on the porch steps. By now, Michael and Caleb will have realized he's not gonna show, and he hopes the two of them have enough done to go ahead without him. All that keeps Vincent going; when he's not so high he forgets, or so absorbed in a videogame he loses touch, is the plan. He's gonna set this right if it kills him.

He might miss the guys, but Vincent's too on edge to just chill at home and decides to go for a ride. Not too far, just in case, but there's really only one place he wants to go. Vincent checks on his mother—she snores peacefully, the photo held against her chest as she curls up with a stuffed toy. That reassures him enough that he can make a quick trip. A minute later, Vincent hops on his bike and takes off through the forest trail towards the old Williamson Farm.

Cut to: a ramshackle old farmhouse in even worse repair than the Trans'. This one has a tree growing through one window with branches reaching out through another. Most of it's boarded up, but that doesn't stop kids breaking in there every Halloween to drink, get high, fuck, and scare the shit out of each other. Vincent isn't interested in the house. He pulls up near the ruins of an old well and ditches his bike a few feet from it.

Enough of the brickwork stands to resemble what it once was, even if it's sealed off. Some respect for his father's sacrifice remains, though, as there's no sign of any tampering or vandalism even if it's been years since anyone beside the Tran kids has left flowers by the well. A plaque bolted to the small section of the rim that still stands reads: In loving memory of Deputy James Tran, beloved husband, father, and hero. He gave his life to save others on the night of February 13th, 1989.

That's it. Two little sentences are all Vincent's father gets for saving the whole damn town. They didn't even call it what it was.

"Fuck Virgin Night," Vincent curses. "Fuck this damn town."

Some nights, Vincent finds himself wishing his father had just let that thing get to town. Why did those fuckers deserve to live while his father dies? Other times he realizes it's not about deserving at all, that fucked up things happen, and there's no real reason for it. Neither of their bodies were recoverable, whatever that means. Too fucked up to move, Vincent reckons, but some stories come around now and then. That when they looked, cleared the rubble, they were just gone. It makes sense, he figures, in a fucked up way. At least for the killer. Nobody knows where the freak comes from, where he goes, and the whole damn town seems too scared even to wonder why. Not Vincent, though; no, he'd love to know where that piece of shit lays his head when he's not slashing and gutting people.

Sometimes, when Vincent doesn't have enough weed to block out the dark intrusive thoughts, he lies in bed and sees it. The blade, the axe, whatever the fucker had, plunging into his father over and over again. It's why Vincent swears that one day, he'll pay him back tenfold.

Placing his hand on the plaque, Vincent promises, "I'll get him for you, dad. I—"

A branch cracking somewhere behind startles him. He turns to see nothing but the dark road leading down to the highway. There's not likely to be anyone else hanging around the old Williamson Farm, nobody else lives this far from town, but Vincent doesn't feel that he's alone.

Another crack, this time clearly from the edge of the forest on Vincent's left. Is there someone out there? Vincent pulls his hand into a fist and marches over to the trees, ready to give whoever might be out there hell for spying on him.

A third crack, deep in, so whoever's there is either heading away or, perhaps, leading Vincent somewhere.

"Hey, dipshit! Fuck around and find out," Vincent warns.

He steps into a clearing to see someone standing on the far side. Only one loser Vincent knows wears a shirt buttoned up that much and a stupid silver cross like a dog collar. "Michael?"

"He made me do it," Michael says with an air of contrition.

"Who—"

"Rarrrgh!" Someone lands on Vincent's back. All he sees are a pair of unlaced Chucks at first. Vincent turns free and pops his attacker right on the nose. Caleb staggers back, holding his face. "Goddamn, Tran! That's a hate crime!"

Vincent cools it, seeing that it's just Caleb. "Christ, Caleb, you're lucky I didn't kick you in the nuts too."

"I could get into that," Caleb winks and shakes off the hit.

"Guys, please, don't take—"

"The Lawd's name in vain!" Caleb proclaims in his best impression of a televangelist, and he drops to his knees, raising his hands to the sky.

Michael stiffens uncomfortably.

"What are you two losers doing here?" Vincent asks.

"We went to your house after you didn't show at the lake house," Michael explains.

"Yeah, and your sister was all like," Caleb puts on a seductive, feminine voice and rubs his chest as he says, "Gee, you boys sure look hungry, how'd you like to snack on my ham wallet." He drops back to his usual self. "And we were like, nah, it's cool, put your clothes back on."

"That didn't happen," Michael states.

"Yeah, no shit," Vincent confirms. "A, because anything Caleb says is an automatic lie—"

"You're lookin' super dope tonight—"

"B, Emilie is at work tonight."

"So she's definitely naked somewhere," Caleb winks.

"Dumont, you want a black eye to go with your nose?"

Caleb puts his arms up. "Hey, don't shoot the messenger; we all know Starsky's a perv."

There's not much worth arguing there; everyone in town knows Starsky of Starsky's Arcade and Pizzeria loves perving on the high-school girls he hires.

"Anyway, I have news," Caleb teases.

"Yes, I was able to get what Caleb needs," Michael says with an awkward smile.

"Michael, honey, you ARE what I need," Caleb fawns at Michael, who stiffens awkwardly. Dropping the bit, Caleb continues. "Home skillet got the deets, for reals, but that's not all," Caleb pretty much sings.

"Yeah?" Michael and Vincent say in unison.

Caleb lets the moment drag out, his eyes darting between his two friends with demented glee. "She's in," he finally blurts out just as Vincent goes to break the silence.

"For real!?" Vincent all but yells.

"We're really doing this then," Michael says with a hint of resignation.

"You bet your fine asses we're doing this, boys!" Caleb says as he puts an arm around each of his friends. "We're gonna kick Virgin Night square in the nuts!"

CHAPTER SIX

THE ROAD to CHERRY LAKE

FEBRUARY 6TH, 1998 - ONE WEEK TILL VIRGIN NIGHT.

Cut to: a Greyhound as it rumbles along the two-lane highway a few miles out from Cherry Lake.

A girl leans her head against the window and stares out at the passing forest from inside the bus. She's seen trees, trees, and, oh, more trees in the last hour than she probably has her whole life. Her hair, pinned up inside a flower-fronted denim bucket hat, spills out a little. Suddenly the treeline breaks, and she catches sight of an empty, abandoned old town almost hidden behind a massive billboard for something called The Church on the Lake.

"That's Old Woodvale, deary," says the kind, older woman sitting just across the aisle from her. The girl turns and sees a big gap-toothed smile, not to mention glasses, too large for the older woman's head. "I used to date a boy from Woodvale when I was your age.

Handsome lad, very quick on his feet. Had to be, or my father would have whooped him good!" The older woman clenches her fists, and the girl in the floppy floral hat thinks it's just adorable. "What's your name, deary?"

"Casey," the girl says, her voice sweet though it's hard to place where she's from, and she holds out her hand. Her fingernails show the telltale roughness of a nailbiter, which isn't a habit you'd associate with such a prim and charming-looking girl, the older woman notes.

"Lovely to meet you, I'm Judy." The two passengers shake hands.

"So what happened to Woodvale? It looks like a ghost town?" Casey asks.

"That's 'cause it is!" A boy springs up over the seat in front, his messy hair held in check by a backward baseball cap. "Whole town vanished back in the fifties. Abducted by aliens." The kid whistles the tune from *The X-Files* while his eyes pop and he waggles his fingers.

"Sit your ass down," says a gruff voice from the seat in front, and the baseball cap kid zips down out of sight. An older, balding man with a thick, muscular neck leans around the side. "Pardon my idiot son, ladies; he's obsessed with that Fox Murder crap on TV."

"Fox MULDER, dad, jeez," the kid pouts.

Casey giggles, "Scully rocks."

The kid shoots back up with a look of pure energetic awe on his gaping face. He points to Casey and proclaims, "The truth is out there!"

"The truth is you don't stop bothering those ladies; I'll tan an X across your hide," the boy's father pulls his son back down once again. "There ain't no such thing as aliens!"

"Nu-uh," the boy says, "Clementine just found water on Mars, so there!"

"I don't care what some Clementine kid said," his dad barks.

"Oh, he's no bother," Judy says. "We were all young once, after all. But it was nothing so exciting as little green men. There was a terrible fire, destroyed most of Main Street," Judy sighs, "and I never saw that lovely boy again. Oh, how I wish I could remember his name."

"That doesn't explain how so many people died at the drive-in, outside of town, twenty-four hours earlier!" the kid chirps.

"Boy, that's it, no more computer time for you," his father warns.

"Aw, man," the kid sulks.

Casey turns back to the window as the ghost town slips from sight behind the tree line once again. Aliens, she thinks? Weirder shit has happened.

"Folks, we'll be pulling over at the last rest stop before Redcastle in a few, be about four hours before we stop again, so do what you gotta," the driver calls over the speaker.

Casey's brow furrows. "Doesn't this bus stop in Cherry Lake?" she asks.

"Nope. Around this time of year, there's always something going on," the man in front says, "roadworks 'n' such."

"Or," the kid, once again, springs to life, "are they hiding some—" and his father pulls him back down before he can finish his thought.

"You're not heading to Cherry Lake, are you, deary?" Judy asks, and though she flashes Casey that gap-toothed smile again, there's a hint of concern laced with the sweet old lady tenor in her voice.

Casey smiles and shrugs. "No, just sounded like a nice little town, thought maybe I could take some pictures." She holds up the camera that dangles around her neck.

"Oh, it is," Judy says, "it is…but you don't want to go there, deary." She smiles nervously. "There's nothing for a pretty young thing like yourself there." Judy takes Casey's hand. "Now, Redcastle, that's where the handsome men are, let me tell you. Back when I was your age, I had a boyfriend from there…"

The Greyhound pulls over into a small rest spot. There's just a convenience store bolted onto a garage and a few pumps out front. Casey steps out, a breeze ruffles her red floral dress. It's freezing but feels good after being cooped up on that bus for so long, refreshing. Most other passengers make a beeline for the restrooms and soda fountains inside while Casey finds her eyes drawn to the old garage. The sign on the front says Walker's, but there's faded, sunbleached letters almost invisible but still there beneath. Casey can just about make out the name "Sam," and she thinks it's worth snapping a picture.

She ducks around the side of the garage, out of sight and into the shade, and when she's sure nobody is looking, Casey slips a small black leather notebook out of her bag. Tucked near the back are a few slips of paper, which she takes out and glances around before unfurling. A crudely drawn map of the town with a circled location on the eastern shore. No directions on how to get there from the crossroads she finds herself at, though.

"Great," Casey mutters and looks around for a clue. Nothing but trees and road as far as she can see.

"All aboard!" the bus driver calls as he clambers back up to the wheel. The other passengers filter back on, some carrying stacks of snacks for the last leg of their journey.

Casey slinks back into the shadows and hopes nobody notices she's missing, not till the bus is on the road and miles away at least. The engine purrs to life and chugs away as the bus idles. It waits for a few minutes after the last passenger gets on board, and then the door closes. As it pulls out of the rest stop, Casey steps out and catches Judy glaring at her. Gone is the pleasant sweetness from earlier, replaced by a stern, disapproving scowl that unsettles Casey long after the bus carries the woman away.

"Kay, Casey, you gotta figure how to get to this shit hole town now," she huffs.

"Missed your bus?" The voice comes from just inside the garage. It's deep and rough, though not threatening in the least.

"Tryin' to get home," Casey lies, "back to Cherry Lake," remembering the warning JuanDongLover gave her about the town's attitude to outsiders.

"Uh-huh," the man says and stands up from his chair, resting his half-empty bottle of Miller on the ground. "Well, you look like a Cherry Lake girl. Which part of town you from?" He's a big man, tall and broad, with a mess of long, curly hair that merges with his beard—all of it kept in check by a torn trucker's cap.

Casey thinks fast, tries to recall something she read to make her story sound more legit. "Yeah, my dad stays in, uh, Old Town."

"So what're you doing out of town then?"

"Went to college," she says, the lies flowing easier now, "didn't take."

The big man mulls it over, then shrugs. "What the hell. No one else is gonna be coming through today. I'll give you a ride up to the Point."

"The Point?"

"Yeah, far as I'm going. My place is up the mountain." The older man scratches his beard. "Local girl like you knows the way from there, right?"

"Of course!" Casey lies. "Thanks. I'm Casey," she says, playing friendly.

"Walker," the man says. "This here's my garage. As you can see, I ain't exactly run off my feet so let me hit the head, and I'll be right with you."

Getting in a truck with a random stranger who's been drinking in the middle of the day might sound like a terrible idea, but Casey doesn't seem concerned. A few minutes later, Casey finds herself in the passenger seat of a truck. She can barely see over the dash to which there's taped a very worn, faded vintage pinup postcard of a voluptuous redheaded woman at the beach. There's some writing, impossible to read through age and wear, save for the last two words: Your Petunia.

"So…you from around here?" Casey asks.

"Eh, more or less," Walker shrugs, "been drivin' these roads for years. Used to be a trucker."

"Yeah? How's a trucker end up a grease monkey out in the middle of nowhere?"

"That, kid, is a story for another time." Walker sees her disappointment and shoots her a wink. "It involves a secret compartment in a wooden leg and an inheritance scam."

"No way! That's some Scooby-Doo sh-stuff right there! When was that?"

"Way back, way too way back. When you got more years behind you than in front, you tend to stop countin', kid."

"Wow, so hey, you must know what happened to that old town back there? Right? The ghost town. What's it called, Woodville?"

"Woodvale," Walker says, and from the way it comes out, Casey can tell there's a lot more he's not saying. "Thought you said you was from the Lake?"

"Uh, yeah, I was stayin' with my mom in the south—"

"Before college?"

"Yeah!" Casey chirps too enthusiastically, forgetting her own cover story.

"Like they say, it was a fire. Didn't have it in them to rebuild, so they moved on. Lots of little towns like Woodvale dotted across this great country. The death of small-town America. Folks don't know what they got till it's gone."

"Dude, you're like a trucker-poet. I love it!"

"I knew a poet once. A real one."

"Oh yeah?"

"Ever heard of Maxwell Lee?"

"Can't say I have."

"Kinda big in the 70s, Bay Area poet. Knew him from way back, though. Here's your stop." Walker pulls his truck over near a dirt trail that leads up an inclined path. "There ain't nobody about, but sure as hell I drive you up to that Point, and some tongue-wagger from town will see. All I'll hear for weeks is how Old Man Walker took some pretty young thing up to Make-Out Point like he was a teenager again. That's all I need…listen, I don't know what your story is, but I ain't no fool. Whatever you're up to in Cherry Lake, be careful. Weird shit goes on round here. The kinda stuff you wouldn't believe."

Casey hops out of the truck and grabs her bag. "Dude, I'm cool, and don't sell yourself short. You ain't passed it yet." She gives the older man a wink goodbye. Casey watches as the truck pulls away, the driver blushing under his wild hair, and waits till it's gone from sight before heading up to the Point on foot.

When she reaches the top, Casey finds herself with an incredible view. She can see the distant remains of Woodvale off to one side. Something about the place unsettles her, and there's not much that gets under Casey's skin. Knowing her destination is in the other direction, Casey marches on. She comes to another clearing and, down below, sits a town that has to be Cherry Lake. It's built around a massive body of water that's mostly circular, except where it thins into a twisting river that leads north. Along the south shore, she can make out several big houses, while on the northwest side, there's the main town with a massive, gleaming glass building that looks like it's built on the lake itself. The contrast between this town and the other couldn't be starker, and from where Casey stands, she can just about fit them both in a single shot with her camera, separated by a sea of trees and open farmland.

The view is enough for Casey to get her bearings, and she heads off towards the place marked on her map.

Cut to: a split-level elegant rustic lake house on the east shore of Cherry Lake, nestled comfortably on the edge of thick woodland. The kind of expensive getaway that costs a lot of money to make it look homely, the lower floor opens onto a deck built out over the lake itself. It's starting to get dark, but there's not a single light on, and the flag out front flaps in the evening breeze.

Casey walks up the steps to the main entrance and peers in through the glass-fronted door. There's no sign of anyone. She tries the handle, but, of course, it's locked. No matter—she picks up a nearby rock, turns it over, and, wouldn't you know it, there's a key taped to the bottom. Casey uses it to open the door and slip inside, pocketing the key for future use.

Inside, the walls are polished pine, the furniture deep, dark wood, and in the middle of the open-plan lounge, a vast stone fireplace goes from floor to arched ceiling. Shelves lined with hardback books fill one wall, while several framed photos dot the rest. A large painting, a family portrait, hangs on the feature wall. It shows a well-apportioned black family of four. A graceful woman sits in the middle, wearing a skirt-suit, while a smiling girl with her thick hair bound back leans in next to her, smiling. They're both beautiful, Casey thinks, like mother, like daughter. An awkward young man with close-cropped hair stands to rigid attention off to the other side, his hand resting respectfully on his mother's shoulder. Casey has an instant urge to undo the top button of his shirt just so the poor guy can breathe. Behind them all stands a powerful man in a fine suit, smiling benevolently, but Casey can't help but feel his painted eyes are passing judgment on her.

"Hello?" Casey calls out, and no one answers. Figuring she's all alone, Casey decides to unpack and get a bit more comfortable. She dumps her bag on one of the L-shaped sofas and takes out a taped together Discman with a fabric CD carrying case. Casey glances around the room, and her eyes land on an impressive-looking music system built into the wall. She flicks through her CD collection and settles on Sexless Demons and Scars with a smirk.

Seconds later, the whole cabin fills with Jessicka Addams' screams, and Casey dances as she pumps her fists in the air. She hurls the bucket hat across the room, and multi-colored hair tumbles free to her shoulders. Casey pulls the dress over her head and kicks the ballet flats off. She takes out a cropped, ripped white t-shirt, scuffed red steel-toe boots, and a black mini-skirt from the bag and tosses them down for later.

In the master bathroom mirror, she applies some black lipstick, then gives herself a riot grrrl roar in time to the music. She fixes her nose and lip piercings back in and twirls out into the lake house's main lounge. Casey headbangs across the room, dancing like the devil with a black dress on, till she turns around and sees three open-jawed boys gawping at her from the front door.

One of them does his best to look anywhere but at the half-naked girl and fails miserably; the second stares with dramatically lined eyes; and the third nods his head approvingly. Like a backward Breakfast Club version of see, hear, and speak no evil.

"Uh, hi guys," Casey giggles in a thick Texan drawl.

CHAPTER SEVEN

10 Things I Hate About Virgin Night

VALENTINE'S DAY, 1997 - THE NIGHT AFTER VIRGIN NIGHT.

The riotous grrrowling of Jack Off Jill gives way to some mumbled pop-punk travesty playing on a sound system where the bass is way off as we cut to a house party in one of the South Shore McMansions.

Teens hang out all over the place, like a Roman orgy with low-rise jeans, band t-shirts, and flannel. A kiddie pool, filled with ice, has two boys and a girl with their arms behind their backs bobbing for beer bottles as a pristine white Miata pulls up outside.

Inside the car, Michael sits formally in the front passenger seat. Even the way his seatbelt crosses his chest is neat and proper. The driver checks her makeup in the mirror, pursing her lips to confirm that everything is applied expertly. It is. She pulls off the headband holding her hair back and then ruffles her choppy, ear-length blonde hair till it sits in a casually effortless bedhead. Michael rubs his hands along his knees and stares out at the party with apprehension.

"Do we really need to go in there? I don't think father—"

"Michael," the girl snaps, "loosen up." She unbuttons her polo shirt, letting the edge of a pink bra peek out. Michael tries not to notice and feels something swirl in the pit of his stomach. "Come on," the girl says and slips out of the car without another word.

"Okay," Michael sighs. He mutters it another twelve times, then says, "Here we go," and follows. Michael takes two steps towards the house and notices his companion hasn't followed. He turns around and sees the girl wrestling with her pleated skirt, pulling it from where it sat, just north of the knee, up high enough that it's more of a belt.

"Kaytlynn, someone will see!" Michael hisses.

"Lighten up," Kaytlynn tuts as she finishes, "Virgin Night was last night." Though it's starting to feel like it's every night with Michael Wallace as her boyfriend. "Take a chill pill." She swings her hips on her way over to Michael and slips her arm around his. He stiffens reflexively but tells himself he's wrong to feel that way and lets Kaytlynn lead him up to the party.

Cut to: the big, open-plan kitchen, where Caleb leads court with a bunch of high-school girls hanging on to his every word. His wild ginger mane is held in place only by a pair of sunglasses perched above his forehead. They're designer, but nobody needs to know he found them dumpster diving. He's telling them all about the last guy he hooked up with, bullshitting much of the story, of course, and they eat up every word he says. From the way a few of them stare at Caleb, they'd like to eat him up too.

"Hey, I didn't know this was a gay bar," a boy says as he pushes through the circle of girls. He wears his Cherry High letter jacket even though it's hot as hell inside the house.

His buddy pushes through on his heels and shouts, "Butts to the walls, boys!"

"Boys," Caleb smiles, "lads, gentlemen, if you will." He puts his hands together and slips into something close to a terrible British accent. "While yes, I do undoubtedly enjoy the company of other men, my presence alone does not make where I choose to partake in alcoholic refreshment a, as you say, gay bar no more than your association makes it a kindergarten."

"What's that mean?"

"He's saying you're dumb."

"Actually, you're both—"

"Fuck you, fag." One of them throws a punch, but the other catches it.

He whispers in his friend's ear, "Not cool, bro, remember what Jam said?"

The hotheaded one nods and then turns his fist into a finger; he points right at Caleb. "You're lucky this is Jam's party, otherwise—"

"Well, we couldn't exactly have a massive rager in your duplex now—"

"Watch it, trailer trash!"

"Let's bounce," the other boy says and drags his hotheaded friend away.

Over the crowd, across the lounge, and at the back, Caleb catches sight of the host of this evening's festivities, Jam, as he watches the party from a raised landing where two staircases come together. His brilliant baby blue eyes meet Caleb's. A smile appears above some chin scruff that clashes with Jam's frosted blonde tips. Jam raises his beer in salute, and Caleb responds with a smirk.

"Those guys were such a-holes," one of Caleb's fangirls says, each word dragged out with more drunken syllables than you'd think were possible.

Caleb swigs his beer. "Lotsa gay guys who ain't ready to come out act like that," he tells his audience. "It's just a way for them to get up and close with another guy without admitting they want to."

"Woah," the girl with abundant syllables says. "Did you, like, ever hook up with a guy who didn't know he was gay?"

Caleb smiles. "Oh, I have a story—"

Cut to: the backyard, where some kids sit with their feet in the heated pool. The night is too young, and no one is drunk enough to have stripped down and gone in. Yet.

In the corner, hanging around a swing set, are three boys almost hidden in a haze of smoke. One of them draped backward over the lower half of a seesaw; another sits with his back to a tree, legs splayed open as he stares up at the leaves, and then there's Vincent, who sits sideways on a swing way too small for him as he puffs on a joint.

The boy on the seesaw giggles, "Man, I am blazed!"

"Anyone who proclaims their blazedness is not truly blazed," the kid on the ground says.

"True dat." The three of them fall into hacking laughter.

"Anyway, what were you saying?" the kid on the ground asks.

"Oh yeah, shit, what was it?" Seesaw tries to recall.

"Something about a movie," Vincent reminds him.

"Oh yeah, cool man, yeah, so they made that movie to, like, plant doubts in people's heads. I'm telling you."

"What movie is this?" the kid on the ground asks.

"*Men in Black*, ain't you listening, man?"

"That movie with the Fresh Prince?" Vincent checks.

"Yeah! For real, like, see, we have all these computers and shit now, and cable TV, so they can't hide all their shit anymore, so they gotta, like, get out in front, get me? Like, make a movie about it, and it's out there. Anybody says shit, and they're like, it's just a movie, bro."

"Who's they?" Vincent asks.

"Aliens, man!" Seesaw throws his hands in the air, "the goddamn Men in Black!"

"You ARE blazed! Ain't no such thing as the Men in Black," the kid on the ground says.

"I've seen them," Seesaw kid insists, "dude's wearing shades even in the rain."

"Could be blind?" Vincent offers, and the thought blows Seesaw's mind.

Over by the house, a few kids take notice of the stoners in the back. "Who invited the burnouts," one of them says, and then, "Hey, watch this." He turns and yells across the backyard. "Hey, Tran! I think I broke my dick off. Can you ask your mom to check if it's still there?" Vincent puffs and tries to ignore it.

Michael and Kaytlynn come around the corner, and Michael's eyes land on the stoners in the back. "Oh, hey, there's Vincent, let's—"

"Ew, as if! We are not being seen with those losers. Come on, let's find Jam," Kaytlynn insists and pulls Michael towards the open sliding doors into the house.

Michael finds a little courage, just a smidge, and plants his feet. "Please, Kayt, he's my friend."

"Urgh." Kaytlyn rolls her eyes. "Whatever. I'll be inside when you're done playing missionary to the degenerates. Come find me, and DON'T let that stinking smoke get all over your clothes, or you're walking home." Kaytlynn detaches herself from Michael and heads into the party.

"'Sup, holy man," says the kid on the seesaw as Michael approaches. He stands far enough away to stay out of the smoke.

"Hey Mikey," Vincent says and nods towards Kaytlynn as she skips up the steps. The boys sitting on them perv up her tiny skirt as she goes. "How's that going?"

"Fine," Michael tells the others. Fine, he tells himself.

"You guys?" the kid on the ground says and attempts to put an index finger through a hole he makes with his other hand. He can't get his finger within an inch of the hole.

"That probably sums it up better than you meant," Vincent says, which makes the three stoners laugh.

"Um, I don't know what you mean," Michael says, totally lost.

"I know you don't, buddy," Vincent says and offers Michael his joint. He knows his friend will decline, but he wants Michael to know he's included all the same.

"No thanks," Michael says, then he's interrupted by the kids by the door yelling again.

"Hey, Tran!" They giggle and shove each other, pushing the shouter on. "Why did your dad throw himself down that well!?"

"Motherfucker," Vincent curses, and the other two stoners giggle uncontrollably. "I'm—"

"Don't, please." Michael holds his palm to Vincent, calming him. "To one who strikes you on the cheek, offer the other also," Michael quotes.

Vincent flicks away his spent joint, about two seconds from violence.

"It's 'cause, hey Tran! It's 'cause it was tighter than your mom's cooch!"

"Hey! Fuckers!" Vincent yells, ready to go, and the chuckleheads all scarper quick.

"They're not worth it. You'll only end up in trouble," Michael points out.

"Yeah, well, what else is new?" Vincent rolls a new one. "You better go find your girl," Vincent says, licking the paper.

"I'll see you boys later," Michael says and heads towards the house.

"Laters, holy man," Seesaw adds.

We follow Michael towards the house, up the steps past the chucklehead assholes, and once he moves through the open doors, the booming bass and music pick up. Michael stiffens up as the sounds grate inside his head.

He catches sight of Kaytlynn over by the stairs with her back against them. Jam leans against the wall, next to her, and from where Michael stands, he can see Jam's brilliant blue eyes stare right down Kaytlynn's open buttons. She doesn't seem to care as she smiles up at him and braces one foot against the railing behind her, rubbing her knee in between Jam's legs.

"Kayt—" Michael begins to shout but is drowned out by the music and one impossibly loud voice.

"Mikey," Caleb declares as he throws an arm around his friend. "I'm drunk," he explains needlessly.

Michael extracts himself from his friend's embrace. "I can see that," he says as he helps Caleb keep his balance.

"Come, drink with me, my friend, and we shall discuss such things. Things and such? I'm drunk," Caleb repeats.

Michael glances back over to where Kaytlynn was and can't see her anymore. He looks around just in time to see her disappear up the stairs. His heart races but calms when he sees Jam's still down at the party, with one of his friends whispering in his ear. Michael doesn't know if it's his paranoia, but they seem to be looking right at him and Caleb. They seem to be smiling.

"I'm drunk," Caleb restates, "and I need the bathroom. Little help?"

"I'll help you find it, but you're on your own when we get there," Michael says and flinches as he lets Caleb put his arm around him again.

"You're a saint, Michael me son," Caleb says in a terrible attempt at an Irish accent, "a SAINT!" Michael gets Caleb to the downstairs bathroom and leaves him there. Once he's sure Caleb can maintain his balance, Michael leaves his inebriated friend to relieve himself everywhere except in the toilet.

When Caleb staggers out of the bathroom sometime later, he comes face to face with one of Jam's buddies. "I'm drunk," Caleb informs him, and the guy doesn't say a thing. He hands Caleb a slip of paper. It takes him a moment to muster the dexterity to unfurl it, but when he does, Caleb finds a message which reads: Meet me in the game room in ten minutes. Alone. Jam.

"Well, well, well," Caleb smirks, "I guess those tips aren't the only thing you want frosted, eh Jammy?" Then he wanders off in search of the game room. Luckily, Jam's parents put plaques on the doors to both the game room and the home cinema, so it doesn't take Caleb all night to find it.

"Hello," Caleb says as he slips inside the darkroom. The only light is what filters in through the half-open curtains. "I'm drunk," Caleb announces as he reaches for the light switch.

"Leave it off," a voice in the dark insists. "It's hotter this way."

"Jam?" Caleb says, recognizing the voice.

"Besides, I don't want anyone to see us," Jam says as he walks out of the shadows and around the pool table.

"Oh, Caleb likey," Caleb says and suddenly doesn't feel quite as drunk as before. He approaches Jam and strokes the little bit of fuzz on his chin. "I didn't know you were into guys?"

"I'm not," Jam says, a little too harshly, before he collects himself. "It's, I guess, I don't know. When I see the way you look at me, it makes me feel uncomfortable. But I like it, all the same."

"Why don't you let me show you what you're missing," Caleb says, and his hand slips behind Jam's head. He pulls the other boy in to kiss, and Jam stops him.

"Not right here. If anyone saw, if my folks found out, I'd be dead."

"Of course," Caleb says, having done this dance with more than a few closeted boys in the past.

"Over here." Jam leads Caleb away from the window to the dark side of the pool table. "Get on your knees," he instructs.

"Yes, sir!" Caleb says and drops down. He reaches up, fumbles for Jam's belt buckle.

"Close your eyes," Jam says, and Caleb obliges. He listens with excited anticipation as Jam undoes his belt and the zipper comes down. The floorboards on either side of them creak. "Now!" Jam yells, and suddenly Caleb feels hot wetness hit him from three different angles. Jets of foul-smelling liquid blast him, some of it getting in his open mouth, and as soon as the taste registers, Caleb knows what they're doing. He falls back, against the pool table, with nowhere to go as Jam and two of his buddies piss all over him.

"Stop!" Caleb begs.

"What's the matter, heard you fags love golden showers," one of Jam's friends says.

"Yeah, drink it up, pussy," the other adds while Jam just glares down with a hateful intensity.

The three of them pin Caleb against the pool table, with nowhere to go, and even with both hands raised, he can't do much to prevent the three of them from drenching him. After a while, he stops struggling.

When they finish, Caleb sits there, slumped on the floor, hair plastered to his face.

"Don't you ever look at me with those faggy eyes again," Jam says as he zips his pants.

"We just gonna leave him there?" one of Jam's friends asks.

Jam smiles; he has an idea. "Nah, boys, you two shove him in that closet over there." He nods across the room. "Put him back where he belongs. I've got someone else to take care of."

"No," Caleb mutters, utterly defeated. "No, please!" The two minions take an arm each, hefting the piss-soaked boy up and dragging him across the room. "Not in there," Caleb begs as they throw him inside and slam the door closed. "No!"

One of them grabs a pool cue and uses it to secure the closet door, locking Caleb inside just as he finds the strength to fight back. The door rattles but holds as Caleb yells, "Let me out, you assholes! Let me the fuck out!" He screams and then whimpers, "Please let me out."

He's not in the closet at Jam's party anymore. He's eight years old, and it's the first time his father caught him taking the clothes off his G.I. Joe dolls. He's twelve years old, and it's the time his father saw him holding hands with another boy at the dump out back of the trailer park. He's fifteen, dragged home after his father found him and another boy making out behind Walker's Garage outside of town. He's all of those ages, and he's locked in the closet, in the sweltering summer heat and freezing winter, of their trailer. Left there for days as punishment for being who he is. A wounded, pained cry escapes his lips.

Cut to: Michael as he wanders the house in search of Kaytlynn. He recalls her going up the stairs but tells himself that she must have been looking for a bathroom. What other reason would she have for going up there? Michael might be an "uptight Jesus fanboy," but he's not so naive he doesn't know what goes on upstairs at these parties.

He stops, asking several people if they've seen Kaytlynn, and the ones who bother to answer all tell him no. Soon enough, Michael bites the bullet and climbs the stairs, his heart racing. The music fades away once he's on the upper floor, gone from overpowering, reduced to a dull, bass hum that only itches at the back of his teeth ever so slightly. The relief is short-lived, as, in the quiet, Michael can hear a familiar voice as it calls out, "Yes, yes, fuck me, yes!"

Michael follows the sound to a bedroom, with the door cracked open slightly, and feels his entire body sink into the floor as he watches Jam, with his pants around his ankles, as he thrusts rapidly between a girl's legs. Her plaid skirt tossed up and polo shirt left on the floor, Jam fumbles at Kaytlynn's hot pink bra, unable to get the thing off while humping and too caught up to stop.

"I'm coming," Jam announces, and Michael throws up in his mouth.

"Not in—" Kaytlynn protests, but it's too late; Jam calls out and pushes hard for a second, then collapses on top of her.

"Fuck, Jam, not again," Kaytlnn complains, "you're paying for it if I have to take another trip to Redcastle, you asshole."

Michael feels the whole world swirl around him, the ground he stands on slips away, and he staggers backward only to come up against something solid.

"Hey Jam," a voice at his back says. "Looks like you got a peeping Tom out here!" the person behind him yells and shoves Michael into the bedroom.

"Michael!" Kaytlynn screams, and she dashes to the floor to retrieve her shirt. "This isn't—"

"Don't bother, Kayt; he's a freak, but he's not a moron," Jam says as he pulls his pants up. "Not like he's going to do a thing about it, am I right?"

Jam's friend's fingers dig into Michael's shoulders. They feel like needles burrowing deep inside his flesh. "I'll tell father, he won't let you be on the youth council anymore," Michael threatens.

"You won't say a thing," Kaytlynn says. "Can you imagine what that'd do to your dad's image?" Michael doesn't respond. "Besides, it's your fault you're too pussy to fuck me yourself."

"Lady has needs," Jam declares.

"Shut the fuck up, Jam; you better hope we're in the clear this time," Kaytlynn says as she puts her top back on and fixes her clothes. She collects her opal ring from the dresser and slips it back on. "I'm gonna go clean myself up," she says. "You go wait for me downstairs," she tells Michael. "We'll have a talk in the car when I'm done."

"O-okay," Michael says and hangs his head as Kaytlynn heads out of the room.

Jam steps over and places two of his fingers under Michael's nose. "Smell that? That's what you're missing." Michael's limp hand forms into a fist. For just a second, a powerful urge to lay one on Jam right in the face takes over, and then it vanishes as quickly as it came. "For the anger of man does not produce the righteousness of God," Michael mutters to himself almost imperceptibly.

Jam either doesn't hear or doesn't care. "You can follow her to the bathroom, get you some sloppy seconds if you like," he scoffs, then wipes his glistening fingers across Michael's shirt.

Laughing, Jam and his buddy leave Michael standing in the middle of the room, slumped in shame, rigid with fear. After a few moments, he heads out the room, with his head hung low, and goes downstairs to wait for Kaytlynn.

Cut to: Vincent, still on the swing out back, as he watches Michael march, eyes to the floor, out of the house and over to the side-gate he came in from earlier that night. It doesn't sit right with him the way his friend looks or the way he moves without paying attention to anyone around him. That's the way Michael used to be before he and Caleb started hanging out with him, and it bothers Vincent to see his friend regress like that. He worries about what could have caused it when screams of disgust erupt from inside the house.

Caleb emerges, soaking wet, and everyone around him acts like they're going to throw up. Even across the yard and lost in a haze of smoke, the stench of stale urine hits Vincent's nose, and he knows that something very wrong has happened to his other friend.

"The fuck is going on," Vincent mutters as he puts out his joint and pockets it. Something inside tells him the shit's about to go down, and he's not about to waste his last one. Caleb heads to the back gate, and when some kid doesn't get out of his way, Caleb shoves him aside, screaming in his face, before disappearing into the night. This whole time, Michael cowers by the gate; he rubs his elbow and stares at his shoes.

Kaytlynn comes out of the house, struts across the yard, and gets in Michael's face. She's telling him something like how a mother tells a child, but Vincent can't make out what from the swing.

"Man, what reeks," Jam calls out from the back porch, and all around him, laughter follows. Not in on the joke; Vincent watches as Jam winks at Kaytlynn and fixes his junk. She holds her right hand to her head and mouths "Call me" as she marches Michael to the car.

Suddenly it all clicks—the stink, his soaked friend. The smirk, the beaten and defeated Michael, regressed years in a single night. Some bad shit, really bad shit, has happened to his best friends tonight, and from the looks of it, one douchebag with frosted tips is the culprit.

That's all Vincent needs. He climbs off the swing and starts across the yard towards Jam. Vincent unhooks the three-row bike chain belt that holds his torn black jeans up and readies it like a whip.

"Hey fucker," Vincent yells, and Jam turns in time to see the end of the belt fly through the air towards him. It wraps across his head, and Jam lets out an involuntary, anticlimactic doof sound before he staggers back. Vincent is on him in seconds, punching his face with his bare hands, enjoying the sound of bone meeting bone, the sweet pain in his knuckles as they pound Jam's face.

It takes a bunch of Jam's friends and two cops to pull Vincent off him.

CHAPTER EIGHT

THE LEGENDS OF CHERRY LAKE

FEBRUARY 6TH, 1998 - ONE WEEK TILL VIRGIN NIGHT.

"Dude," Casey says as the flashing red and blue of the Sheriff's car fades to a flickering fire pit outside the lake house. She's dressed, or what Casey considers that to be. The four of them sit around the swing and armchairs on the porch; a mess of empty Hawaiian Punch cartons and chip bags lies on the ground. "So you got arrested?"

"Yeah," Caleb says, "our knight in shining black eyeliner got taken in defending our honor."

"Luckily, my father convinced the Sheriff's Department not to pursue charges," Michael explains.

"Guess it don't hurt to have a mega-rich daddy on your side," Casey says. "What about this Jam dick? He still a type-a asshat?"

"Nah," Caleb says, "he's too shit scared of Vincent to fuck with us anymore."

"I did get suspended, you know, not like I got off scot-free, all 'cause you and Kaytlynn couldn't say no to a guy who looks like he bleeds Mountain Dew."

"Oh boo-hoo, you got a month off school," Caleb teases. "You were gonna drop out anyway. That'd be like if my Pa went bought me some hung dudes and was like, they're gonna bang the queer outta ya, son. Anyway, the heart wants what it wants. Or is that the dick? I forget."

"Yeah, forgive me if I don't see the appeal of a walking NO REGRETS tattoo."

"And the girl, please tell me you dropped her like a bad habit, Michael," Casey asks.

"Well—"

"Young Michael and Kaytlynn are the poster boy and girl for The Church on the Lake's youth indoctrination, or whatever it's called," Caleb interrupts. "You gotta have seen them on that monster sign on your way in? How has no one drawn a dick on that yet?"

"Youth Council, and we're still together."

"Oh, Mikey," Casey moans with sympathy, "bless your heart, no." Casey reaches out to pat Michael's knee but stops herself when he pre-flinches. "You shoulda kicked her to the curb; she ain't no good for you."

"It's fine," Michael insists, "she's stopped being unfaithful."

"She ain't a lightbulb, Mikey. You can't unscrew a person," Caleb tuts. "Seriously, when are you going to realize that the one who loves you the most is closer than you think," he teases.

"I'm straight, Caleb," Michael states.

"That's what everyone says till they're not," Caleb winks.

"After that night, we decided enough was enough," Vincent explains. "We were done with pretending everything was fine."

"Done with doing nothing," Michael adds, his eyes glued to the floor.

"Cut to the three of us," Caleb jumps in, "hands on hands, swearing a blood oath—"

"There was no blood," Michael states.

"That we were done not getting laid! To the end of Virgin Night!"

"What he said," Vincent nods to Caleb. "I mean, there's more to it, but yeah."

"So boys, y'all gonna tell me the real story?" Casey asks. "The reason why I had to sneak into town dressed like a church mouse?"

Caleb snorts. "I can't believe you did that. We've got ginger Brad Pitt—"

"Bullshit," Vincent coughs.

"And a homicidal guy-liner goth over here. Casey, honey, your piercings and dye job just ain't gonna cut it. Cherry Lake's already got its own homegrown Freak Show!"

"Wow," Casey says, "you are exactly how I figured you'd be."

"I live to please," Caleb takes a bow. "Now, to the legend of Virgin Night!" he proclaims. "But first, pizza!"

"You can't order pizza," Michael states. "Nobody's supposed to know we're here. If my father—"

"Yeah, about that…" Caleb nods down the road as a beat-up hatchback with a Starsky's Pizzeria sign stuck on the roof struggles up the incline towards the lake house.

"Caleb!" Michael tenses up. "What if they see Casey!?"

Caleb shrugs. "We'll just say she's Vincent's sister. Nobody's gonna question why she's hanging around with three dudes."

"Fuck off, Caleb," Vincent snaps.

"And if they notice she's not Asian?" Michael panics.

"We'll just call them racist," Caleb says and waves to the pizza guy as he lifts the boxes from the back of his car.

"Does anyone have any money?" Vincent asks and gets nothing from Casey or Michael. "Seriously, Caleb, do you ever think anything through?"

"Oh, how you hurt me." Caleb feigns being shot. "It's all taken care of."

"How?" Michael asks, a hint of dread in his voice.

"Credit card," Caleb says.

"You don't—Caleb! That's the Church's card!" Michael starts to hyperventilate.

"And we're the needy," Caleb says as he skips down the stairs. "Jesus would approve."

"Jesus wouldn't approve of any of this," Michael says under his breath, keeping his reservations to himself.

Cut to: later, sometime past dusk, to a tottering stack of half-empty pizza boxes sagging over the edge of a coffee table inside the lake house. The four teens recline in food comas as something growly and grungy blasts through the sound system.

"Would it have killed you to order one vegetarian," Vincent says as he picks up a slice of pepperoni and flicks it at Caleb. "We don't all enjoy meat as much as you, you know."

"That meant to be a gay thing?" Caleb sighs. He's reclined on one of the sofas, slouched back with his gut in the air. "I'm too full to deal with your raging homophobia right now. Someone else, slap him."

"On it." Casey playfully hits Vincent on the leg. He smiles, almost unnoticeably, at her touch. "So boys, let's hear it."

"Okay." Caleb half-turns to lift his backside and rips a shotgun of a fart right in Michael's direction.

"Oh, come on!" Michael leaps to his feet and stomps across the room. Caleb chuckles, and then, one by one, the others join in—even Michael, eventually.

"Seriously, boys! What's the deal with Virgin Night?" Casey asks, crossing her legs and looking to each of them for an answer.

"It's the one night of the year when everyone has to live like Michael," Caleb says as he sits up.

"Ha-ha," Michael fake-laughs.

"Insert spooky noises." Caleb ruffles his hair, making it stand out like a mad scientist. "On the night of the 13th of February, if anyone does it like they do on the Discovery Channel inside the town limits, he will come and kill them. Then anyone else who gets in his way before the sun rises." Caleb cackles while rubbing his hands together.

"He?" Casey asks.

"Yeah, nobody knows his name," Vincent answers.

"I hear he prefers Stabby McSlashington," Caleb says.

"Uh-huh." Casey raises an eyebrow. "That's what Caleb told me, but who is he? What's his story?"

"You're just accepting this as fact?" Michael asks from across the room.

Casey shrugs. "I've seen some shit. Weird stuff happens."

"Well, that's narratively convenient," Caleb says while eyeing up some of the leftover pizza.

"What's up with that?" Casey asks.

"What?" Caleb squints at her.

"The movie stuff, that's twice now," Casey says.

"Caleb thinks we're all living inside a movie," Vincent explains. "That none of this is real, and we're all just characters."

"Pawns, toyed with for amusement of The God of Reels!" Caleb proclaims dramatically and waits for non-existent gasps of horror. "I mean, how else do you explain Michael?" He rests his case.

"Fair point," Vincent concedes.

"Come on, guys," Michael sulks.

"And now, as the story requires, it's time for some exposition. Cut—"

—to an old cabin only lit by candlelight. "Though his origin is lost to history," Caleb says in voice-over, "one tale told around campfires and under blankets by flashlight is that he comes from the time of black hats, buckles, and turkeys."

"He means Puritans," Vincent, also in voice-over, confirms.

"Picture a chick, all covered up and shit, but she has those come-fuck-me eyes, you know, the ones Vincent's sister has—"

"Fuck you, Caleb!"

A pretty Puritan girl with come-fuck-me eyes sits by a butter churn. She looks up and sees a big man, his shirt loose and chest hair on raging display, and bites her lip at the sight of him. "She's all—"

"You can churn my butter," the girl says, only it's Caleb impersonating a horny pornstar in a voice-over. "Imagine cheesy Skinemax riffs right about now."

Back in the lakehouse: "And they totally bang, like sweaty, heaving hetero banging." Caleb makes his fists clash into each other.

"I know how sex works," Casey deadpans.

"Cut to nine months later, and her belly is all," Caleb pushes his bloated gut out. "And her father is all," Caleb leaps up onto the coffee table, points right at Casey, and yells, "You whore!"

We cut back to Puritan times as the girl sits before her father, who glares at her with stern, vitriolic hatred. "You whore! You've disgraced this family! This town!" Caleb mimics in the voice-over.

The girl gives her father sad doe eyes. "But papa, I'm a virgin, I swear," Caleb mimics and then, as himself, adds, "She's all, if Mary can get away with this, so can I."

"Do we really need all this blasphemy?" Michael interjects.

The girl is dragged away and thrown into a spartan room. "They leave her till she gives birth. As soon as the kid comes along, they take it away from her." She screams, falls on the floor, begging, "but it's no good. She doesn't even get to name it, and in time, all she can recall is the little birthmark just above his right eye. That's important. Remember that."

"Noted," Casey says. "So what happened to the girl?"

"I'm so glad you asked. Almost as though you were scripted to." We cut back to the lake house. "So, Casey, I'm sorry if this offends your delicate feminine ears, but men have needs. Needs! And sometimes, humping a hole in a tree stump just doesn't cut it. Or it cuts too much. Nobody likes a splinter in their cranny axe!"

"Uh-huh," Casey says. "I think I see where this is goin'."

"Cut back to Puritan times, on a dark and rainy night," Caleb's voice-over instructs. The girl is dragged, by the hair, through the mud. She kicks and screams, but her father pulls her onwards to a dinky little boat with some other men from the village waiting as the rain beats down on their hats. She calls out, struggles, but can't do a thing to save herself as she's hurled onto the boat. They row her out to Black Stone Island and then carry her up to a lonely shack. By the time they reach it, the fight's gone from her.

"See, getting some sweet Amish meat—"

"Amish?" Casey's voice-over questions.

"Don't bother," Vincent says.

"Brought so much shame on her family," Caleb's voice-over explains, "their words, not mine, that she was pretty much dead to them. So whatever they did to her from then on couldn't be a sin. Because reasons."

The shack door opens, and the girl stumbles inside, slamming into the far wall. All that sits within is a bucket and a dirty straw mattress. Her father follows, shuts the door behind them, and then reaches for his belt.

"So whenever a man in Ye Olde Cherre Lafe got the horn, and his wife wasn't doing it for him, he could take a little trip to the love shack. No questions asked."

The girl's father walks out into the rain and gives the other men a nod—the next one heads in.

"Gross," Casey cuts in.

"I could get into it," Caleb says. "So it goes on like that," a montage of different men coming and going to the shack, in daytime and night, winter and spring. "And the girl just loses the will to fight back. To even live. Till…"

The girl, now much older, sits, slumped on the mattress. She stares, dead-eyed, as a man pisses into a bucket in the corner of the room. When he turns around, her eyes wander across his face. They land on something that sparks a memory inside her. A long-lost, painful memory buried by years of trauma and abuse. The memory of a birthmark.

"No," Casey gasps.

"That's disgusting," Michael adds.

"My son," Caleb mimics her raw, ragged voice. "My son…"

Back in the lake house, the other three hang on Caleb's words as he explains. "The guy snaps. Finding out he just banged his own mom will do that. Cries like a little bitch. But see, he grew up big and strong, this momma's boy did, and she reckons he can help her get sweet vengeance on the town. So he goes on a rampage, his momma pushing him on, and after taking out like half the town, a couple of big guys eventually capture and drag his angry ass back out to Black Stone Island. Just before they hang him, right outside the shack they kept his mother in, he curses the people of Cherry Lake and says he will be back…"

"Wait, what happened to his mom?" Vincent asks.

"Oh, shit, yeah," Caleb remembers, "I think she was, like, a ghost all along or something."

"That doesn't make any sense," Michael adds.

"And, how does that fit in with the whole hook-up equals murder-fest thing?" Casey asks.

Caleb shrugs. "I dunno, that's a third-act reveal kinda thing."

"And what act are we in?"

"First." Caleb gives in and helps himself to more pizza. With a mouthful of cold cheese, he adds, "Butdangerouslyclosetotheincitingincident."

"Oh-kay," Casey says. "Was any of that true?"

"Probably not," Vincent relents.

"There a version of this that don't involve some poor girl bein' violated?" Casey asks.

"Tell me about it," Caleb agrees, though not for the right reasons. "Not nearly enough dudes gurgling brogurt." Casey rolls her eyes.

"It's only one story," Michael says. "There are other, less sadistic ones."

"Read: boring," Caleb quips.

"Do tell," Casey says as she leans towards where Michael stands.

"This legend takes place at the height of the Civil War," Michael begins, and we fade to the Cherry Lake of that time. A pious-looking woman does some needlework by a window as she watches squads of soldiers march down the road. "Her husband was sent off to fight, and as her mother was with God, it meant she was alone in the house." A knock at the door sounds, and the woman stands, putting her needlework down carefully. She straightens her dress and then answers the call of her visitor.

"The mayor stands before her," Michael's voice-over explains, "and behind him, a half-dozen Union soldiers. He informs the lady of the house that as she has the room and the nation is at war, it is her duty to quarter some of the soldiers within her walls—"

"I asked in history class; that's not a sex thing," Caleb interrupts. "FYI."

"FYI?" Michael mutters under his breath, still not getting it, then continues aloud. "And so she did as was asked, for she was a Good Woman, a patriot and a follower of the Lord." Two soldiers move in. One a burly bearded man and the younger a handsome yet timid young man. We see the Good Woman prepare meals for them and clean their uniforms.

"But as the months passed, she grew lonesome. One morning the Good Woman going about her chores senses the Young Soldier staring at her." Both look away, flustered. She takes the laundry down to the river and can hear a powerful splashing as she approaches. When her eyes land on the sight of the Burly Soldier, naked in the morning light, the Good Woman drops the basket in shock. The noise draws the Burly Soldier's attention, and the Good Woman quickly gathers the spilled clothing together, ducking behind a tree as the man in the river turns. His thick beard twitches in a smirk as he spots a stocking the Good Woman missed and realizes who it is spying upon him. He continues to wash, though he takes his time while hidden, the Good Woman watches. She feels a stirring within and a deep sense of shame, though the former overpowers the latter.

"She prayed to God for the strength to keep her marriage vows." The door to the Burly Soldier's room creaks open. "And they went unanswered." The Good Woman stands in the doorway, hair down and in nothing but a shift. Flickering candlelight dances across her face, and she either lacks the courage to step in or the conviction to turn away. "The Burly Soldier rousts himself, taking in the sight of the quivering woman—"

"Keep going, man, I'm almost there," Caleb interrupts, then shrieks as Casey hits him.

The Burly Soldier stands and crosses the dark bedroom. With each step, the Good Woman's heart races harder, faster, till they're inches apart, and she can't take it anymore. He pulls her in close, and she melts into his arms. "They began an affair," Michael explains. "Each night she'd sneak into the soldier's room, creeping out in the pre-dawn glow. They carried on this way till one night…" The Burly Soldier and the Good Woman lie in bed, tangled in the sheets when a creaking outside the door startles them. "The Burly Soldier quickly reaches for his rifle and demands whoever is there show themselves." The door opens, revealing the Young Soldier with his head hung low. "Her mind is racing—

now there's a witness to her adultery, and the Good Woman fears her indiscretions will become gossip. Reaching the ears of her husband upon his return." The Burly Soldier laughs, pointing to the bulge in the Young Soldier's long johns.

"Schwing!" Caleb cuts in.

"Her lover turns to her," Michael ignores and continues on, "and suggests letting the younger man join them. A joke, perhaps. She considers it, only for a moment, then throws aside the bedsheet, inviting the young man over."

"Man, that's freaking hot," Caleb butts in.

"There's something deeply, profoundly wrong with you," Vincent says.

While their voice-overs argue, the Young Soldier joins the other two in bed. The Good Woman takes turns kissing each of them while their hands explore beneath the sheets.

"I caught you jacking off to a video game character," Caleb yells. "Judge not lest ye be judged, am I right, Michael?"

The two soldiers begin discussing something with one another wordlessly as the tangential voice-over debate continues.

"That's actually correct, but in the worst possible context," Michael concedes.

"Boys, focus!" Casey cuts in at the same time as the Good Woman demands the same to her lovers.

"Anyway," Michael retakes control of the story, "they carried on like this for some time," and we see the three lovers becoming bolder with their flirtations. One day a cart passes the house on the way to market, and the driver's head turns at the sound of giggling. He catches sight of the three lovers, sharing a blanket, in the shade of a tree. "Tongues wagged, and upon his eventual return, the husband heard the talk."

The bedroom door opens silently in the night, and the husband stands in the dark, observing as the three lovers sleep in each other's arms. "He came home late, quietly, to see if there was any truth to the tales and found them together." The husband pulls back the hammer on his revolver and aims it at the bed. "He shot the older soldier first." The gun goes off, and the Burly Soldier's blood sprays across the other two. The wife shrieks as the other falls out of bed. Fumbling for his rifle, a second shot rings out and causes the Young Soldier to slam against the wall, then slide to the floor. "Lastly, he aims his revolver at his wife and pulls back the hammer." The Good Woman begs, covers herself with the bedsheet as though it could conceal her actions, and with a tear in his eye, he and Michael quote, "If a man is found lying with the wife of another man, both of them shall die, the man who lay with the woman, and the woman." The husband puts a bullet through her heart.

"Well, that turned dark right quick," Casey sums up.

"It didn't end there," Michael adds.

"Oh, joy!"

The house burns, beams cracking, and the roof caving in with the heat as the husband watches. "He set fire to the house, burned it to the ground, and even then, he could hear them whispering about him. Mocking him as a cuckold." The husband turns and marches towards the town as his marital home crumbles behind.

Fade back to the lake house as Michael finishes. "He killed many before he was captured. As he stood on the gallows, moments from execution, he was condemned to Hell by the town pastor. To which the man replied: I'll come back and bring Hell with me. They buried him on

Black Stone Island, out of fear that he might just do as promised."

The lake house is silent for a moment, save for the gentle lapping at the shore outside.

Casey breaks the silence with a shudder. "Did it get cold in here or?"

"Fuck me, Mikey, look." Caleb holds his arm up. "I have goosebumps."

"No thank you," Michael says. "So the legend goes that on the anniversary of the crime, an act of fornication summons him from Hell to continue his vengeance."

"That's a sad one," Casey says to Michael. "Honestly, I mean, I feel for the husband an' all, but y'all don't go shootin' up the place just 'cause your girl is cheatin'." She playfully taps Vincent on the knee. "Story," she insists. "Your turn."

Vincent feels Casey's touch long after she removes her hand. "I could tell you the other version of Mikey's, where the wife isn't so happy to go along with things. Or about the Clancy Gang raiding the town back at the start of the 1800s, folks say they brought this on us. But it doesn't matter which story you buy," Vincent says, "they all end the same, pretty much. Death, vengeance, and Black Stone Island. But those stories make about as much sense as saying Gap-Tooth Mary's behind it."

"Now who's that?" Casey's confused.

"It's just a nursery rhyme," Vincent explains.

"Mary, Mary, Gaptooth Mary," Caleb croaks as he crawls across a sofa, "doesn't care if you don't think she's scary." He hunches over, wiggling his fingers menacingly. "In the light of day, or dark of night," a wicked grin pushes his cheeks up as Caleb edges closer to Michael, "she'll come for you," Caleb twists his head and stares in open-mouthed silence at Michael.

"Caleb—"

"And bite, and bite, and bite!"

Michael yelps and jumps back as Caleb pounces, gnashing his teeth.

"Not! Funny!" Michael insists while Caleb holds his gut, face flushed red with laughter. "You know I hate that!"

"She like a witch or somethin'?" Casey looks at Vincent. "Maybe it's a curse?"

"Nah, there's no record of Cherry Lake ever having anything to do with witchcraft. No records of any native tribes ever settling this land either. Cherry Lake's like a blank spot."

"Aliens!" Caleb wiggles his fingers.

"Fuck off!" Vincent waves Caleb's bullshit away.

"So none of the stories are true?" Casey's even more confused than when they began.

"Actually, I believe they're all true. In a way. It's hard to explain, but there's this video game—"

"Nerd alert!" Caleb yells with his hands cupped together into a makeshift loudspeaker.

"It's called *Final Fantasy VII*, and there's this guy who thinks he's this badass but—"

"Dude, I've played *FFVII*," Casey interrupts. She sits up on her knees and draws Vincent's attention to her outfit. "Tifa's my girl, put this outfit together just like hers."

"Oh yeah," Vincent says and blushes.

"Oh man, Vincent's in love!" Caleb teases.

"Am not!" Vincent protests. "Anyway, these two losers don't get it so, care to explain?"

"Cool, yeah," Casey says. "Right, so this guy thinks he's super kick-ass but later on finds out he's just a nobody with fake memories, and for some reason, everyone around him just goes with it. But with them all believin' in him, he sorta becomes what he thinks he is. Right?"

"Exactly," Vincent says. "Which makes me think, what if all this shit we believe about Virgin Night makes it real?"

"You're losin' me now," Casey says.

"Okay, so, the last time he appeared, one of the survivors said he looked like he was wearing denim, not really a Civil War or Puritan outfit, right? But there's one witness statement from the seventies in an old newspaper I was able to find that says he wore all black. The only thing consistent is that he wears a wooden mask."

"So…" Casey urges Vincent to get to the point.

"He is what we think he is," Vincent suggests. "And the island somehow focuses that into reality."

"So more Freddy Kruger than Jason Voorhees?" Casey asks.

"Exactly!" Vincent all but leaps up. "You get it! Not like these two morons."

"In our defense, neither of us smokes half as much weed as Vincent does," Caleb protests.

"I don't smoke," Michael states.

"That movie was based on something real," Vincent continues. "Some guys died in their sleep after being terrified that a dream demon was waiting for them. They believed it so much they had heart attacks."

Caleb pretends to snore.

"It's a thought-form creature. The more we believe in it, the more it's real."

"By that logic, how can you kill it?" Casey wonders aloud.

"By that logic, all we have to do is believe we can," Vincent explains.

"Well, that's good 'n' all, but I'm going to put my faith in the toys Mikey's father paid for," Caleb says, then turns to Michael. "Has it come in yet?"

"Not yet," Michael says, "I'll check tomorrow morning just in case. We're running out of time."

"Ain't gonna lie, boys, all of this is startin' to sound like a movie. A bad one." Casey sits back.

Caleb shrugs. "I mean, yeah, but they make movies about little league, and that shit's real, so…"

"Can't fault your logic there," Casey smiles. "Either way, I'm in now, come Hell or high water, though I want to know what the actual plan is before we do anything."

"Soon as the equipment arrives," Vincent says, "we'll be able to set things in motion. Till then, we need to keep our heads down and not attract any attention. Got that, Caleb?"

"I'm offended," Caleb says and stands up. "Now, as much as I'm enjoying this little sleepover, I have a date tonight."

"Yeah, I better get home and check on mom," Vincent relents though he makes no effort to leave Casey's side.

"I promised I'd help Kaytlynn with the Purity Prom preparations, and it would be suspicious if I didn't show up," Michael states.

"Great," Casey says, "a girl on her own in a lakeside cabin. That's not how scary movies start, nope, not at all. Say, y'all hear that? Sounds like *ki-ki-ki-ma-ma-ma…*"

"You'll be fine," Caleb brushes her off, "all you've done is flash your titty hammock. If this is a horror movie, then you're all good till you take it off and Michael gets killed."

"That's racist," Michael states.

Caleb shrugs. "Them's the rules. Blame Hollywood."

"That's not even true," Vincent says. "For every movie that does that, there's two that don't."

"Wait, before y'all go." Casey pulls her camera out of her bag.

"Casey, girl, you only need to whip them out; that's a bit far even for me," Caleb jokes.

"Shut up and get in, all of you," Casey instructs, and the boys gather around her. Michael stands behind, chin up and dignified. Vincent moves in beside Casey, and she shocks him by throwing her other arm around his neck, pulling him into a hug, and forming devil horns with her hand. Caleb ducks down below and gives a cheesy thumbs-up, though the second Casey takes the photo, he sticks his tongue out and reaches for her chest.

CHAPTER NINE

HE'S GOT ISSUES

Dolly across town, once more avoiding Black Stone Island, to the glass cathedral of The Church on the Lake, a monolithic megachurch that rests over the still waters below. There's a hubbub of motion as an army of youths in polos and opal rings scurry around the main hall. They carry boxes, pin decorations, and assemble tables.

Kaytlynn Parker stands on the stage; the entire lake gleams through the massive window behind her, but all she has eyes for is the clipboard in hand. Kaytlynn tuts at the volume of work she has ahead of her; she needs the stage ready so the band can have their sound test. Everything must be perfect—this is her chance to impress Pastor Wallace.

"Look out below!" a voice from the scaffolding above the stage yells, and Kaytlynn looks up in time to see a hooked chain hurtle towards her. She jumps aside, falling into a stack of boxed decorations, as the hook whips through the air right where she stood. "Sorry!" the voice above calls down.

"What the hell!?" Kaytlynn yells and, seeing the stares from the rest of the Church Youth, collects herself. "I mean, excuse me!"

"Sorry," the voice yells down, "the brake snapped. Total accident!"

"You could have killed me!" Kaytlynn chides. "Get it fixed!"

"Kaytlynn," one of the younger Church girls taps her on the shoulder.

"What!" Kaytlynn screeches, then as the girl winces, she forces herself to regain her composure. "Sorry, what is it?"

"P-Pastor Wallace wanted to see you in his office," the junior says.

Kaytlynn pinches the bridge of her nose in a vain attempt to stave off the coming migraine. Everything's behind schedule, the stage is falling apart, and now the Pastor wants to see her? How's she supposed to tell him that his son is the reason they're so far behind? He's not much use, she'll be the first to admit, but he's capable of doing what he's told. A rare quality in men, she's found, but it's not like she can say that to Pastor Wallace.

Cut back to the lake house. As the boys head down the path, Vincent drags his heels, an urge to hang around lingers while the other two head their separate ways.

"Forget somethin'?" Casey asks as she watches Vincent from up on the deck. He turns around.

"Why did you come?" Vincent asks.

"Huh?"

"You don't know us. We could be psychos or rapists," Vincent says, "and you came to meet us in an isolated cabin. Either you're stupid, and I don't think you are, or you're hiding something."

"Pretty sure I could take the other two if they tried anything," Casey teases. "You, that's another story. You don't fuck around, huh, Vincent? Why's that?"

"You're doing it again," Vincent states.

"What?"

"Deflecting, you did a few times already. What aren't you telling us, Casey?"

Casey lets out a heavy sigh. "I'll show you mine if you show me yours?"

Vincent nods. "Deal, but put your boots on. We're going for a walk."

"Oh, my," Casey quips, "how romantic."

Cut back to The Church on the Lake, to Creed's office. Like the one at home, there's no door, but unlike at home, his official office boasts a full-sized window for a rear wall, granting a full view of Cherry Lake. Creed rubs his temples over a desk covered in bills and financial printouts. A voice from the speakerphone asks, "Creed, you there?"

"Yes," he sighs, "I'm just thinking, Larry."

"There's nothing to think about Creed," the accountant on the end of the line says. "You're out of money. Something's gotta give."

Indeed it does, Creed agrees. "What are you suggesting, Larry?"

"Long-term? Sell the hotel," Larry advises. "It's a money pit. Some other properties, too. Do that, and you'll be able to tread water for a year or two."

"Short-term?"

"Cancel that party you're throwing," Larry suggests. "Send anyone who refuses to refund you my way, and I'll take care of them."

"That can't happen, Larry," Creed insists. "We, the town, needs it."

"Well, let the damn town pay for it. I don't know why you took that on."

"The Purity Prom will go ahead. Besides, that's on the Church's charge account, not mine."

"Yeah, about that," Larry ruffles some papers on his end, "the Church is overdrawn too."

"What!?" Creed slams his palms down on the desk. How can that be? He budgeted the expenses for the Prom himself. There should still be close to ten grand in that account. "That doesn't make any sense."

"Stand by," Larry says, and a few seconds later, the fax machine spurts to life. It chugs away as a printout slowly spews forth. Creed snaps it out, almost tearing the paper. Larry is correct. "Want me to query the purchases?"

"No!" Creed says, a little too aggressively. "No, that won't be necessary, Larry."

"Creed, I feel like you're not hearing what I'm saying. You're broke. The Church is broke."

"Believe me, Larry, I am aware. How long can you keep them all at bay?"

"Month tops. If you don't start paying up soon, you'll end up in court. Sell the hotel; it's just sitting there, doing nothing but eating money. Buy yourself some time."

"I'll think about it, Larry."

"And cancel the ball, Cinderella," Larry says before Creed hangs up.

He takes a moment to let it all sink in then pushes his concerns to the side. There's nothing that can be done now, but hope is not lost, Creed reminds himself. The Church has plans, ones he couldn't share with his accountant, but all his problems will be solved if they come to fruition.

Soft knocking raps against the wall outside the office, and Creed looks up to see Kaytlynn. "Good evening, Pastor Wallace. You wanted to see me?"

"Indeed," Creed says and turns the monitor off. "Indeed I did, my child. Come, sit." He motions to the seat on the opposite side of his desk. Kaytlynn does as he says. "How are the preparations going?"

"Fine," Kaytlynn lies.

"Be truthful, Miss Parker." Creed leans forward and peers over his knitted fingers. Kaytlynn can feel his eyes pierce her soul. "I am not a man who appreciates supplication, nor do I take satisfaction from falsehoods."

"Well, to be honest, one of the morons rigging the flying angel display nearly killed me with the chain."

"I see, and what of Michael?"

Kaytlynn's eyes narrow. What kind of game is he playing with her? Is this a test? To see where her loyalties lie, with the Church or Michael? She asks herself that, as Creed's eyes bore into her, and she gets her answer. Her loyalty lies with herself. "Michael has been no help whatsoever." Kaytlynn crosses her arms and dares Creed to accept the truth. To her shock, he does.

"Michael is not what I hoped he would be," Creed nods, "believe me, I know. I had such expectations for him, but, alas, the Lord has different ideas. Thank you for your honesty. It's," Creed searches for the right word, "refreshing."

Kaytlynn can't hide the slight smile that brings to her face, and she sits up in her chair, preening.

"Would I be correct in assuming that you intend to pursue a career within the Church after College?" Creed inquires.

"Of course," Kaytlynn says.

"Of course," Creed agrees. "Honesty and integrity, these are essential traits for anyone who walks in the light of our Lord. Remember that, Kaytlynn, and dwell on it before you answer my next question."

"Absolutely, Pastor Wallace," Kaytlynn nods.

"What exactly was your role in the incident that took place at young Mister Starsky's party last year?"

Kaytlynn gulps.

Cut to: Vincent and Casey as they walk north along the east side of Cherry Lake.

"That's my house up there, on the hill," Vincent says.

"You tryin' to get me up to your bedroom Vincent?" Casey teases. "'Cause we had a nice queen-sized bed back at the cabin I called dibs on."

Vincent laughs. "You're not like the girls in town."

"How's that? 'Cause I don't blush when I talk about sex? Even the sweetest little Sunday Suzie goes heels to Jesus. She just says a prayer afterward instead of lightin' one up."

"No, I, um, no," Vincent stammers. "I just mean, you're cool. I feel like I can talk to you, and we've only just met."

"It could be I'm cool," Casey kicks a rock into the lake, "that's not in doubt. But I reckon you don't really try with your fellow townies."

"Huh?"

"Look at me," Casey says, and Vincent meets her eyes. "You've walked all this way with your eyes on the floor, shoulders tensed up. Back there, with your friends, you smiled, joked. There was a spark in your eye. Now you're all broody again. Don't get me wrong, I like broody, but only in movies. In real life, it usually means you're trying to hide from somethin'."

"What do you think I'm hiding from?" Vincent asks.

"The fact you care more than you pretend."

Vincent snorts. "Yeah, don't think it's that."

Casey follows up, "Who hurt you, Vincent? I know pain more than most people, and I can feel it all around you.

There's a whole aura of hurt that," Casey places her hand about an inch from Vincent's shoulder, "yeah, there it is," she laughs. "You've wrapped yourself in it."

Vincent stares at Casey. "Who are you? You're, what, seventeen, but you act like you're way, way older."

"Just an Austin thang, no biggie," Casey says and lays on the twang.

"No more deflection, spill." Vincent doesn't let her back down.

"As I said, you first," Casey answers.

Vincent nods. "We're nearly there."

Cut back to Creed's office.

"I-I'm sorry," Kaytlynn feels her mouth go dry, "what was that?"

"Just under a year ago, Vincent Tran assaulted Mr. Starsky's son in retaliation for what he and his friends did to Caleb Dumont. That is, at least according to Tran and Starsky's statements. I can't help but feel there is a third piece to this puzzle, and it involves my son."

"I don't understand," Kaytlynn says. "What could Michael have to do with—"

"Honesty, Miss Parker," Creed says as he stands, walks around the desk, and comes to stand behind Kaytlynn. He rests his hands on Kaytlynn's shoulders, and though he applies no pressure, the meaning is clear—she has nowhere to go.

Does he know? How? Jam's friends or the asshole himself must have said something. So, if Pastor Wallace knows, he's just testing? Is he that insistent on honesty? Fuck, Kaytlynn, what are you gonna do? she asks herself. If he knows, there's no point in lying. Screw it.

"Michael caught me having sex with Jam—Benjamin. Vincent must have found out and thought he had some stupid, chauvinist obligation to defend his friend's honor."

"I see," Creed remains entirely still. "Why did you do this?"

"Because…"

"Because why, Miss Parker?"

"Because Michael wouldn't. He wouldn't even kiss me. I—" Kaytlynn hides her face in her hands. "I felt so ugly and unwanted. Jam was so kind," she sobs, "and he led me astray."

Creed's grip tightens on her shoulder. "Honesty, Miss Parker."

"Fine!" Kaytlynn yells, the sadness and vulnerability from seconds ago gone. "I fucked Jam because I wanted to. You happy? He's hot, at least he used to be, and I wanted him."

Creed nods silently. "And yet you continue to court my son. Why?"

Kaytlynn doesn't answer.

"Miss Parker?"

"Because he's your son. Son of the head of the Church. And the Church is my life."

Creed releases her. "As I thought."

Kaytlynn rubs her shoulders. They sting from Creed's piercing grip.

"What are you doing tomorrow afternoon, Miss Parker?" Creed asks as he retakes his seat behind the desk. Is this a trick question, Kaytlynn wonders? She's supposed to be overseeing the sound checks. Pastor Wallace knows this. Does this mean she's being removed from her position? So that's it, all of her hard work, gone. Her career, her life thrown away because of one fucking night, a mistake she made a year ago. How is that fair? "Would you be willing to attend a meeting at my home?"

"Why?" Kaytlynn asks, more confused than she's ever been in her whole life.

"I'm holding a gathering," Creed explains. "Only members of the Inner Circle are invited. To discuss the future of the Church and, indeed, Cherry Lake."

"I-I'm not being kicked out?" Kaytlynn stammers.

"On the contrary, my child," Creed looks her dead in the eye, "you're exactly the type of person the Church needs to carry it to even greater heights."

At that, Kaytlynn smiles.

Cut to: the Williamson Farm, where Vincent and Casey stand in front of the well.

"My father died here," Vincent says. "Nearly ten years ago. Played the hero, saved the town."

"Vincent," Casey says, "I had no idea—"

"I'm not asking for special treatment. I don't want sympathy." Vincent's fists ball up. "I just want my dad back."

Flashback to a year ago, to Vincent sitting in a jail cell. He leans on his knees, his hair hanging forward, concealing his face. "The cops treated me better than they should have," Vincent's voice-over tells us as a police officer offers him a Pepsi through the bars. "Out of respect for who my father was. What he did."

It's morning, and Vincent's let out of the cell. Exhausted and still in her work uniform, Emilie throws her arms around her brother. A second later, Vincent hugs her back. "I didn't go to juvie, but the court ordered therapy." Cut to: Vincent sitting across from a kind older woman, gray hair pinned up in a messy bun. Half-circle glasses perch on a pointed nose above an infuriatingly sincere gap-toothed smile. "Anger management, paid for by the Church, of course."

"Well, guessin' that dog didn't hunt," Casey says.

Vincent snorts derisively. "Yeah, you could say that. Was good for one thing, though. She helped me figure out that the reason for my hair-trigger was an unresolvable conflict, that I was projecting my rage onto Jam and others because I couldn't direct it where it belonged. At the fucker who killed my dad." Vincent leans in with a dash of hope in his eyes. "Her solution? Pray."

Casey snorts.

"Pray to God to relieve you of your afflictions," Vincent mocks the therapist. "I, uh, might have told her I wasn't a fan of that idea." Vincent leaps to his feet, giving the therapist both fingers and yelling. "I stormed out."

"Of course you did."

"And she had the balls to say I was lucky. Lucky that I was Jimmy Tran's son. That Pastor Wallace felt sorry for my family." Vincent slams the door behind him, making Emilie, reading in the waiting room, jump.

The SAAB pulls up at Vincent and Emilie's house. Caleb and Michael wait for him on the front steps.

"Lucky," Vincent's voice-over scoffs, "what's so lucky about your dad dying?" The other boys greet Vincent and give him a group hug—even Michael. "I'm sick of hearing that. Hearing about how his sacrifice made it the least deadly Virgin Night on record. Most of those fuckers in town can't even look me in the eye because they know they wouldn't have it any other way. Rather him than them, right?"

"I think you've got this twisted, Vincent. It's awful what happened to your dad, but you can't blame the living for being glad it wasn't them."

"Never underestimate how selfish people can be. Caleb was there that night. Staying at his grandpa's with his mom. My dad died saving them, and you know what she did? Abandoned Caleb. Left him with a drunk, violent piece of shit that locks him in a closet. All because she needed a fresh start, she couldn't bear to look at anything that reminded her of that night. That one fucking night wrecked both our lives."

Cut to: the three boys in Vincent's room. Caleb and Michael sit on the floor in front of a PlayStation, pounding each other on *Mortal Kombat 3*. Vincent stares out the window, joint burning away in his hand, while on-screen, Stryker wails on Nightwolf till he explodes, the word BRUTALITY popping up as Caleb dances on the spot, gloating.

"Do you need to rub it in?" Michael sighs.

"No, Mikey," Caleb smirks, "but I want to," he adds softly. "So, so badly."

Vincent stubs the joint out. "Guys, I need to tell you something."

"If it's about you jerking it to video game characters, we know," Caleb says without taking his eye off the game. "I say this as your friend and a fellow pervert; it's wrong. You need Jesus."

"Saying the Lord's name in vain is a sin," Michael states.

"If we don't sin, then Jesus died for nothing," Caleb shrugs. "Am I right, or am I right?"

"Look," Vincent presses through Caleb's attempts to distract, "when I was beating the shit out of Jam, I couldn't see anything 'cept for a red mist. And there was someone, something in it. You know who." Vincent looks at his bruised hands. "I'm scared I'm gonna lose it one day and kill someone."

"I could give you a list," Caleb jokes.

"I'm serious, man. Jam's in the hospital. What if next time it's worse."

"Have you tried praying away the anger?" Caleb makes the sign of the cross and winks.

"I think you need to confront it," Michael ignores Caleb and speaks up.

"What're you saying, Mikey?" Vincent asks.

"You saw him when you were hitting Jam, correct?"

"Yeah."

"Does that happen every time you get in a fight?"

"Yeah, it does." Vincent thinks about it for a moment. There's been a lot of fights. "Yeah."

"So perhaps you need to face the source of your anger," Michael explains.

"That's what that douchebag therapist said," Vincent agrees. "Not like I can do that, though."

"Mikey, are you seriously suggesting what I think?" Caleb makes a wild leap, and once the words are out, it's too late.

"No, I'm—"

"Pretty damn elaborate way for you to hook up with Vincent's sister, Mikey." Caleb elbows Michael playfully.

"That's not what—" Michael sweats it.

"No, you're right." Vincent steps away from the window.

"You sure?" Caleb leans towards the door. "Emilie, Mikey wants to know if you'll bang him so your brother can fuck up old stabby." Caleb then pulls a lousy impression of Emilie and adds, "Sure thing, boys, just let me finish waxing my beaver for the gangbang tonight." He nudges Michael again. "Take a number, you're in!"

"Fuck off, Caleb, but I'm serious, guys. If there's a way we can do this, take him out without getting anyone else hurt. I wanna do it. I need to."

Caleb and Michael look at one another, both taking a moment to let the enormity of what Vincent's suggesting sink in.

"I think it's too dangerous—"

"I'm in," Caleb cuts Michael off and shrugs. "Fuck it, why not?"

"Mikey?" Vincent looks at him.

"I...only if we can be sure no one gets hurt."

"Thank you, Michael. Caleb. We'll figure this out, come up with a plan, but just the thought of paying that son of a bitch back is making me feel better already." Vincent crosses the room to his friends. He puts his hand out, and the other two place theirs on his.

"Should we be using blood?" Caleb asks. "I'll go get a knife—"

"No, this is enough. A pact among friends. Fuck Virgin Night!" Vincent leads the cheer.

"Fuck Virgin Night!" Caleb joins in, and so does Michael, but he cuts the curse.

"Seriously though, guys, we need a plan that keeps everyone else in town safe," Michael insists.

"If we can't figure this out, or if either of you change your minds, it's cool; we won't go through with it," Vincent agrees. "I promise. And, I also promise that neither of you two dipshits will EVER hook up with my sister!"

We're back in the present, with Casey at the memorial. She could tell there was anger inside Vincent, a lot of it, but now that she knows the truth, she wishes she didn't.

There's an innocence there, too, a wounded boy hidden beneath layers of resentment and hostility.

"Your friends are riskin' their lives for you, Vincent," Casey argues. "Doesn't that count? That's somethin' to feel lucky about."

"I know, believe me, I know," Vincent nods. "Michael might seem like a pushover, but he's the most genuinely good person I've ever known. I wish I had half his strength. Caleb would jump out of a plane without a parachute just to avoid a real conversation, but he's the first guy to step in when someone needs help, even if it means getting his ass kicked too. That's how we became friends. Back in the fifth grade, Michael was still hanging with the other cool," Vincent spits the words out, "Church kids—"

"The way y'all talk about church is weird. I mean, where I'm from, the cool kids wear low rises, Calvins, and thongs."

"It's capital C Church. The Church on the Lake, it's all over these parts, but the heart's right here, in Cherry Lake." Vincent motions back towards the lake. "You had to have seen the massive glass monstrosity they built on top of the damn lake? Mikey's dad does live TV sermons from there every Sunday."

"That doesn't sound like somethin' the Jesus I learned about would be into," Casey says.

"Yeah, well, anybody who's anybody in Cherry Lake is either part of the Church, on the board, or owes them money. So all the rich kids, their mommies and daddies are part of it."

"That's just weird." Casey scratches her head.

"Yeah, so the Church kids are playing dodgeball, only they've got it, so it's most of them against Michael." Cut to: the boys in elementary school, and Vincent continues in voice-over. "They're laughing their asses off at the way he flinches. You might have noticed, Michael doesn't like to be touched, and out of nowhere, Caleb comes in. Nobody knew he was gay, for sure. Hadn't come out yet, but everyone talked. He jumps in front of Michael and tells them all to go to Hell. For a second, they actually stop before pelting Caleb hard, chanting about how much he loves balls, so they'd better give them to him. One of them clocks Caleb hard. He goes down, and there's blood on the floor. Michael's unprotected, so, boom, he gets it too."

"Where were you?" Casey asks.

"Sitting on my own." Cut to: the back of the playground. "Somethin' in me snapped. I walked up to the leader and knocked some teeth out of his stupid grin. Got a few more good hits on the others before the teachers pulled us apart. I got suspended for the first of many times. Caleb showed up at my house the next day."

"Sucks your Pa died," little Caleb says.

"Sucks your grandpa died too," little Vincent responds.

Little Michael comes walking down the path, bruised face to the floor. "He didn't know how to say thanks or really talk to people back then, so he brought me a video game."

"Y-y-you can h-h-have th-is!" Little Michael manages to say, holding out a *Street Fighter II* Super Nintendo cartridge.

"You guys wanna come in and play it?" Little Vincent asks, and the other boys nod.

"That was that. So, yeah, I know they're risking their lives for me, but it's never going to come to that."

"How can you be so sure?"

Vincent clenches his fists. "Because I'm Jimmy Tran's son, and I won't let anyone die. Not Michael, not Caleb, not Emilie, and not you. If I keep going the way I'm going, someone's gonna bite it. It could be me, maybe that'd be for the best, but I can't let it be someone I care about. So, if someone's gotta die, let it be him!" Vincent makes a fist and punches the stone next to his father's memorial. He grits his teeth and eats the pain, letting it calm the fury within. "So, now you know. What's your story?"

After a moment, heavy with consideration, Casey relents. "Okay." Her inner voice says, don't do it, girl, ain't no good comes from getting involved. But this boy, raging at the world and ready to wield that wrath like a sword, might just be what she's looking for. "You're not gonna believe me, though."

"Try me," Vincent insists, so Casey does.

CHAPTER TEN

This One Time At Art Camp

Fade in on a balmy, clear East Texan night. Fireflies dance over a silent field, surrounded by pastel pink and pale blue wooden buildings—distant thunder rumbles, somewhere far off.

"When I was a kid, my parents sent me to art camp for the summer," Casey's voice-over explains.

SUMMER, 1988 - CAMP INKWOOD.

Everything flickers and a grainy, degraded VHS filter comes into play, shifting everything slightly out of focus and distorting the saturation. Tracking lines flicker with the occasional ghost after-image as the sound drops to mono.

We focus on one cabin in particular, the white-painted walls covered in pink and blue handprints.

"One-one-thousand," a girl's voice counts. "Two-one-thousand, three—" The thunder rumbles, and a cacophony of screaming girls joins it. Jump-cut inside the cabin to see six girls hiding under their sheets.

"That means it's getting closer," one girl says.

"Don't say that!" another one protests.

"Y'all a bunch of wusses," a third girl says and throws her sheet off. Even without the bad home dye job and piercings, she screams attitude.

"If you're so brave, Casey, I dare you to go knock on Miss Sharpie's door!" one of the others snaps, and the other four gasp together as silent lightning fills the room with a sudden flash of light.

"Not Miss Sharpie!" a freckled girl with pigtails protests.

"Who's Miss Sharpie?" Casey asks. Thunder rumbles, closer now.

"Don't say her name," Freckles warns. "She'll hear you."

"Miss," a girl with braces says, then lowers her voice to a whisper, "Sharpie was a teacher here. Was. Story goes, kid after kid kept disappearing, year after year, and nobody knew why." Another distant flash punctuates her point.

"I heard she was eating them," a girl missing her two front teeth whistles.

"Well, I heard she was cutting them up and selling their organs to hospitals," another girl says, and they all scream again as the thunder rumbles.

"None of that is true," Braces says and looks from girl to girl before she continues. "Miss Sharpie was an artist. A real one. She sold paintings, and people came from all over to her gallery in Austin. Paid thousands for her paintings. Thousands!"

"Yeah, right," Casey says. "If she's so famous, how come she gotta work at a lame-ass summer camp?"

"I'm so glad you asked, Cra—Casey," Braces says and almost slips out the cruel nickname some of the regular campers have come up with for the new girl. "Miss Sharpie used Camp Inkwood to get the materials she needed to make her best-selling masterpieces."

Some of the other girls pull the bed sheets tight around their heads, but Casey sits forward, her mouth pulled into a daring sneer.

"The owners of the camp tried to keep things quiet," Braces goes on, "Miss Sharpie probably paid them too. But eventually, there were just too many missing kids to cover up, and the police came out to investigate." Lightning flashes, and a second later, thunder follows, just on the edge of the camp. The windows rattle, though no squeals this time as the other four girls all turn their focus to Braces. "When the police forced their way into Miss Sharpie's cabin, there were no signs of the missing campers. No bodies. Just a new canvas, half-painted, with buckets and buckets of red paint...only..."

"No!" Freckles gasps.

"Uh-huh," Braces says with a wicked smile that spreads across her whole face. "Miss Sharpie used the blood of her victims to create her paintings!" Thunder and lightning crash down in tandem, sending the other girls in the cabin into a screaming fit as they duck under their covers. It brings the rain with it, which beats down like it's trying to hammer the cabin into the ground.

Only Casey and Braces remain up.

"B-U double-L honky," Casey states.

"Don't believe me?" Braces shrugs. "That's fine. You don't have to. But if you're so brave, Casey, why don't you go on up to Miss Sharpie's old cabin and have a look."

"Even if that was true, she'd be in jail," Casey points out.

"True," Braces smirks, "if they ever caught her."

Casey rolls her eyes. "Of course they didn't. So, what, she still creeps around here and kidnaps the odd kid, for what? Not like she can sell her paintings anymore. Bet she's got a hook for a hand and dangles dead bodies from trees like this." Casey mimics swaying, hanging, with her eyes wide and tongue out.

"Miss Sharpie was an artist," Braces continues, ignoring Casey's jokes. "She painted because she loved to, not to make money. And, besides, there's bound to be some black market for paintings made from the blood of children."

"She'd have hung her victims upside down, too, like the cows on my daddy's farm," one of the other girls adds. She pulls a finger across her throat. "Cutting them here and letting it run into buckets!"

"Eeeew!" the other girls squeal.

"Urgh," Casey moans. "Where's this cabin?"

"Y-you mean you're going?" Freckles peeks from under her blanket.

"That's not a good idea," Braces warns.

"Save it." Casey rummages in her footlocker and takes out her Polaroid camera. "I'm going there and taking a photo to prove it."

"Well," Braces smirks, "if you insist. Follow the hiking trail till you get to the fork. Don't take either and keep on going straight through the woods. It's the first cabin you'll come across, with the seashells on the walls."

Casey tucks her Zoozie the Space Pirate cartoon pajama bottoms into her boots and jumps to her feet.

She takes her rain slicker from the hook by the wall and throws it on.

"The cabin will be locked, for sure," Braces says, "but take a photo through the window, and you'll see the bloodstains that no matter what, they couldn't clean away."

"You guys are gonna look so dumb when I come back with a photo of garden hoses and shit," Casey says and flips the bird as she heads out into the rain.

Once she's safely out of earshot, Freckles chuckles. "She's so dead." The other girls giggle.

"That's what Crazey gets," Braces sneers.

Outside, the rain pours down so hard Casey can barely see her way. She moves with her head ducked, pausing now and then to look up for bearings, holding her hood out to keep the torrent off her face. She already wishes she laced her boots properly, as they fill up with water and each step comes with a cold squelch.

"If those little bitches' scheme played out like they thought," Casey's voice-over says as her younger self follows the hiking trail, "then I would have crept up on one of the counselor's bunks. Should have known, right? I mean, Miss Sharpie? Really? At an art camp? They figured I'd take a photo through the window, possibly catchin' the counselors changin', and I'd have been kicked out for sure."

"But, you didn't?" Vincent's voice-over asks.

"No." Casey's younger self pushes her way through the woods, coming to a backside of an unpainted, wood cabin with seashells of all different sizes glued to the wall. "Something else happened."

Young Casey creeps around the side of the cabin, finally out of the rain as the awning roof runs it off. The water rolls down like a miniature waterfall, and the noise is almost deafening. Only, very faintly, something sounds like a distant scream. Casey rounds the corner and finds the cabin door slightly ajar. She pushes it open, and a blinding light hits her eyes, forcing her to shield them with her hand as she moves inside. Once the burn wears off and her vision fades back in, Casey claps her hands over her mouth and muffles a scream.

The blinding light comes from a lamp, knocked over on its side, shining at the door like a spotlight. It rests on the floor next to an upturned sofa with a hand hanging over the edge, missing two fingers. Blood drips from the fresh wound, running down the couch and pooling on the wooden floor below.

Casey, trembling with fear, steps around the side and finds the body of one of her teachers sprawled on the floor with a deep gash across her throat. The ground is red all around her sodden and sticky blonde curls, like a bloody halo. A piercing scream from outside beats Casey to her own, and she runs to the door.

Peering around the corner, Casey watches as one of the counselors scoots backward across the clearing, screaming at the top of her lungs. She's covered in mud, or at least Casey hopes that's what it is; in the dark, it's too hard to tell. A flash of lightning streaks across the sky, almost in answer to Casey's thoughts, and informs her of how very wrong she was. Blood runs down the counselor's legs from a deep gouge on her thigh, streaking all the way to her bare feet. A man approaches her; either it's a trick of the dark, or he's impossibly tall, wearing a blood-splattered yellow rain slicker. The rain makes the red run down the smooth coat like it's alive. With the hood pulled down, there's no way to see his face, not that Casey wants to.

"Please," the counselor begs, "please no! We're sorry!"

The Raincoat Killer raises a pair of garden shears, opens them wide, and turns the points down toward the girl.

"Get away from her!" someone yells and rushes at The Raincoat Killer with a shovel. He swings it against the giant's back with all his might, and there's no reaction other than to turn and face the foolish, brave boy slowly. He hefts the shovel back, readies it for another swing, and The Raincoat Killer stops him dead with a solid punch to the face. Even from where she hides and through the rain, Casey hears bone cracking like a tree snapping in half. Dazed, the counselor drops his shovel and staggers from side to side. The Raincoat Killer opens the shears again and severs the counselor's left arm in one powerful snick.

Casey bites down on her hand.

The one-armed counselor somehow remains on his feet as The Raincoat Killer takes his other arm like pruning a tree. At that, the armless counselor drops to his knees, and The Raincoat Killer opens the shears, one more time, to finish the boy off with one clean chop.

Casey feels her legs turn to jelly as the counselor's head rolls back, and his body falls forward. She's so shocked she lets her camera slip to the ground, landing with a thud. The flash goes off as it snaps an involuntary photo of the carnage.

"Shit," Casey curses as The Raincoat Killer's head turns in her direction.

Sensing an opportunity to escape, the wounded girl in the clearing gets to her feet and hops away. Her leg is so mangled that she can't put even the slightest bit of weight on it. She only makes it a few feet before falling, face-first, in the mud. The Raincoat Killer approaches, crossing the distance in two long strides. He grabs the girl by the hair and pulls her head up off the ground. She bares her teeth as she feels the hair ripped from her scalp, then goes slack as the pointed tips of The Raincoat Killer's shears pierce through her throat. He lets her slump to the ground before pulling his weapon free.

Inside the cabin, Casey ditches her camera and runs into the back. She finds herself in a toilet and knows if he catches her here, she's done. Heavy footsteps pound up to the cabin. Jesus, he's faster than he looks, Casey thinks as she searches for a way out. Her only shot is a tiny window above the sink, too small for an adult but not skinny little Casey.

The Raincoat Killer steps into the cabin and reaches down for the Polaroid photo, still developing on the ground, its white edges soaked in blood. He holds it up and watches as the image fades into existence. The distance is too far, but the composition is dramatic, not that the Raincoat Killer appreciates any of that. Tossing the photo aside, The Raincoat Killer crunches the camera underfoot as he heads to the back of the cabin. He pulls open the only door to find an empty bathroom. The muddy boot prints on the sink, scattered toiletries, and open window tell him his prey has escaped.

Storming outside, The Raincoat Killer looks in each direction for where Casey went, but all he can see are footprints coming toward, not away. Confused and angry, he grunts and tightens his grip on the shears.

Flashing red and blue lights steal his focus as a police car comes down the road towards them. The Raincoat Killer does not run, much to Casey's horror as she watches from the gap beneath the cabin, mere inches from where the killer stands his ground.

"Freeze!" one cop yells as he steps out of the car, using his door for a shield as he aims a cocked revolver at The

Raincoat Killer. A second cop steps out of the other side, priming a shotgun.

The Raincoat Killer does not follow their orders and, instead, steps toward them at a calm, measured pace.

"That's far enough!" the first cop yells.

"We will open fire!" the second one warns.

The Raincoat Killer either does not hear or does not care.

"Last warning!" one of the cops yells, and a second later, the one with the revolver opens fire. The shotgun joins in, and both cops empty their weapons into the killer, who shudders with each hit but remains standing nevertheless. As the guns click empty, The Raincoat Killer moves in.

"Shit!" the first cop yells and reaches for the radio while the second reloads his shotgun. Just as he gets a shell loaded and aims it, The Raincoat Killer grabs the barrel, pushes up to the sky, and the blast goes off into the air. The cop yells as he refuses to let go of the gun, and he's off his feet, lifted into the air like a cat with stuck claws. The Raincoat Killer drives the shears into his stomach, and still, the cop refuses to let go, spitting blood all over the ducked hood of the yellow slicker. The killer pulls the weapon out and stabs it in again.

The other cop fumbles for the radio inside the car, shaking with nerves and soaking wet; it takes him a second to grip it and hold down the button. "We—" is all he gets out as the shears come down through his mouth, crack through the radio, and pin both to the seat of the car.

Under the cabin, Casey sinks into the mud, both hands over her mouth, as she can't do a thing but watch.

"Daniel!" a voice calls across the clearing, and both the killer and Casey turn to see another counselor. She stands out by the tree in the middle of the clearing. "Here I am, Daniel! Leave them alone! It's me you want!"

She's nuts, Casey says to herself, and The Raincoat Killer stalks towards her. He stops, though, about halfway to the girl, and Casey can't see why. The other girl stands her ground, and Casey notices she's got one hand behind her back. Whatever weapon she's got, Casey thinks, won't do her any good. He's been shot at least six times, and he's still standing; what does this girl possibly think she can do to him?

"Run, girl," Casey whispers, "run."

She doesn't, though, and instead of attacking, The Raincoat Killer approaches slowly till he stands inches from the girl.

"The hell," Casey mutters as the girl reaches up inside The Raincoat Killer's hood. She pulls it back, and from where Casey lies, she can see what looks like burn marks across his head.

"I'm sorry. For what they did. For what I did," the girl says, "but this has to end, Daniel!" She pulls a knife from behind her back and drives it into the side of The Raincoat Killer's head. He staggers back, dropping the shears as he reaches for the knife.

The girl must have thought that would be enough; it wasn't, and she makes a run for it as The Raincoat Killer pulls the knife free. He quickly comes after her, yet he never even approaches a run, catching the girl as she races up the steps over Casey's head. The Raincoat Killer grabs the girl, causing her to fall hard on the steps, and when her eyes open, they meet Casey's.

"No!" the girl screams as The Raincoat Killer drags her down the steps and throws her on her back.

"No," Casey echoes and realizes she can't just lie there, doing nothing, while another person gets killed in front of her. She rolls out the side while the other girl struggles with The Raincoat Killer. He stabs down with the knife, but the girl ducks her head out of the way just in time—it gouges a chunk of grass and mud less than an inch from her cheek.

Casey runs over to the cop car, looking for one of their guns, and can't find either. Under the driver's seat, an orange handle catches her eye, but when she pulls it free and feels how light and plastic it is, she realizes it's only a flare gun.

"Daniel, no!" the other girl screams, and it's too late for Casey to find something else.

"Here!" Casey yells and tosses the flare gun over. It lands on the grass, inches from the other girl's grasping fingers. The knife comes down through her collarbone, and the girl screams in agony. As The Raincoat Killer tries to pull it free, though, he struggles. The blade is buried so deep in the girl's bone it's stuck, buying her enough time to get her fingers around the flare gun.

Just as The Raincoat Killer pulls the knife free, the girl raises the gun and fires. The flare erupts a blinding whoosh of light as it launches then vanishes—the shot goes clean into The Raincoat Killer's gaping, toothless mouth. He roars as sparks burst from his eyes, out his nose, and he staggers to his feet. Racing across the clearing towards the lake, The Raincoat Killer's whole head catches fire, and he loses his way, eventually dropping to his knees, then falling facedown in the dirt, inches from the water.

Casey runs over to the other girl, wrapping her in her arms.

"It's over," the counselor says. "It's over," she repeats as more red and blue lights appear in the distance.

Fade back to the Williamson Farm, and teenage Casey hands Vincent a Polaroid. "I went back for that," Casey explains, "before the cops arrived." The photo shows a figure in a hooded yellow rain slicker standing in a rainswept clearing, bodies on either side. Only, looking at the picture, the killer doesn't look as tall as Casey described. She was only a kid, Vincent reminds himself. Of course he'd look like a giant to a child.

"His name was Daniel Kleebe, and he was dead. Dead, dead. Years before this all happened. The girl who stopped him and her friends accidentally set him on fire, messin' around with fireworks when they were kids. Yet, there he is, all grown up and angry as all git-out. He," Casey taps the yellow raincoated figure in the photo, "was a Slasher, and the girl who stopped him was a Final Girl."

"Did Caleb put you up to this?" Vincent asks, checking the back of the Polaroid as though it might contain some telltale evidence.

"Look, I know it sounds like a movie, but this shit's real," Casey says and rummages in her bag. She pulls out her black notebook. "This stuff happens; what's goin' on in Cherry Lake, it's been happening for fuck knows how long, but ever since the 80s, it's been happenin' a load more." Casey opens the book on a page with newspaper clippings. Headlines read Seven Slain in Prom Night Rampage; Sole Survivor of The Soot Hill Massacre Speaks; Doll Masked Killer Still at Large; Carnival Chaos at Bonkin's Bonanza; More Mutilated Bodies Found at MacCready's Farm.

"They're real, you know that. Slashers. You and your friends are goin' up against one, and that's why I'm here." Casey locks eyes with Vincent.

"Why?" Vincent still doesn't understand.

"Because you morons need a Final Girl, duh."

CHAPTER ELEVEN

WHAT'S IN THE BOX?

"Bullshit," a shirtless young man declares sometime after midnight. "Why you gotta talk such crap?" He lies on a blanket in a quiet, hidden copse by the shores of Cherry Lake. His pants sit unbuckled, and he begins to button them.

"I'm telling you," Caleb's voice carries from behind a tree somewhere in the dark. "Virgin Night's for real," he says as he comes into sight, strutting around like he owns the place in nothing but boxer shorts and unlaced Chuck Taylors. He sees the other guy fixing his belt and says, "Nope, I ain't done with you yet, stop that." He smirks and does as Caleb says.

"Sorry, my bad. You know, over in Redcastle, we have shootings and stabbings, you know, real crime. Not some made-up country-fried bullshit. You don't have to work so hard to impress me, Caleb. You already got my pants off."

"And yet they're back on," Caleb complains as he lies down on the blanket. He props himself up on one arm and lets his fingers walk down the other man's chest. "Let's fix that," Caleb smiles and begins to tease the belt away.

"You know Redcastle has the highest number of missing kids in the whole state, right?"

"Weird thing to brag about, but sure," Caleb says.

"My point is, you don't have to act so tough about this whole Virgin Night thing. I'm not scared."

"Dean," Caleb says in an uncharacteristically solemn tone, "please just lock up. Keep the lights low. Do what they say. For me?"

"Urgh," Dean moans, "okay, but you owe me."

"Oh, really," Caleb teases and climbs on top; his hair hangs down and tickles Dean's face.

"Really," Dean smirks.

Caleb kisses him on the lips. "Well, I guess I better get started."

"You better."

Caleb kisses Dean's chest. "I think you'll find," Caleb's lips graze Dean's finely haired navel, "that us country folks," he kisses the space just above Dean's belt, "are—"

"Shit!" Dean yells and pushes Caleb to the side as he sits up, in a panic, looking for his shirt.

Caleb rights himself and rubs his chin. "What the hell?"

"It's past curfew!" Dean pulls his shirt on, a short-sleeved white button-up embroidered with the Camp Clearheart emblem.

"Aw, man," Caleb moans. Dean leans over and kisses Caleb. "Just don't pray away all the gay, same time tomorrow?"

"Sure," Dean says as he pulls one of his shoes on. "And I've told you, I'm not gay."

"Could have fooled me." Caleb waggles Dean's other shoe and pulls it away as he reaches for it.

"Getting jiggy with another dude doesn't make you gay," Dean insists, "it only counts if you fall in love with him." He snatches the shoe from Caleb and pulls it on.

"Ouch," Caleb grabs his chest like he's taken a shot to the heart.

"Don't pretend this is anything more to you than what it is," Dean uses his reflection in his watch to tidy his hair. "I know how you roll."

"Oh, yeah?" Caleb raises an eyebrow.

Dean laughs. "Confused boys from the camp make easy pickings, right? And you never need to worry about catching feelings 'cause they're gone as soon as the season ends."

"You make it sound so dirty," Caleb whines.

"It is." Dean kisses him again, but Caleb doesn't reciprocate. "And that's what's fun about it. You know they got a photo of you up there?"

"Not sure how I feel about that," Caleb squints, "wait, do I look hot in it?"

"What do you think." Dean leans in and kisses Caleb on top of his head. "But I've got a wife and a baby back in Redcastle. This is just fun." Dean fixes his clothes and takes a few steps away before turning and confirming, "See you tomorrow?"

"Sure," Caleb says though he's already decided he won't, and says nothing else as Dean hurries back to the camp.

Caleb lies down on his back and stares up at the stars. He watches as one zips across the sky and debates if he should even go home. He still has a half-full bottle of whiskey he stole from his father, and the old bastard's no doubt noticed it's gone by now. "Fuck it," Caleb decides, and he gets dressed, his things together, then heads back to the lake house.

Cut to: the deck outside the Wallace lake house, where Vincent and Casey have the firepit raging again. She has her knees pulled up to her chin, boots on the floor, and the firelight shines in her joyful eyes. On the seat next to her, Vincent insists, "I still say it's bullshit."

"What's bullshit, bitches," Caleb says as he saunters up to the cabin. The other two go quiet. "Did I interrupt something? Before you say yes, now fuck off Caleb so we can have boring straight sex, know this—I have booze." Caleb pulls the bottle of whiskey out of his blanket roll.

"You wanna tell him?" Vincent squints at Casey.

"Go right ahead, my dude," Casey says with open arms.

"If you two lovebirds are getting married, then I claim prima-nata," Caleb waggles a finger at each of them.

"What's prima-nata?" Casey asks.

"Something to do with ballet?" Vincent shrugs.

"It means, as lord of the land, I get to bone whichsoever spouse I choose before the wedding."

"Pretty sure that's not what that's called," Vincent says.

"How exactly is this your land? I mean, it's Michael's lake house, so if anyone's gonna claim it—"

"I peed on it," Caleb points to the wall behind the other two, "so it's mine."

"Ew!" Casey turns and sniffs. "Is he jokin'?"

Vincent looks from the concern on Casey's face to Caleb's smirk. "It's fifty-fifty, honestly," Vincent concedes.

"You're gross," Casey states.

"And you're going to tell me something, right?" Caleb climbs the stairs and plops down in a bucket chair across from the other two.

"What happened to your date?" Casey asks.

Caleb takes a swig of the whiskey before he answers. "Ditched him. Got bored. Talk."

Casey gives Vincent a nod and then lets him explain. "Casey says she's our Final Girl."

Caleb, at first deadpan, erupts with laughter. He points and wipes tears from his eye as he loses control and slides down off the chair. As he sits on the floor, he regains enough composure to say, "Bullshit." He laughs some more till he sputters out.

"And why not," Casey glares at him.

"Well," Caleb has another fit of giggles, "well it's just, Final Girls have certain um," he coughs, "requirements, and I don't think you, uh, that is to say, one cannot be a Final Girl if she partakes in the old hokery and pokery, if you get my gistery."

"Are you callin' me a slut?" Casey raises a brow.

"No," Caleb holds a hand out, "no, please no-hit Caleb. I'm just saying, well, you're—"

"Urgh. Men. Y'all fundamentally misunderstand the Final Girl concept. She don't have to be a virgin or like a nun. She just needs to have good intentions. Y'all gotta stop thinkin' with your dicks."

"Doesn't the whole Final Girl thing mean the three of us guys gotta die?" Vincent points out. "Hence the final part?"

"Man's got a point there, Casey. I mean, we kinda figured that was a distinct possibility going into this, so," Caleb takes a sip. "What makes you the sudden expert on the meta-nature of our very existence?"

"Because this isn't some bullshit movie." Casey takes out her notebook and swaps it for the whiskey bottle. "This shit is real," she adds, and Caleb's eyes go wide as he flips through it.

"Fuck me," Caleb says as the three of them pass the bottle around, and Casey fills him in. "Fuck me with a rusty chainsaw."

FEBRUARY 7TH, 1998 - SIX DAYS TILL VIRGIN NIGHT.

Cut to: a few hours later as piercing sunlight pours in through the windows of the lake house. Casey and Vincent sleep, facedown on opposite sofas, and there's no sign of Caleb. Through the window, we can see a figure heading towards the lake house. He moves fast but rigidly, arms down by his side as he sprints like a robot. As he closes in, and we see it's Michael, we can hear him chanting "You guys, you guys, you guys," over and over till he bursts through the front door and, without stopping to catch his breath, shouts, "You guys!"

Casey and Vincent both jerk awake. Confused, unsure if the voice is real or just part of the ringing in their heads. Both shield their eyes from the merciless morning light, hissing like vampire cats.

"You guys!" Michael yells, even louder, followed by a heavy thud from the dining table. The three of them look over to see Caleb crawling out from under; he rubs his head while putting his sunglasses on.

"Michael, this better be you confessing your undying love for me, or I'm going back under there for the rest of my life." Caleb uses a chair to climb to his feet, cracking his bones as he stretches.

"What were you doing under the table?" Casey asks.

"What were you doing on the sofa?" Caleb fires back.

"Uh, sleepin'," Casey shrugs.

"There you go, now, who wants pancakes? Mikey—"

"YOU GUYS!" Michael yells, louder than either of the other boys have ever heard before.

"Is he sweating?" Vincent observes.

"Thought he was a robot," Caleb notes.

"Maybe it's oil?" Casey suggests.

"That's offensive to robots," Caleb adds.

Michael, with the biggest smile, ignores them and says, "It came!"

Cut to: the Wallace house. Vincent and Emilie's dirty, rustbucket SAAB sits in the driveway, at odds with the well-maintained, elegant surroundings. It drips oil onto the pristine artesian concrete slabs as the four of them stand around some boxes inside the open garage.

"You didn't open them?" Vincent asks as Michael holds the box-cutter, ready to do the honors.

"I wanted to wait for you guys," Michael says.

"What's in the box, Michael?" Casey asks.

"Yeah!" Caleb grabs Michael by the shoulders. "What's in the box! WHAT'S IN THE FUCKING BOX!?" he yells dramatically. The other three just stare. "Seriously, you guys? Brad Pitt? No? Philistines."

The cutter slices through the tape, and Michael pulls the flaps apart. Packing peanuts fall aside as he lifts out a matte, black case. Michael pops the clips, and the four of them stare down into it.

"Where did you get these wonderful toys," Vincent says as he picks up a black baton. With the flick of a trigger, blue-white electric sparks dance around the tip.

"That's a lot of stuff," Casey says.

"Yeah, I was thinking if we're going to Hell, might as well have some fun on the way, am I right?"

Caleb picks up a taser and admires how it sits in his hands. "Hey, do we need to test these," he asks and aims it at Michael's crotch. "Bang!"

"Don't!" Michael jumps away even though there was no shot.

"Relax, Mikey, not like I'm—" The taser goes off, hitting a ball on a shelf and crackling with electricity. The ball pops, making the four of them jump, and fills the garage with the smell of burning leather. "How about that?"

"Let's put that down," Casey guides Caleb's arm till he puts the weapon back in the box.

"Honestly, I'm just surprised you didn't buy a buttload of guns," Vincent says. "None of these boxes looks big enough to hold an RPG."

"It's disappointingly hard to buy guns online," Caleb complains.

"Not sure that's the word I'd use. Or if I like the idea of you with one." Casey gives him the side-eye as she picks up a rescue knife and flicks the blade out. Its matte black edge appeals to her and, when she sheathes it, Casey slips it into her back pocket instead of the box.

"It's cool," Caleb says, "I'll just steal my Pa's," and Casey chokes.

"This doesn't look like everything, Caleb," Vincent notes as he checks out the other box—radios and a motion detection kit. All gear you'd expect the security for a high-profile organization like the Church to require.

"Do you guys want to go all Ruby Ridge? Bring the whole ATF down here?" Caleb asks. "I'm not a moron. Separate orders, separate delivery addresses. Otherwise, the feds would be down here faster than you can say, Timothy McVeigh."

"So, where's the rest of it?" Vincent asks.

"Well, the ammonium and stuff, I got sent to the hotel. Building site's gotta need that shit, right?"

"Makes sense," Casey says and waits for the other shoe to drop. "That's smart."

"Wait for it," Vincent mutters.

"See, you're not gonna like this," Caleb says, "but bear in mind I had to use an address registered to the card."

"You didn't," Vincent's jaw drops.

"Not the Church," Michael panics.

"No! Jeez, guys, what do you take me for, some kind of idiot!? No! I sent it to Mikey's dad's P.O. Box."

Jump-cut, just outside, as Kaytlynn's Miata coasts down the road towards the Wallace House. She's early for the meeting but planned to have words with Michael. The stern kind. As she catches sight of that broken-down old junker Emilie Tran owns sitting in the driveway, she pulls over, the Miata slinking into the shadows cast by the trees on her side of the road.

Kaytlynn watches as Vincent and Caleb head from the garage to the car, carrying boxes around to the trunk. Vincent appears to be shouting at Caleb, but Kaytlynn can't hear them. She turns down Alanis on her CD player and still can't make out much more than "how are we supposed to get it without him." Are they robbing the Wallaces? No, not that she'd put it past them, but it's broad daylight. Michael appears and heads towards the car's front passenger seat, which only concerns Kaytlynn further.

Just as Michael opens the door, Caleb yells, "Shotgun!" so loud even Kaytlynn can hear it clear enough. Then— who the hell is that? A girl appears, wearing ripped-up jeans and a tank-top, her hair streaked with different colors. Who is she, and what the hell is she doing with

Michael? As Caleb and Michael play tug-of-war with the passenger car door, the girl slips in between them, stealing the seat. Both boys stand there, letting her give them both the finger without doing a thing. How dare she!? How dare Michael let her!?

The boys pile in the back seat, and Vincent puts the car in reverse. Kaytlynn ducks down as it passes, and she glances at her watch. There's enough time, so she turns her Miata around and follows the others, keeping back far enough that they don't notice.

CHAPTER TWELVE

STRIPMALLRATS

Cut to: the Cherry Lane Stripmall on the edge of town, just before the two-lane highway. Starsky's Pizzeria and Arcade dominates one whole corner, the giant animatronic above the sign motionless and eerily dead-eyed in the daylight. Along the main strip, there's a nail salon, VHS rental store, karate dojo, Christian bookstore, regular bookstore (both owned by the same person), and at the far side, the Cherry Lake Post Office. The SAAB idles, a few spaces down from that.

"Sometimes I forget, and I have to thank you for once again reminding me that you're one of the dumbest fucking idiots who ever lived. How do you live, actually? Caleb? Seriously, how do you live? Do you have Post-it Notes telling you how to breathe?" Vincent's grip on the wheel turns his knuckles white, temper sizzling near boiling point.

"I am sensing some hostility here, but thankfully it's directionless," Caleb says. "A person's feelings might get hurt if he thought that was aimed at him."

"He mentioned you by name," Michael states.

"Boys, if you're done verbally jerkin' each other off," Casey snaps, "can y'all focus on how we're doin' this? I mean, do we absolutely need this stuff?"

"Yeah, without it, all we have is cow shit and ammonium," Caleb answers. "I don't think flinging turds are gonna do the trick."

"And yet you sent it here, where we're going to need Creed fucking Wallace himself to collect it," Vincent growls. "What the fuck are we supposed to do? Go grab a trenchcoat from the thrift store, stick Michael on my shoulders, and waddle in there like two kids sneaking into an R-rated movie!?"

"In your bitter sarcasm, which only masks your true adoration for me, you have your answer, Vinnie." Caleb holds his hands out like the solution should be evident. It's not. The other three stare at him, saying nothing, till Caleb elaborates. "We don't need Creed Wallace." Caleb turns to the uptight boy sitting in the back with him. "We have the next best thing."

Kaytlynn's Miata pulls into the strip mall, and she sneaks it between two SUVs parked by Starsky's drive-thru entrance. Michael and the others don't notice her, and she slides down in her seat, watching as the three boys get out of the car. Vincent and Caleb are shouting and pointing at each other while Michael drags his heels behind. The girl, the strange one with the dyed hair, leans out of the window and shouts at the three boys.

"Hey, doofuses," Casey hurls at them as we jump back over to the other side of the stripmall.

"Uh, I think you'll find the plural of doofus is doofi," Caleb pontificates.

"Whatever, aren't you forgettin' somethin'?"

The three of them look at one another and shrug.

"Urgh." Casey rolls her eyes. "Did y'all forget that I ain't supposed to be here, and yet y'all brought me to a strip mall!?"

"Oh shit, yeah," Vincent facepalms.

"Ha," Caleb scoffs, "who's the moron now?"

"You do realize she meant all of us?" Michael states.

"Whatever," Caleb says to the two of them and then yells to Casey, "If anyone asks, you're the homeschool girl from Paradise Falls."

"Hey, not bad," Vincent concedes and slaps Caleb on the chest with the back of his hand playfully.

"Good one," Michael agrees.

"I have my moments," Caleb says and hitches up some pretend britches. "Let's go, boys!" He leads them on towards the post office.

Casey slumps down in her seat and huffs as she leans against the open window. "What have you got yourself into, Casey girl," she moans.

Flicking the radio on the car fills with a commanding voice. "Do you feel empty? Alone in a world of sin? The Church on the—" Casey clicks it off and grumbles.

"Uh, what are you doing in my car?" a voice beside the window asks, and Casey looks up to see a confused girl who looks a lot like Vincent, only not so angry and, oddly, with less makeup.

"Uh, hi?" Casey smiles up at Emilie Tran.

Jump-cut to the boys as they walk, in line towards the post office. Vincent and Caleb are doing what they can to pump Michael up, but his shoulders hang in a way that says he's not too sure about all this.

"I dunno, guys," Michael says, "what if they don't believe me?"

"Mikey, it'll be fine," Caleb says with confidence. "I mean, you're practically Cherry Lake royalty. Everyone in town knows who you and your Pops are. It'll be fine."

"Really?" Michael looks to Vincent for confirmation.

"No worries, Mikey," he says, "you got this." The three of them reach the storefront. "Okay, on you go!" Vincent pushes Michael on. He takes a few steps then stops.

"Wait, what? You guys aren't coming with?" Michael panics.

"We'd just make you look suspicious," Vincent explains. "Just remember, all you gotta say is you're here for your dad's package."

Caleb snickers as he holds his fist to his mouth. "I'm sorry," he coughs. "I'll behave."

Michael rocks on the spot, taking deep breaths. "Okay," he says and then twelve more times before pulling open the door and stepping inside. As soon as Michael's gone, Caleb puts his back to the wall, laughing his ass off as he slides to the ground.

"His dad's package," Caleb manages to get out through the tears of laughter. Even Vincent can't stifle a smirk.

Back at the SAAB, Casey flashes a smile at Emilie, who tucks her hair behind her ear and squints in the afternoon sun. "I'm Casey," she says, making an effort to hide her drawl. "I'm, uh, with Vincent?"

"Oh," Emilie says, "oh! Wow, I didn't know he had a, well, wow. Okay. V, nice work. I mean, you're hot-you're-cute," Emilie blushes, "sorry, I mean to say you're lovely. Hi, I'm Emilie. Vincent's twin sister." She holds her hand out, and Casey shakes it. "I'm not hitting on you or anything. We're close, but not that close. Is this weird? This is weird!"

Casey smiles. "It's cool to finally meet you, Emilie," she lies effortlessly. Like it's natural. "Vincent's told me all about you."

"Really? I can't believe he has a girlfriend. I kinda figured he might be, y'know, with Caleb and all." Emilie squints. "I'll stop talking now. Uh, where is he?"

"Huh?"

"Vincent?"

"Oh! He went to go get something from a store."

"Kay, well, I gotta go to work." Emilie models her ridiculous Starsky's uniform, an outlandish love child of vintage candy striper, Disneyland, and Hooters. "And I guess I can forgive him for hogging the car since, you know, date."

"I appreciate that," Casey almost lets her accent through but swallows it at the last second.

Emilie smiles, awkwardly mimes walking on, then shakes her head as she actually heads away from the car. Casey sighs, a quick breath of relief, and then swallows it as Emilie stops, turns back, and says, "Which class are—"

"Home school," Casey says and taps on the side of the car, trying to act cool.

"Oh, okay," Emilie says, and Casey's not sure she buys it. "Cool, well, tell Vincent I said hi and," she gives two thumbs up, "nice job."

"Sure thing," Casey says and waves the other girl off, only relaxing when she's out of sight. "Goddamnit, boys," she curses. "Move your damn butts before it turns into a reunion out here."

As Emilie reaches Starsky's, she hears a hiss calling to her. Turning around, Emilie sees Kaytlynn sitting in her Miata, her face hidden behind her shades. "Kaytlynn?"

"Who's that girl?" Kaytlynn asks and nods her head towards the SAAB.

"That's Vincent's girlfriend," Emilie says with a healthy dose of sisterly pride, then notes how odd Kaytlynn looks. The sunglasses, the slouching down. "Are you stalking them?"

"What!? No! Of course not!" Kaytlynn pouts. "I was just here and saw them come in. I've never seen that white trash bitch before. Don't you think it's weird?"

"You jealous, Kaytlynn? Worried Michael's stepping out on you?" Emilie puts a hand on her hip.

"God no," Kaytlnn sneers.

"Well, he should," Emilie states, and Kaytlynn gasps. "I know exactly what happened that night. When my brother got arrested for messing up your fuck toy. You're lucky Michael isn't like that. He's too good for you." Emilie turns her back and heads toward the door.

When Kaytlynn finishes hyperventilating, she leans out the window and yells, "How dare you talk to me like that!?"

Emilie turns on her heels. "Back off, Parker. I'm not in your little cult, so you can't push me around. Leave my brother and his friends alone."

"Whatever, wage slave. Go clean up some kid's puke or something," Kaytlynn bites back. Emilie ignores her and walks away without another word, leaving Kaytlynn to seethe.

Back over by the post office, Michael comes out empty-handed. "No good, guys, they said my father should have given me his key. They won't open the box."

"Damnit," Vincent kicks the curb.

"Okay," Caleb says, "plan B it is then."

"Plan B?" the other two say at the same time.

"Well," Caleb nods towards the SAAB, "Plan B-cups."

"No, no, no, no, no," Casey says with her arms crossed after Caleb explains his idea. "Did I say no? Sorry, what I meant to say was HELL NO!"

"I'm sensing some resistance," Caleb responds.

"You'll be sensin' my boot up your ass if you think I'm doin' that," Casey warns him.

After the briefest of moments to imagine the possibility, Caleb says, "I could get into that."

"He'd be into that," Vincent mumbles at the same time.

"I could get into a better plan," Casey puts on a deep, faux male voice that sounds nothing like Caleb. "Okay, so, while Casey's all tee-hee looky, my titties just fell out on their own, oh what am I to do, we sneak in and steal the key."

"Team player much, Casey?" Caleb frowns at her like a condescending school teacher.

"Contrary to what y'all must think, but I am not a whore ready to sling it around town whenever it suits." Casey glares at Caleb, daring him to say otherwise.

"Well—"

"Don't," Vincent interrupts. He turns to Casey. "As much as this hurts to admit, Caleb's idea could work."

"I'm not—"

"You don't need to flash anything," Vincent says.

"Let's not take that card off the table—"

"—just flirt a little," Vincent ignores Caleb. "Keep his eyes away from the backroom for a few."

Casey sulks for a moment, then says, "I suppose."

"Awesome!" Caleb gives her a cheesy grin and a thumbs up. "And, Casey darling, if he was into dudes, I'd happily helicopter away in your place."

"Well, there's an image," Casey smirks.

"How would pretending to be a helicopter help?" Michael asks, and none of them can bring themselves to meet his eyes.

"Just remember to hide that gawd-dang accent 'o yours," Caleb says in a mock Texan drawl.

"Despite the situation, not to mention the company I find myself in, Caleb, I am not a moron," Casey hits back and then heads inside.

A few minutes later, she storms out. "You're up, carrot top. Get in there and shake that weenie."

"Huh?" all three boys gawp at the same time.

"Didn't bite, not one bit." Casey seems surprisingly disappointed.

"You sure you know how to flirt?" Caleb jabs.

"I dunno," Casey fixes him a glare, "you tell me." She pushes Caleb to the wall. He goes flat against it, and his eyes widen as Casey runs her fingers up his chest. "Excuse me, sir," Casey teases, "can you help? I'm lookin' for somethin'," Casey pouts, parting her lips slightly and looking up suggestively.

"I, uh, um," Caleb stammers, "w-what are you looking for?"

"A good time," Casey purrs, "care to show me one?" She steps down from Caleb, and suddenly Michelle Pfeiffer is gone. "See, it ain't me, boys. Boys?"

Vincent turns away, pretending to look at something on the other side of the parking lot. "S'good, yeah," he says, trying to hide the tent in his pants.

"Dayum," Caleb nods, "think I like girls now."

While across the parking lot, Kaytlynn growls, "So much for being Vincent's girl."

Jump-cut to the door opening inside the post office, where the clerk looks up as the bell above tinkles. Caleb walks over, leans on the counter, and says, "I hear this is the place to see a man about a package?" Outside the other three facepalm.

The clerk stares in utter bewilderment, and then a slow smile spreads across his face. "You could say that," he says.

Outside, Casey mutters, "Unbelievable."

"This is taking too long," Vincent complains and peeks through the window. Caleb and the clerk are chatting away, but there's no opportunity for him to sneak in. "C'mon, get his back to the door, Caleb."

Inside, the clerk raises an eyebrow and asks, "Are you looking to send or receive?"

Caleb teases his lips with the tip of his tongue. "I could do either."

"Well," the clerk grins, "where do you want your package to go?" He leaves that hanging. "Distance and weight will affect the cost."

Caleb points to the delivery zone map on the left wall. "I'm gonna check the map and see." Caleb walks over to it and leans against the wall, inviting the clerk to come over and join him. "Say I want to send something here, in the blo—I mean blue zone?"

The clerk comes around the front desk and joins Caleb by the wall.

Outside, Vincent pumps his fist. "Yes, it's go time. You two, get around back, and I'll let you in if I can. Go!" Casey and Michael break for it while Vincent crouches in through the door. He opens it slowly, carefully, so as not to ring the bell, and slides through. He crab walks across to the front desk while Caleb and the clerk continue tragically flirting.

"It really depends on how big it is," the clerk meets Caleb's eyes. "How heavy?" Caleb holds his hands about seven inches apart as an answer. "I can work with that," he says as Vincent slips into the backroom.

Vincent gets to the back door and opens it, letting Casey slip inside. "I'll keep watch," Michael says, and Vincent nods.

"I saw the keys back this way," Vincent says and leads on.

"Fuck," is all he can say, though, at the sight of an entire wall dedicated to key hooks, each of them numbered but not a single name on any.

"There's like five hundred of them!" Casey throws her arms in the air. "How are we supposed to know which one!?"

"There's gotta be something," Vincent says, "look around."

Vincent examines the keys, searching for any names or branding that might present a clue, while Casey checks the desk on the far side of the room. She finds a heavy, leather-bound ledger under some unsorted letters, and when she opens it, her face lights up. "Here!" she calls out, and Vincent races over to join her. They look through the ledger together, and Vincent's heart sinks.

"Still no good, there's no names, just the P.O. Box numbers." He shakes his head.

"Yeah, but maybe that's enough." Casey points to the latest logs. "Only three deliveries arrived today, and look, two of them were letters while box 213 has a large box marked," and they say the final word in tandem, "hazardous!"

"213, that's gotta be it, right?" Vincent trembles with excitement.

"Has to," Casey nods.

"I'll be right back," the clerk calls from out front. Vincent and Casey look to each other, then for a place to hide as the clerk makes his way to them.

"There," Casey says and pulls Vincent by the hand to a closet just in time for them to shut the door before the clerk appears. Inside it's dark, though a sliver of light cuts through a slight gap. It lands on Casey's face, across her eye, and Vincent gets lost in the greenness of them for just a second. He never noticed the flecks of dark red splattered through the green before.

"This is kinda exciting," Vincent whispers.

"I can tell," Casey draws Vincent's eye down, and when he realizes what she can feel, pushed up against her so close, he blushes so bad she can tell even in the dark.

"Sorry."

"It happens." An awkward moment passes, the hint of electricity in the air, then Casey says, "Let's go," as she pushes the door open.

Vincent kicks himself and follows her lead. On the way out, they snag the key for box number 213.

"Has to be Vincent," Caleb says back out by the SAAB.

"Why's it gotta be me?"

"Because I can't go back in there without the guy thinking I'm in love with him. Casey's already made a fool of herself, and Michael blew it earlier. You're the only one he hasn't seen so far. Just go in, open the box, get the stuff, and walk out. Don't even need to say a word."

Vincent grumbles and then catches the key as Casey tosses it his way. "Fine," he concedes. "Let's get this over with."

Back in the post office once more, Vincent steps through the door. The clerk looks up, and Vincent gives him a nod. "Good day, sir," he says and instantly regrets it. Who the hell talks like that.

"Good...day?" the clerk responds, confused.

Vincent heads over to the alcove lined with P.O. Boxes, finds 213, and opens it with no fuss. Seconds later, he leaves the post office with the package that's caused so much trouble with no further complications on his end.

The clerk, though, well, he's had a day. First, that kid wanting into his dad's box like he wasn't up to no good. Then that girl, what a weirdo. The cute boy was a nice change of pace, and then that creepy goth kid that spoke like an English gentleman. This close to Virgin Night, he's lucky if he sees one or two customers all day. Never mind four in an hour. The bell above the front door rings—make that five.

"Can I help you?" he asks and looks up to see one of the Church girls standing in front of him. Even though she's a little thing, she gives off an aura that says: do not fuck with me.

"Yes, you can," Kaytlynn threatens. "Tell me what the four of them wanted."

CHAPTER THIRTEEN

THE KIDS AREN'T ALRIGHT

Smash cut to the Lakeview Hotel site as – **BOOM!** – dust and dirt erupt in an explosion that, while small, still causes a hell of a mess: Casey, Michael, and Vincent cough as they shield their eyes. Small stones and debris patter around them, like light hail, while Caleb squints at the tiny crater they've blasted in the dirt.

Behind them, the Lakeview Hotel stands empty and dark. Eight floors of mock Tudor elegance on the outside, mostly bare floors on the inside. Like the South Shore project, the money ran out long before the ambition.

Casey picks gravel out of her hair while Vincent ignores the gray dusting his side-swept long fringe has gathered.

"Look, don't get me wrong, that got me half-hard," Caleb says as he squats down by the small crater. "But, Michael, if you want me to blow my load, I mean really

URGH," Caleb thrusts his hips at Michael, who does his best to ignore him, "I'm gonna need a bigger bang."

"I don't get it," Michael mutters to himself as he looks over his notes. "That should have been…did I get the ratio wrong? What if I—?" Lost in his own world, Michael messes around with more of the homemade explosives while Casey and Vincent step back slowly, only now realizing how close they were standing.

"You okay over there, Mikey?" Casey asks, half ducking behind the carved stone staircase that leads up from the dock to the hotel's grand entrance.

"It's best to leave him when he gets like this," Vincent says as he joins her.

"Mikey's a genius with this shit," Caleb yells over as he joins Michael. "Put a little faith in our boy," he adds, then slaps the table hard—Vincent and Casey duck down, teeth gritted. When nothing happens, when no fine mist made of Caleb and Michael rains down, they look back up.

"He's right," Vincent says when he's sure it's safe to. "This one time Michael was with me when I went to buy some weed in Redcastle. He could tell from looking at the bag that the fuckers were shorting me. He knows his shit."

"Yeah?" Casey doesn't quite buy it. "So why are you hidin' too?" Vincent nods in Caleb's general direction. "Good point."

"Got it!" Michael declares and lifts his new creation like it was his firstborn. Caleb takes it from him and carries it across to where they set the last one off. "Might want to go a bit further this time," Michael instructs.

Caleb gleefully sprints back to the others like a child running down the stairs on Christmas morning. The four of them gather up, huddled low as Michael primes the detonator.

"If we make it through this, we're gonna end up on the FBI's most wanted," Casey groans.

"Nah," Caleb dismisses. "We're under eighteen," he sings, "won't be doing any time."

"Speak for yourself," Casey says without thinking.

"Three…" Michael counts down. "Two…"

"One!" Caleb yells and pushes Michael's finger down on the button. All four of them take cover, huddling together behind the staircase wall as nothing happens. Seconds pass, and they unclench their eyes. "Huh?" Caleb takes the detonator and clicks it again. Nothing. He rapid fires the button, causing the others to flinch again, but still no boom. "Well, that sucks."

"It might be out of range," Michael thinks out loud.

"Let's see," Caleb says and steps out of cover.

"No!" Casey and Michael shout as Vincent tries to grab Caleb's belt, but it's too late.

Caleb takes a few steps away from the others, out in the open, clicking the detonator over and over. Still nothing.

"Michael, you sure y—" WHOOSH! The force of the blast hits them before the sound. It knocks the three still in cover onto their backs again as a wave of heat blasts through the air above. Caleb gets flung through the air and lands in a heap six feet back from where he stood.

"Caleb!" Vincent screams and scrambles over the others. He stumbles to his feet, coughing up dust. Vincent races across to his friend, who lies still on the grass at the far side of the hotel lawn. "Caleb!" Vincent skids to a halt, going down on his knees beside the boy. Caleb sits up, eyes wide, face covered in dirt, hair blasted into something like a mad scientist on a Saturday morning cartoon. Casey and Michael catch up, and the three of them surround Caleb. "Caleb, man, you okay!?" Vincent's hands hover inches away, unsure if it's safe to touch him.

He coughs, spits out some gravel, and then he speaks. "Michael," Caleb locks eyes with him, "I want to put a baby in you."

"You can't. I don't have a womb," Michael states.

Vincent begins to chuckle, as does Caleb. Soon all four of them are in hysterics as they hug Caleb on the lawn. Even Michael joins in.

Cut to: South Shore, to the front door of the Wallace McMansion as Kaytlynn stands before it. She hesitates to ring the bell and takes a moment to straighten her skirt, tuck her shirt in, and fix her crucifix headband. Sure that she's presentable, Kaytlynn rings the bell. While waiting for an answer, Kaytlynn triple-checks her clothes.

"Kaytlynn," Pastor Wallace smiles as he answers the door, "you're here."

Kaytlynn's stunned that he answered the door himself. In all the time she's been dating Michael, his father has never come to the door. Always his wife or his children. That must mean none of them are home. Michael, well, she knows where he is, and she's jonesing to tell the Pastor about that, but Vanessa and Ariella? It is an Inner Circle meeting, Kaytlynn reminds herself and feels a rush at being invited to it; of course, they'd want privacy.

"Good afternoon Pastor Wallace," Kaytlynn smiles and dips her head.

"None of that, my dear." Creed steps aside and invites Kaytlynn in. "Come, the others are waiting." Kaytlynn nods and walks into the house. Halfway into the main hall, she realizes she doesn't know where she's going.

Perhaps noticing her doe-eyed confusion, Creed says "This way" and leads her towards the library.

"Pastor Wallace," Kaytlynn says as the man stops before the large, carved desk by the picture window. "I need to tell you something about Michael."

"Not now," Creed says as he lifts one of two antique boxes from the table and approaches Kaytlynn.

"But he and his friends ordered something, to your P.O. Box then stole it—"

"Kaytlynn." Creed just says her name, but it's a command, loud and clear. "I have no doubt my son is up to no good. He's a lost cause, and I shall deal with him in due time. Now, we have far more important matters to discuss. Please, put these on." He hands her the box.

Kaytlynn, her hands shaking from the rebuke, takes the box and clicks it open. Inside, a wooden mask, just eyeholes with no features, sits on a bed of black silk. She picks it up, confused. The wood is rough, carved from raw bark though it's too dark, too black to be directly from a tree. When she looks at Creed, he's already donned an identical mask and a black silk cloak that covers him entirely.

"When the Inner Circle meets, we do as equals. No marks of our station or person are permitted." He pulls the hood of the robe up, and Kaytlynn feels the weight of his presence multiply. Creed Wallace was always a big man, who projected an even bigger persona onto the world, but now he feels mystical to her. He nods for her to follow suit. As Kaytlynn slips the mask on, Creed takes her robe and drapes it over her shoulders. "When the meeting is concluded, I would have words with you, in private, Miss Parker."

"Oh-okay," Kaytlynn agrees, her lips bone dry. She stands rigid as Creed helps fasten her robe and then pulls her hood up for her.

"Come," Creed instructs and leads the way across the library to a door that Kaytlynn has never, ever seen open before. She always assumed it was just a closet or something, but as Creed leads her inside, Kaytlynn finds herself in a surprisingly sizable windowless room. Sitting around a table built from twisting tree branches are six other masked people who Kaytlynn can't possibly identify and yet gets the feeling they're all very, very important. Six pairs of black, hollow eyes watch as Creed pulls out a wooden, hewn chair for Kaytlynn. She takes the seat and is silently grateful that no one can see her face. See how terrified she is.

Creed takes his seat. "My friends, I thank you for meeting today. As you can see, we have a new member joining us. Like each of you, they will have a part to play in our plans for the Church's future. This great land has become a modern Gomorrah. Harlots are worshipped on television, hedonists are heralded as heroes, and our President is nothing more than a womanizing adulterer. America is in danger of falling to Satan, this we all know. My friends, we cannot shirk this responsibility. We must save this nation from damnation. America needs a new leader, one who will hold office with the blessing of God. You all know this, but to fight the lies of Satan, we must bolster our coffers significantly. To that end," Creed bows his head, "let us begin."

Cut back to the Lakeview Hotel, where Casey scowls at the three boys as they wait expectantly for her feedback. "So this is your plan? Blow him up?"

"You make it sound so stupid," Caleb waves away her doubts.

"That's because it is."

"Yeah, look, this ain't some old-timey dynamite, these are OK-City specials right here, and we've got enough to level the whole damn building."

Casey shakes her head. "Hasn't this thing been shot to bits before, and that didn't do it?"

"Yeah, but there's a world of difference between buckshot and an ANFO bomb," Vincent explains.

"I can't believe you guys." Casey stands in bewilderment. "This is literally stolen from an episode of *Buffy*!" All three boys stare as though they have no idea what she's saying. "Seriously? *Buffy*? The one with the Judge? When Buffy and Angel, y'know," she clicks her tongue, winks, and then mimes humping.

Caleb, aghast with disgust, recoils as he shrieks, "How dare you! Disgusting behavior, you hussy!"

"Y'all never seen *Buffy*?"

"We don't watch that show at my house," Michael states. "It's too Satanic."

Casey holds two fingers to her temples. "We're all gonna die." She stomps over to where they stashed their things and rummages through her bag for the notebook. "Look!" Casey thrusts the book at the boys. "I've been trackin' these things ever since…Camp Inkwood, and you can't kill them that easily! Shoot them, blow them up, makes no difference! I've seen it; it's not that easy."

"It'll work," Vincent declares.

"What makes you think that's even possible?" Casey demands.

"What happened at Inkwood? How was The Raincoat Killer stopped?" Vincent asks.

"They, he, was shot in the mouth with a flare gun," Casey reminds him.

"Right, so somehow that flare did what a hail of bullets and everything else couldn't? I've read your book, Casey," Vincent states, "and I know it'll work."

"When? How?"

"He uses his finger and breaks down the big words," Caleb jokes, and Casey holds her palm to his face.

"The flare gun worked because of who fired it," Vincent explains, "because it recreated the origin of the killer. We don't know where he came from, what made him, but between Michael's toys and what we're gonna rig up in there," Vincent thumbs backward to the hotel, "we'll cover all the bases."

"Oh god, you're ripping off *Home Alone* now," Casey facepalms.

Michael giggles. It's unsettlingly out of character and sounds like it comes from a squeaky little girl and not a large teenager like him. His eyes leak, and Michael wipes them, only then realizing they're all staring at him. "Sorry. I love that movie."

"Anyway," Casey says, keeping a concerned eye on Michael, "What if you're wrong?"

"We just have to believe and, one way or the other," Vincent declares, steel in his eyes, "that fucker isn't leaving this hotel."

Casey relents; there's no changing their minds. It surprises her that she's so concerned. This is no different from every other time, but still, be honest with them, she tells herself. You know their plan won't work, except maybe this is different? Every other case she's investigated had only clueless victims, people with no idea what was coming their way. These boys, they're going into this fully accepting they're up against something dark, something evil, and they're not backing down. Maybe there's something to them? Already they're not following the rules, so could they have what it takes to break them completely? She could put a stop to this right now, but they'd just try it again next year, and she wouldn't be there to help. Besides, if they can break the rules, maybe she can too.

"Okay," she says, "what now?"

Caleb throws one arm around her, one around Vincent, and says, "This is where we'd have the gearing-up montage to the licensed song they'd use in the trailer, so…"

Cue the music as we see the boys setting traps, smashing a hole in the floor, hooking up a bunch of generators, carting around some cans of kerosene—the whole thing smells like teen spirit.

Then the rest of the week goes by: Michael prays in Church; Caleb takes his father's shotgun from under his bed and stuffs it, along with all the shells into a duffel bag; Vincent and Casey walk together along the lakeshore; Dean waits by the meeting spot, but Caleb never shows; small, wicker circlets appear on the doors and windows of a few houses across town; Vincent working at the video store, Emilie at the Arcade; Jam Starsky angrily pumps iron in his garage; Kaytlynn oversees the rest of the Purity Prom preparations, she and Creed nod knowingly to one another; the four kids sitting around the firepit, drinking as the flames dwindle, and we fade to black.

FEBRUARY 13TH, 1998 - TWELVE HOURS TILL VIRGIN NIGHT.

The sun comes up across Cherry Lake, and though the town is still asleep, those with the vital task of isolating Cherry Lake get to work. Chainsaws rev and wires are double-checked. Trees fall, rocks are blasted, and the highway section that leads to Cherry Lake is cut off. The work is done dispassionately, without fanfare. It's routine.

All across the town, homes sit dark, except for one South Shore McMansion. Lights glow in the narrow windows around the top of the garage. Inside, Jam Starsky stares at his sad, distorted reflection in a broken mirror. He sits on the edge of his weight bench, snarling at the freak who stares back. The rising sun burns through the window at the top of the garage. He hasn't slept a wink, and yet he's wide awake, running on rage fuel and Mountain Dew.

Tufts and bald spots—mementos from that night Vincent attacked him wind across his head like a meandering river. His hair juts at awkward angles as it finds ways around the scar tissue. At first, he tried shaving it all off, but that just meant that everyone could see the lumps. Every time Jam has left the house this past year, he's worn a hat, a bandana, beanie, whatever he could, but he knows that everyone else knows what's beneath. Vincent has made him a laughing stock, and no girl in Cherry Lake has come near him since.

He tried calling Kaytlynn several times, just like she asked, but she never picked up. Can he blame her?

At first, his father was livid, gearing up to call his lawyers and bury Tran just like his dumbass father. But then Jam let slip about Michael Wallace. At the very mention of the Pastor's son, Jam's father went ballistic, raising his hand to his own son, screaming at him and yelling at him about how the Church, how Wallace owns everything they have, owns them. That because his stupid son couldn't keep it in his pants, they could lose the arcade, the house, everything. Jam learned that night that his father's love only went as far as his credit line.

That's not all he learned, though. No, Vincent taught him a violently valuable lesson. Strike hard and fast, and make no apologies. So Jam's spent the better part of the last year getting ready, getting stronger, and now the time has come.

Jam takes a trimmer and shaves off his misshapen hair; no more hiding. He checks his bag: hammer, carpet knife, rope, a ball gag stolen from his parents. When night falls, he'll make his move. He will have his revenge. Vincent Tran will pay for what he did, and Virgin Night will provide the perfect cover. He has to start things off first, though. Get the ball rolling, and he knows just how to do that. Fortunately, Jam knows exactly where Emilie Tran will be.

CHAPTER FOURTEEN

THIS IS IT. DON'T GET SCARED NOW.

Michael finds himself staring in the bathroom mirror, eyes wide with apprehension, beads of sweat on his forehead. He's about to break all the rules, do some of the worst things he can think of, and yet that's not what scares him. Michael's afraid he won't have the courage to go through with it, to stand by his friends who've always stood by him. He holds his cross to his lips, kisses it. "So whoever knows the right thing to do and fails to do it, for him it is sin," he quotes and prays to God to keep his friends safe, not once thinking to plead for his own survival.

Vanessa raps on the bathroom door. "Michael, sweetie, come on, or we'll be late. You don't want to keep Kaytlynn waiting, do you?"

"We know what happens if Kaytlynn doesn't get what she wants, when she wants," Michael says to his reflection and stares at himself—surprised that the boy in the mirror would say something so bold, so un-Michael-like. He picks up a small white bottle, one Caleb gave to him earlier that day.

"Down this and make sure you've got a clear run to the bathroom," Caleb's words repeat in his head.

"What was that, sweetie?" Vanessa asks from the other side of the door.

"I'm not feeling well," Michael answers and chugs the whole bottle.

"Oh, I'm sure it's just your nerves, you know how you get."

"I—oh no!" Michael only just makes it to the toilet in time as the entire contents of his stomach rocket up his throat. His whole body heaves as he goes again, retching loud enough for his mother to hear.

"Michael? What's the matter? I'm coming in."

"No—" Michael hurls again. Vanessa opens the door, shields her nose, and melts with sympathy at the sight of Michael hunched over the toilet. But even the risk of getting puke all over her Alexander McQueen evening dress isn't enough to keep her away. "Oh, Michael." Vanessa's heels clack across the tiles.

"I'm-I'm sorry," Michael hurls again, "mother," he finishes and wipes away lumps of bile from his chin.

"Don't be silly, sweetie; I'll go get you some—"

"No! Mother, please. I'll be fine. You go to the Prom with Ariella. I'll be okay."

"Sweetie, are you sure?"

"Yes, mother. Father will be upset if none of us are there." Michael heaves, but nothing comes out.

Her instincts tell her to stay with her son, but Ariella is already in the car honking the horn, and she knows Michael is right. Creed will not tolerate his entire family skipping the Church's first year of hosting the Purity Prom. "Drink lots of water," she instructs. Michael nods. "And call the Church for me if you get worse, understand?"

"Yes, mother."

Vanessa smiles sadly and plants a kiss on the back of Michael's head. "I love you, sweetie."

"Love you too, mother," Michael says, and he holds a smile till she leaves. Even after the complete and total purging of his stomach, he stays in the bathroom until he hears the car start outside. Michael watches from the window as his mother and sister drive away towards town and quietly prays that this won't be the last time he sees them.

"Oh, Jimmy." Cut to: the Tran house, where Vincent watches from the door as his mother turns in bed, mumbling in her sleep. The open bottle of sleeping pills next to her tells him she's not gonna hear a thing, but still, he wants to make sure.

"Mom?" he says, and she doesn't answer. "Mom, I'm gonna do something tonight. I'm gonna make him pay for what he took from us. If I don't make it back, I'm sorry, but...mom?" Still nothing, except that she hugs a stuffed toy even tighter—a faded purple bear in a worn clown suit.

Seeing that it's safe, Vincent creeps into the room and opens the closet door. He takes a tin box down from the top shelf and then carries it out.

"Oh, Jimmy," Debbie mumbles, and, in her dreams, she kisses her husband out on the deck as the kids play behind them.

Inside his room, Vincent opens the box and takes out his father's shield. It still shines and glistens. "I miss you, dad," Vincent says, and his eyes leak. He puts the shield back in the box and then, carefully, lifts his father's gun case out. Cracking it open, Vincent stares at the revolver, at the dozen bullets stored with it, and even though he knows it won't do much good, it feels right to take it all the same. He tucks the unloaded gun into the back of his jeans, covers the grip with the bottom of his t-shirt, and just as he goes to put the gun case back in the tin, he spots a letter at the bottom, marked with the Church on the Lake's logo.

"What the hell," Vincent mutters and can't comprehend why his mother would have a letter from the Church stashed away with his father's things. He slips it out, the seal on the back long broken, but it's the date that gets him. March 1989, shortly after his father's funeral. It's probably some pointless, self-promotional letter of condolences, but why would his mother keep it? She never took a thing to do with the Church. Curiosity gets the better of him, and Vincent slips the paper out, unfolds it, and something falls. An outdated check for fifty-thousand dollars.

"The fuck," Vincent mutters.

"Whatcha got there?" Emilie asks from the doorway. Vincent looks up to see his sister dressed for work.

"Just some old letters. Why are you dressed like that? Aren't you going to the Prom?"

"Starsky's got us getting ready for tomorrow; V-Day's always a headache." Emilie sighs. "Besides, you really think I'd go to the Purity Prom?" Emilie mimes throwing up. "Nah, it's good money for quiet work."

"Yeah, but..." Vincent trails off. He can't tell his sister what's going to happen. She'll put a stop to it, for sure.

"Relax. We're locking down. Might actually be kinda fun having the place to ourselves with Sticky-Fingers Starsky at the Prom." Starsky's has shutters and reinforced doors, sure, and it's way more secure than the Tran house, though the safest place would have been the Church. Michael told him that no expense was spared.

Reinforced steel, tempered glass; it's a shimmering fortress on the lake. Vincent wishes his sister was going there but knows there's nothing he can say to change her mind. "Oh, by the way, she's cute."

"She?" Vincent raises an eyebrow.

"Casey. Your girlfriend," Emilie teases with a slow wink and a grinning thumbs-up. She leaves Vincent embarrassed, cheeks flushed red under his black eyeliner and swooping hair.

FEBRUARY 13TH, 1998 - VIRGIN NIGHT.

The sun goes down on Cherry Lake, and from the roof of the Lakeview Hotel, the four of them watch, black silhouettes against hazy red and orange, their shadows stretched out to impossible proportions. For a rare moment, there's only silence. Caleb is the first to break from the group; he turns away and tucks his hair behind his ears.

"This is it," Vincent says and doesn't need to add any more. He takes a joint from his pocket and flicks a flame from a silver lighter. "Smoke 'em if ya got 'em," he adds and takes a draw. Vincent passes it to Caleb, who takes a pull then holds it out for Casey. After she takes a puff, Casey offers it to Michael, and—just as the other two boys go to say it's cool that he doesn't—he shocks them all by taking it. Michael takes it to his lips, holding his fingers out rigidly like he doesn't know what to do. After the slightest of puffs, Michael doubles over, coughing—sending the others into laughter.

"Hey Mikey, while you're experimenting tonight, you don't suppose," Caleb teases and winks.

"If we're going to Hell," Michael coughs, "might as well have some fun on the way, right?"

"That sounds like something some wise man once said," Caleb ponders.

"You," Vincent states, "you said that."

"So I was right."

"Look, nobody's going to Hell. I just want you all to know, if anyone wants to back down, I'll understand. No judgments. We've had some fun. Pizza, booze, laughs. I'd call that a good time, and if that's all this ends up being, that's okay."

"Hey—" Caleb begins.

"I never had friends, real friends, before you guys," Michael interrupts. They're all stunned by his sudden assertiveness. "Till you took a beating for me," he says to Caleb. "Till you threw a punch for me," he says to Vincent. "No, there's nowhere else I'd rather be. I—it's time I stood up and did something. Greater love has no one than this: to lay down one's life for one's friends," he quotes.

"Thank you," Vincent says and shakes Michael's hand. "It's never going to come to that."

"Well, I can't exactly let you be the hero, dude; my ego won't allow it," Caleb proclaims and tries to hide his tears with a laugh. "I'm with you, bro," he says, then forces Vincent into a hug.

"I'm just here to get laid," Casey offers, caught up in the moment but not sure she's truly part of it.

"Get in here," Caleb demands, and she joins the group hug eagerly. Even Michael places his hand on Vincent's shoulder.

As they disentangle, Caleb dries his eyes. "On that note," he clears his throat and drops into an impression of a game show host, "tonight on Blind Date: Teen

Horror Movie edition, we have Casey from Austin and three very eligible bachelors for her to choose from." The other three laugh as Caleb cavorts around the roof, pretending to hold a microphone. "Time to find out, folks, which gentleman will be putting his dude piston into her gut locker this evening?"

"Gross," Casey shakes her head.

"Will she pick the gorgeous, so handsome he must be gay, redheaded heartthrob?" Casey bites her thumb as she laughs. "Or will she go for the dignified, noble man who spells his name i-n-t-e-g-r-i-t-y?" Caleb jazz hands at Michael, who shuffles on the spot, painfully embarrassed. "Or will she go with suitor number three, the brooding, mysterious dark hero of her dreams!" Caleb throws an arm around Vincent, who squints at him. "Who will she—"

"Vincent," Casey interrupts.

"Oh, thank God," Michael mutters under his breath as Caleb's jaw hits the floor.

"I mean, no offense Mikey, but I couldn't ask you to do that to Kaytlynn, even if she deserves it," Casey apologizes.

"None taken," Michael breathes a sigh of relief.

"You're too cute," Casey says and kisses Michael on the cheek.

"Okay-okay makes sense, I guess," Caleb composes himself. "Of course, you didn't pick me because I'm gay, otherwise—"

"Nah, I'd still pick Vincent," Casey smirks.

A shocked gasp escapes from Caleb. "Is it because I'm ginger!?"

"Vincent has the whole moody Brandon Lee Crow thing going on." Casey smiles at Vincent, who stands rigid and dumbfounded. "That definitely does it for me."

"Well done, lad, well done," Caleb mutters, "it's for the best. Really, it's not like I have a photo of Mikey to stick on the back of Casey's head, after all. Now just don't blow your top like the real Brandon Lee." The other three give him a disapproving stare. "Too soon?"

"Not cool, man." Vincent shakes his head.

"Come on," Casey offers her hand out for Vincent to take. "Let's go."

Vincent's hand is slick with sweat as he takes Casey's, and she leads him towards the stairs back into the hotel. Even though they're about to face a centuries-old undead killer, following Casey down to the room they set up earlier frightens him the most.

Cut to: The Church on the Lake. It shines like a diamond on top of the still, black water. Searchlights dance through the sky above, projecting crucifix symbols onto the cloudless night sky. Cars pull up and park wherever they can. Almost every young person in Cherry Lake makes their way across the bridge to the Church, accompanied by their chaperones.

Ariella bites her lip as she guides Dixie Kong through some tricky platforming on her GameBoy, the screen lit with a screen light snapped over it.

"Sweetie, you'll need to leave that in the car," her mother says as she pulls into their allocated spot in the main parking lot.

"I know, I know," Ariella huffs and sighs as she switches it off.

"Behave tonight, and I'll get you that new one you wanted for your birthday."

Ariella jumps up and down in her seat, the belt barely able to contain her excitement. "Pokémon! No kidding!? But dad said—"

"I know what your father said." Vanessa switches the engine off. "But what he doesn't know can't hurt him," she says with a wink that elicits a wide grin from her daughter. "Ariella, no!" Vanessa snaps when she steps out of the car and sees what her daughter is wearing. Her thirteen-year-old rebel put on the expensive dress her father bought, but instead of the matching shoes, Ariella opted for her tried and true Jordans with mismatching loose laces.

"No fair! If I knew Pokémon was part of the deal, I'd have worn whatever you said. Please, mom! Please don't let this count? Please!?" Ariella tilts her head to the side, her big hair flopping down as she holds a toothy smile.

Vanessa rolls her eyes; this daughter of hers is nothing but trouble, and she wouldn't have it any other way. "The deal stands."

"Yes!" Ariella cheers.

"But you're on thin ice, sweetie. Misbehave once, and your father will chuck you in the lake himself," Vanessa teases and walks with her daughter towards the Church, hand on her back. She catches wind of a strange scent, sniffs the air. "What is that in your hair?"

"Uh," Ariella quickly puts together an excuse, "must be that new shampoo?"

They're greeted by ushers at the main entrance, dressed like usual save for the radios clipped to their belts. Even though everyone in town knows who they are, Ariella and her mother hand over the tickets, taken and counted carefully. They're greeted by Kaytlynn, smiling in a floor-length white dress with loose, gossamer sleeves as they move in through the central vestibule.

"Kay!" Ari yells and runs from her mother's side.

"Ari!" Kaytlynn fist-bumps the younger girl; they bump hips then high-five. "Love the shoes, girl, making a statement."

"Yeah," Ariella wags her less than clean right shoe, "I wanna be comfy," and she giggles. "Oh! I made you this." Ariella slips a handmade friendship bracelet off her wrist and holds it out for Kaytlynn.

"Wow, that's so cool." Kaytlynn holds her wrist out for Ariella.

"Good evening Kaytlynn, don't you look stunning!" Vanessa says as she catches up to her errant daughter.

"Oh, thank you, Mrs. Wallace," Kaytlynn beams, then notices there's no one else with them. "Where's Michael?"

"Oh, honey, I'm sorry, but he's awfully sick."

"What?"

"Poor thing, he was hunched over the toilet when we left. He'll be okay, probably something he ate. He'll be so sad he didn't get to see you in that dress!"

Well, isn't that convenient? Michael is sick on this night of all nights. He, his two loser friends, and that girl who looks like a bowl of baby carrots have been up to something. It doesn't matter though. Soon enough, she won't have any need for Michael anymore. "Oh, that's too bad," Kaytlynn lies, "I hope he's okay."

"I hope this is okay," Vincent says, and we cut to the honeymoon suite on the top floor of the Lakeview Hotel. It's unfinished like the rest of the building, but that hasn't stopped the boys from decorating it up as best they could. String lights hang around the room and frame the wall-to-wall picture window that offers a view across the entire lake. Even from the opposite side, the Church shines bright in the distance.

Casey is impressed by the boys' efforts. A mattress sits by the window covered in layers of different colored blankets. Dotted around the room are dozens of misshaped candles, all of them burning. It's cliché, lame, and possibly the most romantic thing anyone has ever done for her. "It's perfect," she says and can't quite hold back a real, tangible twinge in her heart. Oh boy, she says to herself, this is a bit more than she prepared herself for. "Vincent—"

"This, um, I should say," Vincent stammers as he awkwardly stands by the door. He pushes his fringe out of the way just for something to do. "I've never…you know."

Casey smirks. "Are you sayin' I'm your first?"

"Yeah," Vincent sighs. "Yeah. Have you?"

"This ain't my first hayride, cowboy," Casey answers, "but this is the most effort anyone's ever gone to for me," and she gestures to the room. She walks over to the window and places a hand on the glass. Vincent follows her, standing just to the side. "It's a beautiful town," she says.

"From far away," Vincent adds. "Not everything is what it seems."

"Yeah," Casey's voice wavers slightly. She knows that all too well. "Are you sure you want to do this?"

"Like I said on the roof—"

"Not that. This," Casey gestures to the bed. "Your first time should be special. It should mean somethin'. I don't want to take that away from you." Casey takes Vincent's hand and leads him down to the mattress. "You can back out. I'll even tell the guys it was my decision. Nobody needs to know."

"Casey, I," Vincent searches for the words. "Most everyone I know lost their virginity in some drunken backseat fumble or a basement pool table during a party. I can't think of anything more meaningful than what we're doing." Casey feels Vincent's fingers tense as she weaves hers with his. There it is again, that anger.

"Vincent, I want you to make me a promise." Casey's eyes are grave and solemn.

"Sure."

"Don't let your anger control you. That's no way to live."

Vincent looks away. "Therapists, guidance counselors, everyone keeps telling me not to be angry, like it's a tap I can turn off. Casey, I—"

"Be angry! You can't fight it, so you might as well embrace it. Use it, but don't let what you're angry at define who you are; otherwise, it'll never end."

"What are you saying?"

"That you're not too far gone." Casey puts a hand on Vincent's face and makes him look at her. "Don't write yourself off. Vincent, you're not just the son of a dead man; you're so much more. Those guys out there love you very much. You mean the world to them. Keep them here," she touches his temples, "and here," then his chest.

"Do I have to think about them while…" Vincent smirks.

"Only if that turns you on." Casey kisses him. It takes him a second to kiss her back, and then he lets her pull him down on the mattress.

Through the window, fireworks burst over the sky above the distant Church. Cut across to the Church as the last of the tickets are taken, and the doors are closed tight. They're locked electronically, and Kaytlynn smiles with delight as Virgin Night begins.

Just over two minutes later, Vincent and Casey come down the stairs together, straightening their clothes.

"Jesus Christ, that was fast!" Caleb shouts.

"Blasphemy," Michael complains.

"Was that even long enough to count?" Caleb jokes.

"Fuck you, Caleb—" Vincent begins, and he's interrupted by a high, continuous tone that makes Michael grit his teeth. "Where's that?"

"We have motion out front," Michael declares as he reads the motion detection system's handset.

"It's go time," Vincent declares, and the other three nod. They follow him through the lobby to the main entrance, and none of them can see what tripped the alarm.

"I don't see anything," Casey looks around, "it's too foggy."

"I don't like it," Michael mutters.

"Chill, it's the lake. Fog always rolls in off the lake at night," Caleb explains.

"It's not coming from the lake," Michael points, "look," and he raises his arm to show that the fresh mist tumbles and swirls towards the hotel from the forest instead.

Each of them feels it at once, the evil that lurks beneath the postcard picturesque pastoral of Cherry Lake. A figure emerges with the fog, an embodiment of shadow and hate, and then he steps out into the moonlight.

CHAPTER FIFTEEN

COME OUT AND PLAY

"Hey!" Vincent yells as he goes down the front steps, the others beckoning him back. Everything Casey said disregarded as the sight of his father's murderer makes him come alive with rage. "Fuckwit, you killed my dad!" Vincent raises his arm, pointing in defiance. "You die tonight."

"Vincent," Michael snaps, "stick to the plan!" There's a part of Vincent that wants to rush the fucker, wail on the piece of shit, tear the bastard apart with his bare hands. The way he feels right now, he could do it. If it weren't for Michael's voice of reason, he would do it. Instead, Vincent flips the masked figure a double bird. "Come get some, bitch."

The figure takes one step forward and no more. There is no rush. All will die by his hands this night, as they will for all nights to come. Raising his chin, he looks to the night sky and savors the moment as the Voice in the Fog urges him to *kill*.

Vincent backs off, and he can't help but feel a shred of disappointment. This is not the impossibly tall giant as some stories have told, nor is he the hulking behemoth others have claimed. He looks very much like an ordinary man who nevertheless exudes an aura of bone-chilling heartlessness. The only thing that holds up is the mask. In the moonlight that pours down and bounces off the lake, it's hard to make out precisely what it looks like till a second later when three blasts from hidden floodlights come on. Bathed in sudden, intense luminescence, Vincent gets a good look at him. The mask, made from dark, almost black wood, is virtually featureless, save for the coarse bark, carved, hollow eyeholes, and twisting branches at the top that jut forward like tangled stag horns.

The insolent child stands atop the stairs before the entrance to the husk of a building that shall become his tomb, taunting with a hip thrust. The Voice in the Fog finds this amusing, but he, The Hand, does not.

"Come on, Vincent!" Casey calls from the top of the main staircase.

"He's not coming!" Vincent shouts back. Does the fucker know what we've got in store? "Hey, you gonna stand there and look menacing or actually do something?"

"Yeah," Caleb joins in, "the time you're taking, Vincent here could do it three, no, four more times!"

Vincent? This insolent one who summoned him. The Voice in the Fog commands him to *pursue*, and the masked monstrosity obeys.

"That's it," Vincent whispers, "come right on up." Caleb tries to pull Vincent back, but Vincent shrugs him off. He wants to watch as - **BOOM-BOOM!** - two small explosions go off, peppering the masked thing's flesh with nails, embedding some all the way into the head. It's enough to cause him to pause for a moment and examine the damage. He feels no pain or any compulsion to remove the barbs, so he marches on.

Vincent smirks; first blood is theirs, and there's more to come. He follows Caleb towards the main staircase and regroups with Casey and Michael on the landing above the lobby.

The figure enters the lobby moments later, skin pocked with metallic nail heads. His heavy bootsteps echo through the empty, cavernous room and then soften as they move from stone to plush, red carpet. Another click - **BLAM!** - and he's blasted point-blank, by a shotgun trap hidden beside the door frame. It's enough to make him tilt his head to the side, just. He reaches out, grabs the shotgun with one hand, and examines it briefly before snapping it in two with a single, effortless crunch.

"Aw man," Caleb says from the landing, "my Pa's gonna kill me."

He continues toward the main staircase as the four children scurry away down the corridor behind. They don't elude him for long. As he turns the corner, he catches sight of Vincent slipping through a door. Boxes and mechanical equipment line the hallway; these are of no interest to him. The rabbit is fast but nowhere near quick enough to elude this hunter.

There is no furniture within the room, nothing for his prey to hide behind, and the only closet lies open, with no doors affixed. So, the bathroom. Why do they always hide in the bathroom? He turns, opens the door, takes two strides inside, and has time to see Vincent wave at him before falling through the floor, eyes fixed up at the arrogant brat.

He lands, on his back, in the room below—his fall softened by several inches of water in a room lined with industrial-sized washing machines. A mass of wadded-up towels blocks the door while a deep, gray-metal sink by the wall overflows, water cascading over the edge, flooding the room with ice-cold rivulets.

"I just want you to know that it was my buddy who insisted I say this," Vincent calls from the hole above, hair dangling to obscure much of his face.

The masked thing looks up at the grinning child.

"I'm, shit, what was it, Caleb?" Vincent calls out, and over the rush of water, he can't hear the response. With a snicker, Vincent looks back down through the hole and says, "I can't believe that worked. Honestly. I'm as shocked as you're about to be!"

At that signal, Michael turns on each of the generators hooked up together along the hall outside. The wires that run through the laundry room pump over 1000 volts through the water, right into the masked thing. He goes rigid, hands frozen in arthritic claws as blue sparks dart across his body. For a second, it looks like this might be it, as wisps of black smoke rise and the scent of frying meat fills the air. Then one of the generators blows, and the others quickly follow.

"Fuck," Vincent curses, then heads back to the hall to regroup.

"They blew—" Michael begins.

"It's fine," Vincent states, "we move on to the next stage. Ready?" The other three nod and break for it, heading up the stairs while Vincent goes back to the main hall and waits.

It takes a few moments for him to stop trembling even after the current cuts out. Although pain is not something he understands, he definitely felt what they did to him. Climbing to his feet, he wades through the water to the door. Not bothering to remove the towels blocking the bottom, he grabs both handles of the twin door and yanks them inwards, forcing the weighty towels aside as though they were nothing. A wave of water gushes out into the hall. It does not take him long to find his way back to the main entrance and to the grinning face of the brazen one who sits on the top step, taunting.

"Here's the deal, Treeface," Vincent declares. "You've hurt a lot of people, and I'm more than happy to pay you back for every single one of them, but I'll settle with you just dying. Kill yourself right now, end this."

Treeface? Is that his name? It doesn't feel right, but he knows no other. All that he knows is that this one dies first—even if the Voice in the Fog didn't demand it. Treeface begins to climb the stairs. Vincent stands and backs away with a satisfied smirk.

Once he's put a few floors between himself and the slowly advancing killer below, Vincent takes his radio out and calls the others. "You guys ready? I'm bringing him up."

The radio crackles, and then Casey's voice comes through. "Shit, no, the thingie broke. What? Not now, Caleb! We need time to reset."

"What did Caleb say?" Vincent asks into the radio.

"I said," Caleb's voice crackles through the tiny speaker, "that's what Vincent's sister said."

"Very fuckin' funny, Caleb!" Vincent snaps. "I'm gonna lead him around the fourth floor for a bit."

"Gotcha, I'll radio when we're good—"

"No," Vincent cuts Casey off, "I might have to hide. I'll check in when I can."

"Vincent?" Casey's static voice wavers. "Be careful, you hear?"

"Of course," Vincent reassures her, "who do you think I am? Caleb Dumont?"

"Hey! I resemble that remark," Caleb whines over the radio.

Through the gap in the stairs, Vincent sees Treeface step out from the third floor. Backing halfway down one corridor, Vincent preps the stun baton, holds his position, and waits for his stalker to arrive. It doesn't take long, and Vincent cracks the rod to draw his attention. "That's right, this way," Vincent whispers, but for some reason, Treeface doesn't follow. Instead, he looks up as though he can tell the other three are waiting. "Shit," Vincent mutters to himself, "he's not buying it."

Instead of following or heading up, Treeface disappears into the opposite corridor and vanishes from sight. "Damn it!" Vincent grabs his radio. "Guys, I've lost sight of him. One of you keep an eye on the stairs at all times."

"How the hell did you—" Casey starts.

"Fucker can move when he wants to, be careful," Vincent says and clips the radio back onto his belt. "Okay, Woody," Vincent raises the stun baton, "let's play." Vincent creeps along the corridor Treeface went down moments ago. It's lined, on either side, with crates, building supplies, and boxes containing disassembled furniture—so many possible places for an ambush. The plastic sheets covering much of the unopened supplies rustle in the breeze that whistles through the empty window panes. This place did not feel this spooky till just now, Vincent thinks as he swings his head from side to side, baton at the ready.

Unseen, Treeface watches, correct in assuming that there is some purpose to the bold one's defiance; he would not be on the hunt now, otherwise.

Something clunks to the floor; Vincent jumps and thrusts the baton at the sound, filling the corridor with a staccato of blue-white light. Just a can, only a rat, and Vincent's breathing rushes to catch up with his heart. He's no sooner caught his breath when a hand suddenly wraps around his neck—a single, human hand with the grip of a machine. Treeface lifts him off the ground before even a gasp can escape. The stun baton, dropped at the shock of the attack, clatters on the floor. Vincent's feet kick desperately as he uses both hands to try and pry even a single finger free. His vision blurs, and it gets difficult to even bat, lifelessly, at Treeface's arm.

Then Vincent finds himself on the floor; air rushes back into his lungs but, even so, he can still feel enormous pressure around his throat. Treeface jerks to the beat of rapid clicks and, as Vincent scrambles free, he sees Casey standing with the discharging taser in hand. She drops it, runs over, pulls Vincent to his feet, and drags him down the corridor as Treeface recovers from the shock.

There she is, he notes, the insolent one's mate. Of course, she had to be somewhere nearby. The boy smells of the lake, but she does not. There's something different about her. These are the ones who brought him out of the Fog, and they shall be the first he sends back there tonight. He crushes the stick the boy tried to defend himself with underfoot and follows after the both of them.

Casey leads them around the corner and then pulls Vincent into a room. He goes to thank her, but Casey puts her hand over Vincent's mouth. He can taste the salt of her sweat on his lips. Outside the room, heavy footsteps round the corner and march closer. Both Casey and Vincent hold their breath as the stomping gets louder, louder, and then fades, somewhat, as Treeface passes them by.

"Here's the plan," Casey whispers, "I'll go back the way we came, make some noise. You go the other way, do the same. We'll confuse him and then break for the stairs."

"Is it ready?" Vincent whispers back.

"Let's hope so," Casey answers. "Michael said he's figured somethin' out, but he wasn't making much sense. Ready?"

"Ready," Vincent nods.

Casey returns the gesture and slips away. Seconds later, a clutter of paint cans crashing to the floor sounds from the way they came. The stomping of heavy steps racing toward the sound follows. Vincent sprints the other way as soon as it passes, knocking over some unassembled scaffolding on purpose. He watches, over his shoulder, to see Treeface reappear and pursue. Vincent races on, jumps over a stack of fallen wooden slats, and pauses at a heavy pallet leaning against the wall. Treeface closes in. Just as he gets within reach, Vincent pulls the pallet down, both stunning and momentarily trapping the killer. Vincent can't suppress a laugh, watching the killer stuck there—stumped by a simple wooden pallet. He almost wishes there were a few more around here so he could lead Treeface on a loop, crashing them down on him again and again.

Back where the corridors meet the stairs, Casey waits, bouncing on the spot. "He behind you?" she asks.

"Yeah," Vincent answers, "and he's gonna be pissed."

The two of them race up the stairs; Casey takes a comfortable lead, and Vincent almost regrets the sheer volume of weed he's smoked over the years. Almost. When they reach the second-to-top floor, they see Michael messing around inside the open elevator door as Caleb stands over him, hands on either side, keeping it open.

"What happened?" Caleb and Vincent ask each other at the same time.

"The bar snapped," Michael answers. "I can't get the door to stay open on its own. One of us will have to hold it."

"Caleb, swap places with me," Vincent commands and waves his friend away.

"Not happening, like what your sister said when the Redcastle Knights bus broke down by your house, I'm all over this."

"Caleb!"

"Deal with it!"

"Fuck," Vincent runs his hands through his hair. "Okay, how's this gonna work now?"

"Takes maybe four seconds for the door to close once it's released," Michael explains. "Caleb will just have to get out of the way the second we hit him."

"Okay." Vincent picks up half of the broken steel pole they had used to prop the door open earlier. "Casey, Michael, you two get out of sight. On go, you two charge him, and Caleb gets out of the way."

"You mean when you say go, or after you say it?" Caleb jokes.

"Actually, it would make sense for us to go as you say it and for Caleb to dive after. The slight delay would allow for—"

"Michael, not now!" Vincent snaps. Footsteps echo up the dark staircase. "He's coming." Casey and Michael scramble out of sight, taking cover in an open storage closet beside the top of the stairs. Vincent tests the weight of the pipe in his hand and waits.

Treeface comes around the bend, a chunk of wood embedded in his shoulder.

"Oh fuck," Vincent gloats, "that must have hurt." Treeface reaches up and yanks the rough shard free, and though no blood seeps from the wound, a fine black mist rises as it heals over almost instantly. Even though his eyes are nothing but jet-black hollows, Vincent can feel them narrow as they land on him. Treeface begins to climb the final set of stairs between them.

Lure him up, keep his attention away from Caleb, and bail as soon as he's in position. That's the plan, except this pipe sure feels good in Vincent's hands, and this fucker did kill his dad. Treeface reaches the final stair and then stands on the landing, within spitting distance of Vincent. He takes a step forward, then another, and then he's in range, but Vincent does not move. No, he ignores Michael and Casey's silent urging to go and instead readies his weapon.

"You killed my dad, you piece of shit," Vincent yells and swings the pipe. It connects with Treeface's shoulder and does nothing. That doesn't stop Vincent from taking another swing, then another, and another. "You killed him!" Vincent screams as he loses control, all his hate and fury flowing into his attacks.

Realizing Vincent's lost control of the situation, and himself, the other three act almost instinctively.

"Grab him," Casey yells, and Caleb dashes forward from the elevator. Wrapping his arms around Vincent, Caleb throws them both to the side as Vincent screams. Treeface stabs the shard of wood down, sticking it deep into Caleb's shoulder before both boys hit the ground.

Casey and Michael rush Treeface from behind; the two of them shove him with all their combined strength and propel the monster through the closing elevator doors. Just before they close, Casey steps in and wedges them open with her body.

At the bottom of the shaft, Treeface lands in a pile of loose, metal containers that clunk like they're full of some liquid. A sharp scent almost overpowers him.

Blood pours from Caleb's wound, even with the wood still stuck in him, staunching much of the flow. Vincent's eyes settle on the damage done to his friend, and his stomach drops at the realization it could have been so much worse.

"Caleb, shit, I'm—"

"Boys! Hurry!" Casey interrupts. Snapping back to the task at hand, Caleb hobbles over to the elevator with Vincent's help. All four of them stare down into the black abyss of the empty shaft. "Got a light?" Casey asks. Vincent takes out his lighter, flicks it to a steady flame, and drops it down the shaft. The tiny little glow gets smaller and smaller till it vanishes into the black, and then a wall of heat whooshes up, blowing Casey, Vincent, and Caleb's hair back as a mighty fireball surges up the shaft. When it passes, the four of them look down to see a raging fire consume the body at the bottom.

Michael crawls away and comes back a moment later with a backpack. He fidgets around inside and something within beeps. "Do you want to do the honors?" he asks, holding the bag out for Vincent to take.

He nods. "Thank you," Vincent says as he takes the bag. "Thank you all, I—"

"Speeches later, boom-boom now," Caleb says through gritted teeth.

Vincent pushes a button inside the bag, and the homemade explosive inside begins to beep rapidly. "Fuck off, Treeface," he says and drops the bag down the shaft.

All four of them dive to the ground and cover their ears.

As Treeface crackles and burns within the flames at the bottom, he feels something land, inches from where he lies, and then nothing at all as the bomb goes off.

It blasts out through the hotel's entire ground floor; first, an invisible wave of pressure and heat obliterates almost everything in its path, then raging flames burst forth from every window and door.

All the way at the top, the four of them feel the very foundations of the hotel shake and then crumble as the supports holding the second floor give way.

"How much did you put in that bag?" Casey shouts over the ringing in her ears.

"Huh?" Michael holds his hand to his ears.

"How much—"

The whole hotel trembles, and they all feel it move, slightly off-axis.

"I think I put too much in—"

"Run!" Vincent yells, and the four of them race down the squared, spiral staircase as the Lakeview Hotel begins to come apart. "Fuck, fuck, fuck!" they yell as they go; Caleb falters, falls behind, and Michael and Vincent take a shoulder without a word. They keep going, around and around as dust falls, then chunks of masonry.

They reach the lobby, cross it in seconds, and are almost to the bottom of the steps outside when the interior floors begin to crumble, cascading down like a house of cards till the inside of the Lakeview is just a mountain of wood and stone. Dust billows out, covering the whole clearing a layer of gray.

The four of them collapse on the dock in a fit of hacking gasps for air.

As the dust settles, the hotel remains standing, though the debris that now clutters several floors' worth of windows confirms that the same cannot be said for the interior. One by one, starting with Casey, they begin to laugh. Relief washes over them, their mission accomplished, and all of them alive to see it. The rush of victory even dulls Caleb's pain enough for him to get in one last quip. "Fuck off, Treeface? That's the best you could come up with?" And that sets them all off, again.

The ruin of the Lakeview Hotel begins to settle. Chunks of granite and charred timber slip through cracks and holes. Smaller sections still crumble as the weight they hold becomes too much to bear, setting off declining cascades of debris. Juts of flame burn here and there, though not enough to pose any real threat to the nearby forest.

"Hey, look," Caleb smirks and nods to flames flickering on what was once the top of the hotel. "The roof, the roof, the roof is on fire..."

Vincent smiles, honest and goofy, then nods. "The roof, the roof, the roof is on fire," he joins in, and together they sing the third line, "the roof, the roof, the roof is on fire." Both raise a middle finger to the building and sing, "We don't need no water, let the motherfucker burn." They punctuate each word with a thrust of their fingers, "Burn, motherfucker, burn!"

CHAPTER SIXTEEN
END CREDITS

And so, we pull up from the four heroes to a sparkling night sky as the boys' singing leads into the real thing, a licensed Bloodhound Gang song that'll make overpriced collector's edition remasters problematic in all sorts of ways in a few decades. We don't gotta worry about all that right now, though. Just enjoy the credits as we dolly in, real slow, over the lake towards the Church.

Written, Directed, and Produced by
(yeah, because fuck Hitchcock's Holy Trinity, right?)
Christopher Robertson.

Starring
Vincent Tran - James Edward Duval
Caleb Dumont - Edward Furlong
Michael Wallace - Keenan Thompson
Casey - Brittany Murphy

We're getting pretty damn close to the Church now.

Kaytlynn Parker - Melissa Joan Hart
Emilie Tran - Thuy Trang

Ariella Wallace - Vanessa Lee Chester
Jam Starsky - Devon Sawa
with
Laurence Fishburne as Creed Wallace

Scratch-cut to a private penthouse-style room at the very top of the Church. Each wall is, of course, made of glass, affording a spectacular panorama of the entirety of Cherry Lake. Even the distant lights of Redcastle, but all the gathered members of the Inner Circle aren't interested in the scenery—their eyes are focused on the bed-like ritual table in the middle of the room.

Creed stands up, naked except for his featureless wooden mask, his powerful body dotted with specks of sweat. "It's done," he proclaims, and one of the Inner Circle approaches, draping a black silk robe over his shoulders. Kaytlynn covers her own nudity with another silk robe on the bed, slipping into it not because she's embarrassed or feels vulnerable but because there's work to be done.

Creed walks towards the window wall that looks down upon the Church's entrance without bothering to fasten the robe. "Has he been sighted yet?" One of the Inner Circle holds a phone to their ear, listening. They shake their head at Creed's question. "Strange," Creed ponders, "it should only be moments before the fog forms, and yet all is clear." As each minute passes, Creed becomes more concerned. "Something has gone wrong," his eyes narrow.

"Was it me?" Kaytlynn asks, suddenly afraid that she failed in her role—that her place within the Inner Circle is in question.

"No, my dear," Creed offers scant reassurance and doesn't even turn his head as he speaks. "You performed your role perfectly." Creed glares down at the town before him. "Others must have summoned him."

"How?" Kaytlynn climbs off the bed and holds the robe closed as she crosses the room. "No one in Cherry Lake would be stupid enough to…" she trails off. "No," she mutters, "even they're not that dumb."

"Speak up," Creed commands, and suddenly the room rattles as it's bathed in a flash of orange light. It comes from behind—from the forest across the lake. All of the Inner Circle rush to the back window wall. There's only a taught silence as they watch fire and smoke billow from the distant Lakeview Hotel.

"Morons," Kaytlynn growls, hands balled into fists so tight her nails press into her skin. A large, strong hand lands on her shoulder.

"Tell me what you know," Creed demands.

If only you'd listened to me the other day, Kaytlynn considers saying, but the vibe the Pastor is giving off doesn't imply he'd take that well. She's not going to sugarcoat it, either, though. "Your son and his delinquent friends smuggled some whore into town." I tried to tell you; she doesn't add. For a second, it feels like Creed might snap her collarbone clean in two, and then he relaxes.

Creed declares, turning to the others, "This is merely an inconvenience. The salvation of the Church, and Cherry Lake, will still be made real. Gather the Devoted, and go forth. If any of them still live—they must remain so till I say otherwise." All of the Inner Circle, barring Kaytlynn and Creed himself, leave the Watchtower in silence. "My dear, I dare not ask any more of you this night," Creed says as he lifts Kaytlynn's mask to look her in the eyes. "You have fulfilled your role, with splendor, and may make your way to the Sanctuary till this is over." He finds no fear in her eyes, though, only a cold resolve.

"No, Pastor Wallace," Kaytlynn insists, "you're going to need me."

"My dear," Creed says and raises his mask. "You are a gift from God," and he kisses her while the Lakeview Hotel crumbles in the distance behind them.

Fade in, across the lake, as Vincent helps Caleb to his feet. "Well, come on then, what would you have said?"

"I dunno," Caleb grimaces as fresh blood seeps out between his skin and the embedded wooden shard. "Anything's better than 'Fuck off, Treeface.' How about Hasta la vista, Mister Tree."

"Okay, one, that's awful, and two, he wasn't a fucking tree, just had a mask like one."

"I'd say it was more bark with branches than a tree," Michael states.

"Even better! How about, You barked up the wrong tree—boom, there you go! Hey, if we ever do a remake, we'll use that line." Caleb hobbles forward with Vincent's support and then manages a few steps on his own. "No! No! I got it. Hey, Treeface, remember when my dad dropped a well on you? How about a whole building! Yeah, that's good!" Caleb prods the wood, sending a sharp twinge of focused pain through half his body. "That's not so good." He starts to laugh, even though it hurts like hell, and can't find his words through the hysteria.

"What's so funny," Casey asks, dusting her clothes off.

"I-I can't," Caleb tries to control his breathing, sounding like a woman about to give birth. "I'm gonna die if I say it."

"Oh no," Michael states.

"Don't—" Vincent warns.

"Bet-betcha Vinnie's sister's pissed she missed out catching this wood!" Caleb yells through wild, uncontrollable laughter. He has to sit down before he falls and can barely see through the tears that are equal parts joy and agony.

"You're lucky you got staked, or I'd kick your ass," Vincent threatens.

"Yeah, guess we can rule out Caleb being a vampire, huh?" Casey teases. "I mean, that looks like it could reach your heart."

"If he had one," Vincent grumbles.

"Everyone has a heart," Michael states.

"Hey! I'm not the one who just had to pick a fight with Jason Voorhees in a Wicker Man cosplay," Caleb wipes his eyes, "this is your fault, buddy, now help me yank it out." Caleb smirks. "Then take care of this wood."

"Shit," Vincent's eyes drop to the floor, "I don't know what I was thinking, Caleb. Guys. I could have, fuck, I'm sorry."

Casey slaps Vincent over the back of his head. "There, even," she declares.

"No way!" Caleb protests. "I'm the one who got stabbed! I wanna hit him."

"Urgh!" Casey moans. "Fine, you can slap him later, once we're outta here." Caleb raises his hand like a school kid. "Yes?"

"A slap is hardly fair compensation," Caleb counters. "One kick, right in the dick titties, no blocks."

"Fine! Deal! Let's go!" Casey goes over and helps Caleb back to his feet. He points to Vincent with a grin then swings his foot.

Vincent turns to the ruins once more and looks it over for signs that Treeface might still be alive.

"We dropped a building on him, Vincent," Michael reassures. "He's not walking out of that."

"All the same," Vincent takes out the revolver and loads it.

"That won't do a thing," Michael reminds him, "even the shotgun to the head didn't work."

"I know." Vincent closes the chamber. "It's not for him."

"Man, that's dark. Even for you," Caleb jokes.

"What? No! Jesus, Caleb!" Vincent puts the gun back in his belt. "I'm gonna stay behind and watch, just in case. If he isn't dead, I'll fire three quick shots if he gets out of there. You guys should be able to hear them; sound carries over the lake even in fog like this."

"Vincent, that's not a good idea," Michael tries to persuade him.

"No, someone has to, Mikey," Vincent stands firm, "and this was my idea, so I'll take watch."

"If the gunshots can be heard, then the explosions must have been too," Casey realizes.

"I'll keep out of sight," Vincent promises, "won't be hard with the fog. I'll meet you at the lake house at sun-up. Go take care of Caleb; he looks like he's gonna pass out."

"That's the plan," Caleb grimaces.

"You sure?" Casey asks. She doesn't like the idea. "Don't folks get themselves killed when they split up in these kinds of movies?"

"Movie's over," Vincent turns to the ruins of the Lakeview Hotel. "I'm just sticking around for the credits."

Jump-cut to the front seat of a black SUV with tinted windows and a gold crucifix attached to the dashboard as it speeds along a forest road. Kaytlynn holds a blocky cellphone to her head. "Send people to the Tran house and the trailer park but just watch, I don't expect them to be that stupid, but after tonight I'm having doubts." She's swapped her dress for the usual Church uniform except that she and each of the Devoted surrounding her have bare, wooden masks; Kaytlynn's rests on her knees at the moment.

Behind her SUV, three more follow as they head south, around the lake.

"Remember, alive. The other three you can rough up, but lay a finger on Pastor Wallace's son, and you'll regret it." Kaytlynn hangs up with a sigh. Why couldn't this have been easy? Those idiots, why would they do this? Michael covers his eyes at sex scenes; how the hell did he let them talk him into this? And Vincent Tran, you'd think he'd know better. It's the girl, that trashy little thing with the daddy-issues hair. She's done this, led them into this, and for what? Kaytlynn does not like being in the dark, and she will have answers.

Cut back to Michael, Casey, and Caleb as they make their way along the shore through the fog. Casey and Michael each have one of Caleb's arms.

"We need a hospital, or a doctor at least," Casey argues.

"Nearest hospital's in Redcastle," Michael explains.

"Then a doctor? You gotta have one, at least, in town?"

"Of course—"

"No doctors," Caleb insists, "they'll ask questions."

"So? We'll just make somethin' up," Casey says, "like you fell off your bed trying to suck your own dick."

"That adds up," Michael states.

"One, I don't need to do it myself. I have plenty of willing partners, thank you very much," Caleb snorts.

"And, two, fuck you!" That gets a brief laugh from the others. "Just get me back to my trailer. My Pa's always coming home drunk and beat up; he'll have shit we can use."

"He won't be home?"

"Nah, it's the weekend. Virgin Night or not, he and his buddies will be locked in at Tillman's, drunk as shit by now. Won't see him till the morning at least."

Casey looks up the hill to their right and sees a familiar building. "That's the Williamson Farm, right?"

"Yeah," Caleb nods, "not far to mine now."

Casey brings them to a stop, slips free from Caleb, and takes a few steps towards the house on the hill. The place Vincent took her to tell his story, the place where his father gave his own life to save others. She glances back at where they came from and realizes that Vincent's doing the very same thing, taking it upon himself to stand between death and everyone else. Something inside her twists—this isn't right; this isn't like her; she's seen dozens of these scenarios play out and hasn't ever felt this way before. Every instinct she has tells her to keep going, follow this to the end and move on, like every other time. Casey can't, though.

"Michael, can you get Caleb the rest of the way yourself?"

"Sure, but why?" Michael looks at her, confused.

"I'm going back," Casey states. "We, I, can't leave Vincent alone."

"But Vincent said—"

"Mikey," Caleb interrupts, "let's go."

"But—"

"Keep him outta trouble," Caleb says to Casey, and she nods before taking off back the way they came. After she slips from sight into the fog, Michael and Caleb turn around and resume their journey at a markedly slower pace.

"Well, Mikey, it's just you and me now. Let's go take care of my wood."

"You've already used that joke tonight," Michael notes.

"Aw, gimme a break; I'm wounded over here."

They don't talk too much more as they move along the shore, then cut up a path to the road. It's not that far now, thankfully. The pain must be worse than he's letting on if he's so quiet, Michael considers.

Neither of them sees the lights approaching from behind. Caleb's grunting disguises the approaching engines till it's too late for them to hide. As their shadows grow suddenly longer and more angular, Caleb and Michael both look over their shoulders. The Church's SUV skids to a halt on the road beside them. The doors pop open, and the Devoted pile out, wearing weird masks they're too freaked out to recognize.

"Grab them!" one of the Devoted commands, and two of them close in on the boys. They grab hold of Michael and, as they pull him away, Michael shoves Caleb free.

"Run!" Michael yells as two Devoted drag him back towards the SUV. It takes a second for the rest of them to come around the car, and that gives Caleb a moment to decide if he's going to run or fight. Save himself or save his friend. The second he tries to move, needles of sheer anguish shoot straight to his wounded shoulder, and in the time it takes him to wince, Michael is dragged into the back of the car, kicking and punching. "Run!" he yells one more time before a bag's pulled over his head.

It's too late, Caleb tells himself, and he sprints back down the path towards the lake, running into the forest instead of following it all the way. Too late, he repeats and focuses on that, so he doesn't have to wonder if the pain stopped him from rushing to Michael's aid or making a break for the trees sooner.

Smash-cut from Caleb tumbling through the shrubs to Vincent kicking aside chunks of stone at the Lakeview ruins.

"Come on," Vincent mutters, "I know you're in there. Where are you?"

He uses a broken plank of wood to wedge free a sizable concrete slab, sending dust up in a thick cloud that causes him to turn away, coughing. As it settles, Vincent narrows his eyes and peers into the chaos of ash and rubble. In that, beneath it all, something that looks very much like a charred hand lies still. A sly smile spreads across Vincent's face as he watches for any sign of life and finds none.

"Got you good, you piece of shit," Vincent spits, and then something catches his eye. Lights, pairs of them, approaching from a distance. "Fuck," he mutters and turns to run towards the treeline in the opposite direction. He completely misses the burned hand, blackened bones sticking through ravaged flesh twitching back to life.

As the Church SUVs pull up at the site, Vincent slinks into the shadows, backing away as he watches the mask-wearing Devoted climb out.

"The fu—" is all he gets out as a hand wraps around his mouth.

CHAPTER SEVENTEEN

MASK/OFF

Everything's pitch-dark, almost, save for tiny pinpricks of light. Heavy, panicked breathing, then a sudden surge of blinding light forces Michael's eyes shut. He opens them, one at a time, carefully. It takes him a few seconds to realize where he is. The cream leather couches, luxury wood paneling, and the gentle swaying that's triggering his seasickness—his father's boat.

"Hello, Michael," Creed says and drops the sack that covered his son's head to the floor. He's tied to a chair and can do little but struggle pointlessly.

A masked Devoted in Church attire dips in and collects the discarded sack. Creed doesn't even acknowledge his presence, or the other two Michael can see. What's up with those masks, Michael wonders. They look just like—

"I apologize for the roughness," Creed states, and he signals to someone behind Michael. A second later, his hands are free, and Michael rubs his raw wrists. "There was simply no other way, no time to explain."

Michael wants to say, "You've never apologized for anything in your whole life." Instead, he asks, "What's going on?"

"Follow me, my son," Creed instructs. He marches out onto the deck, not pausing for his son to follow, confident that the boy will regardless. He's right.

Cut outside to see a Baglietto 25m yacht moored to the dock beneath The Church on the Lake. Close in on the name of the boat: *The Sanctuary*. Michael emerges to see his father already standing on the bow, looking out to the lake with his arms behind his back. Glancing to the dock, Michael considers making a run for it, but more of those masked guards stand at attention; there's no way he'd make it. Resigned, Michael makes his way along the gunwale; suddenly grateful Caleb's concoction emptied his stomach earlier. The sidelights glimmering over the surface below, not to mention the slapping of water against *The Sanctuary*'s hull, make him want to dry heave.

"Exactly what were you and those imbecile friends of yours thinking," Creed demands to know, not bothering to face his son.

"Father, I—"

"Do not even think of lying to me. I know you, the dropout, and that white-trash waste of space were at my hotel with some unknown girl. I can't even begin to tell you how disgusted I am with you." Creed sighs. "But you are my son, and I cannot deny the role I had in shaping you into such a disappointment."

"I-I'm sorry, father." Michael hangs his head.

"That's good, my son." Creed turns, granting Michael a cold, domineering glare. "Now, tell me everything."

Cut to: the edge of the forest, where the hand over Vincent's mouth tastes familiar.

"It's just me," Casey reassures him, though the way she holds the rescue knife ready to stab him in the chest is unsettling. She lets go but keeps the blade in hand. What would she have done with that if it wasn't me? Vincent wonders if he wants to know. Or if he cares. "Who are they?" Casey nods out to the SUVs and masked Church members taking over the site.

"Those are Church uniforms, but fuck knows about the masks," Vincent answers.

"They look a little familiar, right? I'm not the only one seein' it?"

"Yeah, they look like Dollar Store Treeface knock-offs," Vincent agrees.

"We're really goin' with Treeface?"

"Why not?" Vincent shrugs. "You really gonna tell me your Raincoat Killer is more original?"

Casey pauses, looks away, then concedes, "No. I guess you're right."

One of the Devoted finds what they're looking for amidst the rubble and waves the others over. Several of them gather around the section where Vincent uncovered the burned, dead hand of Treeface. Some of their heads turn as one of them yells, and they move out the way as a masked girl pushes through; the way she carries herself says she's way above the Devoted.

"They've found his body," Vincent whispers.

"How can you be sure?" Casey hisses back.

"Because I found it after you guys left. Are the others—"

"They're fine; what do you mean you found it? Is that why you stayed behind!?"

"I had to be sure!"

"We can't let them dig him up." Casey sighs; knowing what she knows about these creatures, Vincent isn't

193

wrong. You can never be too sure. Still, he's starting to worry her.

"Agreed," Vincent nods. "Plan?"

"Spook them? Make them crap their pants and run. Somehow," Casey suggests. Both look around the site for inspiration. Casey's eyes land on the three SUVs on the far side. Two are well within the clearing, while the third blocks the road out. "Okay, see the cars?"

"Yeah," Vincent nods.

"I'll slash the tires on the two over by the side. Can you think of somethin' to fuck with the one on the road," Casey asks, "something that'll scare the shit out of them?"

Vincent smirks. "Yeah, I think I do. We blow it the fuck up."

"How? We don't have any bombs left."

"Easy, stick a rag in the fuel cap, light it and run."

"You've done this before."

"Maybe."

"How though, you used your lighter in the hotel?"

Vincent slips a cheap, plastic lighter out of his jacket pocket. "You think a burnout like me doesn't carry spares?"

Casey grins. "All right, wait for my signal before you light 'er up."

"Got it," Vincent nods, and the two of them creep along the outside of the clearing, using the forest for cover.

They pass the middle and move closer to where the Devoted gather and hear the one in charge yelling. There's something distinctly familiar in the commanding screech of her voice. "I don't care how hard it'll be; get digging now!"

"God, what a bitch," Casey mutters. "Okay, watch for me," she says as the two of them split up. Vincent heads on while Casey ducks out of the woods and plunges her rescue knife into the first SUV's front right tire. It hisses stale air as it slowly sags down, and once she's satisfied with the damage, she moves on to the back end.

Vincent reaches his car and peers inside the open door, searches for something to stick in the fuel tank, and when he comes out empty-handed, he rips the bottom of his shirt, tearing off a chunk with little effort. As Vincent stuffs the cloth into the tank, he can't suppress the smirk that spreads across his face. A premature joy, though.

Casey glances up from slicing the right rear tire on her second car to see a big, masked Devoted come up behind Vincent. She wants to call out, but all that'll do is give her away, and there's nothing for it but to let the big guy grab Vincent, lifting him right off his feet and holding him up in an arm lock. "Fuck," Casey mutters and watches as other masks gather around. The female one in charge marches over, and though she can't quite hear what they're saying, Casey can tell from the harsh slap she gives Vincent, not to mention the fuck-you grin on his face, that whatever it was pissed her off. That brings a smile to Casey's face and makes the dilemma she faces all the worse for it.

"Fuck, fuck, fuck, fuck," Caleb pants as we cut to him, hobbling through the dark towards the mish-mash of lights illuminating the Paradise Falls Trailer Park.

He arrives to find the front gate chained shut. It's not much, nothing like the bars and shutters the rich folk in town can afford to protect their homes on Virgin Night, and while it wouldn't do much to stop an undead stalker, it completely blocks a teenage boy suffering from severe blood loss. Even thinking about trying to climb sends hot shudders of pain through his shoulder.

"Fuck!" Caleb rattles the gate. "Hey! Hey! Anyone! Let me in!" he calls out, but if anyone hears him, they pretend they don't. Then, there's no other way; Caleb resigns himself to using the back door. Slouching around the side, Caleb picks his way through the trash-heap of discarded junk to a wooden board, pinned to the fence by an abandoned and torn-up La-Z-Boy. He grits his teeth and growls as he pushes the chair aside. As much as that hurt, Caleb gulps; here comes the hard part. Moving the wooden panel aside, Caleb exposes a hole in the fence with a long-forgotten refrigerator pushed against the other side. The back is missing, rusted away mostly, but even so, it's a tight squeeze under normal circumstances, never mind with a piece of wood wedged in his shoulder.

"This is gonna suck," Caleb moans and takes a deep breath. He slips sideways in through the back of the old fridge. Even with his back flush to one side, the tip of the wood scrapes across the other. The noise is almost as bad as the pain. Caleb pushes the door open with his right hand, grunting with effort, but as he goes to slide out, a sudden pang of intense stabbing agony stops him as the end of the wood gets stuck on the lip of the door. Attempts to angle his body to allow passage only end in more searing spasms, the stake twisting in his shoulder, gouging the wound open even more.

"Oh fuck me," Caleb groans as he realizes the only way out of this predicament. "Okay," he pumps himself up, "okay-okay-okay," and he leans into the other side, pushing the wooden spike in even farther, and screams as his whole body trembles. Cold sweat runs down his forehead, fresh rivulets of warm blood down his chest, but it works, and Caleb all but falls out the other side of the fridge. He somehow manages to stumble across the park to his trailer, climb the metal steps up, and collapse inside.

"The fuck happened to you," Horton says as his son falls onto their ratty sofa.

"F-f-fell out a tree," Caleb manages, "watching girls ch-changing."

Horton is in no mood for his son's horseshit, and there isn't time for it. He helps Caleb lie down on the sofa and then looks at the wound. Even touching it lightly causes his boy to jerk and kick. "Relax, dipshit," Horton tells him and stands up, "I've seen worse, but, boy, we gotta get that outta you soon afore it gets infected. No way we're making it to a hospital tonight, so pucker up, buttercup, this ain't gonna be fun."

Horton goes to the cupboard over the sink and pulls out a bottle of whiskey. He pops the lid, but as he approaches Caleb, his boy shakes his head, no. Taking a whiff from the bottle, Horton notes that this whiskey doesn't smell half as strong as it should. "You little pissant," Horton grumbles, realizing Caleb's been stealing and watering the rest down. Instead, he puts the bottle back and goes to the fridge, taking out two tallboys. Horton cracks his first, downs half in one go and wipes his mouth with a satisfied exhale. "This ain't gonna do half the job, but that's your own damn fault." Horton opens the other and holds his son's head up to help the boy drink. "Now, don't be a pussy," he says as he uses one big hand to pin Caleb down and the other to yank the wooden shard free.

Caleb screams, his body arcs, his legs kick out wildly, and then he collapses into blissful unconsciousness.

"The hell are you doin', girl," Casey mumbles to herself as we cut to her, hiding behind one of the SUVs. "Just go; it's over now." Part of her, though, refuses to run. For some reason, she can't bail on these guys, and that means she's gonna have to do something she'd really rather not.

"Screw it," she says and flicks the rescue knife around, pointing the tip down. "No more fuckin' around."

The closest Devoted doesn't hear her coming. All he feels is the arm around his neck, then stab-stab-stab-stab—his white polo shirt blossoms with blotches of red, and just as he attempts to call out, the blade glides across his throat. The only sound he makes is a hiss, then a dry rasp as he drops to his knees. Casey leaves this one and kicks the back of the next Devoted's knee, bringing him to heel. She drives the knife down through the crown of his skull with ease. The third mask gets a scream out just as Casey sticks the knife in through the side of his head, the sound alerting the ones huddled around Vincent.

"Stop!" the girl in charge yells, and Casey looks up; the bloodlust still surging through her comes to a crashing halt at the sight of a gun pressed against Vincent's temple. "Drop the knife. Now!" Casey tosses it aside. "We only need one of you alive, so don't try anything. Knees. Now!" the masked girl commands, and Casey obeys, fighting every instinct she has. Turning to the big masked guy, the one in charge says, "Get him in the car," and Casey can't do a thing but watch as Vincent's dragged out of sight. The masked girl approaches. "Do you have any idea who you're fucking with?"

Casey spits. "I'm guessin' you're the STD riddled slut Michael's too nice to kick to the curb."

"And I'm guessing you're the skank who let those three morons go to town on her," Kaytlynn says as she stands over Casey, "though the why escapes me."

"Jealous, bitch?" Casey growls.

"Hardly." Kaytlynn nods to someone behind Casey, and she turns her head just in time to see the pipe race to meet her.

"No," Michael states as we cut back to *The Sanctuary*.

"What do you mean, no," Creed demands, surprised by his son's sudden defiance.

"I mean no, father, do what you want to me, but I'm not talking," Michael trembles. His voice isn't very convincing, and Creed suspects it would take mere minutes to persuade him otherwise, but all things considered, this brings a smile to his face.

"Though an army encamp against me, my heart shall not fear; though war arise against me, yet I will be confident," Michael quotes. "Though an army—"

"I'll confess, my son, I find this sudden backbone you've grown intriguing." Creed smiles, and it chills Michael more than the coldness of the lake ever could. "It's all together inconvenient, but you misunderstand the situation. I do not need answers from you. Whatever games you and your companions played tonight were merely a diversion, a simple bump in the road. My plans will come to fruition; all your efforts will amount to are a few more steps in the process."

Creed walks toward Michael, and the boy winces, readies himself for the smack to come, and even though all Creed does is place a hand on his shoulder, he still jumps. "W-what do you mean, father?"

"Come with me, boy," Creed orders, "I have something to show you."

Cut back to the hotel as the SUV carrying Vincent and Casey disappears into the fog. Several Devoted work together to unearth the body hidden below the debris. Their uniforms are stained with dust and ash; they work in line, lifting and passing on concrete and wood chunks.

"I can't do this," the one at the front declares and takes his mask off. "Can't breathe in this damn thing."

"Pastor Wallace said we must not take them off," one of the others points out.

"Yeah, well, Pastor Wallace isn't here, is he?" the maskless one says. "Not like anyone's gonna see us here either." He wipes the sweat from his brow and goes back to work, grunting, hefting debris, and passing it down the line. "Jesus wept," he shouts as he uncovers the upper part of a body. It's burned and charred beyond identification, whatever clothing it wore fused by extreme heat with what passed for flesh. "What did they do to him?" Something's odd about the corpse, though. The mask, the faceless bark mask with the horns made from twisting branches, isn't even scratched. "That's strange," the maskless man says, and he leans in to examine it.

The dark, hollow holes suddenly come to life as a pair of bloodshot, rage-filled eyes open within.

Debris clutters as the charred, boney hand shoots up and grabs the maskless man's face. He screams, begs for help, but the other Devoted just stand around, frozen in horror. The maskless man feels his left cheek pushed up, the bone cracking as it covers then punctures his eye. He sees rushing red, then nothing at all, as the three fingers on his forehead crunch through his skull. The maskless man remains alive long enough to fully experience the sensation of Treeface crumpling his entire skull with one hand.

The others in the clearing run in any direction they can as Treeface drops the lifeless body of this night's first victim. It's not the ones he wants, but it is his purpose, and he will kill all who cross his path.

He frees himself from the rest of the rubble and stands, for a moment, in the unforgiving spotlights that shine on the former hotel that had, however briefly, become his tomb. No one in his entire existence has put up such a fight. If he were capable of such things, this would bring a smile to the face beneath the mask. He can sense the two of them; there's nowhere in Cherry Lake they can go he cannot follow, and so he does.

Lights in the sky soon catch his attention, though. The Voice in the Fog whispers eagerly as the mist curls towards it. Treeface does as he's told, as always, and marches towards the glowing crucifix, high above the treeline; heavy footsteps reverberate through the night as he passes a sign that reads Camp Clearheart.

CHAPTER EIGHTEEN

THIS ONE TIME AT BIBLE CAMP

Cut from Treeface's mottled feet to a well-shined, immaculate pair of black brogues last seen dangling between Caleb Dumont's fingers lakeside. They clack and echo along a white-tiled corridor till Dean pauses to look in one of the locked rooms, confirming that the solo occupant is visible and asleep. Under normal circumstances, Camp Clearheart has a strict curfew and shut door policy, but on February 13th, it's even more draconian. Instead of 10 p.m., all residents must be secure in their rooms one hour before sundown. Something to do with a stupid superstition the town has, and Dean's had enough of it.

Four weeks in, and he's yet to even be in the same room as Pastor Wallace; it's been nothing but a waste of time. He thought volunteering at the camp would be a great way to boost his profile in the Church, hopefully securing him charge of one of the outreach projects in

Redcastle Heights while giving him a few weeks of peace from the constant drama back home.

Dean enters the counselor's office at the end of the corridor, where he'll sit and wait till his next round is due. Even if he got nothing else, he'd hoped the post would be a distraction, a change of scenery, and it certainly was, thanks to Caleb. Dean eyes a poorly photocopied photo pinned to the wall, showing a sneering young man with wild, untamable hair. Do Not Admit, it reads, and between the attitude and messed up clothes, Dean guesses it was taken under duress, probably as Caleb was forcefully evicted from the camp.

Despite how things have played out, he can't suppress a smile as he recalls the warnings and the stories about Caleb Dumont. At first, he assumed them to be grossly overblown, pure farce, but after meeting him, well, if anything, they undersell just how rapacious Caleb can be.

One year, they say, Caleb disguised himself as one of the residents and was caught making out with two boys simultaneously. The following year he was found, along with four other residents in various states of undress in the utility shack out back, in a fugue of marijuana smoke. Dean found the stories amusing and the "don't give a fuck" attitude of the photo intriguing. The touching through the fence, the late-night rendezvous by the lake, Caleb made this otherwise boring job exciting. Of course, he had to ruin it, didn't he? Had to throw his weight around and take charge, like always.

Dean sighs, looks to the phone on his desk, and talks himself out of calling his wife. He really should at least check up on her and the baby. It's been over a week since they last spoke. Dean reaches into his pocket and takes out his wallet, unfolds the photo of his wife with their newborn son in her arms. He does love them, but he's starting to worry that he might love Caleb too.

"Two more weeks," Dean mutters. The sooner his post ends, the better. He can't wait to put this whole damn town, its dumb superstitions, and whatever this is he's feeling behind him.

As Dean puts the photo back into his wallet, it slips and drifts to the floor. He has to go under the table to pick it up, and as Dean ducks out of sight, he misses the shadow marching past the window beside him.

Cut to: another window in a white bunk room adorned only by a single wooden crucifix as a shadow flicks by the window. Screams echo from somewhere inside; a voice begs, "Please, please God, no—" and a distraught gurgle follows.

A young man, dark-skinned with a head full of thick, wavy hair, hides behind an upturned bed, clutching a crucifix around his neck as he mumbles prayers for his salvation. Steel gray eyes wide with terror. Outside his room, he can hear rapid footsteps, someone running, and the crash of wood as whoever it is yells, "You bastard!" Seconds later, there's another ear-piercing scream and the sound of bones cracking.

"I wasn't much older than you when it happened," Creed's voice-over explains.

FEBRUARY 13TH, 1961 - VIRGIN NIGHT.

"I was a volunteer youth counselor at the very same camp you seem to take issue with. Back in the sixties, it was purely for Bible study and prayer, though evidently, some couldn't follow the Lord's teachings. As a result, almost thirty people lost their lives that night."

Behind the upturned bed, young Creed cowers as another scream ends abruptly, replaced by a scraping of metal.

"I was the only survivor." Footsteps approach where young Creed hides. "A miracle, I thought at the time." From where he cowers, young Creed can see another counselor crawling across the floor, his hair and face covered in gore. His sticky red hands land on the tiles with a slap as he pulls himself along; only when his lower body comes into view can Creed see he's missing one leg below the knee. The counselor half-turns as the attacker closes in and holds his hands out for mercy. He almost gets the chance to beg for his life before a fire axe comes down, parting his skull not quite in two. "Divine intervention, I know now."

With both hands over his mouth, young Creed trembles and feels warmth spread down his legs.

"That's when I saw something I couldn't explain. My undetected proximity allowed me to gain an insight no other had before."

A fine, red mist floats in the air as the killer pulls the axe free. It could be blood, only it doesn't spray or gush but floats, wisp-like, up towards the man who towers over the fresh corpse. He stands still, almost as though waiting. The nearly imperceptible mist spirals and twists towards the black bark of the branch-horned mask.

"We've all heard the legends, of course," Creed's voice-over continues, "and yet none of them mention this. I believe he takes more than just his victim's lives; he absorbs their essence. I didn't know that at the time, but in the years that followed, I found answers, Michael, and I found hope."

Cut to: Creed, a little bit older, as he sits in a grand, ornate library with tall, wooden bookshelves packed to bursting. With a pair of reading glasses perched on the end of his nose, Creed searches through one open book while several more tower next to him.

"I found it curious that our town's historical society had such incomplete records regarding the preternatural demon that plagues it," Creed explains, "and how reluctant the historians were to provide answers, so I sought them elsewhere. Abandoning my path to priesthood, I pursued history instead, though, in time, my studies would become more...esoteric."

Young Creed scratches a three-day build-up of stubble as he sits behind a pile of books, alone in a vast library. Sensible heels clack, and an elderly librarian places a book before him. "This what you're looking for, young man?" she asks with a gap-toothed smile.

"Perhaps." Young Creed takes the tome and runs his fingers across the title: *A History of Disasters*. He flips through it, past The Great Woodvale Fire of 1959 that shows photos of the town's burned-down Main Street. Past the Paradiso Drive-In Pile-Up of 1959, he lands on a page that reads Mass-Poisoning at Camp Hope, 1961.

"The official story, recorded in the history books, is that on February 13th, 1961, a toxic substance leaked into the water supply at the camp. It was ruled accidental. It did not take me long to find a string of fires, building collapses, and mysterious explosions throughout our town's history all occurring on February 13th of a given year."

Young Creed flips through the book to the earliest entry on record that corresponds with the town and date. 1802 - Clancy Gang Shootout.

"I thought I had the answer, you see. That either this cowboy gunfight or some event around that time resulted in our town's burden. How wrong I was."

Young Creed dumps more historical volumes on the table, a mad smile on his face, the booming sound earning disapproving glances from the other students.

"Looking back, I am ashamed of how naive I was, looking for such answers on the written page. In the end, I came to conclude; I would have to return to Cherry Lake."

A bus pulls away from a stop, leaving young Creed standing in the dust it kicks up. A bag strapped tight to his back, he smiles and marches towards the town hall. Inside, Creed combs through the town's public records.

"A little older, somewhat wiser, I focused my investigation, not on the deaths and incidents themselves, but on the events of both the following and preceding years. Sadly, I could find little documentation of the town's fortunes prior to the commencement of the 19th century. The town's fortunes changed for the better when the reward money for bringing down the Clancy Gang enabled unprecedented expansion and development. Blood, it seems, is always the answer. As interesting as that was, it did not satisfy me. I vowed not to give up and stayed in town to continue my research."

Cut to: young Creed, bowing his head in a small, modest chapel. Pull out to see it sits on a hill overlooking Cherry Lake to the west. It stands on the same ground the Lakeview Hotel would later fall on. "I turned to God for answers, and my devotion was rewarded."

As young Creed walks out of the chapel, he stops to tie his shoelace in a hillside graveyard. Looking up from the ground, something on one of the gravestones catches his eye. The date of death: February 13th, 1780.

"A coincidence, surely. Not all who die within this town, on that date, can be attributed to the curse. And yet…"

Young Creed checks another grave, then another, and the sun begins to go down by the time he stops.

"1801 was not the first occurrence. Merely the first to be covered up. The question then was, why? Searching that decrepit graveyard, I saw a familiar pattern forming—groupings of deaths around a certain date. This death curse that haunts Cherry Lake goes back further than any town records, and, eventually, I found an answer in an old letter sent by our first Mayor. After several months passed with no word from his brother, he came in search and wrote of finding a town abundant with life but devoid of settlers. Homes vacant, as though their occupants spirited away in the night, and yet fields ripe for tilling. Seizing the opportunity, his letter invited others to join him and, in 1762, they resettled Cherry Lake. Entirely ignorant of the darkness awaiting them."

In his room, the walls covered in papers, the desk and bed filled with open books, young Creed studies by lamplight. He's unwashed, unkempt, and deliriously focused.

"It was a breakthrough, yes, but still not an answer." Young Creed pinches the bridge of his nose and rubs his eyes. He opens them, blinks a few times to get rid of the dry itch, and then they land on two crossed pages from separate books, lying beside him on the bed. Steel eyes widen as he leans in.

"The Clancy Gang Shootout resulted in a substantial financial reward for the town. I then noticed similar synchronicities. Each tragedy preceded some financial boom. The greater the loss of life, the greater the prosperity that followed." Young Creed charts it all on the wall of his boarding house room. "The Christian in me couldn't believe in such a thing. Human sacrifice. Yes, the Bible speaks of Pagan demons, the likes of

Moloch, but these were just tales told by unwashed heathens, or so I thought. But the scholar, he couldn't deny the evidence before my eyes. It sent me spiralling."

In his room, Creed takes shot after shot of whiskey.

"Eventually, I knew I had to leave Cherry Lake if I was to find something which I could combat this evil with. Find others who stared down the demons in the dark."

Cut to: a bedroom at night, as a young girl in a nightgown floats several inches above her bed. A little older now, Creed stands at the back of the room, horrified, as black, bilous gunk flows out of her mouth and fills the air above her, like foam made from hydrogen.

"I saw a demon exorcised from a young girl in Louisiana and consulted with a priest who informed me of the pacts men make with the Devil and how breaking them is no simple thing."

Cut to: a campfire in a desert. Creed sits with a Shaman as they look to the sky. Lights, shifting colors, dance around in impossible patterns, forming a triangle, and a hazy, alien world glimmers through it. Green-gray rocks float through the portal, and the Shaman plucks one from the air.

"I've glimpsed other worlds, impossible realities," Creed's voice-over continues, "and seen miracles performed with the profane things taken from them."

The Shaman crushes the strange, glowing rock into a mortar, grinding it into a paste he then takes to a gravely ill child in a bed. Gently tipping the solution to the child's lips, Creed assists the Shaman and watches in awe as vitality flows back through the skinny, emaciated body in seconds.

Cut to: a purple and blue neon-lit bar. Creed stands with a tall, mustached man whose hair reaches his neck and a burly, bearded man in a trucker hat. Shadowy, clawed figures surround them, and the three men prepare for a fight.

"I faced creatures from the depths of fevered dreams."

Cut to: Creed, who looks to be about forty, returning home to Cherry Lake.

"All of it, and none of it, prepared me for what I did next," Creed's voice-over laments. "My travels and studies all suggested there must be some nexus for the events in this town, something or somewhere from which it stems. Think, Michael, what do all the stories you children love to tell have in common?"

Creed's forty-something self pushes a rowboat out into the waters of Cherry Lake and climbs in.

"Black Stone Island?" Michael suggests.

"Black Stone Island," Creed's voice-over agrees as his slightly younger self rows, through the gray mist, towards an island that barely pokes through gaps in the fog. "In the depths of the South, I saw how demons are part of our world, and in the wastes of the West, I learned how to bend the demonic to man's will. And so I sought the heart of Cherry Lake's evil, not to destroy it—I am not so bold as to think a man such as myself is capable of such—but to find a way to wield it for the betterment of all."

As Creed drags his boat ashore, he can't see beyond his arm's reach. From afar, the island looks small, though large enough to have a cluster of trees at the center.

Despite this, Creed walks for close to an hour before coming to a clearing. "I ventured to what I took to be the heart of Cherry Lake's evil." A black tree sits in the middle, tall and twisting, its bark almost jet-black. "And, I was not alone there."

"It's been some time since one of you has come," a voice that creaks with age calls from the mist, and an old woman emerges from the fog, dressed in mismatched, ragged clothes.

"Who are you?" Creed demands.

"Oh, just an old hermit. I live out here. Nice and peaceful, you know," the Hermit says and cranes her neck to the tree. "On you go."

"How does it work?" Creed feels the tree call to him, but he wants answers first.

"He hunts those who summon him. And all others on his path are forsaken," the gap-toothed Hermit caws. "You know this."

Creed does, and wheels begin to turn in his head, not so much a plan but the beginning of one. Black, rotten seeds of evil are already taking root. He walks to the tree and begins to form the impression it is not what it appears to be. It looks like a tree, but one imagined and designed, not the product of nature but of something sinister camouflaging itself, like a viper hidden among rocks.

"Take some," the Hermit says with a gap-toothed smile. "It won't mind."

A chunk of bark comes off with ease, and Creed examines it. He runs his hand along the bark; it feels smoother and more alive than appearances suggest, and Creed thinks he can sense a heartbeat for just a moment. When he turns back to the tree, there's no sign of damage whatsoever.

"It likes you," the old Hermit says, and when Creed turns to ask her what she means, there's no one there.

"As I held that black, undead wood in my hands, I felt it speak to me," Creed's voice-over picks back up. "As though whispering through the fog, and I knew what I had to do."

Cut to: a car, windows steamed up as the radio plays. It rocks, from side to side, rapidly, then slowly, then not at all.

FEBRUARY 13TH, 1979 - VIRGIN NIGHT.

Jump-cut inside, and we see Creed, sweating away on top of a heavily made-up woman. As he climbs off, he hangs his head, resigned. It doesn't bother the woman much; she's seen this countless times. Married men with regrets, lonely losers sinking back into depression. As long as they pay up, she couldn't care less how they feel. Still, sometimes they like to talk after, and since she charges by the half-hour, why not?

"That was wonderful, hon," she lies, pulling her underwear back up. "Why the sad face? You want some more cheerin' up?"

"I don't relish doing this; I want you to know that," Creed says, unable to look her in the eye.

"Well, jeez, hon, that ain't on me, I've never had no complaints. Ever!"

"You misunderstand; it is not your performance. You're wonderfully skilled. I would rather this didn't have to happen at all."

"Uh-huh. You got a wife? Kids?"

"Yes." Creed can't suppress a smile. "A son, just a babe in arms."

"I get it, hon," she says as she finishes fixing her clothes, reasonably sure she's not going to talk him into paying for another half-hour. "Screaming baby, wife's in no mood for it. You don't gotta feel bad for finding some lovin'. If you don't want to pay for another half-hour, then you gotta settle up, though."

"Of course," Creed says and hands the woman a roll of notes.

"Woah, hon, this is way more than I said," her eyes pop at the cash. Easily three times her rate, though, that doesn't stop her leaning down and tucking the money safely inside her knee-high boots before Creed asks for it back. When she looks up, she's greeted by a featureless mask made of almost black wood. "What the hell!?" She's heard of weirdos like this, and she thought she was too clever to end up in a car with one.

"I am sorry," Creed says, and for a moment, she's confused; he sounds like he genuinely means it.

"Please don't hurt me," she begs.

"I won't," he states, and a second later, an arm crashes through the window, pulling the screaming woman out into the rain.

"No, no, no!" she yells, and then there's only silence following an audible crack.

Creed exits the car on his side and approaches slowly. The killer stands over the twisted, lifeless body—her mouth ripped open, leaving her head trapped in an eternal scream. Creed comes within inches of him, and they stand face-to-face for what feels like the most prolonged moment of his life. The killer turns and begins his march towards the nearby lights of Cherry Lake, and only once he's gone into the fog does Creed breathe.

Fade back to *The Sanctuary*, where Michael's eyes water at the impact of what he's hearing.

"Before that experiment, I invested what little money I had in properties around town. By the end of the year, I had enough money to establish the Church," Creed states. "It's real, Michael. Whatever power dwells on that island rewards our sacrifice."

"That's evil," Michael protests.

"No, it's simple mathematics, my son. Blood sacrificed for prosperity. This is the way of the world. Life is not precious; it's currency spent in transactions carried out by those in power every day. This is no different."

"N-no," Michael stammers. "It's not right."

"Had James Tran not prematurely ended the sacrifice of 1989, tonight may not have been required," Creed laments. "The boon, you see, is proportional to the sacrifice. As such, we have treaded water; I could delay this no further."

"Father, you, this, can't be…" Michael feels his knees give way.

"Had you and your friends not played silly games, we would have contained him, kept him isolated, and when the sacrifice was complete, prevented him from causing further harm."

"What are you saying, father?"

"You and your friends set him loose on the town while we intended to keep him confined."

"Where?" Michael demands, but he already knows in the pit of his stomach. Built like a fortress, but to keep people in rather than out. More than half the town already gathered there, like lambs to the slaughter. "Where, father!?"

"Where else, my son," Creed looks Michael dead in the eye.

CHAPTER NINETEEN

THE FINAL GIRL

Fade in on little Vincent and Emilie, playing in the lounge. The sofa cushions cover the floor, some of which form a makeshift fort. Both parents stand on the deck through the glass patio door, though neither child has noticed their father yet.

"Die, Shredder, die!" little Vincent screams as he throws himself off the back of one sofa, arms and legs spread wide as he attempts to body slam his sister. Emilie rolls aside, and Vincent crashes flat onto the cushions. He grunts, and then again as his sister plops down on top of him. She bounces on her backside, pinning Vincent in place and making him yelp.

"Ha-ha! Got you now, you worthless Turtle!" Emilie growls in a mock, macho voice.

Vincent struggles, wiggles from side to side but can't dislodge his sister. "Lemme go," he demands.

"Nu-uh," Emilie teases.

"Yeah-huh," Vincent protests, "you gotta. The good guys always win."

"Not always, Vincent," a grown-up voice whispers in his ear. It's not his sister, and it speaks with a pleasant Austin twang. "You gotta wake up, Vincent," she says, and everything goes black. "Vincent, wake up, ya gotta wake up, now!"

Vincent's eyes shoot open, and the pounding ache all across his head crashes down on him. He's in the same room from his dream, only it shows nearly ten years of neglect and disrepair. Both Vincent and Casey are tied to chairs placed side by side in the middle of the room. "Oh fuck."

"Do you know where we are?" Casey whispers.

"Yeah," Vincent sighs, "this is my house. Shit! Mom!" He looks around, as much as his restraints will allow, but there's no sign of Debbie Tran. Or any of those masked Church weirdos.

"Vincent, cool it," Casey urges harshly. "You ain't gonna do her any good tossin' around like a fish in a boat."

"What am I supposed to do then!?"

"Just listen." Casey double-checks; they're still alone. "I nearly got your rope free on this side. When I do, you gotta run for it. Don't wait for me."

"Casey—"

"Listen! They thought I was out when I wasn't. I heard them talkin'. These freaks call themselves the Devoted; they need us for somethin'. Got orders to get us to the Church. You run, they'll follow. It's the best shot we got."

"But my mom?"

"I haven't seen anyone else, but if they wanted to hurt her, they would have already. Best thing you can do for her is lead them away, far away. Got it?" Vincent doesn't answer. "Got it?"

"Okay! Fuck!" Vincent struggles.

"Just run. Don't stop, don't fight. You hear me?"

"You're not making much sense, Casey."

"Just trust me? Worst thing you can do right now is fight."

Vincent sighs. "Okay," he relents, "okay."

Casey goes back to trying to undo some of the knots. Twisting her right hand in an unnatural, painful angle that cuts off her blood flow, she's able to work at Vincent's binds with her nails. "It's a good thing these culty fucks don't seem to know what they're doing. Anyone with half a brain would have kept us apart."

"You sound like you have some experience being tied up." Vincent can't help a smirk.

"Let's just say I ain't exactly opposed to the idea under more enjoyable circumstances."

"Yeah." Vincent smacks his lips, his mouth suddenly bone-dry at the prospect, not to mention the absurdity of what he's about to propose. It's now or never, though. "About that. If we make it out of this, I don't suppose, I mean, it's kinda dumb since we already, you know, but I guess I'm sorta, kinda, asking if you'd maybe want to go out with me. Like a date. A real date."

Casey goes silent for a moment. "That's a pretty big if, Vincent."

"Yeah, true, but we've survived a crazy Slasher and a building falling down on us; I think we've got a decent shot, all things considered."

"That's not a guarantee."

"And that's not an answer."

"Vincent...you don't know me," Casey's voice drops. "Not really."

"I know some, and what I do, I like. I like a whole lot."

"I'm not what you think—"

Footsteps from the stairs cut the conversation off. Two Devoted come down, then move to take positions by the front and back door. Slow, uneven plodding steps follow a moment later. "Move it!" Kaytlynn demands and pushes Debbie down the last few stairs.

"Mom!" Vincent yells.

Debbie falls against the wall, pulling a side table over as she staggers into the room. Kaytlynn shoves her onto the sofa, and the woman falls face-first. "Urgh," Kaytlynn moans, "she stinks."

"If you—"

"Oh shut up." Kaytlynn struts across the room and slaps Vincent. "What are you going to do?"

"Should I find more rope?" one of the Devoted asks.

"What, for her?" Kaytlynn looks at Debbie, drooling facedown on the sofa, and laughs. "There's no need. The junkie bitch is wasted. Look at her; she's not going anywhere."

"Oh, Jimmy," Debbie mumbles as, wherever she is inside her head, she embraces her husband.

"Miss, um, Ma'am," one of the Devoted speaks up, "Pastor Wallace said to—"

"I know what he said," Kaytlynn cuts the Devoted off, "but I'm in charge here and—"

Vincent snorts with laughter. "You gotta be fucking with me. You? In charge? What is this, a fundraiser? I don't see any shitty sandpaper cupcakes." Kaytlynn smiles, tilts her head, then bites her lip as she slaps Vincent again, this time with enough force to knock him and the chair to the floor.

"Besides," Kaytlynn composes herself, "we only need one of them."

"Are you sure it wasn't one of the other two—"

"Of course it wasn't!" Kaytlynn motions for one of the Devoted to pick Vincent up while she gets right in Casey's face. "Michael doesn't have the balls to even touch a girl, never mind fuck one, and that little queer

Caleb Dumont couldn't get it up for a real woman, never mind this rancid little gutter slut." Casey just smiles at that. Kaytlynn doesn't like it. "What?"

"Just wonderin', do all the boys make you wear the mask, or do some just flip you over instead?"

Kaytlynn smiles. "Oh, this?" She taps the black, wooden mask that sits on top of her head. "Just you wait and see what these are for."

"He's here!" One of the Devoted crashes in through the kitchen door, cutting the conversation off as he falls into the room. "He's coming!" the Devoted yells, then rushes to the nearest window to watch, bouncing with nervous energy.

The other Devoted look to Kaytlynn. "Trust in Pastor Wallace," she commands, and she lowers her mask. "And stay true."

"What's with the fog," the Devoted by the window asks, and no one answers.

"No way," Vincent's heart sinks, "we dropped a building on him." He can't believe it, and yet those footsteps on the deck outside land with the same murderous intent as the ones Vincent heard stalk the halls of the Lakeview Hotel mere hours ago. The whole house trembles at Treeface's approach.

Some of the Devoted look ready to run; they inch further and further away from the door, and yet they remain resolute just as Kaytlynn commanded. Even as Treeface steps in through the open doorway, they hold their ground. One of them within arm's reach of the burned, bark-masked monster. Grab him, Vincent urges silently, rip his fucking head off. Yet Treeface does nothing, even when he stares directly at the Devoted; it's as though the creature can't see the shaking, masked Church freak at all.

"The fuck?" Vincent gasps. He tastes the scent of burnt flesh in the air.

"It's gotta be the mask," Casey mutters, "they're the same as his. Almost."

"For a cheap slut you're not so dumb after all," Kaytlynn teases as she slips behind Casey, wrapping her arms around her as though they were suddenly best friends. Casey sneers and recoils at the other girl's touch.

Debbie sits up on the sofa, her head swaying from side to side as she blinks repeatedly.

"Mom—" Vincent tries to call out, and he's cut off as Kaytlynn places one hand over his mouth. He spits against her palm, his raging protests muffled.

"Watch," Kaytlynn commands, and she places her other hand on Vincent's forehead, pulling up with enough pressure to force his eyes open wide. "I want you to know something, Vincent. If you and your friends didn't interfere, if you'd just been good little losers and sat around, killing your brains with dope and video games, then this wouldn't have had to happen. Your mother would have lived through the night. If you can call what she does living. This is all on you."

Vincent screams, tearing his throat raw, near inhuman rage muffled by Kaytlynn's firm hand.

"Bitch!" Casey spits.

Debbie stumbles to her feet, almost falling back down to the sofa but keeping upright with the contradictory ballerina-like balance of a life-long drunk. She smacks her lips and looks around the room as though only just becoming aware of where she is.

Treeface takes three strides across the room and stops, mere inches from Debbie.

Casey looks down and closes her eyes.

Vincent's chair rattles and Kaytlynn holds him in place tighter. Red veins pop in the whites of his eyes.

Debbie reaches the black bark mask and runs her fingers across it, tracing along where a cheek should be. Her hands slide along the side of his face, stroking the mottled, fused mess of skin, bone, and wood as though it belongs to someone beloved. In Debbie Tran's head, it is.

Treeface, likewise, places a hand on either side of Debbie's face. "Oh, Jimmy," she laughs, a smile spreads across her face, and Treeface spins her neck around in one swift crack.

Vincent is forced to watch the smile on his mother's backward-facing head as she falls to the ground, dead, and the fight in him dies with her. He slumps, defeated, and broken.

"She's better off this way," Kaytlynn purrs without even a shred of empathy.

Treeface stands over Debbie, his head bowed as though silently considering his handiwork.

"You're a monster," Casey states. "And believe me, I know."

"You can think whatever you like," Kaytlynn smiles. "You're dead meat anyway."

"No!" Vincent slips his mouth free from Kaytlynn's grasp and protests. "No!"

"Leave her," Kaytlynn instructs, "take him to the car, out the back door."

"No!" Vincent cries. One of the Devoted cuts the ropes binding Vincent to the chair, and the other joins in restraining him as, even with his legs and arms still tied, Vincent struggles hard enough to give them hell. They drag him through the kitchen, towards the back door, as he knocks over everything in their way.

"Wait!" Kaytlynn orders. "Hold him there a minute." She turns Casey's chair around, the legs squealing across the floor. "Say bye-bye to your boyfriend," Kaytlynn says to Casey as she pushes her around to face Vincent. Something in the kitchen catches her eye.

"Casey!" Vincent screams as black eyeliner streams down his face. "Casey, no! Please, don't! Take her! Leave me! Please!"

Kaytlynn picks up a chef's knife from a block in the kitchen and admires the polished blade. It's so clean she can almost make out the reflection of Treeface moving towards the bound, helpless girl. Treeface stops abruptly as Kaytlynn steps between him and Casey. The Devoted all hold their collective breath, but nothing happens. Kaytlynn holds the knife out for him, and he takes it. Holding it close, his emotionless mask examines the blade. His blackened flesh and bone hand grips the handle.

"Vincent," Casey speaks with an unnerving calm that cuts through Vincent's hysteria. "Vincent, promise me one thing."

Kaytlynn steps away, leaving nothing between Casey and Treeface.

"Don't let your anger control you. That's no way to live," Casey says with a smile, and the chef's knife pierces her heart from behind, the tip bursting through as her body arches forward with the force of the thrust. Blood runs from her still grinning mouth as she and the chair she's bound to crash down.

"No!" Vincent howls, and the whole world slows to a crawl. Kicking, screaming, he makes the Devoted fight for every inch as they drag him to the car, waiting, ready to go, out on the lawn. Kaytlynn skips to join them. Before the door swings closed, Vincent sees Treeface stoop to pluck the knife from Casey's back. A pool of red already surrounds the girl's limp body.

The Devoted wrestle Vincent into the back of the car, and through the rear window, he watches Treeface stand on the back steps, knife in hand, his head turning to follow the fleeing vehicle.

The car disappears into the night, but it matters not. He has already taken one of them, and soon the Child of the Lake will join his mate. His internal compass leads him into the night and along a quiet, desolate highway. The fog comes with him, as always, and whispers all the while. Soon enough, though, the chatter stops as an erratic chain of lights breaks through. *More*, the Voice in the Fog whispers inside his head, *more*.

He approaches the lights and, in one swift pull, rips the chain free from the gate of Paradise Falls Trailer Park.

"I'll kill you all for this," Vincent growls in the back of the car, wedged in between two Devoted who can barely keep him subdued.

"Shut him up," Kaytlynn orders from the front, and the Devoted on either side of Vincent force a gag in his mouth and a bag over his head. He bites one, headbutts the other, and everything cuts to black.

CHAPTER TWENTY

PARADISE FALLS

Jump cut to James Van Der Beek's smiling face, hair parted in an effortless carefree way, pinned to the wall in Caleb's room as he jerks awake. His breathing is labored, hair slicked back with a sheen of sweat on his forehead. It takes him a second to remember where he is and then another to recall what's already transpired. He's shirtless, with a strapping of blood-spotted bandages fitted tight across his chest and collarbone. Even thinking about touching it makes his eyes tremble.

Sliding off the bed, Caleb makes his way over to the mirror fixed onto the back of his door. Slipping two fingers inside the top of the bandage and wincing, Caleb peels it down to examine what his father has done with the wound.

"You gotta be shittin' me," Caleb snorts. He expected maybe fishing wire, but, nope, Horton patched Caleb's stab wound together with staples. Basic, everyday staples. "That ain't gonna hold." Caleb grits his teeth as he gently lets the bandage fall back in place.

The door opens, causing Caleb to take a step back to avoid getting whacked—the sudden motion causing a twinge of pain, but it's mild compared to what it was before. Horton pokes his head through, looks his son up and down, then sneers. "Ain't the worst thing I ever caught you doing in that mirror." He moves into the room and sets a bottle of pills down on the computer desk. "Don't take them all at once."

"NOT all at once, damn, that's where I've been going wrong, thanks, Pa!" Caleb snarks as he takes a seat on the edge of his bed.

"If somebody hadn't already kicked seven shades of shit out of you, I'd whoop you one for that," Horton says, and yet there's almost a hint of concern to it. "You gonna tell what happened? Got caught chompin' on the wrong meat pole?"

"The right ones just don't do it for me," Caleb says as he pops the lid off the bottle and then dry swallows two pills. "Would you believe me if I said we were getting chased by Churchies in weird masks and—oh shit, Michael! They got Michael!" Caleb jumps to his feet, clenching his eyes to suppress the pain. "I gotta—" Dizziness overcomes him, forcing Caleb to sit back down.

"You ain't doin' nothin' in the state you're in, boy," Horton says. "'Sides, if you and your buddies are in shit with the Church, he's gonna be fine. Wallace ain't gonna do nothin' to his own boy."

"You believe me?"

Horton shrugs. "I don't doubt that Church does some weird shit, and you didn't exactly stick that piece of wood in your own self. Less that's some kinda queer thing?"

"Eh," Caleb groans, "fifty-fifty." He lies down on the bed, the painkillers beginning to take effect. "I gotta phone Vincent and see…oh, yeah," Caleb trails off as he remembers his father cut the phone off. "I guess we got stuff to talk about, huh, Pa?"

"Yeah, boy, we do. Not now, though. When I give you an ass-kicking, I don't wanna have to hold back."

"That's nice." Caleb closes his eyes, and a second later, they jerk wide. A scream pierces through the air.

"The shit was that," Horton mumbles and goes to the window, pulls down the blinds, and peers out. "Some kind of commotion out there."

No, Caleb's heart sinks, no fucking way. They stopped him, they—

"Stay here. Gonna take a look." Horton heads out, through the rest of the trailer and out the door. Caleb forces his body to get up and cross his room to the window. He looks through the curtains but can't see anything with Higgins' trailer so damn close. Another scream bounces off the tin walls.

Caleb reaches the main section of his trailer as Horton barges back in through the door. The look on his face, Caleb's never seen his Pa look so scared. That's it then; it has to be. They failed. Horton doesn't say anything; he just pushes past his son and goes straight into his bedroom. Caleb watches as his Pa slides out the case where he keeps his shotgun, then grimaces as Horton opens it, finding nothing but an indent where the gun should be.

Horton turns and looks over his shoulder. He doesn't need to ask. The look on Caleb's face says it all. "You dumb bastards," Horton growls and shoves the case aside. Instead, he picks up a metal baseball bat and gives it a test swing. "You got some back door out of here, right? That's how you sneak in and out, thinking I don't notice?"

"Y-yeah, Pa," Caleb stammers.

"Get your ass to it, show folks the way out, and don't come back."

"But Pa—"

"You heard me." Horton pushes past Caleb without another word and heads out with his bat in hand. He marches down the steps, out into the middle of the park. Paradise Falls isn't that large, consisting of a dozen trailers spread out in a double-layered half-circle pattern. Horton follows racing shadows that move behind thinly curtained windows, and then a thud so powerful the trailer moves. More screams and the sound of glass shattering comes from the first trailer by the gate.

Around the park, curtains twitch as other residents spy on the unfolding carnage. Lights go out; locks are bolted. "Ain't gonna do any of you any damn good!" Horton yells. Caleb emerges from their trailer, a t-shirt thrown over his bandage, though he's irritated the wound enough for little red spots to soak through. "My boy'll show you the way out back; anyone with a mind to should grab what you got and help buy them some time!"

A trailer door across the lot is kicked open, and an older man clinks down the steps, one leg in a squeaky metal brace. He readies a bolt action rifle and nods. "Horton."

"Dickie," Horton nods back.

Dickie hobbles over and stands beside Horton. "This bitch killed my friend," Dickie says.

"Killed a lot of folks," Horton points out.

"So what's two more then?" Dickie agrees.

"Three," a large woman wearing a pink dressing robe adds. She joins the two men. Her hair is bound up in curlers, and the robe barely fastens, but the look on her face says, don't fuck with me. She loads two shells into the double barrel cradled in her arm.

A bunch of kids stream out the trailer behind her, the youngest just a baby carried by the oldest one among them. "Y'all follow Caleb now, you hear? Momma's got an ass to kick." The children flock to Caleb. Others join too, some adults with them, those unwilling or unable to fight. Caleb locks eyes with his father, who urges him to go with a nod.

"This way," Caleb says and leads them all towards the back of the park.

The trailer by the front grows silent, and a moment later, the door opens. Treeface steps out into the night, and more fog drifts in from the road.

"Jesus, somebody fucked him up good already," Dickie says as the three of them get a good look at the burned, mangled masked monstrosity.

"Yup," Horton agrees and feels the oddest drip of pride that his boy did that kind of damage.

"I've seen you do worse to your burgers there, Dickie," the robed woman teases.

"Brooke, I ain't ever hit a woman, but I reckon I got just enough time left to fix that," Dickie jokes. He raises his rifle, takes steady aim, and fires one clean shot. It hits Treeface flat in the chest and does nothing besides cause a slight jerk at the impact.

"To hell with this," Horton declares, grips his bat tight, and rushes to meet the monster head-on.

Caleb reaches the fridge by the back fence and pulls it open. "Okay kids, first—" and he's cut off as Higgins barges through, shoving everyone aside and forcing his way into the fridge to a cacophony of protests. "What the hell!" Higgins only grunts in response as his bulk gets wedged, stuck halfway through.

Gunshots erupt from the other side of the trailer park. The first, single shot, freezes them all in place, and the second double blast that follows kicks them all back into action.

Caleb grabs Higgins' flailing arm, along with one of the older kids, and they try to pull him back out. "No!" Higgins resists, grabbing hold with his other arm. "Push me through!"

"That ain't," Caleb grunts, "gonna work!" He collapses against the fence, more red spots spreading across his shirt. "You're too big! You gotta find another way—"

"The fence," the older kid says and points up, "we can boost the little ones over?"

Caleb follows his hand; the problem is there's barbed wire. He glances around and his eyes land on a rug hanging on a nearby washing line. "That could work," Caleb claps the older kid on the shoulder and runs over to appropriate the carpet. He tries to throw it over, but the pain in his shoulder surges, and he only manages to hurl it a foot from his body.

"We got this," the older kid says, and his sister helps him toss the rug up over the fence, pushing down the barbed wire below. They cover a wide enough space for the older kid and another to stand side by side and help boost the others over the top.

"Get me outta here!" Higgins demands as the others reach the top of the fence. Caleb looks over the heads of the ones waiting to climb as more gunshots ring out.

Horton swings his bat so hard, so fast, that when it connects with Treeface, the sheer force he puts into the blow causes Horton to fall aside as the bat bounces off, clattering to the ground. The hit did nothing at all to the masked bastard.

Brooke lets off both barrels, hitting his chest with little more than puffs of burnt skin to show for it. Dickie pulls back the bolt on his rifle, aims, and fires again—this time shooting for the head. The bullet just ricochets off the mask, not even leaving a mark. All the while, Treeface only stands, watching, as the fog unfurls around them.

Horton scrambles away and back to his feet. He rejoins the others as Treeface begins to step towards them. Two more shots from Brooke's gun slow his approach for a half a second.

"Now what?" Dickie asks. "Kicking his ass ain't in the cards."

"Never was," Horton states. "Ain't nobody lays a hand on my boy 'cept me, though."

"Father of the year," Dickie scoffs.

"Ain't too late to run," Horton points out.

Dickie taps his rifle to the leg brace, metal clinking against metal. "Left my running shoes back in my trailer."

Brooke loads two more shells into her gun. "We doin' this or what, boys?"

Horton nods then steps up again to meet Treeface. He swings a punch, and the second it connects with the mask, Horton feels all the bones in his hand shatter. "Fuck," Horton curses, and before he grabs hold of his broken hand, Treeface grabs it around the wrist. Horton howls as Treeface lifts him; even though Horton's taller, the killer has no problem lifting the man. He might as well weigh as much as a balloon for all the effort it takes. Horton feels a sudden sharpness, and his ribs break as a large knife goes all the way to the handle through his abdomen. Horton kicks free before Treeface can pull it out, falling on his ass, blood pouring into the dirt.

The smell of gunsmoke hits his nose as both Brooke and Dickie fire, in tandem, at point-blank range over

Horton's body—muzzle flashes cutting through the fog. Brooke reloads and goes to fire again but only gets off one shell, which she fires directly into Treeface's reaching palm. He grabs the front end of the barrel just as Brooke fires the second shell, causing the whole gun to explode in her hands. She screams, recoils, blinded by the flash, and raises bloody mangled flaps of skin and bone where her hands used to be. Brooke cannot see as Treeface pulls the blasted remnants of the double-barrel back, but she feels it for sure when he forces it through her screaming mouth, breaking her neck in the process and sending her crashing to the ground.

Since there's no time and no point anyway, Dickie swings his rifle like a club, and Treeface catches it with one hand. Dickie tries to pull it free but loses his balance and falls to the ground. Treeface tosses the gun aside; it clatters somewhere in the fog as Dickie tries to crawl away. He knows there's no escaping him. He pulled it off once, got away nine years ago thanks to Jimmy Tran, so this is just fate catching up with him, he reckons. Treeface brings a foot down on Dickie's braced leg. The man howls as the killer stomps bone and metal together into a twisted, agonizing mash. Dickie forces himself to turn on his side, look upon Treeface with his own eyes, and spit one last "Fuck you!" at him through gritted teeth.

Treeface brings his foot down, again, this time crushing Dickie's skull with a single, mighty step.

The fog draws his attention towards the back of the trailer park, drifting its dreamlike tentacles towards the escaping residents.

"Fucker," Horton spits, "I ain't dead yet."

Treeface turns to see the man standing, somehow, on his own two feet. Horton pulls the knife free from his abdomen, ignores the torrent of blood that comes with it, and rushes Treeface with the blade. He manages to stab the monster a few times before he loses steam. Treeface catches Horton by the knife hand and feels his wrist crack, breaking as Treeface squeezes—the knife drops and sticks in the dirt. Horton remains on his feet as Treeface stoops to retrieve the weapon despite it all. He even spits a mouthful of blood and calls him a "Pussy." Then Treeface slices his neck open.

At the back fence, it's down to just Caleb and the older kid. Higgins still whines for help, but they've managed to tune him out. "You go," Caleb says and forms a cradle with his hands as he braces his back to the fence. "Come on."

The other kid takes in the way Caleb struggles to keep the position, not to mention the growing patch of red that sticks his t-shirt to his chest. "No, man, I got you," the kid says and adopts the same position as Caleb. "There's no way you'd make that fence on your own."

Caleb wants to argue, but the pain in his shoulder tells him the kid's right. The silence from the front of the park means he doesn't have time to argue, either. "Okay," Caleb says and lets the kid boost him up, over the fence. He lands on the other side and looks back through. "Shit." A figure stands, a silhouette in the fog, between two trailers just behind them. "Move it!" Caleb yells.

True to his word, the older kid manages to scramble over the fence just as Treeface comes into view. Caleb knows that means his Pa is dead, but there isn't time to think about that right now.

"Don't leave me!" Higgins begs, his hand sticking out, waggling for help. For a second, Caleb is ready to run. *Just like you did with Mikey, huh?* And then what his Pa just did stops him. Horton Dumont was a racist, homophobic, hate-filled monster, and he still had enough humanity left in him to do the right thing when it came down to life or death. What the hell would Caleb be if he did any less?

"We can't leave him," Caleb says to the other kid, who nods in agreement. The two of them rush to the backside of the secret escape and take hold of Higgins. They try to pull him through, but it's still no good. There's simply no way the man can fit. "George, man, there's no way."

"You have to!"

"Shit," Caleb curses. There's no other option. "Higgins, we're gonna push you back through—"

"Wait! No!"

"At least you'll be free; you can run for it!" the older kid points out.

"No! Pull me harder! Get! Me! Out!" Higgins grips the inside, making it impossible for the boys to push him back through. So they give it one more shot. Caleb takes Higgins' arm while the older kid grabs onto Caleb, and they pull as hard as they can. "No!" Higgins screams, "no!" But he budges, gives way, and with another almighty tug, the boys pull him free, falling to the ground under the momentum.

Except for it's only half of Higgins that comes with them. The rest remains wedged in the fridge, steaming guts slopping down into a mushy pile of gloop. The rest of him flops to the ground, all that was inside Higgins splattering over so much discarded junk. Treeface looks through just as the other kid hurls all over himself.

"No time," Caleb says and pulls the other kid to his feet. "No time, no time," he chants as they race through the night, around and back to the main road leaving the carnage and chaos of Paradise Falls Trailer Park behind them.

Treeface watches them go. *Leave them,* the Voice in the Fog whispers. And he does, turning and heading towards town, as the fog points him in the direction of the insolent one, the Child of the Lake. Soon the gaudy, whacky blue and yellow plastic of a fake spaceship gleaming through the fog, like a beacon in the night, catches Treeface's attention. The Voice in the Fog commands that he makes one more detour.

CHAPTER TWENTY-ONE

ONE NiGHT AT STARSKY'S

Fade in on Emilie, splashing water on her face, steam rising up from the barely functioning bathroom tap. Starsky's allergy to getting things fixed means it has two settings: ice and fire. Emilie's eyes meet their reflection and see in them boredom, the desire to give up entirely. Trying to scrub the smell of stale puke and soda out of the arcade's nearly ten-year-old carpets is not an achievable goal, not for three minimum wage workers with a bucket and off-brand cleaning products. If Starsky weren't so cheap, he'd at least supply them with decent gear. Then again, if he weren't so tight, he'd replace the damn carpets. The arcade's name, woven into the pattern of planets and asteroids, is almost unreadable these days.

"I need a change," Emilie sighs in the mirror. Maybe her hair? She teases the fringe out, then cups the back, trying to imagine herself with a short bob but then realizes she'd look way too much like her twin brother. "Ugh," she moans, "why does Vincent have to look prettier than me?" Emilie tilts her hair, noticing how the pale blue neon light of the bathroom tints the sheen, and wonders if she should dye it a different color. Could ask Vincent to ask Casey to help her, plus that'd be a way she could get to know the girl better.

Still bewildered that Vincent managed to get a girlfriend, never mind such a cute one, Emilie heads back to work. She exits the bathroom and heads left towards the stockroom at the back. It's a stark contrast to the front, just rows of simple metal shelves holding a vast stockpile of paper plates, candy, reams of paper tickets, and the prizes worth less than the paper kids will exchange for them. Since tomorrow is Valentine's Day, and the place will be full of couples on dates, Emilie's boss has already stocked up on the trash and adjusted the ticket payout, of course.

Grabbing a box of the dumb, fluffy things, it hits Emilie just how cold it is in the back. There's no heating there, so it's chilly at the best of times, but she can just about see her breath. Glancing to the back wall, Emilie checks the rear door is, in fact, shut. Starsky would kick their butts if any of them left it open, not because he's worried about anything happening to his employees. God, no. Even though it's Virgin Night, he's far more concerned about shrinkage than the safety of his staff. The bastard would seal them all in for the night if he could get away with it. As it stands, the back door is the only way in, the front all shuttered up, and just the fire exits for emergencies.

Carrying the teddy bears back towards the main arcade, Emilie doesn't notice the tall shadow standing motionless behind her. "Shit," she curses and remembers the other reason she went into the stockroom—paper towels for the bathrooms. Emilie turns on her heels, going back the way she came, with no sign of the ominous shadowy figure.

Heaping two large rolls on top of the box, Emilie heads on her way, and because the pile she carries blocks her vision, she misses the leering creature with a long snarling snout packed with rows of oversized teeth. It watches Emilie use her butt to push open the stockroom door, and then it follows.

In the corridor by the bathrooms, Emilie loses balance; she stumbles, trying to keep everything she carries from toppling, but it's for naught, and it all comes crashing to the floor. "Aw, man," she moans and puffs her hair out of her eyes with a sharp, annoyed breath. As she kneels to gather everything, the creature from the stockroom stands just inside the hallway.

Nearly seven feet tall, covered in furry lime green scales and dressed in blue shorts with a Starsky's t-shirt: Charlie Chomper. The anthropomorphic space-lizard mascot watches Emilie, bent over with her butt in the air, with feral glee. It moves forward, claws ready to strike. Fluffy talons pad silently across the floor, giving Emilie no warning as it closes in. Charlie Chomper's oversized paw reaches down and pinches Emilie's butt.

Emilie jumps at the touch; it feels like she brushed up against a stuffed toy or something, and it's only when she turns to see the snarling mascot raising its arms to pounce that she screams. Scrambling forward on her hands and knees, Emilie clambers to her feet and races towards the other side of the hall only to find it blocked by Charlene Chomper—the lazily gender-swapped female mascot counterpart whose main distinction from Charlie is the color of the shorts and a flower glued to its right ear. Both costumes are just cheap, generic crocodile ones, given a half-assed space twist to fit Starsky's theme, which hasn't changed since the 80s. Anyone unlucky enough to have seen the short-run commercial featuring the mascots will have their off-brand wrongness and that awful theme song stuck in their heads. Caleb once told Emilie that some who saw it kept giggling and giggling until they died. The stories and costumes never bothered Emilie all that much. Not till the two of them cornered her in a corridor.

Skidding to a halt, Emilie finds herself with nowhere to go. Both mascots have cut off her exits and even the possibility of running into one of the bathrooms. Together, both mascots rush her, pinning Emilie between them, and savagely dry hump her with wild abandon.

"Aw yeah, give it to me, baby," the person inside Charlene Chomper sings, the words and speaker muffled by the stuffed mask.

"Work that ass," the one inside Charlie adds, and both mascots come together, making over-the-top insanely gratuitous orgasmic grunts till Emilie pushes them apart.

"You guys are assholes!" Emilie declares as she rips the head off Charlie, revealing the grinning, bespeckled face of a brown-haired teenage girl.

"You shoulda seen your face," the other says as he pulls Charlene's head off. "You were all," he pulls a stupidly dramatic, horrified grimace.

"I don't know whose ass I'm gonna kick first—"

"It was Clyde's idea!" the other girl declares, pointing her soft clawed hand at her accomplice.

"Nu-uh!" Clyde protests.

"You know what, I'm inclined to agree. This has Jade written all over it." Emilie turns to the girl still wearing the Charlie Chomper bodysuit. "Come here so I can kick your ass!"

Jade turns around and bends over, waggling her butt and tail. "Come and get me!" she taunts. Emilie accepts the challenge and takes a running start into a firm kick that propels Jade forward a few steps. "Ow!" She rubs her backside. "I actually felt that!" Jade climbs out of the suit and rubs her behind again. "I bet that's gonna bruise. Take a look."

Emilie lifts her friend's skirt to check. "Oh, shit," Emilie's face drops.

"What!?" Jade panics.

"This," Emilie says and slaps Jade's exposed butt cheek.

"Ow, cut it out!" Jade slips away and backs herself against the wall, a wild grin across her face.

"You're gonna stink of B.O. all night after wearing that," Emilie points out, and Jade sniffs her clothes to see if she's right.

"Oh, yuck," Jade says, sticking her tongue out and then yells, "Smell me!" as she leaps on Emilie, rubbing herself up against her.

"Ew! Get off me, you pervert!" Emilie pushes her friend away.

"You're mine now; I've scent-marked you," Jade teases and then notices Clyde just standing there, staring at the girls, still in the Charlene suit. His cheeks are flushed red. "I don't think Clyde's gonna be able to get his suit off," Jade points to his crotch.

"Is that a front tail you got there," Emilie teases, "or are you just happy to see us?" Clyde tries to hide his hard-on with little success, and the girls erupt with laughter.

"Anyway," Jade changes the subject, "looky what I got," she dangles a set of keys between her fingers.

"Jade, no! We'll get fired!" Emilie's eyes pop.

"What old man Starsky doesn't know, come on, it's free play all night!" Jade skips down the hall towards the arcade.

"What about this mess?" Emilie motions to the boxes and the discarded mascot costume.

"Clyde will clean it up," Jade states.

"I will?" Clyde asks.

"Yeah, it'll give you time to get rid of that boner." Jade sticks out her tongue and backs her way into the arcade.

Jam waits till the Purity Prom is well underway, till an hour after his parents have left. He didn't make any excuses for why he wasn't going, and he wasn't asked. That's fine; it suits me, he says to himself, even if it's only because his father's worried about upsetting Pastor Wallace. His kit bag is already in his truck, and Jam fights the urge to check on it for the tenth time. It's all there, it's all good, and he just has to wait.

He hopes Vincent lives through the night; he doesn't want him to die. Not right away. Not till he sees what fucking with Jam Starsky has cost him. Thinking about what he's gonna do to Vincent's sister gets him fired up. Jam's hand finds its way to his pants without thinking, and he has to make an effort to stop. He hasn't touched himself for weeks, saving it all for this—and he's not going to kill the buzz at the last minute.

Sure that the coast is clear, Jam gets in his truck and drives out of his parents' South Shore mansion. He makes his way north but keeps to the byroad, staying out of town as much as possible. He pulls onto the main road just before the crossroads where the Cherry Lane Stripmall sits. Jam kills the lights and parks his truck around the back of the arcade, out of sight. No one will know he was here and, even if someone did see his truck by chance, so what? His dad owns the place, and in the morning, everyone will assume the Virgin Night Killer did it. Vincent Tran will only learn the truth moments before Jam finally decides it's time for the loser to die.

Dense fog rolls in, enveloping his truck and the whole arcade. That's even more perfect; Jam smiles and makes his way to the back door. He punches in his father's access code, then pulls the heavy steel door open as it buzzes. As it swings closed behind him, Jam doesn't notice the seared, boney hand that stops it from sealing shut.

The arcade blasts to life as Jade flips the main breakers, filling the place with the sounds of pinballs, game music, and claw machine jingles. Jade flips another switch, killing the overhead fluorescent lights, and whirls through the empty arcade. All the sounds blend into a single glorious cacophony of chaotic electronic joy.

"What do you want to play first?"

Emilie smirks. Smash-cut to a montage: Jade butt-bounces Emilie to distract her while they duke it out on *X-Men vs. Street Fighter*; Emilie managing to clip Jade's fingers at the air hockey table; the two of them laughing while racing each other on *Daytona USA*; Jade putting her name down as ASS on the *Zoozie* pinball machine's high score; then striking badass poses as they gun down some zombies on *The House of the Dead*.

Cut to: Clyde, dumping the mascot costumes in the security room with a grunt. He swears the girls are making this night especially tough for him since there's no way he's gonna get any. "Yeah, not like that's gonna happen any other night either, Clyde," he moans to himself and thinks about how long he's been dropping hints to Emilie that he'd like to be more than friends. Why do they gotta act like that, though? All touchy with each other, it drives him wild.

Clyde catches sight of the two girls on the security cameras and pauses to watch. Emilie looks especially cute with that gun. Clyde glances around; there are no cameras here, no one else in the building, and no reason at all why he can't just have a little Clyde time, right?

Pulling the chair over as close to the monitor as he can get, Clyde unzips his pants, pulls it out, and starts to beat off as he watches Emilie on the monitor, totally missing the hooded figure who enters through the back door. Or the masked one who follows, just behind.

Cut to: Jam as he creeps through the stockroom. He can hear the sounds of the games out front, which covers his approach, though they shouldn't be on. Naughty girls. Jam's smile is a delightfully cruel slit that cuts across his face; they'll have to be punished. He knows from stealing a look at the schedule that Jade Pulaski will be working tonight, too, and though Emilie's his target, he doesn't mind having a little fun with Jade also. He fantasizes about making them do things with each other before joining in. After all, he's gotta make it look legit, right? Then he'll pin the whole thing on that dunce Clyde Harlow, and when the killer shows up, nobody will look twice. They'll figure Clyde and the girls got it on, summoning the Virgin Night Killer.

Now comes the hard part. Jam pauses by the door to the arcade. He has to make sure none of them see him cross to the power closet. Fortunately, it sounds like the girls are really into the game. He can hear Jade calling for Emilie to cover her while she reloads. Man, this is gonna be fun, Jam tells himself and slips into the arcade.

Clyde grunts and moans in the security office as he picks up the pace, but he's not getting there. It's the picture; it's too damn small. He starts fiddling with the settings, and a single image of just the front door fills the screen.

"No! What did I do!" Clyde starts mashing buttons on the keyboard, and the picture changes to the arcade interior, though he can't see the girls on it. He hits the key again, and the screen changes just as a crouched figure moves into view. It's now the shuttered pizzeria section on the monitor. "Come on." Clyde starts mashing the button, and the images flick by so fast he doesn't notice the masked figure strolling through the stockroom. It lands on the girls again.

"Yes!" Clyde cheers and picks up where he left off. The close-up image does the trick. It's close enough for Clyde to see Emilie sticking her tongue out the side of her mouth like she always does when she concentrates. Man, that drives him wild. And the way she stands with her legs apart, all business with that plastic gun in her hand, oh boy! They must have beat a level because Emilie gives a one-arm pump cheer, and then Jade pats her on the butt.

"Oh, god!" Clyde moans as he shoots his load all over the screen. The lights go out, and Clyde only catches the briefest outline of a reflection standing behind him before a knife comes through the back of his throat— splattering the screen with his blood too.

"What the hell!?" Jade yells in the suddenly dark arcade, the only light coming from the emergency strips along the walls and floor.

"Did we blow the breaker?" Emilie suggests. "Starsky's gonna kill us if we did."

"Nah, it'll be that LOSER Clyde fucking around with us," Jade decides as she slams the plastic gun back into place. "I'm gonna kick his ass."

"I'll watch," Emilie adds, and the two of them set off.

Jam keeps low, ready to follow behind as they pass, his hood up to cover his face, though only for the element of surprise. These girls aren't gonna be able to say a word by the time he's done with them. He plans to grab Jade, hold the knife to her throat and then make Emilie handcuff herself to one of the pinball machines. If it comes to it, he'll kill Jade if she puts up a fight, but he'd rather they both live for a while.

"Wait." Jade comes to a stop, still some distance from where Jam waits. "Did you hear that?"

"What…" Emilie holds her breath, and when Jade doesn't respond, she hits her friend on the arm. "Stop messing with me!"

"I'm serious!" Jade insists. "I heard something from the back."

"It's just Clyde—"

"If Clyde turned off the breakers, then he can't be in the back, can he?"

"That's…a good point." Emilie suddenly feels very exposed in the cavernous dark of the arcade; the emergency lights and glow-in-the-dark decorations do little to help. The back doors slam open, making both girls jump and squeal. They hold onto each other as they creep around, trying to get a look at what caused the noise.

"Damnit," Jam curses under his breath, "fucking Clyde Harlow," and he follows the girls.

Emilie and Jade come to a sudden halt, and both stifle screams as they see Treeface standing in the blue glow of the emergency lights, a blood-stained knife in his hands. There's no doubt it's him; no thoughts of Clyde pulling another prank cross their minds. They both can feel the hate, the cold-hearted malevolence pouring off him like the wisps of fog that waft around the monster's feet.

The girls back away slowly at first, but once they're out of sight, they make a break for it. Emilie crawls under the pinball machines while Jade slides into the ball pit, carefully lowering her body beneath the multicolored surface. Jam is confused at first, then he too lands eyes on Treeface. "Fuck," he mutters, "how!?" Of course, he knows how, just not the details, but that doesn't matter. There's no way Jam's letting that fucker kill Emilie; she's his. That means he's gonna have to get her out of here. How, though?

Treeface stalks between the machines. He knows there are others here. He heard them moments ago with his own burned ears.

Jam glances at the pinball machine Emilie hides under as Treeface makes his way in that direction. Unless she can keep her cool, which Jam very much doubts, he'll find her. He'll kill her. This thing doesn't give a shit who it kills, which gives Jam an idea. He ducks behind the prize counter and rummages around till he finds a box of Fun Snaps. Kids love this shit, Jam says to himself; let's see if undead psycho killers do too. Taking a handful out, Jam tosses them across towards the ball pit.

The scatter of tiny bangs causes Jade to jump, and a cascade of balls scatters. The noise draws Treeface right over. Stomp-stomp-stomp, and before Jade can even think to clamber out of the ball pit, Treeface steps in and starts stabbing like he's playing a game of *Whac-A-Mole*. He can't see where the girl is and misses more often than not, but when the blade connects with flesh, a scream bubbles out between the clatter of plastic.

"Oh god," Emilie trembles, then barely covers the shriek that escapes her mouth when all the lights and games come on at once. The joyful chirping of arcade machines drowns out Jade's dying screams. The game they were just playing declares it's "The House of the Dead," in a deep and very poorly timed groan while the Starsky's Arcade jingle plays.

"Emilie," a voice growls behind her, and she jumps, smacking her head on the bottom of the machine. She winces, then looks up to see Jam Starsky holding a hand out. "Come on, I'll get you outta here," he promises, and given what's just happened, Emilie doesn't even think to question why he's there. She just takes Jam's hand and lets him lead the way towards the back of the arcade as Treeface climbs out of the ball pit.

A few balls spill to the floor, rolling across the sticky carpet, strawberry splashes all over the place.

CHAPTER TWENTY-TWO

THE FINAL BOY

Jump cut from Emilie and Jam's sneakers beating across the stockroom floor to the main highway as Caleb races to catch up with the rest of the Paradise Falls refugees. The older kid from the trailer park leads by a few feet but slows to let Caleb catch up. The blood soaking through Caleb's shirt concerns him.

"You okay, man?" the kid asks.

Caleb wheezes, "Yeah," and takes a few more breaths, "all good." He grits his teeth and pushes the pain down. "Could do this all day."

The rest of the escapees wait ahead, clustered and huddled against the dark.

"Where are we going?" a little girl clutching a teddy bear asks, and it takes Caleb a second to realize she's talking to him. They're all looking at him as though he's in charge. Well, shit, he thinks as he looks from face to face, guess I am.

"We'll just keep going this way," he points ahead, "till we're outta town. Till we find help." No one argues. It's miles to the nearest town; Caleb knows that. They all do, but none of them want to go back towards Cherry Lake even if there's nothing this way but a ghost town, a rest stop, and Old Man Walker's garage—that's it! The crazy old guy lives up the mountain pass, over the town line. They'll be safe there. "We'll go to Old Man Walker," Caleb says.

"He scares me," the little girl says, "and he smells funny."

"Nah." Caleb pats her on the head, thinking of the time Walker saved him from a solid ass-kicking. "He's all right. Come on, let's go." A short while later, though, the group passes the turn-off for the old Williamson Farm, which means Vincent's house is only a few minutes away. They were supposed to meet there; maybe Vincent and Casey are waiting? The group notices him stop and halts, too, looking at Caleb as he stares off into the night.

"Caleb?" one of them asks.

"Keep going on this road, first left up the mountain will take you to Old Man Walker's place. He'll know what to do."

"You're not coming?"

"I gotta go check on someone," Caleb says and looks to the others. "You guys go; I'll be alright."

The older kid nods. "Be safe."

"Hey," Caleb holds his arms out as he walks back towards the trail, "look who you're talking to!"

The Tran house sits quiet; all the lights are on, but Caleb can tell no one is home even from down the hill. The front door sits open as he climbs the steps to the porch, which sets off alarm bells. Caleb creeps along the outer wall and peers inside. There's no sign of anyone, so he enters and, after two steps, comes to a dead stop.

"Oh, shit." He runs over to the lifeless body of Debbie Tran. "Oh, fuck no!" Caleb drops to his knees, holds his hands, inches above her body, torn by the conflicting desires to help and not harm her any further. When he sees her neck, he knows neither is possible. "Vincent…" Caleb's head falls into his hand. It had to be Treeface; who else could spin a person's head around like that. At least it would have been quick, right? Though Debbie's body lies facedown, her head faces up and to the side, towards the kitchen. She's still smiling, and Caleb can't bring himself to look at her anymore.

He glances around and then grabs a throw blanket from the nearby sofa. He covers Debbie's body, looking away from her twisted, smiling face as he covers her head. "Sorry, Mrs. Tran," he says, wishing there was something, anything he could do to turn this whole shit show back. "The fuck am I gonna tell Vincent," Caleb asks himself, and then, remembering why he came here, calls out, "Vincent!" There is no answer, so he goes back to the door and out onto the deck. "Vincent!" Caleb yells into the night, "Casey!" Nothing but crickets.

"Shit." Caleb kicks the door as he heads back into the house. "No way he'd just leave his mom like that unless…" Caleb doesn't want to think about it. They can't be dead, not them too. It can't be just him left; it can't. That's when he sees the large pool of blood leading into the kitchen. "Fuck." Caleb follows it and nearly slips in his haste.

Almost the entire kitchen floor shines, coated in fresh, dark blood. A chair stands to one side, loose ropes dangling from it, and another lies on the floor. There's so much blood, no way whoever lost it is still alive. One of them must have gotten hurt, and—Caleb hops over the gore and out the back door. "Vincent! Casey!" he screams, but still nothing. And, for all that blood, not a single drop of it outside. Whoever's it was, never left the house. "The fuck?" None of this makes any damn sense. Caleb brushes his hair back, over and over, to help gain some focus.

"The fuck do I do now," he asks, his sanity on the verge of collapse. He feels dizzy, and it's not just the blood loss. The weight of all their stupidity begins to crash down, and if Caleb doesn't keep moving, it'll bury him. He gets his answer as a distant light catches his eye—a glowing crucifix atop the phone tower at Camp Clearheart. "Oh shit." Caleb realizes that if Treeface came through Vincent's house, then he would have passed the camp first. "Dean!" he yells and takes off towards the distant light.

Cut to: Emilie and Jam, bashing through the arcade's back door as they hear Treeface stroll into the stockroom.

"My truck!" Jam shouts as Emilie stands dazed, lost in the suddenly thick fog that laps against her and the building. She spots the pickup as Jam points and races to the passenger door.

Jam's already behind the wheel as Emilie climbs in, and he turns the key just as Emilie slams her door closed. The headlights come on, cutting through the fog, and Emilie screams at the sight of Treeface, just inches in front of them–his blackened, burned form like an inhuman shadow in the glowing fog. Jam puts the truck in reverse and floors it, though the car only jerks back and then comes to a halt.

"What are you waiting for! Go!" Emilie yells.

"I am!" This bitch, Jam growls to himself. The engine roars, and both can hear the wheels spin, but the truck still goes nowhere. Slowly but steadily, Emilie and Jam feel the front of the vehicle rise. "No way," Jam mutters.

Nobody is strong enough to lift his truck, not like that, not so easily. Soon enough, it's undeniable, and both of them feel the truck approach 45 degrees of verticality.

"He's gonna flip us over!" Emilie realizes.

"Nobody can do that," Jam insists as he pushes his foot down.

"Tell him that!" Emilie points through the windshield as the truck's front rises up his chest; all they can see is that black bark mask with the branching horns now.

Jam rummages through his bag and pulls out a taser, spilling the ball gags and plastic zip-ties to the floor. "Shit," he curses, but fortunately for him, Emilie is too freaked out to notice. "Here," he holds the taser out for Emilie. "Take this and zap him." Emilie looks at Jam, then at his hand. What's he doing with a—"Take it, Emilie! Now!"

Emilie grabs the taser and leans out her window, though she can't get a clean shot. She has to put her entire upper body out just to get enough of an angle to shoot. Emilie fires, the taser connects, and as it clicks rapidly, Treeface halts, not by much, but it's enough to make him drop the front of the truck. It bounces to the ground with enough impact to dislodge the fender. Emilie jerks, her shoulder slams into the top of the window, and then she falls out, down into the fog.

Jam faces a dilemma—he could just drive away, get the hell out of there and leave Emilie for that creepy masked fucker to finish. Vincent would still lose his sister, but that's not enough for Jam. Nowhere close. So Jam puts the truck into drive, revs the engine, and charges the beast forward. The truck catches Treeface dead-on and slams him into the back wall of the arcade.

"Like that? Huh, fuckface!" Jam switches to reverse back halfway across the lot, then flips back to drive and revs forward. Treeface only just steps away from the wall as the truck catches him again, slamming him so hard, this time spiderweb cracks appear where his body meets the wall. "Yeah!" Jam cheers and reverses once again, this time as far back as he can.

Emilie gets to her feet as the truck pulls back past her; she sees what Jam's about to do and yells, "Stop!," sure that he'll kill both himself and the masked monster.

Jam waits, the truck back in drive, for a sign that Treeface is still alive, hoping that the piece of shit gives him another excuse to ram him. Seconds pass, and then Jam's face glows with violent delight as Treeface extricates himself from the small crater in the wall. He's not on his feet more than a second before the headlights race to meet him. Jam's untapped bloodthirsty scream is audible over the howl of the engine. Treeface is rammed back into the wall as the truck's front crumples around him. There's a crunk of shattering brick, a crunch of metal, then silence as the engine dies and the lights go out.

"No!" Jam bashes the dashboard and turns the keys over with little more than mechanical wheezing in response. "No, damnit!" He slams both fists down on the wheel.

Emilie comes around and clings to his window. "Leave it," she tells him, "we gotta go!"

What's the damn rush, Jam thinks, no way he's—and he loses his train of thought as he looks up to see Treeface grip the accordioned hood with both hands. "No fucking way!" He can hear the metal groan and brick separating as Treeface begins to push the truck free.

"Now, Jam!" Emilie demands, and he doesn't argue. Jam climbs out of his wrecked truck, the shock of it being totaled still sinking in, and makes a run for it with Emilie.

By the time Treeface pushes free of the wreck, the two of them are gone from sight. He listens for the Voice in the Fog to tell him which way as he stalks across the parking lot. It draws his masked eyes to the glittering, shining diamond glowing in the near distance, above the rooftops of Old Town, unable to contain its excitement. Both can feel them; more souls gathered together than ever and, above that, the Child of the Lake. Emilie and Jam are forgotten as Treeface heads to the Prom.

Caleb arrives at Camp Clearheart and finds nothing short of a massacre. White-tiled walls splattered in blood; a body hanging through a smashed window, shards of glass staggered across his back; three bodies on the floor of the chapel, as though they tried to crawl to the front before dying; a pool table broken in two with a counselor in the middle, pool cue embedded in his chest. However, all of the horrors pale compared to the sight of Dean's body in his office chair. The phone in one hand, a photo on the desk an inch from the other, and Dean's severed head on the desk between them. The picture shows a smiling woman in a hospital bed, proudly displaying her new baby.

"No," Caleb drops to his knees, "fuck no."

Dean is dead, and it's his fault. All of this is his fault. He could have stopped it. No, he was too busy cracking jokes and making light of every little thing, doing all he could to avoid dealing with something real. And now, Dean is dead. Vincent and Casey, they're probably gone too. Michael, he let him down, ran when he should have fought. Isn't that just me, Caleb admits. Talk big, run fast.

Part of him just wants to give up and die; his body is ready to. That photo, though. Dean's wife and baby, it haunts him. This place should have been locked up tight, lights down low, but Dean didn't listen. Why should he, anyway, after Caleb ghosted him. All because he can't handle people leaving him. Caleb has to be the one to decide when it's over. Ever since his Ma left, he's been this way, and it sickens him to be so needy all the damn time.

"I'm sorry, Dean," Caleb mumbles weakly and hates himself for it. Sorry doesn't do shit, his Pa, another person he's gotten killed, used to say, and of all the things Horton Dumont was dead wrong about, that wasn't one of them. "Sorry ain't gonna do shit, though," Caleb says to the corpse of his former boyfriend. You put up or shut up; Caleb remembers his Pa's words. And, since you don't know how to shut the fuck up, you better put up boy, 'cause runnin', that's only good for wearing our yer shoes.

Caleb picks up the photo, looks at the face of a child who'll never get to know who their father was at all, and places it back into Dean's cold, dead hands.

"I'm sorry, Dean. Pa. Shit, you too, George," Caleb runs off the names of the dead. "Vincent, Casey, Michael. Michael!" He's not dead, at least as far as Caleb knows, and since it was those Church fuckers who grabbed them, there's a good chance he's alive. He only got a quick look at them when he ran, but those damn shirts and slacks, even with the stupid masks, are dead giveaways. There's fuck-all Caleb can do for the others, but Michael, he's still alive; he has to be. They'll have taken him to the Church, Caleb figures, but it'll take him well over an hour to get there on foot even if he was up to it. The run over to the camp must have popped some of the staples out—Caleb can feel the blood seeping out, and when he catches sight of his reflection in a window, he sees one whole side of his t-shirt soaked in blood.

"Gotta be another way." And then, through the jet-black window, he finds his answer. As the clouds clear and the moon shines down on Cherry Lake, Caleb sees, moored to the dock by the edge of the camp, a single motorboat remains.

Moments later, Caleb limps down to the dock and climbs in. He unhooks the boat and pulls the engine cord. His hair blows in the wind, the water spats his face, and he races towards the glowing glass palace of The Church on the Lake.

Cut to: sweat pouring down Emilie's face as her feet pound on the pavement. She's a few feet ahead of Jam as they race down Witt Street, the heart of Old Town, and there's not a soul in sight. Not a light on in a single store or apartment. Even the theater is closed up for the night. At least the fog's gone, Emilie thinks between breaths. She looks over her shoulder to see if they're being chased and slows to a halt. Jam leans against the theater wall, hunched over and out of breath.

"Are you okay," Emilie asks as she jogs over to him.

"Yeah," he says, though it doesn't sound like it. Jam puts his back up against the wall, right between posters for *Shakespeare in Love* and *Deep Rising*. "Just need," he wheezes, "a break."

Emilie looks back down the street. There's no sign of Treeface, but that doesn't mean anything, she tells herself. He just appeared back there, like out of the fog. She wants to keep on running till they find help, but one look at Jam tells her that's not possible. "Okay, we'll rest up."

"No, you go on," Jam insists. "I'll just," he coughs, "slow you down."

"I'm not ditching you," Emilie refuses to budge.

"Just help me into the alley?" Jam leans his head to the side, indicating the small lane between the theater and Campbell's Hardware next door. "I'll lie low there till I'm good."

"Okay," Emilie says, though she doesn't like it one bit. She likes it even less when, once they're in the dark of the alley, she feels a blade against her back.

"You stupid bitch," Jam sneers, all traces of exhaustion gone. "You know you'd be dead twice over if it wasn't for me?"

"Jam!? What the hell are you doing!?" Emilie is forced against one wall as Jam points the knife at her throat.

"Payback," Jam says, and he brings the tip of the knife down Emilie's throat, between her collarbones, the end just scraping the surface of her skin.

"I've not done anything to you." Her whole body trembles, and she wills it to stop, afraid a single involuntary twitch will cause the knife to plunge.

"Not you!" Jam pulls the knife away and then yanks his hood back. He points the blade at the scar tissue crossing the top of his head. "Payback for what your fucking brother did to me!"

Emilie makes a run for it as soon as the knife points away and pelts down the alley. She only makes it a few feet before Jam wraps his arms around her torso. He drags her back as she kicks and screams. Jam throws her against the wall, hard enough to crack the back of her head. Emilie feels the impact in her teeth, and even with her eyes closed, everything flashes white.

"Shut. Up," Jam demands, the knife once again pointed at Emilie. "If I wanted you dead, you would be," Jam lies. "Do what I say, and you'll live."

"W-what are you gonna do?" Emilie asks, fearing the obvious.

"I am going to fuck the shit out of you. You are going to do everything I say. When I'm done, I'll leave something for your brother to remember me by. How big a mark, where it is, that's all down to you, Emilie. Be a good girl, and it'll be as painless as possible." Jam steps back and lowers the knife but keeps it ready for use. Just in case. "Now, let's see how well you listened. Panties. Off. Now."

"Please, Jam—" Emilie screams as Jam whips the knife across her outheld palm. She clenches her fist to staunch the flow of blood.

"Panties. Now."

"Jam—" He raises the knife to take another swipe— "No!" Emilie cowers. "No, please, I'll do it. I'll do it." Jam lowers his knife hand slowly, never breaking eye contact with Emilie. When the blade comes to rest against his hip, dripping with her blood, Emilie gives in. She reaches down with her uninjured hand, past her knee, as her stomach turns and body shudders. Bracing it against her body to fight the tremors, Emilie slides her hand up her skirt till her fingers reach the waistline of her underwear. It takes a few attempts for her fingers to hook, they twitch all on their own, but she manages to get a grip and then slides them down. And then Emilie stops, decides she'd prefer the knife to Jam's dick. "You know what I heard?"

"Panties," Jam flicks the knife.

"I heard when you were pretending to make out with Caleb, he touched you, and you were hard as shit." Emilie spits in Jam's face.

"Bitch!" Jam grabs her by the throat and pulls the knife back, ready to stab.

"Hey!" a third voice yells, and Jam only half-turns before a fist meets his face. He staggers back as the attacker lands another punch in his gut, causing him to double over. Jam slashes with the knife, but the shadow catches his arm. He feels intense pressure like his attacker could snap his wrist in two if they chose, and he drops the knife.

"The fuck are you—" Jam manages to say just as the attacker kicks him in the knee, causing Jam to limp then fall on his ass, pulling a trash can with him. His attacker closes in, and as they move out of the shadows, he sees it's a girl—just a girl. His confusion is replaced with an ear-piercing screech as the girl brings a heavy boot down on his balls with enough force to crush them completely. They explode in a single crunch, shotgunning blood and meat in his pants. Jam howls in utter agony and then shuts up forever as his own knife whips through the air and lands in his throat, deep enough to embed itself in the concrete on the other side—the humming from the impact.

Emilie staggers away from the wall, struggling to keep her balance with shock; the other girl catches her, helps Emilie keep her footing, and, as Emilie looks up at the face of her savior, she recognizes..."Casey?"

CHAPTER TWENTY-THREE

Purity Blues

As the fog rolls across Old Town, bringing with it the silent avatar of death, reverbs of heavy bass puncture the night. Not only can he see the Church from afar, but hear it, feel it too. The pulsing drone of the distant music and the vibrant, vital life of so many bodies sing to him in perfect, harmonious union. It's almost as though the Purity Prom, and the Church itself, were an invitation meant just for him. The Voice in the Fog chitters excitedly as his hand grips the knife, and the fog swirls—not far now.

The flashing white tiles on the floor and subtle yet bright, hidden mood lights make the tall glass walls into jet-black mirrors inside the Church. Adults and young people dance, eat, drink—all the while unaware that they're the mice in this terrarium and that the hungry snake is on its way.

Vanessa gives Starsky an awkward smile as he tries to dance up against her far too close for her liking. Not wanting to be rude, she shuffles over a few steps, but Starsky doesn't take the hint and follows. There's not supposed to be any alcohol here, but she can smell the booze wafting out between his lips as he whispers something she's glad the music covers. Something like, "Where's the mister?"

Ariella saves her mother, taking her hands and leading her away, right to the middle of the dancefloor. Suddenly there are a lot of eyes on them, and Vanessa feels all elbows and knees.

"Come on, mom!" Ariella shouts and kicks her Jordans out; she throws her hair back, ponying with her arms in the air. Vanessa wonders where her daughter gets her boldness from, and not for the first time. Michael is his mother's son; Ariella is like her husband if he was carefree and joyful—in a word: unstoppable. People start to clap. Oh, no, they want me to join in! In front of everyone! Vanessa is fine shuffling awkwardly at the edges of the room, but not in front of an audience. "Mom!" Ariella takes her by the hand.

Oh, to fudge with it, Vanessa says and joins in. She starts with a lukewarm hustle, only really using her legs, and after a second, when Ariella takes it in, her daughter copies, only she throws her whole body into it. "Old-school moves, mom!" Rising to the challenge, Vanessa throws in some arm moves, starting to lose any concerns about looking silly. Ariella butt-bounces her mother, then rocks her body into an effortless Reebok, leaving the woman stunned and challenged. "Do it like this, mom." Ariella rocks three times on her left side and waves her arms, slowing down enough for her mother to copy. Once Vanessa looks like she's got the hang of it, Ariella picks up the pace.

The crowd around them claps along, and, fortunately, some other kids join in—giving Vanessa a moment to catch her breath and slink back into the group. She wouldn't have to be playing the host role so much if her husband was anywhere to be seen. "Where are you Creed," she asks under her breath.

Cut to: the Church's security room, above and beside the pulpit's fly loft. A wall of screens shows more than two dozen perspectives of the party below and some external shots of the building. Pastor Wallace stands before them, arms behind his back as he observes. A slight smile twitches across his face as he sees wisps of fog begin to encroach in the furthest reaches of the external cameras. "Finally, it begins."

Fierce, muffled cries of distress sound from behind, and Creed turns to the hooded boy tied to a chair. He nods to Kaytlynn, who then walks over and pulls the hood off. Vincent's bloodshot eyes glare with unbridled fury and hate. Kaytlynn pulls the gag out of his mouth, a stale grasp for breath follows. "Fuck—"

Kaytlynn shuts Vincent up with a firm slap.

"Miss Parker, enough," Creed states, relaxed and calm. "There is no need for cruelty." Kaytlynn doesn't like that, and it shows.

"Cruelty!" Vincent spits. "You bastards led that monster to my mom! You killed her! Killed my friend!"

Creed hangs his head. "I want you to know Miss Parker's actions were against my instructions, and she will be punished. You have my promise." Kaytlynn bridles but remains silent. "I hope that you can accept my apology for what happened to your mother and Mister Dumont."

"Fuck your apology!" Vincent fires back and then realizes Creed thought he meant Caleb; he doesn't know about Casey. So Caleb could be—

"Pastor—" Kaytlynn tries to speak up.

"Silence, Miss Parker!" Creed snaps; his voice booms around the room, bouncing off the steel doors and walls.

"If you don't accept my apology, then know, at least, I am grateful for your mother's sacrifice. I wished no harm on her, even after your father ruined the last ritual."

"The hell are you talking about?"

"Your father's actions, however heroic, only hastened the need for tonight. Had he let the last sacrifice run its course, perhaps... Still, I endeavored to ensure your family's suffering was lessened. Your mother wouldn't accept our money, but I personally ensured she would have access to all the medication she needed."

"You killed my dad! Turned my mom into a junkie! You're a fucking maniac!"

"I am a leader of men!" Creed towers over Vincent. "And a sad fact of life is that sacrifices must be made."

"Yeah? Don't see you making any!"

"I am." Creed turns back to the monitors and watches as Treeface approaches. "Believe me, my child, I am."

Cut to: the front of the Church as Treeface sets foot on the boardwalk. He can feel the waters of Cherry Lake below as The Voice in the Fog pushes him on.

Tendrils of mist curl up against and rebound off the glass doors; they begin to spread around the building, moving to wrap its circumference. Try as it might, though, the fog can't find a way in, which means neither can he. The dancing crowd within, unable to see him, revel in this blissful ignorance of what waits just beyond the vestibule.

A small light above the door turns from red to green, and the two massive glass panels slide apart like magic. That's all the invitation he needs.

Treeface steps through, his heavy footsteps suddenly muffled by the elegant carpet within. The door slides closed behind him, severs his physical contact with the fog, but not the bond they share. Nothing can break that rope. The light above the door turns red again.

Nobody in the main hall notices him, not at first. They're all too happy, too caught up with the music and the fun to see the masked stranger walk up the steps. It's a cheerful young man, not looking where he's going, who crosses his path first. The young man nods to his friends, calls out something inaudible to them, and turns to head down the steps when he comes face to face with a demon. He screams, but no one hears the young man over the music. No one hears Treeface cut the young man's throat so deep his head lolls back like a PEZ dispenser. Treeface grabs the gelled, spiky bird's nest at the top of the young man's head and pulls it free; the body drops to his knees before tumbling down the stairs.

No one in the main hall notices a thing. Not till Treeface launches the head across the crowd and one girl catches it. Her face switches from confusion to horror as the top of her dress turns red. She inhales; her mouth opens wide, and she screams.

Cut to: the security room. Creed watches the crowd back away, pushing together as one huddled mass.

"You're gonna let your wife die? Your daughter!?" Vincent growls.

"I am making a sacrifice—"

"You're making nothing! They're the ones dying! For what! What the fuck is the point of all this!?"

Creed ignores him. "Miss Parker, once the sacrifice is complete, you know what to do."

"Yes, Pastor Wallace," Kaytlynn nods and steps up.

Creed puts a hand on each shoulder and kisses her on the forehead. "The reaper will come for him," Creed nods his head towards Vincent, "seal the room. We shall meet at *The Sanctuary* and watch the dawn of a new era for the Church together."

"What kind of bullshit is this!?" Vincent rages.

Creed picks up a wooden mask, places it securely over his face. "Blessed be their sacrifice."

"Blessed be their sacrifice," Kaytlyn responds as Creed leaves.

"Come on, you know you want to brag; what the fuck's this all about?"

Kaytlynn smirks. "Look around, Vincent." He does what she says, though it provides no answers. Metal walls, monitors, panels, and the only decorations are those little wicker circle things. They look like they're made from the same kind of wood as the masks. Vincent's head twitches as the dots begin to connect. "You've noticed. He's afraid of it," Kaytlynn purrs. "It keeps us safe. Keeps him at bay. Once he's done down there, he'll come up here looking for you, and, when he does, he'll be trapped."

"You think some dumb wood and metal doors will keep him down? Bitch, please, we dropped a fucking building on his ass—"

"And we will drop him, and the whole church, down to the bottom of Cherry Lake," Kaytlynn interrupts. "This is kinda how your dad died, right? Throwing his life away, thinking he's a hero. Achieving nothing but misery. Do you think he'd be proud?"

"Don't you talk about him," Vincent growls, "you don't deserve to!"

"Think about it this way," Kaytlynn smiles, "you'll get to see him again soon. Your mom and your skanky little girlfriend too."

"I promise," Vincent vows, "you die tonight." He starts to laugh madly, deliriously, as Kaytlynn pushes his chair up to the screens. It staggers Kaytlynn; Vincent's defiance cuts through her façade and niggles at the insecurities within.

She takes her mask, slips it half over her head, but she can't just walk away. "What's so damn funny?"

"It's just," Vincent chuckles, on the edge of sanity, "I'm guessing he fucked you?" Kaytlynn's silence says it all. "So, if that Treefaced bitch comes for the ones who called him, and we weren't part of the plan, how did the Pastor expect to lure that masked fucker up here?" Kaytlynn doesn't have an answer for him, and she storms out while Vincent's laughter continues to taunt her.

Cut back to the main hall, where a half-circle of party-goers almost surrounds Treeface. They push into one another, crushing the ones at the back. One man somehow gets the nerve up to take the initiative. He roars and charges at Treeface, throwing a wide punch. Treeface catches his fist, killing the man's momentum, then, with a flick of his wrist, snaps the man's arm back, forcing the bone through the elbow into a sharp point. He wails, then Treeface rams the man's pointed bone through his own eye.

That triggers the rush, and everyone makes a break for it. Treeface is surrounded by bodies rushing around in every possible direction.

People race to the exits only to splat against static electronic doors. That doesn't halt the stampede behind them as wave after wave of bodies slams against the sealed exit. The ones pressed up at the front feel the pressure build behind them; it gets harder to move then breathe as the mass pins them in place. "Stop!" one woman begs, but it's no use. The pressure mounts, her head pinned between the glass door and the mounting wall of bodies behind, till her skull cracks against the tempered glass.

A teenager gets the idea to fight back, pulls a fire extinguisher from the wall, and charges at Treeface with it, holding the red canister like a battering ram. He trips over the leg of a body, lying motionless on the floor, and stumbles into a fall, landing just before Treeface. The last thing he sees is the burned rubber at the bottom of a boot before Treeface curb-stomps him.

Ariella climbs up on top of the speakers on the stage, high enough to see over the crowd. She watches as Treeface grabs hold of a boy running past, as the masked monster holds the kid up by the collar and quickly stabs more times than Ariella can count. She yells, "Mom, where are you!? Mom!"

Starsky, looking over his shoulder, runs faster than he thought he ever could. He bumps into a snack table, almost tumbling over it, and then gets an idea. Flipping the table over, Starsky pushes it to the side and then clambers over, cowering behind the cover. The whole table jerks, and Starsky whimpers as something heavy impacts his improvised barricade. Glancing around the side, he sees a person, still alive, staring at their bloody hands—their body impaled on the table's top leg. Starsky crawls back into his hiding spot and closes his eyes.

Cut to: elevator doors opening to reveal Creed, in his mask, as he reaches the Watchtower on the top floor of the Church. The Inner Circle's masked members all sit around a carved wooden desk, much like the one back in Creed's house, watching the carnage unfold on a large screen. Just before Creed steps out of the elevator, he turns a key, takes it out, and even after he leaves, the doors remain open.

"It's begun," one of the Inner Circle states, "at last."

"It's beautiful," another adds.

"It has," Creed agrees, "and it is."

Each of the Inner Circle members makes a sign of the cross and raises their masked faces to the sky. "Blessed be their sacrifice," they all chant as one.

"Blessed be your sacrifice," Creed intones, and before any of them catch what he said, he pulls a pistol from inside his jacket. Creed puts two bullets in the closest member of the Inner Circle while they're all still praying. He shoots another in the head just as the others react.

The Inner Circle scatter, most of them racing towards the elevator, piling in. One of them bashes buttons, but the doors remain open. Too late do they realize they're trapped and can't do a thing as Creed empties the rest of his clip into the elevator. Without a word, Creed reloads and turns to the one remaining member of the Inner Circle. She crawls back into the far corner until there's nowhere else to go.

"Why, Pastor Wallace!? Why!?" she begs to know, and the only answer Creed gives her is one bullet to the heart and one to the head.

"Mom!" Ariella yells, and we cut back to the bloodbath at the prom. "Mom!"

"Ari!" Vanessa calls out, and Ariella's face lights up. She scans the chaos, the directionless hoard of racing bodies circling their doom hopelessly, but there's no sign of her mother. "Ariella!" A hand shoots up out of the crowd.

"Mom! Up here!" Ariella bounces up and down on top of the speaker, waving her arms like she was doing jumping jacks.

Vanessa pushes through. Her dress ripped, she's bruised and distraught, but the second she sets eyes on her daughter, safe and alive, she smiles like she's never smiled before. "Baby!" She opens her arms. Ariella jumps down and runs into her mother's embrace.

Out on the floor, three men surround Treeface. "Jack him up!" one of them yells.

"Hurt him bad!" another adds, but none of them wants to be the first to rush in. All three glance nervously at each other, daring the others to make the first move. A group roar builds between them, some non-verbal cue to go, and all three rush at Treeface together.

Treeface catches one with the knife, stabs it through his eye in a backhand jab, then uses the body to sweep another one aside—the last of the three wails on Treeface, landing punch after punch, with no effect. As Treeface turns to deal with him, he jumps back, turns, and bolts. Treeface follows, slashing at passing bodies on his way—leaving wounded and dying in his wake.

The man reaches the turned-over table and vaults over, landing out of sight on the other side. "Get out!" Starsky shouts and shoves the man away, causing him to fall back into view. Treeface grabs the man by the foot as he tries to crawl, hoists him up like he weighs no more than an infant. Movement catches his eye, and Treeface turns to see Starsky scuttling away behind the upturned table. Treeface boots the table with one mighty kick, stunning Starsky and trapping him against the window. The upside-down man punches at Treeface, then the monster whips him through the air, like a ragdoll, spins him around right into Starsky—turning both men into splatter with the impact and still not a dent in the glass.

"This way!" Ariella pulls her mother by the hand up onto the stage.

"Where are you going?" Vanessa cries out, letting the child lead the way to the backstage door. Unlike the main doors, this one isn't electronic, and though it's shut tight, Ariella and her mother give it all they've got.

Others in the crowd see what they're doing and rush over to help. One woman knocks over a toolbox and grabs a hammer. She's able to wedge it into the lock, and then, working together, others join in and pry the stage door open. More people see what's happening and race over. Soon enough, those who remain alive and on their feet flock to the stage.

Treeface watches them all run, then follows.

Vanessa holds Ariella close, both of them realizing they're still trapped, just in a maze of white cinder block corridors instead of a glass slaughterhouse. People scatter and split through the back corridors, with no idea where they're going. Some of them pound on the fire exits, rattle the door bar, but they can't get it open. There's no way out, but maybe up? "Ari, honey," Vanessa meets her daughter's eyes, "the stage ladder!"

Ariella leads through the corridors, the sounds of bones breaking, flesh ripping, and screams following. She looks over her shoulder and sees her mother falling behind. Vanessa balances on one foot, then the other, and pulls her heels off, throwing them aside. She races barefoot to catch up with her daughter and promises to never complain about Ari's shoes again if they make it out of this.

They reach the ladder to find it closed off, the gate secured with a heavy padlock. There's no time for how odd that is to cross her mind; Vanessa searches for another option. The fence goes up maybe six feet, and there are no grips. No way to climb it, but if Ari stood on her shoulders? "Ariella, honey, listen to mommy; I'm going to lift you up on my shoulders, and then you climb."

"But, mom—"

"Listen! You climb, honey, and you don't look back!" Vanessa doesn't give Ariella time to argue; she hugs her daughter, kisses her, and breathes in the scent of her hair before hefting the girl up. Ariella's feet find purchase on her mother's shoulder, and she's able to get a grip of the ladder above the barrier. She climbs a few rungs and then looks down.

"Mom?"

"I love you, with all my heart," Vanessa says, then turns her head to see Treeface come round the corner. Vanessa takes a few strides away, down the corridor. "Go, baby, go!"

"Run, mom!" Ariella yells and watches as she disappears around the far corner. As Ariella starts climbing, she feels a sharp tug on her right foot. She looks down and sees Treeface up close, gripping her ankle. Ariella screams.

Vanessa hears her daughter, and realizing Treeface isn't just behind, her heart sinks. "No!" She grits her teeth. "No!" Vanessa smashes a nearby fire axe box with her elbow, not giving two fucks about the glass, and takes the weapon in both hands. "Leave her alone, you bastard!" Vanessa yells as she races at the monster with the axe overhead. She screams with the raw fury only a mother can muster and buries the axe in Treeface's back.

It does nothing, relatively, to him, but it lets Ariella wiggle free and climb. Her daughter safe, Vanessa snarls at the killer. "Come get me!" and runs for it.

Treeface pulls the axe free and holds it in one hand. He weighs it against the knife and finds the heavy weapon preferable. Dropping the blade to the floor, Treeface takes the axe in both hands and heads down the corridor in pursuit.

Ariella makes it to the top of the ladder, her heart going a mile a minute, and she struggles to keep her balance on the walkway. The catwalk sways from side to side, and Ariella tries not to look at the massacre below.

Someone blocks her path. Ariella looks up, both hands on the railings for support, to see a familiar skirt and polo shirt, and though she has a strange mask on, Ariella recognizes the friendship bracelet right away. "Kaytlynn!" Ariella cheers and races over as quickly as she can, throwing her arms around the girl.

Kaytlynn lifts her mask and looks down at the child. She puts her arms around her back and holds Ariella close.

"I'm so glad you're safe, Kaytlynn," Ariella, smushed voice laced with tears, sobs. Kaytlynn strokes Ariella's hair, comforts her, then grips a fistful of the girl's curls. "Ow! Kaytlynn," Ariella pulls away, and the cruel smirk on Kaytlynn's face chills her to the bone.

"I'm sorry, kid," Kaytlynn says and then drags Ariella by the hair across the catwalk. She screams, begs her to stop, but Kaytlynn ignores it all. They reach a break in the railing, and Kaytlynn throws Ariella back down into the nightmare below.

CHAPTER TWENTY-FOUR

THE CRUELEST INTENTION

The little motorboat cuts across the black lake as the radiant cathedral towers above. Caleb tells himself that even if the Churchies have gone all *Red Shoe Diaries* with the masks, they're not going to hurt Mikey. The Church, though, glowing like a lightbulb in a dark room, is a five-story tall sign for an all you can slay buffet. Caleb can't shake the idea that's the whole point.

Beneath the Church, Caleb steers his motorboat around the side, and the hidden dock below comes into sight. "Fuck me sideways with a crucifix," he mutters, "that's some James Bond shit right there," he adds at both the secret berth and the massive leisure yacht docked within. Caleb maneuvers his little boat close enough to toss the rope ashore and climb up. He doesn't waste much time securing it; he just throws the rope around the post and heads toward the far stairs at a clipped pace.

Several blinking lights draw Caleb's attention and curtail his speed. They're all across the tops of the extensive, wooden supports that hold the Church up. It doesn't take a genius to figure out they're bombs, though these are a bit more sophisticated looking than Michael's homemade efforts. "What the fuck." Caleb can't quite put the picture together, and commotion aboard the yacht stops his train of thought from going any further. It sounds like a hurried, muffled cry for help. Caleb clambers up onto the stern, grunting as he feels another staple pop lose. "Ah, shit, that ain't good." Caleb puts his hand to his shoulder, and when he takes it away, it's slick with fresh blood.

A boy in a button-up shirt, a little worse for wear but still oddly neat with a sack over his head, sits tied to a chair inside the yacht on the boat. "Mikey!" Caleb cries out in joy and rushes over to his friend. He feels his heart lift, and his very steps lighten. "Mikey!" Caleb pulls the sack away and then yanks the gag out of his friend's mouth. "Mikey, I'm so happy I could kiss you!"

"Please don't," Michael says, and Caleb gives him a massive hug instead. "Caleb—"

"It's a friendship boner! Honest!"

"No, Caleb, we have to hurry," Michael states as Caleb pulls out of the embrace and begins to untie him. "We're in trouble."

"I'm way ahead of you, buddy; let's get this beast started and sail outta here like a bunch of bankers who just killed a hooker."

"We can't." Michael stands up, rubs some feeling back into his numb limbs. "The Church, no, my father's going to kill everyone at the Prom."

"Yeah! No shit, I've seen the bombs."

"Bombs?" Michael narrows his eyes. Caleb leads him out onto the deck and points to the rigged supports. "So that's how he's going to cover it up."

"What's going on here, Mikey?"

"My father believes that those who are killed on Virgin Night are a sacrifice to bring the town wealth. He's going to let Treeface—"

"Treeface," Caleb mutters under his breath, "come on, man."

"—kill them all, then, I guess, blow it up to hide the evidence."

Caleb gives out a nervous chuckle. "Man, was I right about that James Bond thing. Okay, what's the plan then?"

"First," Michael runs back into the boat, to the controls, and pulls the key out of the ignition, "let's make sure my father can't get away so easily." Michael pockets the key. "Now, there's a security room that controls the door locks. We can open the doors and let everyone out."

"What makes you think," Caleb rolls his eyes at the name, "Treeface is inside?" A blood-curdling scream echoes from above. "Nevermind."

As the two boys head towards the stairs, Michael looks around. "Where's Vincent?"

Caleb freezes. "Mikey, man…"

"No." Michael looks to the floor.

"Casey, Mrs. Tran, it was a bloodbath."

Michael's whole body trembles as his hands form fists. Veins pop in the whites of his eyes. Then it passes, and Michael returns to himself. "We have to put this right."

"Yeah," Caleb agrees. He keeps the "How though?" to himself.

Cut to: the private elevator as the doors open, and Creed emerges into a white, cinder-blocked hallway. Kaytlynn waits for him, leaning against the wall. Creed masks his confusion quickly, but Kaytlynn notices.

"Miss Parker? Why are you here?"

"What was the original plan, Pastor Wallace?" Kaytlynn doesn't look him in the eyes. She knows Creed well enough by now to not give him any way to assert dominance.

Creed smiles and holds his hands out. "This is the plan, my child. Soon the sacrifice will be complete, then you and I—"

"If we didn't have that dropout upstairs to lure the reaper into the safe room, who would it have been?"

"Miss Parker—"

The sound of Kaytlynn pulling the hammer back on the stolen revolver silences Creed. "It was me, right? I was gonna be the final sacrifice?"

"God's plan—"

A shot shuts Creed up; he ducks to the side as chips of brick explode next to his head. The ringing persists even after he clears the debris from his ear.

"No more almighty horseshit, Pastor. Yes or no, would you have let me die?"

"If God willed it, yes." Creed holds his hands up. "But hasn't he shown otherwise?"

"You know what," Kaytlynn sneers, "I'm fucking sick of God," and she fires. Creed dodges aside, but the bullet clips him in the shoulder. A spray of blood lands on the white walls like fine red spittles. Creed takes off down the corridor, and Kaytlynn follows, gun arm outstretched. She shrieks and ducks back around the corner as a hail of bullets fly her way.

Creed feels the blood soaking through his silk shirt, though the material helps staunch the flow. He can hear Kaytlynn close behind and stops to fire some more wild rounds, then runs as fast as his feet will carry him to *The Sanctuary*.

Emilie's heart pounds to the beat of her sneakers as she tries to keep up with Casey. "W-w-wait." A stitch in her side kicks in, and Emilie doubles over, growling through gritted teeth. "Casey, wait."

Casey slows to a jog and stops. She bounces on her boots as she turns. The girl is wild, covered in blood, and there's something wrong with her eyes. They don't have the same sparkle from when they met in the parking lot; in fact, there's no color to them at all. They're dead eyes. "We don't have time," Casey states, cold and severe.

What is she made of, Emilie wheezes to herself. Not even a drop of sweat on her. "I can't; it hurts."

"If you don't hurry, your brother's screwed," Casey says. "Royally."

"Okay," Emilie punches her side, pumps herself up, "okay." Even though it hurts like hell, she starts to run.

We cut to the two of them as they come in sight of the Church. It emits a red glow, mistaken at first as mood lighting. It's only as the girls close in that they see the horrifying reality. From within, the brilliant white light is tinted crimson through the splatter, smears, and streaks covering the walls. Hands beat against the glass, adding red handprints to the bloody mural.

"Oh my god." Emilie stumbles. "What happened?"

"We don't have time." Casey starts to kick the door. It vibrates as though a tremendous force was applied but holds firm and steady. Those still trapped in the main hall bang their fists against the door at the top of the vestibule.

"Is there any other way inside?"

Emilie stares in open-jawed horror.

"Emilie!" Casey shouts, and the other girl snaps out of it.

"I don't think so," Emilie answers. "I haven't been to Church in forever, though."

Casey looks around for something she can use, but there's not even a trash can. Out of options, she resumes her assault on the door, though it's entirely in vain.

"Fuck!" Cut to: Caleb and Michael as they stumble into a room filled with bodies, heaped on top of each other in a tangled mass of white shirts and twisted arms.

"We're too late," Michael mourns, but there's something unusual about these corpses. They all wear Church uniforms; there's not a drop of blood on them and, scattered across the room, as many wooden masks as bodies.

"I don't think our stab-happy friend did this," Caleb says. "This has a real *Heaven's Gate* vibe to it."

"There's nothing heavenly about this," Michael states.

"Mikey." Michael looks over to Caleb. "Never change." Caleb then begins to tiptoe around the room, trying not to touch anything.

Creed runs along the dock, one hand pressed to his wounded shoulder. He looks behind and almost stumbles, but there's no sign of Kaytlynn. This sensation, this fear, it's entirely alien to him. As bad as things have turned, though, the plan is still salvageable. All he needs to do is get to *The Sanctuary*, get far enough away, and hit the detonator tucked safely inside his jacket pocket.

Creed climbs up onto the yacht and heads below deck. It doesn't even register that Michael isn't there anymore; his focus is entirely ahead. He reaches the cabin, grabs the wheel, and his hand reaches to turn the keys instinctively, only to grasp nothing but air. That's not right. Creed checks his pockets and the usual places around the cabin he might keep the keys, all the while knowing he left them in the ignition specifically for this purpose. Glancing over his shoulder and finally realizing his son is nowhere to be found, it sinks in—Michael took the keys.

"No!" He slams his fists on the wheel. "No! No! No!"

That boy! That worthless walking disappointment! If he had the time, the things he'd like to do, but he does not, so Creed puts aside his wrath, for now, and looks for another way out. As he climbs back down onto the dock, he sees a motorboat moored to the other side. Creed has no idea where it came from but thanks God for providing as he heads across the dock.

A gunshot echoes and wood splinters erupt from the decking in front of him.

Kaytlynn stands at the bottom of the stairs, revolver gripped in both hands. "Going somewhere, Pastor?" she says and fires again.

Creed throws himself down, narrowly avoiding the shot and dropping his gun. Kaytlynn runs over and kicks it, sending it skidding across the deck. She aims her revolver at Creed's back.

"Turn around," Kaytlynn orders.

Creed does as she asks, with a devilish smile on his face. Creed never smiles, not like that, and it's so disarming that Kaytlynn takes a step back even though she has the upper hand, or so she thinks. A glance at his hand makes her reconsider that position. Creed clutches the detonator, his finger over the button. "Shoot me, my child, and it'll be the last thing you do."

"Yeah," Kaytlynn pulls back the hammer, "maybe that's worth it."

"Let me go," Creed climbs to his feet, carefully keeping the detonator ready, "and we both live. The sacrifice will still be complete. You'll be richer than you could ever imagine."

Kaytlynn doesn't trust him, yet what Creed offers is too tempting to decline. "How do I know you won't blow this place as soon as you're safe?"

"Get in the boat with me."

"Hah," Kaytlynn laughs, "as if! Here's what we'll do; you hand me the detonator, and I'll let you go."

"And what guarantee do I have you won't just shoot me after?"

Kaytlynn holds her gun out to the side, over the water. "I'll drop it as soon as you put it in my hand."

"Agreed," Creed says and holds the detonator out. He lowers it towards Kaytlynn's outheld palm but stops just short of giving it to her. "The gun, Miss Parker."

Kaytlynn's eyes narrow; her gut tells her this is a bad idea, but she drops it all the same. The second she does, that same smile flashes across Creed's face, and she realizes her mistake. Wide-open and defenseless, Creed punches her with his free hand. A blow from a man his size should have put her down, but the shoulder wound causes Creed to pull his punch at the last second. The distraction is enough, though, and Creed makes a break for the boat.

"You fucker!" Kaytlynn grabs her bloody nose. By the time she opens her eyes, Creed's almost at the boat. "Come back here, you wrinkly dicked old fuck!" She gives chase but spots Creed's gun, just on the edge of the dock, and goes for that instead. "Bastard!" She fires widely, bullets hit the dock around Creed, causing him to flinch and drop the detonator.

For a second, neither of them breathes as it falls through the air. Even the lake seems to go still and silent as they both watch it tumble and then clunk to the ground—the sound echoes forever, but no explosion follows.

Creed leaps in, removes the rope, pulls the engine cord, and the boat surges forward out of the dock.

"No!" Kaytlynn screams and chases him along the dock, firing at the boat.

Creed covers his head, letting the boat go wherever, as shots plop harmlessly into the water. Except for two. One chips off the side, doing no real damage, while the other hits the engine. It coughs and sputters; the speed dips considerably with black smoke billowing forth but keeps chugging nevertheless.

Kaytlynn reaches the end of the dock, but it's too late. Creed's too far away; she'd never make the shot. "Fuck!" she screams and then yells indeterminable curses as she stomps on the decking.

Kaytlynn stops to pick up the detonator on her way back to *The Sanctuary*. As tempting as it is to blow this place to hell and be done with it, she wants at least some personal satisfaction, so Kaytlynn pockets the detonator and climbs aboard. Fine, she says, if she can't kill Creed, she'll do the next best thing—his son.

Her sneer turns to fury as Kaytlynn also discovers Michael has vanished. She bites her lip so hard it bleeds, and then a wicked smile takes over. She realizes exactly where he'll have gone.

"Vincent!" Caleb cries out as soon as his eyes land on his friend. Caleb has his arms around the boy in a second, squeezing the life out of him. "I'm so happy to see you!" Caleb kisses him on the cheek as Michael enters the room.

"Caleb—"

"It's a friendship boner—"

"Guys!" Vincent feels a wave of pure joy—it caps the simmering anger within. "You're both, oh thank fuck. Mikey, we gotta get the doors open right now."

"On it," Michael states and rushes to the security console. He starts tapping buttons, but nothing happens. "Uh, I think."

"Michael, man, hurry. It's a slaughterhouse down there," Vincent urges as Caleb finds the knots around the back of the chair.

"My-my mother? My sister?" Michael pauses.

"I dunno, man," Vincent lowers his head, "last I saw, they were alive, but it's chaos, and I couldn't watch for any longer. I'm sorry."

"Is Casey..." Michael trails off. The look in Vincent's eyes says it all.

"He, they, killed her. Killed my mom—"

A heavy, guilty silence settles upon them, halting all action. Caleb breaks through the grim barrier of remorse and pushes past Michael, taking over at the console.

"Move aside, Mikey-boy, I got this." Caleb cracks his knuckles and stretches like he's about to go for a run.

"Today, Caleb!" Vincent snaps.

"You know what you're doing?" Michael asks as he sets about untying Vincent.

"You're talking to the guy who ordered all our shit without getting caught and still had time to find naked photos of James Van Der Beek," Caleb states as his fingers fly over the keyboard. "I got this." Boxes and windows pop up all over the screen, a red glow from them deepening Caleb's smug grin, and his eyebrows peak thinking about those images.

"They were fake," Vincent points out.

Caleb shrugs. "My boner wasn't, and, like your sister said to the three dudes with empty bacon bazookas in the back of their panel van…" The screen turns green. "Done!!" He turns and gives the others a cheesy thumbs-up, a big grin across his face.

"Don't you ever shut up?" Vincent groans.

There's a joke on the edge of Caleb's lips as he heads to help with Vincent's bonds. Something cocky, contentious, and comfortably Caleb.

A boom bounces off the steel walls, echoing like a whip crack.

Blood splats across Vincent's face.

The world slows to a crawl as the shot brings in a cold void of near silence, heavy heartbeats, and a ringing drone.

Caleb staggers, drops to his knees before Vincent, still smiling.

Vincent bares his teeth in silent rage, a ragged snarl painted with the blood of his friend. Words don't come, just a grunting, hopeless rasp.

Kaytlynn stands in the doorway, the cruelest of smiles on her face; this couldn't have worked out better. She moves the smoking barrel towards Michael, frozen in horror—his neat shirt sprayed with the blood of his best friend. Kaytlynn's thumb pulls the hammer back, and her tongue dances across her lips, savoring the moment. She pulls the trigger again.

The world kicks back into gear, and Michael dashes aside, just in time, as the bullet hits the panel. Sparks fly, the air fills with static, gunsmoke, and Vincent's anguish.

"Run, Mikey!" Vincent screams as Kaytlynn takes another shot. She misses, but it's close enough to make Michael jump. He pushes through the door and out onto the catwalk. Kaytlynn follows but pauses just long enough to whisper in Vincent's ear.

"Don't cry," she taunts him with a kiss. The boy's body rocks with furious, helpless despair. "You oughta be used to it by now."

The dam breaks, all that was Vincent Tran is awash with savagery and rage. He wants to rip Kaytlynn's neck out with his teeth, push her eyes through the back of her skull with his bare hands. But he can't do a thing, still tied to the chair. Blood wells from between his clenched fists as his fingernails dig deep into his skin. Vincent's eyes fall to his friend, bleeding out on the floor.

Still smiling, Caleb laughs a spurt of blood to a joke only he knows.

A crowd of desperate Prom guests streams out of the Church as the light above turns green, and the massive doors slide open. Both Casey and Emilie scan the crowd, looking for any sign of Vincent, Caleb, or Michael. The surging tidal wave of bodies races at Casey, and she jumps aside to let them flow down the stairs.

As the rush dies down, it's clear the boys are not among them.

On the catwalk, Michael's pounding footsteps cause it to sway like a drunk, and he's about halfway across when another gunshot booms; the bullet pings off a stage light, and it brings him to a stuttering halt. There's no way he'll make it to the other side before Kaytlynn pulls the trigger again, so Michael puts his arms up and appeals to her mercy.

"On your knees," Kaytlynn demands. "Now," she punctuates the command with a pull of the hammer. Michael complies though his uncontrollable shakes, and the wobbling catwalk makes it a challenge. Once he's down, he gulps hard and begins to whisper The Lord's Prayer. He repeats it another twelve times as Kaytlynn slowly approaches him. "I want you to know something before you die." She puts the barrel against the back of his head, the metal burning his skin. Kaytlynn leans in, a few inches from his ear, and says, "I fucked your dad."

A pair of dirty, blood-spackled unlaced Chucks steps on the catwalk behind Kaytlynn.

"Hey, bitch," a voice calls, and Kaytlynn whips around to see a deathly pale ginger boy who should be dead, giving her a shit-eating grin. "Same."

Caleb shoves her as she turns, pushing Kaytlynn over the edge of the catwalk—the revolver firing one more time, aimlessly into the air. Kaytlynn's belt catches on a hook, and as she tumbles towards the stage, it snaps, yo-yoing her through the air, causing her mask to fly off and clatter to the floor.

Caleb collapses on the catwalk, coughing up more blood. Michael rushes to his side but doesn't know where to place his hands. "Don't move, I'll—"

"Mikey, man, this is it." Caleb spits. "I've lost too much blood. Look at me, man," he snickers, "I'm wetter than Vincent's sister on a Saturday night."

"Caleb—"

"Don't gimme that. I'm good," Caleb smiles. "You guys are alive. That's—" He twitches.

"No, I mean, did you really have sex with my father?"

"What!? No," Caleb chuckles, "I just couldn't think up a good line. Do me a solid, make up a better one when you tell this story?"

Michael nods.

"And make sure someone hot plays me in the movie?" Caleb coughs. "Not some fuckin' loser like Eddie Furlong. Brad Pitt or bust, baby."

"Is there anything you want me to tell—"

"Yeah," Caleb manages a slight smile, "tell Vincent what I said about his sister."

"Of course." Michael takes his hand.

"And, I'd like a kiss. From someone who loves me. I've never had one of those."

"You've had lots of boyfriends."

"Yeah, but none of them loved me. Not like you guys do. I know it's not the same kinda love, but...."

Tears run down Michael's cheek, and he nods. He can do this; for his friend, who saved his life, he will do this. Michael leans in, closes his eyes, and puts his lips out, only to feel a lifeless slap against his cheek. He opens his eyes to see Caleb grinning up at him. "Ha," Caleb smirks, "gay," and then his head lolls to the side.

CHAPTER TWENTY-FIVE

DEATH BECOMES HIM

Blood runs along the catwalk, turning into thick fat droplets that swell and fall, pattering on Kaytlynn's back as she dangles helplessly. She flails, but the hook has hiked her belt up high, and all the twisting makes her suspended body swing wild.

Soon enough, Kaytlynn gives up, and she sways to something close to a stop. The stage is only a few feet below, but it might as well be miles. Her predicament's indignity and humiliation frustrate her almost as much as her failure to finish off both Pastor Creed and his loser son. The only consolation is the look of utter defeat on Vincent Tran's face, burned into her memory as she shot that white-trash piece of shit Caleb in the back.

The stage vibrates, and the boards creak with heavy footfalls.

"Oh, thank God!" Kaytlynn sighs. "Help me down!"

The footsteps come closer and then stop. Kaytlynn gulps, "H-hello?" They circle, and, at the height she hangs at, Kaytlynn comes face to face with Treeface. Her heart pounds through her ears as her eyes dart to the mask on the floor.

There are no threats Kaytlynn can make, no cruel barbs or insecurities she can exploit to manipulate her way out of this one. There are no subservient, weak-willed followers to command—there is nothing Kaytlynn can do to save herself, but she'll be damned if she lets herself become a victim. "Well! Come on! Do it!" Kaytlynn yells into his face. "Do it!"

Treeface only tilts his head up in response, following the chain to the catwalk above, like a child trying to understand something new and fascinating.

"Do it!"

Treeface steps around and examines the hook. He lowers his axe, drops it to the floor, and grips the curved end of the metal in one hand.

Kaytlynn almost laughs. For a second, she thinks he's going to let her down? She wonders if the mask still has some effect even on the floor and then wails as Treeface begins to drive the pointed tip of the hook through her back. Kaytlynn's lips pull back into an agonized snarl as the rounded metal tip bores through her skin—pushing into a deep hollow before finally bursting through her flesh.

Treeface braces his other hand on her stomach and pushes, keeping Kaytlynn's body still as he works the hook. He twists and jerks the metal, helping it bore through thick muscle and tissue.

Kaytlynn's back arcs, her throat jerks up as blood spurts out—she can barely breathe as her throat fills, and her screams turn to spluttering gurgles.

The hook comes through the other side, just below Kaytlynn's rib cage, slick and red.

Kaytlynn looks down; she doesn't want to but can't stop herself. Her fingers tremble as she dares to touch it, sending a bolt of disgust and horror surging through her body. Kaytlynn instinctively grabs the hook as Treeface lets go, and her body weight drives her down, ripping an inch-long gash and cracking several ribs before the hook finds purchase.

Treeface backs away, as though admiring his handiwork. He almost hears the Voice in the Fog chuckling in delight from beyond these glass walls.

Letting go of the hook, Kaytlynn goes limp and dangles, suspended in the air like a macabre piñata. She manages the strength to look up and stare into Treeface's mask. "Kill me," she demands with blood-stained teeth. "Finish it. Do it!"

Blood and bile drip to the floor below, almost forming a pattern as Kaytlynn sways back and forth. Treeface stoops and picks up his axe.

"Do it!"

He takes one long look at her, axe in both hands, then walks away.

"No! Pussy! Don't leave me!" Kaytlynn begins to cry as her strength fades. It hurts more with each passing second—the hook dragging incrementally up her body.

Suddenly all the lights come on, the carnage in the hall put on full brutal display with blasts of unforgiving fluorescence. Kaytlynn tries to look up at the catwalk, but the stage lights blind her for a second; then, as her vision returns, Kaytlynn watches the doors open across the hall, and survivors begin to flow out.

The cover of a table near the stage ruffles, and a small person crawls from beneath. Kaytlynn smiles. "Ari," she reaches out, "help me, please."

Ariella climbs up on the stage, her jaw set and eyes narrow. She approaches Kaytlynn's outstretched hand, dragging a painfully twisted foot. Ariella grits her teeth with each labored step till she reaches Kaytlynn, then, without a word, rips the friendship bracelet off—beads clattering to the floor, never breaking eye contact with Kaytlynn.

"Ari, please," Kaytlynn begs as the girl hobbles away. "Please," Kaytlyn cries as she dangles above the stage and on the edge of death.

Michael, shaking, works the last of Vincent's bonds free.

Vincent sits on edge. His bottom jaw jutted and tense, teeth grinding so hard he tastes blood. The second there's enough slack, he takes off, shoving free and making for the door.

"Vincent?"

There's a softness to Michael's voice, a quiver of vulnerability that brings Vincent to a halt. "Get the hell out of here, Mikey; I got this."

"But—"

"Listen, Mikey! He's coming for me. I can lead him away, and I have an idea; I think I can really hurt the fucker. I—"

"Refrain from anger, Vincent," Michael begins to quote, "and forsake wrath—"

"Enough with the Bible shit! Fuck! Michael! All this and you still believe! How!?"

"How? How can I not!?" Michael draws Vincent's eye to their dead friend. "Caleb, he's...he's in a better place. I have to believe that. I have to!"

"Yeah? Well, excuse me while I send the fucker behind this to a much worse one."

"How?"

"The masks, the shit they're made of, that bitch said he was afraid of them, maybe if I shove one down his fucking throat—"

"The masks come from a tree on Black Stone Island," Michael explains. He doesn't want to, but Michael can't help but tell the truth, say things as they are. "My father discovered it. He's been behind all of this. He's gonna blow the supports, sink the Church, to cover it all up. We have to leave." Michael reaches for Vincent's arm, only for Vincent to shove his hand away.

"Get out," Vincent growls.

"No," Michael refuses, and Vincent grabs him by the shirt, pulling him in close. "Get out now!" he demands and shoves Michael, sending him stumbling back a few steps, then down to the floor, hard.

Michael lands on his arm, hissing with pain. He doesn't get up and cradles his arm as his large frame shudders with sobbing pleas. "Please, Vincent, I don't want to lose another friend."

As the red mist clears from Vincent's eyes, he's left with nothing but shame in its place, stunned by the cruelty, the indifference of his anger. Vincent stares at his friend on the ground, trying to come to terms with the fact that he did that. He hurt Michael, the kindest, gentlest of them all. Vincent looks at his shaking hands, not recognizing them—they belong to a monster. It used to dwell within and now has a claw in the door with that single transgression.

"I'm sorry." It's pathetic, but it's all Vincent has to offer. He kneels next to Michael, reaches out, and feels a stab in his heart as Michael flinches. He's afraid of Vincent, and there's no going back. So be it then; it was only a matter of time anyway. Vincent always knew he'd hurt the ones he loves, but if he can take out that bastard downstairs, then it'll be worth it—right?

Something glitters on the floor next to them. A set of keys, with a buoyant keychain, inscribed *The Sanctuary*.

Creed's boat. He can use that, Treeface will follow, and Vincent can bring him to the island. To this tree. If the masks hold sway over him, what will the source do?

"No!" Michael shrieks as Vincent snags the keys. "Don't!" He grabs Vincent's hand but can't stop his friend from taking them, and, once again, Vincent pushes him away.

"Fuck off, Mikey." Vincent stands. It's too late to be anything other than the monster, but maybe that's what they need. If he has to hurt Michael to keep him safe, so be it. He's too far gone to see how wrong that is.

"Please," Michael begs, "please don't throw your life away."

"I..." Vincent doesn't know what to say. Even after everything, the blood, death, and even hurting Michael as he did, the boy still only cares for his friends. He truly is the best of us, Vincent says to himself, and that's precisely why he has to do this.

Michael climbs to his feet, Vincent still too stunned to offer any help. He looks Vincent in the eye, something Michael's never done before, and reads him like a book. Michael nods, a single tear racing down his cheek, then gives up. There's nothing more he can do to save his friend—he's lost Vincent to wrath. Michael turns his back and heads out to the catwalk. He stoops, picks Caleb up into his arms. He's surprisingly light, and Michael has little trouble lifting him. "I'm not leaving him here," Michael states, "I'm not losing any more friends."

"Mikey..."

Michael walks past Vincent, refusing to look his way. Without turning, he says, "Caleb wanted me to tell you that he was wetter than your sister on a Saturday night."

Despite it all, Vincent snickers. "Yeah, I bet he did. I'll see you later?" Vincent offers weakly.

"Sure," Michael says and walks on. He doesn't look back; he can't bear to see the lie written across his friend's face.

"Ariella!" Vanessa stumbles around, the rough ground cutting into her bare feet, and she doesn't care one bit. "Ariella!" she screams, her dress torn half off and hair drooping in a clumpy mess. "Ari—"

"Mom!" Ariella squeals as she staggers out the front of the Church. Vanessa rushes over and catches her daughter just before she falls, then spins her around in circles laughing with pure relief. She kneels and hugs Ariella so tight neither of them can breathe, and if it wasn't for what she sees coming out of the Church next, they might have stayed like that forever.

"Michael!?"

Ariella, her mother, Casey, and Emilie all turn to watch as Michael emerges from the Church, Caleb's body in his arms. The four of them rush to Michael as he stumbles, helping him lay the dead boy down on the ground.

"Oh, no…" Emilie touches her face, unsure what to say or do.

"What happened, Michael?" Casey snaps.

"He saved me." Michael drops to his knees and brushes Caleb's hair out of his face. "Saved us all."

"Oh, honey," Vanessa says and joins her son. Ariella hugs him from the other side.

"Michael, where's Vincent?" Casey asks.

Michael shakes his head. "He insisted. Thinks he can kill him."

"Where, Michael!?"

"My father's boat," Michael tells them, "Vincent's going to lure him to the island."

"Fuck!" Casey curses. "How do I get there?"

"Through the back and down, but it's too late—"
Casey takes off at a run.
"Wait! I'm coming!" Emilie shouts, and Casey stops.
"No, get them somewhere safe," Casey nods to the others.
"He's my brother," Emilie insists.
"Not for long." Casey runs off, weaving through the last stragglers making their way out of the Church.

"There you are." Cut to: Vincent facing off with Treeface in the back of the Church. "Looking for me, right?" Treeface twirls the axe in his hands. "Yeah, come get some!" Vincent flips the bird and takes off down to the dock.

He doesn't look back, doesn't need to; Vincent can feel him coming. This bond, whatever it is between them, it's getting deeper, and though it should scare the fuck out of him, he feels alive. The dangerous confidence that comes with not caring if you live or die; it makes anything feel possible. Vincent makes it to the cabin and slams the door shut. He blocks and locks the door. Won't keep him out for long, Vincent figures, but maybe it'll buy enough time to get to the island; he turns the key.

Jets of water bubble up as the engine comes to life, and the whole boat rocks as Treeface jumps aboard.

"All aboard, asshole," Vincent laughs, "now let's go see what you're so scared of, tree fucker." Vincent fiddles with the different levers and buttons. He has no clue what he's doing, but *The Sanctuary* jerks forward, nevertheless, and some experimentation makes the yacht pick up speed.

Casey pounds down the steps just as *The Sanctuary* pulls out of the dock. "Shit!" She races to the end of the pier, and even though the yacht is too far and picking up speed, she doesn't stop. She reaches the end and leaps, soaring through the air and rolling to a stop on the stern.

Treeface, pounding his axe against the cabin door, turns around at Casey's presence. *Her*, he wonders, *how? I killed her*, and yet he feels her. There's that scent again, too, something he can't place. The Voice in the Fog chitters, almost nervously. *Careful*, it warns, but what choice does he have? Treeface heads out to face her.

Kaytlynn's hand finds its way into her pocket, twitching and trembling as the last of her life ebbs from her. She manages to grip the detonator and pull it out. "Fuck you all," she mutters, and Kaytlynn Parker goes out with a bang.

Beneath the Church, all the charges attached to the supports beep as the flashing light turns steady and explodes as one.

On the streets of Old Town, the survivors all flinch at the blast. Still on his knees over Caleb's body, Michael watches with wide eyes as the Church tips like a slowly collapsing iceberg. There's a tremendous groan of wood bending then snapping, like a massive gunshot that echoes off the historic brick buildings of Old Town. As the Church slides into the lake, the boardwalk breaks apart, and waves crash up over the promenade.

"Vincent..." Emilie gasps. "Casey."

"They'll be on the boat," Michael states.

"H-how can you be sure?" Emilie's on the verge of tears.

"I just am." Michael takes one last look down at Caleb's face. He's still smiling, somehow. Like it's all one big joke, and only he knows the punchline. "Can you stay with Caleb?"

Emilie nods. "Where are you going?"

"My father," Michael stands, "he did this," and he looks to the scared, confused survivors scattered across the street. "I can't let him get away."

"How do you know he's not—" Emilie looks at the sinking remains of the Church.

Kaytlynn's last words repeat in his head, and something someone else might have missed hits home. I fucked your dad, not killed, the consistently literal Michael notes. "He's alive."

"Yeah, still alive, surprised?" We cut to Casey, pulling her knife out of her boot. She plays with the blade and licks her lips. "So, wanna dance?"

Treeface charges her, but the second he swings the axe, the whole boat surges forward, hit by a massive wave. Both Casey and Treeface go sprawling to opposite sides. Casey almost tumbles over into the lake but manages to hang on. Just as she's righting herself, the axe whirls past, clipping her hair and landing in a safety bar with a twang. Casey takes advantage of his stuck weapon and jabs at Treeface in a furious blur, the knife fluttering like a dozen stinging bees. Treeface pulls his axe free, ignoring his wounds as Casey charges, drop-kicking with both legs, sending Treeface back across the deck.

As Casey gets to her feet, she spots something odd. Trickles of blood seep from the stab wounds. "That's new," Casey teases and points the tip of her blade at him. "You know what they say? If it bleeds—"

Pull back, and we can see that *The Sanctuary* is halfway to Black Stone Island. *The ritual must be finished*, the Voice in the Fog commands, so Treeface readies the axe again. He can feel it, both the island and the coming dawn; he must kill this one quickly.

Casey runs at him, jumps off the wall, and dives into a full-throttle punch. Treeface moves aside with surprising grace, and Casey realizes her mistake too late. He brings the axe up with a backswing, catching her in the arm. Casey crashes down, the knife skidding across the deck. In seconds she's on her feet with a gash from wrist to armpit. Her skin flaps like a gutted fish as blood pulses out, running down her ruined arm in a spindly crimson cascade. Casey lets the ruined arm droop and snarls.

Treeface comes at her again, and this time Casey keeps it simple. She runs right at him, faster than he can swing the axe, and lands a jumping headbutt that sends Treeface stumbling back. The boat hits a rough wave, and the sudden jolt finishes the job; Treeface crashes down, dropping the axe.

Casey screams like an animal and runs at him, grabbing the axe with her good arm, swinging it overhead, burying the blade in Treeface's chest. She backs away, holding her wounded arm. "C'mon, get up. Don't pull that play-dead bullshit with me; I know what you are, you piece of shit. Get up!"

Treeface jerks up and pulls the axe free from his chest with little effort. The Voice in the Fog urges him to *finish this now*. Casey charges again, but he's ready. Instead of dodging, Treeface lets her launch herself at him, punching and kicking like mad. He feels it, actually feels the blows beat against him. It's a strange sensation, like something familiar from long ago. It reminds him of somewhere dark and wet. The second Casey begins to slow down, Treeface pops her in the head with the axe handle.

Casey stumbles back, momentarily dazed, and Treeface strikes. The axe cuts through the air, then Casey's wounded arm, severing it in one clean hit. "Fuck!" she roars and falls to the deck. She kicks backward as Treeface looms. He raises the axe for one final overhead swing, and as Casey closes her eyes in anticipation, the whole boat rocks. It tilts up as the bow hits land. Casey rolls back over the edge and into the lake as Treeface stumbles, dropping the axe.

The yacht comes to a stop at an uneven angle, beached on the shore.

Treeface stands and approaches the back of the stern. He looks down at the black water below and sees no sign of the girl.

"Hey!" Vincent shouts as he steps out onto the deck. Treeface turns to greet him as Vincent wraps his three-chain belt around his right fist into a makeshift knuckle duster.

This one, the Voice in the Fog insists, *I want this one.*

Shreds of red light begin to break over the horizon; the night is almost over. One way or another, this must end soon.

Vincent charges, and Treeface allows it. It's time. With a scream that tears his throat raw, Vincent unleashes all of his fury, the red mist descends, and he sends Treeface to the floor with a right hook. Vincent straddles his chest, seething with bitterness and rage. Vincent roars in his face.

"You killed my dad!" Vincent yells and punches the mask. The bike chain cuts into his skin, and the pain is delicious. "You killed my mom!" Vincent hits him again, and a crack appears in the mask. "I'll kill you!" Vincent punches, again and again. Over and over, he beats down on the mask, immune to the pain as the fire consumes him, as the hate flows.

Casey clambers up onto the deck, rolling on her back as she lands.

"Stop!" she yells as she tries to get to her feet with only one arm.

Vincent doesn't hear her. He punches more and more till the split in the mask widens, spreads from top to bottom—till the mask cracks in two and falls apart. Even then, he doesn't stop at the sight of the face beneath. It doesn't even register. His free hand finds the axe, and Vincent raises it above his head. "Die!" he screams.

"No!" Casey dives in, grabs the axe with her one hand, and stops Vincent from bringing it down. She manages to yank it free, and Vincent snarls at her like an abandoned feral dog who's forgotten what it used to be. Her face, even with the cold, dead eyes and the impossibility of her presence, is enough to halt the brutality. A shred of Vincent returns. It's enough.

"Casey?"

"Stop," Casey sighs, "don't," and she looks to the beaten, bloody man beneath Vincent.

He follows her eyes, looks at the face beneath the mask.

"No." Vincent crawls aside. "No, it can't be!"

The lifeless face of Jimmy Tran stares, glassy-eyed, at Vincent.

"Dad!?"

CHAPTER TWENTY-SIX

SAY IT AIN'T SO

FEBRUARY 13TH, 1989 - VIRGIN NIGHT.

Jimmy Tran stares up from the bottom of the well as the world crumbles above, as the monster in the wooden mask falls on top of him, followed by a rain of brick and stone. He smiles through the pain. "You're not going anywhere, pal," he spits out with a mouthful of blood. "Just you and me now." That brings him little comfort as the monster takes out its frustration on him, but Jimmy's okay with that; his wife and kids are safe. A fair trade, he reckons.

Are they?

The voice comes with a sudden halt in the monster's assault. Before Jimmy can even think to ask who—he hears it again.

Do you want to keep them safe, James Tran?

"Who's there?" It's not coming from the monster; it just stares at Jimmy like a well-trained attack dog told to sit. No, this voice is as intangible as the fog that dances through the gap between them.

Do you?

"Yes," Jimmy screams, "of course I do!"

Then take it. Take the mask.

Jimmy reaches out, and half expects the monster to grab his hands and shatter them. To his shock, it allows Jimmy to place a hand on either side of the mask, and it comes free as though nothing was holding it in place. The face beneath is familiar, someone he hasn't seen in years. Someone who died last Virgin Night...

But how? This monster's been haunting Cherry Lake since forever, and here he's looking into the face of a guy he went to school with, how—

Put it on.

Jimmy stares into the back of the mask, the jet-black wood that smells of blood as he brings it closer and closer—the second it touches his skin, it latches on, and Jimmy cries out as dry, sharp roots pierce his flesh, worming their way inside, and the voice comes through clearer now. Commanding.

Become the Hand, James Tran. Release them...

Without thinking, Jimmy takes the blade from the killer—no, it's given to him willingly, and Jimmy drives it through Dan's heart. The body exhales a dry gasp, and streams of red flow from it, the fog drinking every last drop.

"My kids," is all Jimmy can think to say as he loses himself to the fog; "they're safe. They're safe..." he tells himself as the fog envelopes him.

"No," Vincent shakes his head. "No, it's not; I'm losing it. I'm—"

"Vincent." Casey puts her hand on his shoulder.

"Don't touch me!" he yells and pushes her away, jumping to his feet and pacing the deck. "How, just how? It's not possible. He died, he—"

"Vincent—"

"You died!" Vincent grabs Casey by the shoulders. "You died! I saw it." A sudden fog begins to rise around them, drifting out from the island, moving faster and more purposefully than any mist should.

"No, you didn't, I—"

"No! Enough of your bullshit, Casey, tell the goddamn truth! You took down those Churchies like the Terminator on coke, survived being stabbed through the heart, and you're standing there with one arm like you just left the other one in your purse. What the fuck is going on? Am I losing my mind?"

"You're perfectly sane, child," a strange voice carries through the fog, echoing through the wispy, rising tendrils.

"Who said that?" Vincent spins around. "Did you hear that?"

"Yeah." Casey prepares herself for another fight.

"This way," the voice beckons, and a path through the fog clears, inviting Vincent and Casey further into the island. Vincent collects his bike chain belt while Casey grabs the axe, and then, side by side, they follow the path, and the fog closes behind them. The two of them meet each other's eyes and nod.

It feels like they walk for ages before it clears, and they come to stand in a nearly lifeless expanse. A pale moon hangs overhead, though neither of them is all that sure it should be there. It's not so much that everything in the circle is dead; it's that life avoids it. Grass retreats and the trees grow outward as though the very ground is corrupt, the air toxic.

Above a rock so black, so perfectly formed it cannot be natural, stands a single twisted tree, its crooked naked branches striking out like dead man's fingers; its bark as black and its presence as distant as starless midnight.

"Where are you?" Vincent calls out, his grip on the belt turning his knuckles white.

An older woman with ragged clothing, pieced together with scraps from different decades, appears behind the Black Tree. "Welcome, Vincent, Son of the Lake. Casey, Daughter of Cain." She grins wider, her skin like tanned leather creasing with the effort, showing a crooked, rotten gap-toothed smile.

"Daughter of—what does that mean? Do you know what I am?" Casey steps forth.

"Indeed," the woman chuckles, echoes of her cackle rebound through the fog. "Deary."

"I know you!" Casey suddenly realizes where she's seen this woman before. "You were on the bus!" The kind older woman, what was her name? Judy? Now that she thinks about it, Casey can't recall the woman ever sitting next to her. She was just there.

"No shit." Vincent recognizes her too. "She's that damn therapist! Pray on this" He flips her off.

"What am I!?" Casey demands. "I'm not like that puppet of yours!"

"No, your kind is born of hate and pain, while my Hand comes from a fool's hope and desperation: either way, both serve the Fog." The Hermit grins at Casey. "It has been almost two centuries since a Child of Cain has dared enter my domain. I was...curious and so glad we allowed you to play with the boys—most amusing. Particularly in how you deceived poor, lovestruck Vincent."

Casey turns to him. "I didn't want to lie to you; honestly, I didn't. At first, yeah, but after you showed me where your father...I didn't want to lie to you, Vincent, but I had to."

"Well, stop then," Vincent says.

Casey nods. "Okay—"

Flashback to Camp Inkwood—grainy filter and all. The Raincoat Killer stands over the body of the impaled police officer.

SUMMER 1988 - CAMP INKWOOD.

"Casey!" A girl runs out into the rain. Her voice calls through the night, barely audible over the rattling drone of rain on the police car roof. The killer hears it, though. The voice pierces their cold, dead heart, and the killer turns in answer.

The girl, standing out by the tree in the middle of the clearing shouts, "Here I am, Casey! Leave them alone! It's me you want!"

The Raincoat Killer pulls down her hood, and the rain lashes Casey's face, washing over her lifeless eyes.

"It was an accident," Casey's voice-over explains.

Cut to: Camp Inkwood again, only it's a sunny day, and little Casey's out in the field with the girls from her cabin. She pushes one of them over, sends her down to the dirt. "What's the matter, Freckles? Huh?" The other kids are scared of her. One of them moves to step in, and Casey raises a fist. "You want some too, Braces?"

"I didn't fit in with those rich kids," Casey's voice-over laments. "I wasn't like them. They pushed me around, so

I pushed back, ten times harder. But they got their revenge."

Cut to: a Camp Inkwood night, as Casey creeps through the woods with her camera in hand. "That shit about the killer art teacher, going to her cabin—I did that." A flash, and Casey's dumbfounded face. She drops the camera and runs. The cabin door opens, and a counselor picks up the developing photo—the image fades in and shows an older woman with a young male counselor, half-naked in each other's arms. "I accidentally took a photo of the camp manager with one of her staff. She was cheating; he was sixteen, all kinds of wrong. They got the photo but had to make sure I kept quiet."

Little Casey runs through the woods while a pair of flashlights dance through the foliage behind her. She reaches the edge and realizes that there will be nowhere to hide if she heads out into the clearing. So little Casey clambers up a tree, then onto a branch. Clinging on she makes herself look as small as possible.

Below, the lights catch up, and Casey can make out a panicked argument. Then the branch cracks. Everything goes black. "I fell. The next thing I know, I wake up," teenage Casey's eyes pop open in a clean, white hospital room, "and it's ten years later." She's hooked up to all kinds of machines. "I can't explain it. I shouldn't have been able to get up after that long in a coma, but—" Casey climbs out of bed and walks to the mirror. "Something was callin' me. It woke me up, and there was this pull, dragging me back to Camp Inkwood." Teenage Casey steals some clothes from a hospital locker room, throwing on a yellow rain slicker before leaving.

Cut to: Camp Inkwood; only there are no children, just adults sitting around a bonfire. "It was the ten-year reunion, just an excuse for a get-together before college.

There they all were, the girls who pranked me, who accidentally sent me to my death." The Raincoat Killer stands in the forest, watching the former campers and counselors drinking and chatting. "I was dead for those ten years. Sure, machines kept my body going, but I was gone. Even if they'd left me in the woods, I think I'd still have come back. As I watched them smile, joke, laugh, talk about old times, about what happened to me, I felt this urge, this calling. I had to kill them. Something deep inside demanded it."

"No!" the Final Girl screams as Casey sits across her chest, ready to bring the knife down. She stabs, hard and fast, and drives the blade into the earth instead of the girl's head.

"I couldn't," Casey's voice-over sighs, "I couldn't finish it. And she couldn't finish me. Because I still loved her, and she still loved me."

Flashback to little Casey smiling as she sits on a log in the forest. A little redhead girl with equally red cheeks, dotted with freckles, tucks a flower behind Casey's ear. Casey kisses the girl quickly on the lips, and after an awkward moment, they both giggle. The other girl kisses back. "She was my first love, I was hers." Another kid, the one with braces, spies on them from afar. "And when someone saw us together, word got around fast."

Girls surround Casey and the little redhead girl on the field, pointing and chanting, "Gaycy loves Becky!"

"She, uh, took an out," Casey's voice-over explains, and Becky shoves little Casey.

"She forced me! It was gross!"

"My heart shattered into a thousand pieces," Casey's voice-over laments, "and I snapped." Little Casey climbs to her feet, shoves Becky to the ground, and lands two punches as a counselor races over to break up the fight.

"They made us apologize to each other, nobody told the whole story, and I figured she, Becky, would let it go. I was wrong."

Fade back to Black Stone Island as Casey says, "So now you know. I'm not a Final Girl; I'm a killer, a monster. I'm a fucking Slasher. Something broke when Becky couldn't kill me. When I couldn't kill her, it's like a disc that got scratched and won't play no more. I can't die; no matter what happens to me, I just wake up in one piece again. I've been seventeen for ten years. Ten years I've spent lookin' for others like me."

"Why?"

Casey wipes tears from her eyes. "Because I want to die, Vincent. I want it to end. This pain."

"Casey—"

"It hurts all the time. Havin' to live with what I am, what I've done. Killin' dulls the pain, but that only makes it harder to stop. I want to die, and I can't." Vincent takes her in his arms, and Casey drops the axe. "Then I felt your pain that night we met, and it's the first time I've felt anythin' in a long time. I'd forgotten what it was like, being alive. Hanging around with you guys, I could pretend I was human. That's why I half-wished you'd stop."

"But you went through with it anyway?" Another weight is added to Vincent's shoulders, more pain, more suffering he's created.

"For you," Casey trembles, "for myself. So I could convince myself I was your friend. I don't usually interfere, I—"

"Casey," Vincent smirks, "shut up. Of course, you're my friend." He holds Casey at arm's length to look in her gray eyes, and the color fades back in. "You're one of us now, a card-carrying member of the Cherry Lake Freak Show."

"Thank you." Casey feels something glow deep down in her heart. A sensation she's long forgotten; warmth.

"Oh how my heart weeps for you, truly," the hermit groans, "to be young and beautiful forever."

"Yeah, well it ain't exactly cool getting carded by some kid half my age." Casey goes to wipe a tear on her one good hand, and Vincent offers her his sleeve.

Looking over Casey's shoulder, Vincent sees the delighted grin on the older woman's face. She's enjoying this. "Can you help her?" Vincent asks.

"I can," she croaks, "but why? Doesn't her betrayal anger you, Vincent?"

"I don't care. Help her and I'll do whatever you want!"

"No!" Casey pulls away and puts herself between the woman and Vincent. The woman flashes her a rotten, gap-toothed smirk. She tries to grab the woman, only for her to turn to fog in Casey's fingers. "What the hell are you?"

"Just an old hermit," she caws.

A Voice in the Fog—the words find their way into Vincent's ear.

"We can't hurt her," Vincent says as more fog rolls around him. He tilts his head; faint whispers float through the air, drawing his eye to the Black Tree. "They're...connected...it's not—"

It speaks to you, doesn't it, Vincent?

"I—" He falls to his knees, and as the Fog takes root in Vincent's heart, he flashes back to—

CHAPTER TWENTY-SEVEN

Virgin Night: 1758

FEBRUARY 13TH, 1758 - THE FIRST VIRGIN NIGHT.

Three stern-faced colonial men row out, through dense fog, to Black Stone Island. They face forward, eyes of steel, as though approaching Death itself. It's midday, and yet the sun barely breaches the mist, forcing the colonists to light their way with torches.

They step onto the island and the fog parts, pulling back as though clearing the way.

"August, this bodes ill," one of the men says, but their leader only braces himself and accepts the unspoken invitation. With hesitation, the other two follow, and the fog seals the path behind them. "This mist is not natural," the man says, "we are being ushered unto the Devil's garden."

"Aye," the leader, August, states, "perhaps this means Old Scratch will be inclined to listen."

"This is wrong! God will—"

"God has abandoned us, Levi," August snaps. "What choice have we but the Devil?"

The three men approach the clearing to find a beautiful native woman humming enchantingly on an obsidian rock decorated with a myriad of animal furs. She whittles something mask-like from a block of wood; dark hair with the faintest threads of silver runs almost the length of her body, curving down her back and halting just before her ankles. Behind her, a dead tree rots lifelessly.

"I know why you're here." She smiles without looking up. "I've been waiting."

"August, let us return. This land is cursed! That wench is naught but evil incarnate," one of the men insists. "Thou shalt not suffer a witch—"

"Enough, Levi!" August snaps. He turns to the woman on the rock. "My name is August Lee, and I stand for the good men and women of Cherry Lake. We are in desperate need of salvation. We have no food to feed our young, to trade with—many have starved already. Sickness takes us, and no physic provides succor."

"A tragedy, to be sure." The native woman blows shavings from the mask she carves, a flicker of a gap-toothed smile between breaths.

"Is it possible then?" August demands. "Can your magic save us?"

"Of course." Her voice is like silk, her English impossibly flawless. Her gap-toothed smile enchanting. "For a price."

"What is the cost?" the third man demands to know. "Speak, Devil, what would you take from us? Our souls belong to the Lord."

The woman laughs. "Why would I desire something so trivial? No, you," she stands and walks towards August with a finger pointed right at him, "are a striking and beautiful man." Much of her tanned skin shows through the loose furs and gaps in her hair. "Would you lay with me, break your marriage vows, if it were to save your people?"

August gulps. "Aye."

"August! You can't!"

"I must! If it saves but one life—"

The native woman's laughter cuts through their argument. "I shall save you further indignity; you are too old for me. I prefer younger, more virile lovers. You have a son, correct? What is your word? A shaver?"

"Aye," August gulps, "he is of age."

"Tell me, August Lee." The native woman pads across to the men silently on bare feet. She moves like a cat, each step purposely graceful, and furs shift, revealing swaths of flawless, tanned skin. Each of the three men do all they can to hold their gaze forward and fail. She comes around behind August and goes on tiptoes to whisper in his ear, "Is he as beautiful as you?"

"He is a handsome lad, aye," August states, eyes fixed ahead.

"And betrothed to my daughter!" Levi steps in.

"Perfect!" the native woman purrs. "Send him to me, this eve, as the sun is swallowed by the mountains. Give your son to me for one night, and I shall give the Children of the Lake the means to prosper for as long as desired."

"Agreed," August nods.

"August! We should take no part in these heathen ways!"

"What would you have me do? These are dire times, and God does not answer our prayers."

"So you would give your son to the Devil!?"

"Oh, I'm hardly the Devil." The native woman walks between the men, stroking August's chest with a long, delicate finger. "Just a lonely heathen," she chuckles, "who speaks with the Old Gods."

"There is but one God!" Levi insists.

"If you men believed it so, then why come here?" The woman returns to her seat and resumes carving the black wood. "Go now, say what prayers you must, console yourselves however you like. I shall wait." Once they are gone, she takes up the mask again and continues her work, shaping the wood. "Fools."

The sun fades behind the mountain range, and the boat returns to the island with but one passenger. The single occupant is a beautiful young man, quivering as he climbs out. He lacks his father's full beard, and thick curls fall around his eyes. The young man follows a trail of torches through the trees to the clearing, the fog holding back, shifting with excitement as he passes.

His eyes soon land on the native woman, lying naked on the pile of furs beneath the Black Tree. Her body is covered in dancing shadows, flames reflecting faintly in the near gloss-black of the stone beneath, and she wears but a simple mask hewn from dead wood. The native woman pushes her hair over one shoulder and turns on her side, presenting the young man with an uncompromised display of her flawless form.

A conflicting turmoil turns the young man's stomach. He is pledged to another and knows the Lord's teaching prohibits what he has agreed to do. It was easier when he saw this as nothing more than duty, but the sight of this woman causes stirrings that bring shame and, worse, a deep desire to embrace it. The native woman pats the fur before her, stroking it provocatively, and the young man utters a prayer before he disrobes then walks towards her. He stops at her command, and she takes in his body with a delighted smile. A voice whispers from the edge of the clearing, urging him to **go to her**, and so he does.

The native woman holds a similar wooden mask to her own, adorned with twisting branches that form stag-like horns. The son of August Lee takes it, places it over his head, then climbs on top of her.

They make love in the firelight, in the shadow of the Black Tree, and at the moment of climax, it happens. The mask bites into the young man's skin; he pulls away from the woman as he screams, trying to remove it as splinters of wood pierce and worm their way deep inside. The native woman tosses her mask aside and laughs as the fog circles them, as the roots of the Black Tree sink into the young man's soul.

He drops to his knees and looks upon her with silent compliance as she hands him a crude knife made from stone and rough wood. "Go forth, Hand of the Fog," she instructs.

Kill for me, the Voice in the Fog echoes.

Naked but for the branching stag mask, the Hand of the Fog marches into the cold water, not slowing or hesitating as each step takes him deeper and deeper. Sometime later, screams ring out across the lake.

Through the eyes of his mask, they run, the men, women, and children of Cherry Lake. Their cries for mercy are met with cold silence and a swift blade. One by one, they fall, slaughtered in their homes, their beds, their cribs, till only one remains. Naught but a child, a young girl barely come of age who faces the Hand in defiance. The feeble rake in her hand poses no threat to him, and yet as he swats it from her grasp and raises his blade for the kill, he stops.

No, the Voice in the Fog instructs, **you must release...**

The girl takes this for hesitation and strikes, knocking the blade from his hand; she takes it up, herself, and drives it up through his chin, where wood and flesh meld. The wooden mask clatters to the floor as though not even attached at all. The son of August Lee drops to his knees, gouts of blood flooding down his naked body.

"Brother!" the young girl gasps and braces him from falling. Looking into his dying eyes, she begs, "Why!?"

Hush, little one, a voice whispers in her ear.

The child glances around, eyes landing on the mask. It's in her hand before she realizes, and as her brother's blood soaks into the wood, the gray turns jet-black as though coming alive.

Are you lonesome? Afraid?

The girl nods.

Put it on, become my Hand, and you shall never walk alone again.

Tears in her eyes, surrounded by the dead bodies of all she loved, the girl places the mask on her face.

On Black Stone Island, the native woman kneels, nude before the tree. Her fingers dance through the air, swishing the fog, conducting it as the scenes from the mainland play out behind her eyes. From the cruel gap-toothed smile she wears, they must be bloody. She teases wisps of red from the fog, making it move like string, guided towards the roots of the old, dead tree.

The bark begins to crack as she mutters words in a language not spoken by any living being. From beneath its husk, something breaks through, something in the shape of a tree, and yet it is not. The black bark pulsates as though made of flesh, as though a heart beats within. The shell of the dead tree crumbles, and the Black Tree breathes. Perhaps it was always there, dormant and waiting for one who speaks the dead tongue to revive it. Or whatever foul magic occurred that evening twisted the natural into something profane—it matters not.

A small fruit grows from a single branch, like a blood-red droplet; it ripens in seconds.

Plucking the blood fruit, the native woman gives thanks in her dead tongue and takes it into her mouth. She swallows, and her eyes flash with all the life the Hand has taken that evening. Their energy flows through her.

The last survivor of Cherry Lake approaches, and the native woman turns. Where seconds ago stood a mature woman now stands a youth, barely older than the child who has become the Hand.

"Come, sit, Hand of the Fog," the native girl gestures, and the masked one obeys. And, together, they wait.

The crops that year grow thick, hearty, even though none live to yield. A bargain is a bargain, after all. It will be sometime before others settle this land, this the native woman knows, but that's fine. She has plenty of time.

CHAPTER TWENTY-EIGHT

COME OUT SWINGING

Cut back to Vincent, gasping with ragged breaths and staring with faraway eyes. Casey kneels beside him. "Vincent?"

"I saw it," Vincent tries to catch his breath, "how it started. She tricked them."

"Nonsense." The Hermit reforms from the fog, waving her hands. "Tis but what they desired. The means to their salvation. What's one life for the sake of others? That was your forefathers' philosophy, not mine. All it takes is a sabotaged harvest here, a whisper in an investor's ear there, and your people come, begging. And, what's the harm? We all gain from a little spilled blood."

"What happened? What did you see?" Casey helps Vincent to his feet.

He points to the Hermit. "She," Vincent catches his breath, "banged some old-timey dude's son under the tree, and he became Treeface. The first one."

"Gross, but kinda hot."

"Yeah, I think Caleb could have gotten into it," Vincent agrees.

"So that's it? All this insanity so you could get some? That's kinda stupid," Casey taunts the Hermit.

"It really is when you think about it, right?" Vincent adds.

"I saved your precursors from extinction," the Hermit sours, "then and forever. They need only reenact the ritual on this sacred eve to renew the bargain."

"Yeah, what do you get out of it?" Casey demands. "I mean, you ain't been doin' this for two-hundred years for shits and giggles, right? Wait, was she all—"

"Nah, she was hot," Vincent answers without Casey asking. "Like, *Playboy* hot."

"Damn," Casey pictures it and shrugs. "Nice."

"Yeah, it makes her young again. Shit, lady, you know you can get work done in Redcastle for half the hassle you're going to here, right!?"

"Enough of your prattle, Vincent! Dawn approaches." The Hermit points a crooked finger to the edge of the clearing as Jimmy Tran shuffles in; battered and subdued, he falls to his knees. "You've come so close, Vincent. All those years, all that hate, and here he is. Don't you want your revenge?"

Kill him, the Voice in the Fog whispers in Vincent's ears, though the Hermit's lips remain frozen in a sneer. He clenches his fists.

"It's time." The Hermit's eyes narrow. The mask is in her hand, once again whole—she holds it out for Vincent.

Become my Hand, the Voice in the Fog whispers. He feels a connection forming, like thousands of strings made of smoke, all of them leading back to the Black Tree.

"Don't you hate him?" the Hermit chides.

With the face of Jimmy Tran, the Hand stumbles forward and drops to his knees. It speaks, "I only jumped down that well to get away from you and your worthless mother."

Vincent steps forward involuntarily at those words spoken from his father's mouth. Casey tries to hold him back.

"I wish you and your sister were never born. You trapped me here, in this town. Death was the only escape."

"Take that back," Vincent growls.

"Vincent," Casey's confused. "She didn't say anything."

"Not her. Him," Vincent nods to the Hand. "It."

"Nobody's talkin' Vincent, I don't know what you're hearin', but it's not real."

The Hermit smiles as Vincent's face turns pale, his mouth goes slack, and his voice warbles. "Caleb?"

The Hand lifts a body from the fog; it hangs limply in his hand—as lifeless as a ventriloquist's dummy, and a telltale mop of red hair gives away its identity before it flops to life. The dummy sneers, twisting Caleb's face into something he never was in life—bitter and spiteful. "You got me killed, man. Pretty sure that's like a hate crime or something."

"Caleb, no." Vincent's hands tense into fists. "I didn't mean to, I—"

"Vincent! It's not real!" Casey yells, and Vincent pulls free from her grip.

"It's all your fault," the dummy says with Caleb's voice.

Vincent closes his eyes, hears the Voice in the Fog call, and knows what he must do. His hands find the axe handle.

"Vincent, don't! Listen to me!"

Vincent screams and charges ahead with the axe. The Hand of the Fog raises its neck, presenting itself for the final sacrifice—for the release. The Hermit's eyes fill with cruel delight, anticipating more souls than ever—then her triumphant grin turns to absolute horror as Vincent rushes past the Hand and goes straight to the Black Tree.

"No!" the Hermit screeches, and the fog rises in a panicked flurry.

Vincent swings the axe into the base of the tree. The wood cries out like a wounded animal, and branches recoil like stick-thin fingers; the squeal reverberates through the clearing, amplified by the fog, bringing the Hermit to her knees. Vincent pulls the axe out; a sticky blood-like substance coats the blade and seeps like dark red sap from the wound.

"Stop!" the Hermit begs as though she, too, were being cut down.

Vincent chops again, cutting even further into that black, sick wood, and more blood wells, dripping with the consistency of honey. The tree's branches twist, reaching out for salvation, and the fog rushes around in every direction, conducted by the waving limbs.

"Stop him!" the Hermit commands the Hand, and the revenant rises once more.

"Nu-uh," Casey cracks her neck and blocks the way. The Hand punches her, but Casey takes the hit, barely giving any ground. She looks up at it, licks the blood from her lips, and smiles. "That all you got, bitch?"

Vincent screams and chops till the axe cuts halfway through the trunk. He can see the pulsating organs of some impossible creature in the gap, squealing and squirming like a tube stuffed with worms. He's about to throw up when Casey's scream grabs his attention. Vincent looks over to see her shove the Hand back, only for it to stand and move forward like some burned, lifeless machine. No, that's not right; it's not a machine—

it's a puppet—a broken toy belonging to some primal, malignant power.

"Casey!" Vincent yells and hurls the axe through the air. Casey catches it, spins with the momentum, and drives the blade into the Hand with unimaginable force, cleaving the monster in two. Its legs take a few steps and then collapse into the dirt.

"Stop!" the Hermit screams, her voice both ancient and youthful simultaneously.

The Hand's torso crawls towards the Black Tree, ignoring Casey altogether. She kicks it onto its back and brings the axe down on one arm, then the other. Its torso wiggles on the ground like a turtle fallen on its shell.

Vincent kicks at the Black Tree, trying to make it topple. It squeals like a dying pig, and blood spurts from the stump in thick, viscous globs. Casey runs over and joins him, their eyes meet, and as one, they tear the Black Tree from the earth.

"What have you done?" The hermit falls to her hands and knees, aging rapidly into nothing but dust.

What have you done... the Voice whispers as a wall of fog surges from the ruins of the Black Tree. The twisting mist races at Vincent and Casey, and before they can even brace for impact, they're consumed.

CHAPTER TWENTY-NINE

A SHAPE IN THE FOG

Vincent opens his eyes, and he's home again. White light streams in through the windows, and for a second, he almost believes all is well, that the previous night was just a nightmare. Then he realizes he's, once again, tied up in the middle of the room. Casey is next to him, asleep with her chin on her chest. His mother lies facedown on the sofa, gentle snores sputtering now and then. It's morning, though, and there's no sign of Kaytlynn or the other culty Churchies. Vincent allows himself to imagine for just a second that everything past that point didn't happen, that Virgin Night is over, that his mother is still alive. Then the front door opens.

He realizes that it's not morning light strewing forth but a bright, white haze. Wisps of fog curl over the threshold, and a masked-up Kaytlynn steps through.

Vincent tries to speak. He screams, but no sound comes out. Kaytlynn says nothing either; she simply walks over and lifts Debbie off the sofa with one hand, as though the woman were as light as the mist hissing around the room. Suddenly she's not Kaytlynn anymore; Treeface stands with Debbie's head between both hands, and Vincent looks away as the monster silently snaps his mother's neck once again.

When Vincent looks up, it's Kaytlynn once more, and she turns her mask calmly, like an owl, to face him as she pushes a knife slowly into Casey's heart. Vincent fights against his bonds and spits curses at Kaytlynn but can't break the deafening silence. It's so quiet he can hear the threads of Casey's clothes rip, her flesh open. Blood drips from Casey's lips as she turns her accusatory, dead eyes to Vincent.

I'm sorry, Vincent mouths, and some unseen force pulls his chair away towards the back door, and suddenly there are two more bodies on the floor. Caleb and Michael join Casey in silent, dead-eyed judgment.

Some great force drags Vincent outside, and the fog envelops him. He squeezes his eyes shut tight, fights back the pain, and then opens them again to see he's back home in the lounge, tied to a chair.

No, Vincent silently begs, no. The scene resets, and, once again, the door opens. This time it's not Kaytlynn that steps through; it's himself. This Vincent sneers with gleeful contempt as he snaps his own mother's neck; he grabs a handful of Casey's hair, yanks her head back, and kisses her while plunging the knife into her heart.

The other Vincent leans in, face to face with the real one.

FURY.

The voice comes from everywhere the fog touches, booming through Vincent's very soul.

"Yeah," Vincent says, his voice returning, "you're right. I fucking hate him." The other Vincent grins without blinking, without moving an inch. "If it wasn't for you, my father wouldn't have gone out there that night, wouldn't have felt he needed to play the hero. If it wasn't for your stupid, self-centered need for vengeance and validation, my mother and Caleb would still be alive."

The ropes binding Vincent slacken and fall to the floor. He brings his arms around and finds the knife used to kill Casey in his hand.

HATE.

Every part of Vincent wants to cut his own throat; of all the deaths that night, his would be the most deserved. His anger, his rage, Vincent realizes, has been grossly misplaced all this time. The world would be a better place if he were to turn that fury inwards and end the real monster here. Vincent brings the knife up to his doppelganger's throat.

Casey's accusatory eyes agree, but her lips move, and though no sound escapes, Vincent can hear the words. The same ones she said before. "Don't let your anger control you. That's no way to live."

Vincent turns back to the copy; a small trickle of blood runs down from its neck, along the blade, and onto the real Vincent's hand. Still, it does not move, doesn't so much as blink, as it waits for Vincent to finish.

"No," Vincent says and drops the knife to the floor. The second it hits, everything vanishes, and Vincent's eyes open—an unimaginable weight lifted from him.

"You're alive!" Casey exhales and leans over to hug him as he lies on the ground. "I thought," she doesn't finish and helps Vincent to his feet. The rest doesn't need to be said.

It takes him a moment to realize he's no longer on Black Stone Island. They're nowhere at all. There's nothing to see but hazy whiteness no matter which direction he looks. "Where are we?" Vincent asks; his voice echoes and lags behind his mouth.

"I don't know," Casey looks around, "but I've been here before."

"When?"

"When I died, back at your house, I didn't go where I usually go; into the dark. I was here, in this fog, and there were others. So many of them, I think they were all the Treefaces. Whenever this is, whatever, I dunno, it isn't hers. She was just using it, somehow."

"What do you think it wants from us?" Vincent's words echo then each syllable races to catch up.

"I don't think it wants anything…it just is."

"And the others?"

"They're gone now. I think we set them free." Casey smiles. "One of them looked just like you, only older and less, you know—"

"Goth?"

"Angry."

"Same thing."

"He whispered, don't let him end up one of us. Please, save my son. I had to stop you from crossin' the line, but you did that yourself." Casey smiles.

"I had help." Vincent takes her hands in his, only now noticing she has both again. "Is that normal?"

Casey shakes her head. "None of this is normal. We should go."

"Yeah, Vincent agrees, "but where?" There's no scenery, no distant landmarks to head towards, nothing but the endless fog.

They pick a direction at random and walk. It feels like hours pass, or it could be minutes; it's impossible to tell.

"This is getting us nowhere," Casey points out. "Got any ideas?"

"Ideas were Mikey's thing." Vincent looks at his feet. "Not sure we can punch our way out of this one. Do you know if—"

"He got out." Casey's head drops. "I'm sorry about Caleb."

"Yeah," Vincent nods, "me too." And then Vincent's eyes notice something as they rise. A dark silhouette stands in the fog, far away but distinct. "Do you see that?" Vincent points, and Casey turns.

"Yeah...what is that?" The silhouette turns and walks away, vanishing into the fog. "Should we follow?"

"You got a better idea?" He shrugs, and they follow.

They only catch glimpses of the form as it leads them away, but whatever it may be, its intention seems benign. Ahead of them, eventually, the figure stops. It half-turns, letting Vincent and Casey watch as it salutes, almost cockily, and then falls back into some invisible hole, long, wild red hair rushing up around it as it goes.

"Was that..." Casey can't bring herself to say it.

"I think so." Vincent smiles. "Come on." He takes Casey by the hand, and together, they take a leap of faith.

They land on the soggy shore of Cherry Lake, safely back on the mainland. There's no sign of Vincent and Casey's ghostly guide except for imprints made by a pair of Chuck Taylors, each lighter than the preceding till they outright disappear.

Vincent and Casey collapse, side by side, and roll on their backs to watch the sun come up over Cherry Lake. They don't say anything for a while, just lie there together as Virgin Night comes to an end.

"How did you know it wasn't real?" Casey eventually asks, turning to face Vincent. "Back on the island. I thought you were gonna kill him."

Vincent smiles. "Just something he said."

He quietly flashes back to the security room, where the fatally wounded Caleb climbs to his feet. We can see Kaytlynn fire over Michael's head through the door, forcing him to stop. Caleb whispers in Vincent's ear, "It's not your fault." He grunts. "I love you, man," and he staggers off toward the catwalk.

For a moment, there's nothing but the gentle lapping of the lake—then a shout pierces the serenity. Vincent and Casey turn towards the source, toward the Wallace house further along the shore.

Cut to: Creed as he rummages through the safe in his office, the morning sun streaming through the stained glass window casting the room in shades of red and blue. Duffel bags sit on the desk, stuffed with bundles of clothes and rolls of cash. Creed runs from the safe to the desk, pressing more documents and money in, not taking the time to clean up papers that spill to the side. A bandage hastily applied to his shoulder seeps red and yellow, his silk shirt soaked with damp spots, and his face is slick with cold sweat.

"Father," Michael stands in the doorway, "you can't do this."

"Michael!" Creed runs to his son and puts his hands on the boy's shoulders. "I'm so glad you made it, my son."

"Don't," Michael pushes his father back, "don't lie to me."

"Michael, I—"

"No! You left me for dead! Mother! Ariella!"

Creed reels; this is not the Michael he knows. "But you lived! It's God's plan, don't you see? You and I can start anew—"

"Mom's alive. So's Ariella."

"That's," Creed fumbles for the words, "that's fantastic. God's will—"

"You know nothing about God!"

"I am your father! I am Pastor of The Church on the Lake!"

"Pastor of the Church IN the Lake! You left us all to die!"

"No," sweat pours down Creed's face, "no, Michael! I-I checked the boat, but you were gone. I knew you'd escaped, I knew God—"

"GOD HAS NOTHING TO DO WITH THIS!" Michael screams, the words coming from deep within. From years of swallowing hypocrisy, of keeping quiet and saying nothing as his father lied and sinned.

Creed looks to the side, nodding. "You're right, my son. I'm just a man, a sinner like everyone else. Don't I deserve a chance for redemption?"

Michael wants to tell his father where to stick his redemption, but the appeal to Michael's faith works. "Of course you do, father."

Creed approaches his son, smiling like a drunk used car dealer. "Come with me, son. We can start a new life. I'll send for your mother and sister once we're settled—we can be a family again, son. A new start."

Michael looks at his father's outstretched hand. "Do you truly want forgiveness, father?" Michael then meets his father's eye. "Confess, accept responsibility for your actions, and God will forgive you."

"Michael, I can't do that—"

"They're already on their way," Michael nods to the window, "I called them. They know everything, father. Repent therefore, and turn again, that your sins may be blotted out—"

"And do not be deceived! Bad company ruins good morals!" Creed roars. "Do not think to quote the word of God to ME! No, Michael, not when you keep the company you do. One boy ready to burn the world down, the other consumed by his own ego—you have fallen, my son, into the company of devils!"

"They're my friends," Michael refuses to move, "and better people than you'll ever be."

"Michael, I don't have time for this." The distant sound of sirens testifies to that. "Move aside or come with me."

"No."

"Michael—"

"No!"

Creed's eyes narrow. "Fine." He backhands Michael, but the boy holds his ground. Creed pulls a fist in threat. "Don't make me hurt you, son."

"You already have," Michael growls, "father," he spits the word, the taste of it foul on his lips.

Creed punches Michael in the gut, but he takes it without going down. Michael does not retaliate and stoically takes another hit to the face, only raising his arms to grab the door frame. Creed, desperate, wounded, and exhausted, swings a punch that Michael catches. He holds his father's arm without applying pressure.

Creed yanks his arm free, grabs Michael by the throat, spins his son around, and slams him against the nearest wall. Framed photos clatter to the floor as the plaster cracks. Creed bares his teeth as he chokes Michael, yet the boy does not raise a hand. Through the heat of the moment, Creed realizes he's about to murder his son; it's one thing to push a button or sentence hundreds to death, but taking the life of his blood with his own hands is not so easy. He falters for just a second, and Michael pushes free. Creed stumbles back towards the desk, trips over one of his bags, spirals, and lands facedown on his letter spike. Michael gasps as the pointed tip pierces through the back of his father's head.

"No…" Michael staggers forth. "Father, I-I didn't mean. Father?"

Creed slides off the desk, pulling a bag of money with him, sending notes scattering across the room. Michael races to his father's side, gliding through the slick paper, and takes his hand. "Father?"

Creed twitches uncontrollably, and before he dies, he lands his disapproving eye on his son one last time. "Fail…"

"The fuck!?" Vincent calls from the doorway, Casey right behind him. "Mikey, what happened?"

"I-I-I it w-was an accident," Michael stammers, "I-I didn't mean—"

"Shit," Vincent curses. He can see police cars coming along South Shore Road from the window. "Cops will be here in no time." Vincent looks to his friend on the floor, holding his father's hand. It doesn't matter the circumstances; this will ruin Michael's life. Another innocent who's paid the price for his personal crusade. No, Vincent decides, not him. "Casey, get him outta here. Don't let the cops see either of you."

"What are you gonna do?" Casey asks.

"The right thing. For once."

Casey nods and helps Michael to his feet. He's too shaken and distraught to put up any resistance and lets Casey guide him downstairs.

Vincent closes his eyes, sighs, then follows. He takes a seat on the front step outside the house and waits as flashing red and blue lights get closer. He watches as Casey and Michael slip into the woods just before the police come into sight and smiles.

He's lost much, both through his actions and those of others, both worldly and not. There's nothing he can do to change that, and the world makes even less sense than before, yet because of this, Vincent arrives at a simple, comforting truth. His anger, his hate, his pain—these things can only define him if he allows it, and thanks to his friends, he had the strength to face that evil and say "No."

Vincent thinks about how there were many monsters on that island, and the ones who made it off did so more human than they arrived. He feels something strange settle upon him—not quite peace, but acceptance. Of who he is, what has been, and what will come. It's a new sensation, but not an unwelcome one.

CHAPTER THIRTY

EPILOGUE: I GUESS THIS IS GROWING UP

17 YEARS LATER.

Cut to: a Greyhound bus traveling along the highway towards Cherry Lake. It passes a billboard for The Church of Cherry Lake, showing church members building houses.

A digital clock near the front of the bus reads 12:05 2/13 2015.

Vincent leans his head against the window, slight hints of silver in his slicked-back hair and chin stubble. He likes the feel of sunlight on his face and smiles as the bus turns left when it reaches the old strip mall. It heads past what used to be Starsky's Arcade, now a Starbucks drive-thru, and the irony isn't lost on him. The world's a drastically different place since he went away, and it amazes him.

Something about taking a bus into the heart of Cherry Lake hours before what used to be Virgin Night makes Vincent feel more liberated than when he walked through the gates of Westview Penitentiary the day before.

There was a care package waiting for him and a note saying, "Hope these are still your style." They were, and Vincent looks a little like his old self in a black shirt and jeans. Only a little, though—like Cherry Lake itself, they're the same and yet altogether different. Names on stores have changed, men wear skin-tight jeans, and there's not a pair of low-rises in sight. Some change is for the best, Vincent figures.

Posters for sequels to movies Vincent's never heard of line the theater's wall—but this is still Cherry Lake, and Vincent is home.

The Greyhound comes to a stop, and Vincent waits for the others to get off first, enjoying the sight of carefree people walking around. He waits till the bus pulls away before throwing his bag over his shoulder. When he looks across the street, Vincent's greeted by the sight of a large man with a big smile. His hair has pretty much given up and sought fairer climates, but no one in the world can tuck a shirt in that tight and still move around.

Michael crosses the street and laughs. "You got gray?" He points to the tiny threads of silver at Vincent's temples.

"You got fat," Vincent points to Michael's burgeoning stomach.

"I was always fat," Michael states, and Vincent bursts out in tears. Suddenly he's seventeen again; they both are, even if just for that moment. Michael puts his hand on Vincent's shoulder. "It's good to have you home."

"Yeah," Vincent wipes his eyes, "it's good to be home."

As they walk through Old Town together, Vincent spots the Church emblem on Michael's shirt pocket. "I'm still surprised you didn't give all that up."

Michael looks at the pin and smiles. "No matter how damaged the foundation, we can always rebuild."

"That your new slogan?"

"Our philosophy. The Church is strictly non-profit now. We have a lot to atone for."

"Yeah, I get that," Vincent agrees. "Had a lot of time to think about all my fuck ups."

"I don't know how to thank—"

"No," Vincent cuts in. "Don't. I only did what was right. For once."

"You gave up nearly seventeen years for me, Vincent. You have to let me—"

"And I took so many from others."

Michael nods. No matter what he says, he knows Vincent won't let him say the words, so he vows to find ways to show it instead. "What was it like? Inside?"

"Honestly? Best place for me; I got to work through my anger issues, and my cellmate was decent. For a guy accused of killing his girlfriend and her family."

"Did he?"

"I dunno, hard to tell. Westview's full of innocent men if you hear them tell it, but he was pretty broken up either way. Few folks there had family who died that night. Looked out for me. Hell, even the judge seemed like he wanted to let me off. But I needed to be away from people. For a while."

Michael chuckles. "I still remember your lawyer's face when you demanded the judge give you something."

"Yeah," Vincent smirks, "he threw his pen at me."

"In retrospect, it's a good thing Caleb wasn't there for that," Michael muses. "He always did suspect they wore nothing under those gowns."

"I dunno; he'd have gotten at least a few years for indecently assaulting a judge while shouting something about the people needing to know the truth. We could have hung out in the yard."

Vincent and Michael pass a café as the owner comes out the front door. "Evenin' Pastor Wallace," an older man says as he takes in the outdoor A-frame sign advertising that day's specials.

"Evenin' Earl," Michael returns the greeting. "Closing up early?"

"Yeah, you know," Earl falters for a second as he realizes who the man with Michael is. He doesn't know what to say, so Earl just nods and returns to locking up his store. Few people in Cherry Lake blame Vincent for the crime he took the fall for, but he's a cold reminder of what used to be. Of what they lost.

"Some folks still can't believe he's gone," Michael explains. Squeals break the solemn mood as teenage girls run past Vincent and Michael. They watch the girls pile up against the ticket booth at the theater.

"They don't even know what it was like." Vincent smiles. The two of them walk on towards the promenade. "So, Pastor, don't you find that kinda, you know?"

"A good friend once did a brave thing for me. Showed me to own what I am." Michael taps the pin on his shirt. "Here we are."

Michael and Vincent stop before a tall, black monument. It reads In Memoriam and lists the names of all those who died on Virgin Night 1998. Vincent traces down the list and stops on Debbie Tran. "You didn't need to do that," Vincent holds back the tears, "that one was on me."

"Come on," Michael puts a hand on Vincent's shoulder, "he's waiting."

Cut to: the two men walking through a graveyard.

"Have you heard from her?" Michael asks.

"She sent me letters for a while. She's still out there, hunting them, helping people now. Saving them." Vincent takes a photo out of his jacket pocket. "She sent me this as soon as I got to Westview," he holds out the polaroid Casey took in the lake house. She has her arm around Vincent, with Michael beside them and Caleb pretending to honk her boobs.

Michael chuckles. "I was such a dork."

"Was?"

"And look at you? Could you have been more in love? You'd only just met!"

"Hey, screw you, Mikey! At least I saw her in her underwear before proposing."

"Are you going to look for her?"

"Yeah, think that ship's sailed, Mikey. She'll still look like a teenager, and I'm just an old fart now."

"I don't know, Vincent, you still got the looks. Not many men over thirty can pull off emo."

"What the fuck is emo?"

The men walk up to a well-maintained gravestone. It reads Caleb Dumont. 1981-1998. Hero. Best Friend. Purveyor of the finest "your sister" jokes.

"Nice," Vincent smiles at the last statement and then feels the void, the emptiness where a person used to be, deep in his heart. "Not a day goes by where I don't miss him."

"Me too," Michael nods. "I like to think he lives on inside us."

Vincent snickers. "Inside you, maybe. Did you really try to kiss him?"

"He asked me to!"

"Yeah, sure, hey man, whatever turns you on."

"Well, you know—"

"Don't say it! Don't you dare!" Vincent warns and then turns back to the grave. "I hope wherever you are, buddy, there's hot dudes and cold brews everywhere." Vincent puts the Polaroid down between some fresh flowers. "Those are nice."

"Folks from town," Michael explains. "He saved a lot of people that night. Myself included."

"Me too," Vincent sniffs away the sorrow welling up, "in more ways than one." The dam breaks, and the tears flood. "I fucked it all up, didn't I?"

"Vincent," Michael kneels beside his friend.

"I got him killed; that's on me."

"No, it's not," Michael comforts him. "It wasn't you, or even the Hand that took him from us."

"Yeah, but she, the Church, wouldn't have come after you guys if it wasn't for me. If I hadn't started it all off—"

"Then tonight would be the same as before. Because of what you and Casey did on that island, kids will play on the streets tonight, lovers will kiss and not fear the monster waiting in the fog. I did what I thought was right, too, and my father ended up dead. How are we any different?"

"I still don't feel good about it."

"You don't have to." Michael helps Vincent to his feet. "But you can't go back, so you might as well go forward."

Vincent smiles. "When'd you get so smart?"

"I was always smart," Michael states. "So, there is the matter of the—"

"Yeah, yeah, I know." Vincent takes a deep breath and works himself up. He stands with his legs apart. "Just give me a countdown."

"Would Caleb?"

"No you're—fuck!" Michael gives Vincent one swift kick in the balls, as promised all those years ago outside the remains of the Lakeview Hotel. He drops to his knees and whimpers. "Goddamnthathurts."

"Well, boys, I guess this is what growing up looks like," Emilie says as she walks over and joins them.

Vincent looks up at Michael, eyes wide like this is gonna hurt worse than the kick. "Sorry, you know what she's like; I couldn't not tell her."

"No, I know what you're like, Mikey!" Vincent turns to his sister. "I guessed you wouldn't want to see me."

"Oh, really? So it's been me refusing visits and calls?" Emilie scowls with her hands on her hips.

"I guess I figured you'd hate me." Vincent sits on the grass, spreading his legs to ease the pain.

"I did," Emilie crosses her arms, "for a while," then she relaxes. "I don't blame you, not anymore. You're my brother and all I have."

"Not strictly true, now is it," Vincent says as Michael helps him to his feet.

"Mommy! Mommy!" a small boy yells as he runs across the grass, "Mommy, I saw a ghost! A real one!" He leaps up, and Emilie catches him. "He was old and had a beard and had a funny hat on."

"Vincent, I'd like you to meet your nephew," Emilie turns to the little boy. "C.J., say hi to your uncle Vincent."

The boy shies away, taking a careful sideways glance at Vincent. After a moment, he giggles and jumps down, then runs over. "Hi! I'm Caleb James Wallace!"

"We were going to go, James Caleb, but J.C. is a little too on the nose," Emilie smiles.

Vincent shakes the little man's hands. "Do you know you're named after two heroes who saved a lot of people?"

"Uh-huh," C.J. says, "a looong time ago."

"That's right, back when your daddy had hair!"

"Daddy had hair!"

"Hey now," Michael complains.

"Oh, I have stories to tell you! Like the time Uncle Caleb—"

"No Uncle Caleb stories till he's sixteen!" Emilie insists.

"Eighteen," Michael states.

Vincent picks C.J. up by the arms and hugs his nephew for the very first time. Over the boy's shoulder, Vincent's face turns to disgust at what he sees. "No, no, none of that when I'm here!" He points to Michael and Emilie, who have their arms around each other. "Emilie, Michael doesn't like to be touched!"

"He doesn't seem to mind," Emilie giggles.

"Enough!" Vincent pushes in between them. "None of that!"

Somewhere, watching over them, they're sure Caleb's laughing.

"Come on, let's go eat," Michael says and nods towards the car.

"Sure, I'll be right there," Vincent puts C.J. down. "Just want a minute alone, if that's okay."

"Of course," Emilie says, "we'll be in the car."

Once they're out of earshot, Vincent touches the grave and talks to his dead friend. "So what would you do next? Can't stay here, not for long. That thing on the island isn't gone, not totally. It's still got its roots in me. Felt it as soon as I crossed the county line. If I stay too long, well, I guess you can't go home again, huh? So what would you do? Go chasing the mad dream girl who, for all I know, still looks seventeen. Yeah, I know, you could get into that," Vincent smiles. "I think I know what you'd do, buddy."

"C'mon, Unca Vincent!" C.J. yells. "We're getting pizza!"

"Just a second!" Vincent calls back and turns to the grave. He strokes the photo.

C.J. runs in circles, chanting "Pizza-pizza-pizza!"

"You'd do the right thing. Grab a slice and have a good time with the people you love. Thank you, Caleb. For everything. I love you too."

Vincent stands and then walks over to his nephew, who chews on a finger, waiting for him. "Race you to the car!" Vincent yells and takes off with a squealing C.J. on his heels.

We pull back and up, taking a view of Cherry Lake as the sun hangs low. The night's not far off now.

Roll credits.

CREDITS

Virgin Night was the hardest thing I've ever done. Yeah, I know, that's what Vincent's sister said. These guys were the best friends I never had, and this was a hard book to finish, not because I didn't have an ending in mind but because I didn't want to say goodbye. I love them all and broke down in tears when I finished the first draft. They got me through a tough time in my life, and I didn't want to say goodbye to them. I hope you loved hanging out with them as much as I did.

Now to some real, living friends to whom I owe a great deal.

No stranger to these pages, Craig Walker is the best friend I've ever had. I know if I asked him to help me kill a centuries-old undead Slasher, that's precisely what he'd do. He'd sigh, shake his head, and be there—that's just the kind of guy he is. His TerrorScope counterpart, Walker, got a little more screen time this release. As always, thank you for reading each draft and listening to my dumb ideas. You're the voice of reason in my life, and I'm sorry I don't always listen.

And to the other beta readers, Casey (no, not *that* Casey, but you'd be forgiven for the mistake since they're both total badasses who kicked my ass into getting this book in shape), and Rob. Thank you for not sugar-coating your opinions and your endless support. Casey, you're awesome. And thank you for being there from the start, Rob, taking the time to read *Virgin Night* and your feedback. I'm glad I made both of you laugh and one of you cry. I'm not saying who, Rob, don't worry.

Thanks, also, to Derek Eubanks, who put the cover together and made those awesome chapter titles. You're the Billy to my Stu. Is it just me feelin' woozy over here?

One of the book's most tragic and bittersweet moments is the way Debbie clings to the love of her husband. "Oh, Jimmy," was an innocent, loving phrase that I tried to corrupt, but nothing could be as perverted as the true origin. No, that comes from my good friends and fellow gamers, Rob and Jane, from one drunken game of SMITE. The story behind that is best left unspoken...but thank you both, and the real Jimmy, for the inspiration.

A lot of people showed me a lot of love this year, cheering me on with heartwarming support. So here's a big thank-you to: Steph, Samuel M. Hallam; Jamie Stewart, the immensely talented author of *I Hear The Clattering of the Keys (And Other Fever Dreams)*, a friend who once called me the "Ryan Reynolds of Indie Horror"; Alana K. Drex who crazily put *The October Society: Season One* on her top 10 of 2021.

And a big thank-you to the early readers who read the synopsis for *Virgin Night* and said, "Fuck it, I'm in anyway": Kathryn Owen (@kathryngraceloveshorror); Damien Casey (@damienthulhu and author of the choose your own adventure novel *The Village of Gill*), and Bret Laurie (@brettymachette) who also edited the second edition.

Of course, the biggest thank-you to Dexter. You're a good boy.

So what's next for the TerrorScope universe? It's still some time before *The October Society* will gather once more, and there might be something surprising on the way this summer in the meantime. Something wickedly sweet this way comes...

About the Director

Christopher Robertson has been called the "Ryan Reynolds of Indie Horror" and "some Scottish Dr. Frankenstein." He doesn't care that they were joking. He writes cinematic horror that has been described as wholesome and gruesome in the same sentence multiple times.

You can find him on: Instagram as @kit_romero; TikTok @terrorscopestudios and he'd love it if you stalked him or visit his website

www.terrorscopestudios.com

FIND OUT WHAT *REALLY* HAPPENED TO WOODVALE IN...

MY ZOMBIE SWEETHEART

Once upon a time at a drive-in...

TERROR! From outer space comes crashing to Earth, giving rise to creatures of pure-

HORROR! The likes of which the quiet little town has never seen and the-

NIGHTMARE! That befalls two old friends as they struggle to survive against impossible odds!

It's Friday night, date night, in the quiet little town of Woodvale. For Suzie Palmer, this means hanging out at the All-Night Diner and maybe cruising up to Make-Out Point with her sweetheart. Little does she know there's something on its way to Woodvale. Something cruel and insidious. Something... out of this world...

MY ZOMBIE SWEETHEART is a love letter to 1950s sci-fi movies like *The Blob* and *Invasion of the Body-Snatchers*. It's a tale of young love and alien invaders coming soon to a drive-in near you!

The October Society

Halloween approaches, and ***The October Society*** gathers.

They come to share their stories.

Tales of dark magic and crooked lies.
Of tragic pasts and wicked cruelty.
Of misguided misadventure and sinister pranks…

Collected here are the first six episodes of the spookiest show that never was. A series only found in the static between channels, that can only be watched on broken TVs in dusty attics and damp basements. Tune in, if you can, because the author of ***My Zombie Sweetheart*** welcomes you to ***The October Society***.

THE COTTON CANDY MASSACRE

The book you are about to read is an account of the tragedy that occurred at the reopening of Bonkin's Bonanza one day in the summer of 1989.

Some came looking for fun, like Candy Barton and her best friend, Leigh. Others, like Rocky Rhodes and Sully Sullivan, came looking for a second chance. Instead, they would find a twisted, funfetti nightmare.

For many of the thrill-seekers and families visiting Bonkin's Bonanza, that day would be their last. And the events that unfolded would go on to become infamously known as ***The Cotton Candy Massacre***.

Milton Keynes UK
Ingram Content Group UK Ltd.
UKHW021322211223
434787UK00026B/1218